Praise for
Craig Shaw Gardner's
Dragon Circle Trilogy

Dragon Sleeping . . . Dragon Waking . . .
Dragon Burning

"Delightful . . . fast-paced action . . . abundant witty
repartee . . . his clear enjoyment of the proceedings should
be infectious. [Has] a singular supporting cast: rival
'brother wizards' named Nunn and Obar, a race of beings
called the Anno, and several other sentient characters
whom Gardner imbues with particularly distinctive
personalities."
—*Publishers Weekly*

"Recommended . . . Cross-world fantasy is growing in
popularity, and this latest example seems likely to add to
its appeal."
—*Library Journal*

"Engrossing."
—*Science Fiction Chronicle*

"Consistently entertaining."
—*Locus*

"Appealing."
—*Booklist*

THE DRAGON CIRCLE

DRAGON BURNING

CRAIG SHAW GARDNER

ACE BOOKS, NEW YORK

This Ace Book contains the complete text of the original hardcover edition. It has been completely reset in a typeface designed for easy reading, and was printed from new film.

DRAGON BURNING

An Ace Book / published by arrangement with
the author

PRINTING HISTORY
Ace hardcover edition / October 1996
Ace mass-market edition / October 1997

All rights reserved.
Copyright © 1996 by Craig Shaw Gardner.
Cover art by Glenn Kim.
This book may not be reproduced in whole or in part,
by mimeograph or any other means, without permission.
For information address: The Berkley Publishing Group,
a member of Penguin Putnam Inc.,
200 Madison Avenue, New York, NY 10016.

The Putnam Berkley World Wide Web site address is
http://www.berkley.com

Make sure to check out *PB Plug*,
the science fiction/fantasy newsletter, at
http://www.pbplug.com

ISBN: 0-441-00478-4

ACE®
Ace Books are published by The Berkley Publishing Group,
a member of Penguin Putnam Inc.,
200 Madison Avenue, New York, NY 10016.
ACE and the "A" design are trademarks
belonging to Charter Communications, Inc.

PRINTED IN THE UNITED STATES OF AMERICA

10 9 8 7 6 5 4 3 2 1

Major Players in The Dragon Circle

The Neighbors

Nick Blake
Joan Blake, *his mother*
George Blake, *his father*
Todd Jackson
Carl Jackson, *his father*
Rebecca Jackson, *his mother*
Mary Lou Dafoe
Jason Dafoe, *her brother, now the Oomgosh*
Rose Dafoe, *her mother*
Harold Dafoe, *her father*
Bobby Furlong
Margaret Furlong, *his mother*
Leo Furlong, *his father, now lost inside Nunn*
Evan Mills, *currently inhabited by two others*
    (Rox and Zachs)
Constance Smith
Old Man Sayre, *now the Lawn God*
Charlie, *a dog*

The Islanders

Nunn
Obar   } *three wizards*
Rox

Oomgosh
Raven
Zachs, *a creature created by Nunn*
Owl

The Captain, *formerly Nunn's second-in-command, and, as Douglas, the original leader of the Newton Free Volunteers.*
    The Wolves
    Renegades drawn from Nunn's forces

The Newton Free Volunteers, composed of
    Thomas — *now dead*
    Wilbert
    Stanley
    Maggie

Nunn's soldiers
The Anno
The Dragon
    Garo, *the Dragon's servant*

Visitors from the other islands
    Snake and his men
    Sala
    The Red Furs

Those who hold the eyes:
    Nunn (two) — *a wizard, currently controlled by Carl Jackson*
    Obar — *another wizard*
    The being who is part Evan Mills, part Rox (a wizard) and Zachs (an energy being, originally part of Nunn)
    Constance Smith — *an elderly neighbor*
    Mary Lou Dafoe — *a younger neighbor*
    Todd Jackson — *another young neighbor*

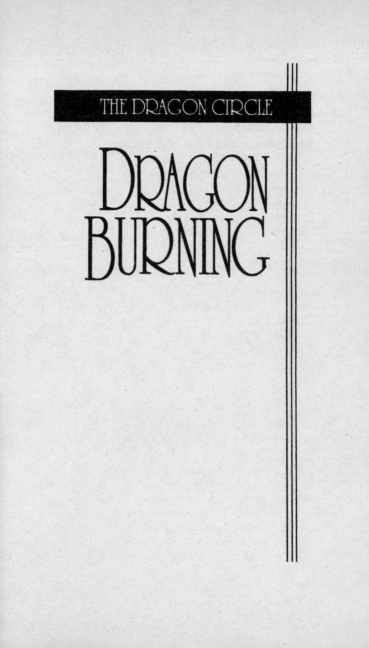

THE DRAGON CIRCLE

DRAGON
BURNING

O Prologue
Watching the Owl

The Owl is watching.

You see it, half-hidden among the trees. The bird sits on a high perch and seems to regard everything—you, the clearing you stand in, the whole world beyond the clearing—with large, dark eyes; eyes the same color as a cloudless night. You did not see the Owl land on that perch, and you doubt that you will see it leave. You feel as if the Owl has always been there, hidden by the deep green shade, until the sun rose to just the right height to reveal it. Perhaps a minute from now the shade will swallow the great grey bird again.

The Owl is waiting.

The Owl's feathers may be as many shades of grey as there are colors in the rest of the world. The bird blinks, and stretches its great wings. You are sure that those wings would make no sound, the Owl silent as death as it swoops down upon its prey.

The Owl knows.

Somewhere, deep within those dark, dark eyes, are the answers. How great is the Owl? How small is the rest of the world? Yet the Owl has suddenly appeared, as if it had come out of a great darkness, like the shadow of a waking dragon's wing.

You have seen the signs. The dragon is waking. The great creature is ready to take flight, a flight that will change the world.

Maybe the Owl is a part of that change. Or maybe the Owl has always been there, waiting.

The Owl is lost in shadow as the sun slips toward the horizon. The long day is almost over. And the Owl owns the night.

BOOK ONE

○

At the Dragon's Door

○ One

The battle was over. And the Oomgosh was dead.

Jason ran. He was following Raven, because Raven had told him to follow.

No, that wasn't the only reason. If he ran, no one had to see him cry. The warm tears hurt as they ran down his cheeks, tears that wouldn't stop, tears that made him want to close his eyes, to fall down and hug the ground.

He hadn't cried like this since he was a kid. Heck, he had turned fifteen over a month ago. What would he do if Bobby or Todd or Nick or even his sister Mary Lou saw him like this?

The Oomgosh had been more like his father than his father. Tree-tall and strong, not just some stumbling, mumbling human. The Oomgosh had made Jason feel like he belonged here, in a way he'd never felt he belonged back on Chestnut Circle.

Chestnut Circle? It had only been a few days ago, but it felt more like weeks or months, like a whole different lifetime. Jason felt older now than he ever had with his home and school and family back in that other place.

But if he was so old, why was he crying?

Even tears gave to the earth.

The thought came into his head as if it had been there all along. It was the sort of thing the Oomgosh would say.

And now Jason was the new Oomgosh. Or so the tree man had told Jason before he died.

How could that be? Sure, the great tall Oomgosh had shown Jason how to listen to the earth, to hear what the trees and birds and insects were all saying, to feel the shifts in wind and

5

water. He had given Jason a new calmness, a new meaning, a real place to be.

And then the tree man had died.

The Oomgosh always knew where he was, and what he was doing. How could Jason be the new Oomgosh if he was so confused?

"Oomgosh!" Raven called from overhead. "We stop here."

Jason let himself stumble to a halt. To his surprise, his tears had stopped as well.

They were surrounded by the woods that covered most of the island. There was nothing special here that he could see. "What are we doing here, Raven?"

The great black bird cawed softly down at Jason. "We are waiting for someone." The bird ruffled his feathers as he settled onto a tree branch. "You'll remember. You are much better at this than I." He lifted his head to survey the surrounding trees. "That Owl is back again."

It was only when Jason went to rub whatever tears remained from his eyes that he realized there had been another change. He wasn't wearing his glasses. He must have lost them in the battle. The thick lenses with their brown plastic frames were gone. And he could still see everything. If anything, he saw more clearly than he had before.

He looked up at Raven.

"What's the owl?" Jason almost asked. No, that was wrong. Instead, he asked "Who is the owl?"

"Exactly the way Owl would say it," Raven agreed, cocking his sleek, black head to one side. "There are almost as many stories about Owl as there are for Raven. Owl brings something, on that all the stories agree. But the stories do not agree what that something is." Raven shifted his weight back and forth on the branch, as if searching for just the right position to tell his story. Raven was very fond of telling stories.

Satisfied with the branch below him at last, Raven continued, "Maybe the something Owl brings is wisdom." Raven made a cackling sound in the back of his throat, his opinion of those who believed the first story. "Or maybe the coming of Owl simply means that the world will change." Raven paused again, this time to shake his great black wings. "But others believe that whoever sees Owl will soon see death."

Jason shook his head. He didn't want stories. He wanted to know what was really going on. "Aren't you Raven? Don't you know everything? Which one does the owl really bring?"

"Oh, all three, of course." Raven chuckled. "Not that we have to fear death, of course. Raven and the Oomgosh both live forever."

Forever? Now Jason wanted to laugh. It was a different view of forever than any Jason had heard. But something inside him kept him from complaining to the bird, something new. He wanted to learn more.

"And it's up to us to meet the owl?" he asked.

"We certainly can't leave it up to the wizards. Wizards never notice things like owls." Raven nodded, more to himself than to Jason. "But then, what do wizards know?"

What do *wizards* know?

If Jason really had become the Oomgosh, was he better than the wizards? He certainly would be different. Jason thought about how strong and happy the old Oomgosh had always seemed. He supposed there were worse ways to spend your life.

He looked down at the fine green veins that now crawled across the back of his hand. But he had never asked to change this way!

Then again, he supposed that no one, the neighbors on Chestnut Circle or the other beings on this island, human and otherwise, had ever asked to be brought to this place. They had all been brought here by the dragon.

And they all had a purpose.

They all had a purpose. That sounded like the great tree man, too. A lot of Jason's thoughts were turning that way. It seemed to be hard to think depressing thoughts when you were the Oomgosh.

The black bird swiveled his head around to survey the surrounding sky. "Perhaps Raven is too soon. Sometimes Raven is too quick. Owl is not ready."

"Then why do you worry?" Jason asked. "What if the owl doesn't want to see you?"

"Not see Raven? Ah, Oomgosh, why else would Owl be here?"

Why else except to see Raven? Jason started to laugh.

"Now, my Oomgosh," Raven replied, "you are beginning to sound more like yourself."

Jason's laughter stopped abruptly.

"Someone *is* coming," Jason said, surprising himself that he could know something like that. He could feel it through his feet, as if the roots below were sending messages about the island around him.

Raven cocked his head again, as if listening for something beyond Jason's hearing. "You are right, my Oomgosh. Somewhere between two and five of them, purposely moving deeper into the forest." The bird cawed softly down to Jason. "They must be looking for somewhere private to talk. They must be talking about something interesting."

Jason frowned. What did "interesting" mean? What if the newcomers were Nunn and his men? He didn't feel enough like the Oomgosh yet to go up against a real wizard. "Should we leave?"

"Certainly not. How do you think Raven knows everything? He listens! We'll just stay around here."

Stay—out in the open like this? Jason felt panic rising in his chest. "Won't they see us?"

The bird shook his glistening, black-feathered head. "What is there to see? Raven is part of the sky. And what is the Oomgosh but another tree in the forest?"

"A part of the forest? I don't—"

Raven stared at Jason with an eye the color of the nighttime sky. "You know, my Oomgosh, you know."

Jason blinked as Raven looked away. He took a deep breath. The panic was gone. Maybe he did know.

"Now we listen." Raven hopped up a branch, his feathers blending in with the shaded leaves.

Jason found himself stepping back into the trees, until he was deep in the shade of the forest.

People were coming. But Raven and the Oomgosh were out of sight.

Todd Jackson was getting angry all over again. After all, he had only been trying to help.

He should have known it wouldn't work. Didn't his father always tell him that everything he touched would turn to shit?

Yeah. That's what his father would say. Todd had to remind

himself that his father was as responsible as anyone for what had happened.

The dead—human and not-quite-human—were everywhere. The clearing looked like the end of the world.

Todd also had to remind himself that there hadn't been much of a world here in the first place. This was the clearing where the neighbors from Chestnut Circle had tried to make a home for themselves. With the help of a bunch of Daniel Boone lookalikes called the Newton Free Volunteers, they had built a couple of rough lean-tos, with roofs of gathered branches to protect them from the elements.

That was before Nunn's troops attacked; Nunn's troops, led by Todd's father, Carl Jackson. Now the only things left here were mud and bodies.

"What say we dispose of some of this?"

Obar's voice startled Todd. He hadn't noticed the old wizard in white walk up behind him.

Todd realized that for the first time since he'd gotten to this island, he wasn't ready to jump at the first noise around him. He was no longer on edge, waiting for the worst. The worst had already happened. Now Todd was only exhausted.

Todd glanced over at the old man in white as the wizard stepped up next to him.

"I'm afraid I can't do it myself," Obar admitted. The mouth behind his long white mustache was set in a frown. "But I thought perhaps, more than one of us, working together with our eyes, might be able to get the job done."

"So we all work together, right?" Todd asked. As if he should trust any of the wizards. It had only been a few minutes since another wizard had threatened Todd and demanded that he give up his own eye. That was a wizard named Rox, who somehow was wearing the body of Mr. Mills, one of the neighbors from Chestnut Circle. Todd thought that was what had happened, but he didn't begin to understand it.

Todd unclenched his fist and looked at the small green jewel he held there, the dragon's eye, a magic thing that gave its owner power. And that power supposedly came from the great dragon itself. Now Todd held one of his very own, just like Rox and Obar and Nunn. He held the same power as all these crazy wizards, and he could use it any way he liked.

"Yes, work together, most certainly," Obar went on in that

way he had, sounding more like he was talking to himself than to anybody else. "Except we seem to be missing a participant or two."

Todd turned away from the pile of bodies at the clearing's center. Mr. Mills was nowhere around. That didn't surprise Todd at all. And Nunn had vanished when they'd beaten his armies; both the human army and the second one full of red-furred apes. But that still left four of them who held the eyes; Obar, himself, Mrs. Smith—

He spotted the old woman, up against one of the great trees, sitting next to Sala. Both of them were fast asleep. Sala was, if anything, even prettier than when Todd had first met her. She had a half smile on her peaceful oval face; a face surrounded by a mass of red-gold curls that looked an awful lot like a halo. Funny, he thought, that he could compare her to an angel when the tavern where she had worked for her father was a lot more like hell.

But if Sala looked like the best thing in life, Mrs. Smith looked a lot more like death. The woman had been frail as long as he'd known her, all his years growing up back on Chestnut Circle. She was pretty old, too. In her sixties, Todd guessed, much the same age as his own grandmother.

But Mrs. Smith had changed after she came to this new place, this world full of islands and a huge dragon that seemed to keep just out of sight. She had been the first of the neighbors to get one of the dragon's eyes, and it had made her strong and sure, as if her age didn't mean a thing and she could do anything.

That is, until the eyes suddenly lost most of their power. With the magic snatched away from her, Mrs. Smith had seemed to shrink back into the frail old woman from Chestnut Circle. No, worse than that. As he looked at the old woman's sleeping form, her pale skin laced with light blue veins pulled taut across her face and hands, she seemed as old as anyone Todd had ever seen, as if the eye had taken years from her life in exchange for its magic. Mrs. Smith half looked like she would never wake up again.

"I think Mrs. Smith needs to rest," Todd said.

"Hmm?" Obar jumped slightly at Todd's voice, as if the wizard was surprised to be having a conversation. "Quite right. The jewels can only do so much. Our Mrs. Smith has expended great effort these past few hours. Besides, we have two young and vigorous eye holders.''

He waved to the sixteen-year-old girl on the far side of the clearing. ''Mary Lou! Would you come here for a minute, please?''

Mary Lou—the last of the four here with a dragon's eye—pushed her long brown hair out of her eyes and looked up from where she was staring at the ground. In the hours since she'd come back from wherever she'd gone, wherever the dragon had taken her, she seemed to be doing an awful lot of staring at nothing in particular.

She looked older than she had before, too; more like an adult than the teenage girl he'd known before. She was certainly much more serious than before. Todd didn't think he'd seen her smile since she'd come back.

He felt differently about her now, too. How much he had wanted her, the pretty girl next door, back when they lived on the Circle; how he'd even tried to push himself into her life. Now that all seemed changed. Maybe it had something to do with his finding Sala. But maybe it also had something to do with both Todd and Mary Lou holding dragon's eyes. Todd felt like the two of them were connected now, like they were related in some way closer than brother and sister.

Todd guessed he had changed some, too. Everybody around him was changing, from the dog Charlie, whose bones were bending him into something that looked prehistoric, to that other kid his age from the circle, Nick, who had gotten a sword that somehow made him a great warrior, but also seemed to be driving him crazy.

Mary Lou stopped between Todd and Obar.

''Yes, my dear,'' Obar began as soon as she stepped between them. ''We need to do something with all of this. Otherwise, we might encounter some—most unsanitary conditions.''

''What would you like us to do?'' Mary Lou asked quickly. She seemed very ready to help. Todd guessed he was, too. But he kept watching the way the magician would glance at Mary Lou's hand, the hand that held the eye, as if he might snatch the jewel away at the first excuse. After all, it was Obar who told them never to trust a magician.

The magician pulled his gaze away from Mary Lou's fist

and nodded like he was going to start one of his lectures. "Normally, when the dragon's power was in my gem, I could lift the bodies, and stack them neatly in only a moment. A quick spark from my gem, and we'd have a grand funeral pyre in no time. Now, though, what with the dragon interfering with the power of the eyes, almost as if it were taking back part of the magic—"

Mary Lou frowned back at the wizard. "The dragon has its reasons."

Obar stared back at Mary Lou for an instant, mouth open. He blinked, his mouth snapping shut. "No doubt," he said with a shake of his head.

Todd wished he didn't have to listen to Obar's speeches. After he had some control over this eye of his, he wouldn't have to listen to anyone. No. Todd forced himself to take a deep breath. That was his anger again. For now, it seemed safest to stick with the others, at least until they figured out how Nunn would attack them next.

He looked down at the eye in his hand. Maybe he should be more worried about an attack from the dragon. But how could you worry about something you couldn't do anything about?

Todd had no time to worry. He had to learn to use the dragon's eye. Starting with the bodies.

"Then we have to burn them?" he asked the wizard.

"Thomas would like that," Wilbert said. Todd was surprised to see the Volunteer standing nearby. He had been concentrating so much on the others with the eyes, he wasn't paying attention to the rest of those in the clearing. Todd felt like he was getting as absentminded as Obar.

"Like the Vikings, sort of," Wilbert went on as he scratched at his beard. He nodded at the body of his fallen comrade. Unlike the other corpses spread across the clearing, Thomas had been carried beneath the trees. His arms had been folded across his chest, his eyes shut, as if he might have found some kind of peace.

"A proper farewell to a warrior," Wilbert concluded with a shake of his head.

"We can't bury them," added Stanley, his face set back into its perpetual frown, from where he stood at the clearing's edge. "You dig down far enough on these islands, you hit water."

Wilbert and Stanley would know what Thomas wanted. The large, bearded man and his thin, sour-faced companion were two thirds of the remaining Newton Free Volunteers, a group that had been brought here by the dragon a long time before the people from the Circle had shown up. Thomas had been their leader until he, along with the tree man called the Oomgosh, had died in the battle.

Todd frowned. What had happened to the tree man's corpse?

Todd thought he heard a whispering in the distance, the rustling of leaves on the vines at clearing's edge. Todd remembered the time the soldiers had cut the vines when they first brought the neighbors; those vines had made a sound almost like a human cry. Now it sounded like they were talking again, not quite loud enough to be heard.

Vines talking? Todd snorted. The leaves were rustling because they were blown by the wind.

Except there wasn't any wind. Besides the whispering vines, the place was as still as Todd had ever seen it, no breeze, no birds, no insects, even; like even the air wanted a moment of silence for the dead.

Todd knew what had happened to the Oomgosh. The vines had taken him. He was absolutely certain that's what had happened. Had the eye told him that, too?

He wondered if the others knew about this. As certain as he was of the tree man's fate, he didn't want to be the first person to say it aloud.

"Where's the Oomgosh?" he asked, hoping for some sort of explanation.

"I think he's gone with Raven," Obar replied.

What the hell did that mean? Obar specialized in answers that seemed to have nothing to do with the questions. Todd half wanted to throw his jewel away and sock the wizard in the jaw.

"These bodies grow no fresher while we talk," Obar added, as though he wished to end the conversation.

Wilbert shook his head at the wizard. "Are you sure you wouldn't want a hand? The Newton Free Volunteers have moved a body or two in their day."

Obar shook his head in return. "No, magic will be easier."
The wizard frowned at that. "Well, it *should* be easier." He
lifted his hands into the air.

"The Anno believe eating your enemy makes you
stronger," Mary Lou remarked as she watched Obar.

There was no expression on her face, but Todd thought he
saw a smile in her eyes. Maybe she didn't like the way the
old wizard took control of things, either.

Obar's hands dropped. He tugged at a sleeve of his once
white clothing. "We are not the Anno."

"That's what you say. But what are we, then?" Todd demanded.

"Well . . ." Obar began. He seemed at a loss for words
again.

Mary Lou answered instead. "We are waiting for the
dragon."

She had that look in her eyes, as if she was looking at
something the rest of them couldn't see. Todd remembered
thinking about how they had all changed, but Mary Lou was
acting downright weird.

"The bodies," Obar repeated. "We really should dispose
of them, don't you think? I believe, with a bit of effort, I
should be able to move one at a time."

Most of the bodies here belonged to the enemy. Half a
dozen of the corpses here were Nunn's human soldiers. There
were three times that many of the red-furred apes.

Todd watched carefully as Obar placed the small green gem
between the palms of his hands. The wizard raised his hands,
placed palm to palm as if he might be praying, so they were
between him and the nearest of the corpses. He lifted his
hands, and the body lifted as well, floating a dozen feet to a
pile of three other dead. The floating corpse dropped abruptly
on top of the others as Obar staggered back, his hands waving
about as if he was about to fall over.

But the magician didn't fall. Instead, he hunched forward,
fists resting on his knees. He gasped for breath as if he had
just run a mile.

He glanced over at Todd.

"Would you care to try?"

Just like that? Todd thought. He was actually hoping to get
a bit more in the way of instructions. Still, he had used the

jewel before. If not for him and his dragon's eye, their ship would have been sunk by some tentacled thing out at sea. The gem seemed to sparkle the slightest bit in his hand. Maybe everybody had to figure out how to use his eye for himself.

"You already know how to do it," Obar called. "Just picture what you want to do with your mind."

So he already knew, did he? Maybe it would work if he just followed Obar's lead. He placed the green stone between his palms and pointed his clasped hands at the next of the corpses. He thought about floating bodies, and lifted his hands toward the sky.

Nothing happened.

He was doing something wrong. But the dragon's eye had helped him out a couple of times already. Of course, he was never quite sure exactly *why* the eye had helped him—He took a deep breath and glanced over at the wizard. Obar was smiling ever so slightly. Was it a smile of encouragement, or was Obar already making fun of him?

Why couldn't the wizard just show him what to do? Todd really wanted to walk over there and wipe the smile right off of Obar's face. But punching out the wizard wasn't going to get his dragon's eye to work. He thought about the gem resting between his palms. He pictured what he wanted to do with the eye, but did he really believe it? What was he missing?

The dragon's eye seemed to work best for Todd when he got angry. Maybe, instead of thinking about punching Obar, he should consider punching the corpse.

He thought about how the soldiers had tried to kill them all. How had that made him feel?

"Maybe I should try," Mary Lou said softly from where she stood by Todd's side.

Todd's head snapped around to look at the girl. He wanted to shout at her, to tell her to get out of his way. But he knew she was trying to help him, to give him some time to understand his own eye. He had to be careful just where his anger went. He had to calm down and concentrate.

Mary Lou didn't even try to imitate Obar's movements. Instead, she stared directly at an ape corpse sprawled a bit farther away than all the others.

The corpse stirred, and shook slightly, as if the ape creature was really only twitching in its sleep. Somebody, maybe Mary

Lou's mom, cried out as the body lurched upward.

But the body was still only a body; limp within that invisible force from Mary Lou's eye. The body rose up, and kept on rising, gaining speed like some object pushed down by gravity. Except this object was flung straight upward until it was only a dot between the clouds. And then the body was gone, too far away to see.

Mary Lou blinked, and shook her head. "I couldn't stop it," she whispered.

Nobody spoke for a moment. Wilbert coughed, and said something about not needing a fire after all. Sort of a joke, Todd guessed. Nobody laughed.

Todd wasn't going to be left behind. Mary Lou had lifted up that body, like she had an extra pair of invisible hands. Well, he could do that, too.

He made a fist around his dragon's eye and reached out toward another of the corpses, one of the human soldiers.

Those soldiers had worked for his father.

His father, who couldn't come home without bringing a bottle. His father, who, when he was drinking, liked to yell at both his wife and son, liked to tell them both how worthless they were, how much they dragged him down. His father, who, when he was really drunk, would stagger around and hit whatever was in front of him. And, if you didn't get out of his way, he'd hit you, too.

Work! he thought at the jewel in his hand. Damn it! Work!

The corpse shifted on the ground.

Yes! He lifted the arm that held the gem.

The body jerked a few inches off the ground.

It was working. But the body felt so heavy, like he was carrying the whole weight on his fist.

He was worrying too much about the body. He had to remember Chestnut Circle.

Todd thought about the hatred in his father's eyes. How his father had had another drink and told his son how everything Todd did forced his father to hit his mother. His father let him know it was all Todd's fault. How much better it would have been if he had never been born.

Todd squeezed his fist as hard as he could, like he wanted to crush the jewel inside.

And the body danced before him. An arm jerked one way,

a leg another, the head flung back, then forward. The corpse capered through the air like some sort of rotting puppet, dancing faster and faster, until its movements were too fast for Todd's eyes to follow. But he could see splits appear in the soldier's torso, bits of red showing through the uniform, as if some invisible beast was tearing the body to shreds.

"Get back!" Obar cried to the others. "It's going to shake itself apart!"

Todd realized the magician was right. He couldn't stop his magic any more than Mary Lou could halt hers. He took the hand that held the eye and threw his arm high overhead.

The shaking body flung itself away from those in the clearing, a blur of arms and legs. It exploded above the trees at clearing's edge, raining blood and bits of torn flesh on the leaves beneath.

"My," Obar said softly. "If I had ever wanted to demonstrate that the dragon's magic can work in different ways . . ."

Would that old man never shut up? Todd spun to face the magician. And Obar was thrown into the air, tossed a dozen feet back across the clearing.

The magician in white made two fists of his own and settled quickly back to earth.

"You must learn to control this magic," he called to Todd, "or the magic will possess you."

Obar wiped his nose with one of his fists, then looked down at his knuckles. His nose was bleeding.

Todd couldn't stand this anymore. The rage that he had poured into the jewel flowed back into him. He was glad that corpse had been ripped apart. A part of him wanted to rip everything apart. The hand that held the eye started to shake. His anger had to go somewhere, or it would tear him apart as well.

"Get away from me!" he shouted as he waved the fist with the jewel above his head.

The others didn't move. They stared back at him, as if what had happened was too much for all of them.

This wasn't the place for his anger. He had to find his father.

But first he had to get out of here.

Todd ran for the trees.

○ Around the Circle:
When Birds First Got Colors

Once there was a time when each bird was like every other, for none of them had yet taken colors for their feathers to tell one bird from another. But, as the animals had taken different coats before them so that one might now be called Bear, another Seal, a third Fox, and so on, to include all the many things that walked, now were the birds called upon to do the same for the many things that flew. So it was that all the birds were called to the place where the colors were to be chosen.

But clever Raven had seen what had passed with the animals and knew that the same would pass with birds. Before the words were fully spoken, Raven had taken flight so that he might be first among those to do the choosing. And Raven's wings beat so strongly and so quickly that he was the only bird in the sky, and so he swooped quickly down to the choosing place before another bird might draw a breath.

Now, at the center of this choosing place was a great tree, and on the greatest branch of this tree was a lamp to show all the birds the way. What better place of honor, Raven thought, than to perch right beside this lamp?

But as Raven settled upon this branch at the very center of the place, he noticed another bird was there already, perched in the shadows where the lamp's light did not quite reach. This other bird sat upon the limb with eyes closed, perhaps asleep, as if it had been there a very long time.

Raven cried out in surprise, but it was not a loud cry, for Raven was short of breath after his arduous flight.

But the other bird's eyes snapped open, two dark orbs so large that Raven's own gaze might be lost in them.

"I am Owl," the other bird said simply, "and we are first

18

to the clearing so that we might help choose the colors for all.''

Raven chafed at this, for he was used to getting his way. "How do we do that?"

Owl blinked, turning her great head away from Raven to stare at the legion of birds who now approached the clearing.

"Simple," Owl replied. "We ask each of the birds which colors they would like."

So the birds came and chose their colors. Many of them took coats of brown, mixing the bark of trees with a lining of old leaves to blend in with the forest. But some took bits of the spring snow to give them tufts of white, and others gave themselves necklaces of wildflowers so that they might add red or green or yellow. And others flew up above the great branch, taking coats the color of the fluffy clouds or the bright red dawn or the blue of the sky itself; their coats coming in as many different patterns and colors as there were birds to wear them.

So had all the birds chosen colors except for the two on the branch.

"Come, we shall help each other pick colors as well," Owl called.

"And what would you like?" Raven called, for helping to make the coats of all the other birds had put him in a better mood.

Owl stared deeply at Raven and replied, "What would you suggest?"

With that, Raven knew just what was needed. He would fashion owl a coat that was worthy for one with so forbidding a stare. So Raven took the brown of earth, and the white of snow, and flecked both with the color from the time when there is no color, in that darkest of moments just before sunrise.

Owl looked down at the coat Raven had given her. "This is a wondrous thing," she proclaimed. "You have given me colors that will be instantly noticed, and yet might blend with the shades of either summer or winter."

At that, Raven preened. "Of course," he replied. "Wasn't it made by Raven?"

And Owl replied, "You have made me such a fine coat, I can do no less for you. What color is your innermost desire?"

Raven realized that he had been so busy helping the other birds that he had given no real thought to a coat of his own. But surely, Raven thought, I must have the finest coat of all!

So Raven looked at all those things the other birds had used before him. Which should be his?

"Perhaps," Raven said after a moment's thought, "I could be such a blinding white that I may rival the sun."

Owl stared at Raven for a moment before she answered. This would not be an easy task. "If that is what you desire."

But why, Raven thought, should he limit himself to only one color, no matter how brilliant? He thought about all those colors around him, and thought of a coat that was one part snow and one part bark, one part cloud and one part night.

"Or perhaps," he added quickly, "I should have a bit of every color, so everyone will know Raven is here."

Owl regarded Raven for another instant before replying. To gather every color might take a very long time.

"Ah, then, if that is what you truly—"

But Raven had already had another thought, for Raven was used to making as many choices as he wished, even if that meant choosing everything.

"Or perhaps I should be a color different from all the rest. A shade that everybody knows, but still has no name; the color of a child's laughter or a maiden's tears."

This, Owl thought, might be even more than difficult. Still, after receiving such a fine coat herself, Owl could do naught but try. "If that—"

"Or perhaps—" Raven began again.

But Owl had had enough. Raven would never decide! With that, Owl screeched her frustration and spread her wings to rise up from the great branch. And, as she flew away, her talon hit against the lamp, knocking it over, so that it spilled thick, black oil over Raven.

So it was that Raven gained his coat, and Raven gained his wish as well, for every color that Raven sought is reflected in that black.

But then, doesn't Raven always get his way?

○ Two

"Todd, wait!"

Sala didn't realize what was happening until it was too late. Todd was the only one she really knew out of all these strange new people, and now he had disappeared into the woods without even a glance her way. But so many men always promised her one thing and did another. Why should Todd be any different?

She looked away from that place where Todd had vanished in the surrounding forest, and stared down at her hands, slender fingers above small wrists and lean arms. Her father had laughed at her, called her scrawny and useless. She sometimes marveled that men wanted her at all.

She looked around her at the clearing and all the people she had barely met. Todd *was* different; she had known that from the first time they had looked at each other. He looked at her, touched her, even kissed her in a different way. Todd saw the real Sala, with all her faults and all her problems, and he didn't seem to care. If he had had to leave, he had a good reason. She expected him to come back, too; so different from so many people in her life.

Back in the port town where she had been born, refined people always looked down on her. She was a tavernkeeper's daughter. She was gutter trash.

Why would these people be any different? The Volunteers, the wizards, the ones Todd called the "neighbors," all pretended to like her. But Sala had seen them stare at her when they thought she wasn't looking. She had heard them talking, their voices low to keep the words from carrying in her direction. She knew what they really felt.

"Don't worry," a girl's voice said by her ear. Sala looked up, surprised that someone had gotten so close; where she had grown up, it was important to know who was moving behind your back.

But people around here didn't always move by the most normal of methods. She'd seen a couple of the magicians just disappear, and the oldest woman here seldom walked, but rather floated from place to place. On the island she had come from, the dragon had seemed only a story to scare children. Here, the dragon was very close.

Mary Lou, the girl close to Sala's age, smiled down at her. Sala didn't think she could trust that smile. She certainly couldn't trust any of those girls back in the town where she came from. And Mary Lou had a dragon's eye besides.

"What do you want?" Sala asked. From what Todd had told her, wizards got their dragon's eyes from killing other wizards. Could a girl Sala's age be a wizard? The neighbors were different from the wizards, weren't they? Old lady Smith and the others seemed to be given their eyes by the dragon itself. Sala had seen Todd simply walk up and take one of the glowing green gems for his own in her father's Tavern. She guessed that Mary Lou and the old woman got their eyes in more or less the same way.

Sala stared back at Mary Lou. What made a girl so special that she would get a gift from the dragon?

"He has to adjust to his new power," Mary Lou replied, as if that answered Sala's question.

"You mean Todd?" Sala asked. "He went somewhere because of that—stone?" There were many things here that didn't make sense, including a lot of things these other people talked about. She hoped Mary Lou was right, and Todd would hurry back.

Mary Lou nodded. "I feel sometimes like I've got to throw out everything I've learned and start all over again."

Sala knew what that felt like. She had left her home to come to this strange new island, but Mary Lou had come from someplace even farther away. Maybe Sala had more in common with this other girl than she thought.

Sala looked away, up at the clear blue-green sky. How could she answer Mary Lou? She had never been really comfortable talking with girls her own age. They always laughed at her and pushed her around. She was the tavernkeeper's daughter. She had to be put in her place.

She turned to stare back at that place in the woods where Todd had disappeared. How she wished he would walk back between those trees!

"Don't leave the clearing," Mary Lou said sharply. "There are things out there—small creatures called the Anno—that I think like to eat people."

Was Mary Lou telling her what to do now? Sala glared back at the other girl, all of the good feelings gone. She couldn't stand someone taking that tone with her; she knew how to take care of herself. She had had enough lectures and punishment and people laughing at her back on that other island to last her entire life. She would go wherever she wanted!

But Mary Lou wasn't even looking at Sala anymore. The other girl was already wandering away, as if she could no longer be bothered with what stupid Sala might do.

Sala had had enough of these *neighbors*. If Todd wouldn't come back for Sala, she decided, Sala would go out and find Todd. Who cared what someone like Mary Lou said? Sala had taken care of herself in worse places than this. Sala stood up, her back to the retreating Mary Lou, and marched toward the edge of the forest. She'd show everybody what a tavernkeeper's daughter could do.

Not that she could move very fast. How could anybody get anywhere with all these vines snaking between the trees? But she was too angry to stop. She wanted to scream at the vines for being in her way, at Mary Lou for being such a bitch, at Todd for leaving her all alone.

She stopped when she heard something; a small noise, like she had startled something with her crashing through the underbrush. She half expected to see the little cannibal creatures Mary Lou had talked about, waiting for Sala with big smiles filled with pointed teeth.

There instead, standing in the shadows beneath the first of the trees, was the boy who had the same red hair as she. Nick, that was his name. He looked up at her as she approached, his down-turned mouth both sad and apologetic at the same time, as if he was sorry she had seen him, or maybe just sorry he had ever been born.

He took a step away, glancing quickly to either side, as if

there might be some way he could still escape into the shadows.

"What are you doing here?" she blurted, afraid of losing him.

Nick gazed straight at her then. "I didn't feel comfortable with all the people chattering around me in the clearing." He twisted his mouth into something that, if not for the look in his eyes, might have been a grin. "I don't feel like I belong anymore."

This was the second of the young people here saying something that might have come out of Sala's own mouth. Sala almost laughed. These neighbors seemed so much more civilized than her father and his cronies, but everybody here seemed to be sitting on something. Todd looked half the time like he wanted to hit something. From the look on Nick's face, he mostly wanted to hurt himself.

She had seen Nick's sword in action, the blade somehow feeding on the blood of its victims. In return for the blood, it gave Nick tremendous skill and power.

Nick saw her looking at the sword. His hand stopped just short of the hilt, as if he was afraid even to touch it. "It's going to make me into some sort of monster, but here it is"— he patted his scabbard, his eyes slowly closing—"still hanging from my side. Is it any wonder I want to get away from everybody?"

A small shudder ran through his body as his hand finally encircled the hilt. Nick opened his eyes. "Maybe you should get away from me, too."

But Sala wasn't scared at all. She wished she could find some way to help. He was even more afraid than she was. With his red hair and the sadness in his eyes, Nick could be her brother.

She took another step toward him. The vines felt slippery beneath her feet. Something rustled by her side. She glanced over, ready for danger, but could see nothing in the shadows. It was probably one of the little creatures that lived in the underbrush, running away from her big feet.

Sala felt something move underfoot.

She looked down, afraid of what she might have stepped on. But she saw nothing there but the ever-present vines, full of dark leaves, more purple than green. As she watched, the vine nearest to her foot shifted. She looked about to see if something had pushed it toward her, and realized that all the vines were moving, twisting and writhing about, as if the whole forest floor was covered with snakes.

"Look out!" Nick called. Then he saw it, too. She wanted to look up at him, ask him what was happening, but the shifting vines were making it difficult to keep her balance.

Something grabbed her leg. It was one of the vines, curling around her ankle, reaching for her knee. She tried to pull away—her muscles were strong from long nights waiting tables at her father's tavern—but the grip of the vine was stronger. There must be some way to break free of this thing. Todd had promised her a knife, but he had disappeared before she could get it.

The vine jerked at her leg, pulling her to her knees. Other vines reached for her hands, her arms, her shoulders, her face. She tried to thrash around, to somehow loosen the grip of these things, but everywhere she turned, another tendril pushed forward, lacing through her fingers, braiding through her hair. The vines yanked at her again, pulling her toward the ground. They would smother her.

She used all the strength she had left to lift her head enough to look away from the ground, up toward the forest.

"Nick!" she called.

He stood in front of her, only an arm's length away. Nick had drawn his sword, and he was laughing.

Where was Raven when you needed him?

When Jason looked back to the clearing, he saw two people had arrived quite suddenly, without any noise. Like magic, he thought. One was Mr. Mills, the vice-principal at their high school, back when they were on a world that had a high school.

But the other one was Nunn, their enemy, who had tried to kill or control them since they had gotten here, either through his magic or with his soldiers. And now he had brought Mills here . . . to do what?

Jason wondered if there was something he could do to protect Mr. Mills. Not that he would know how to protect him; Raven had told Jason he was the new Oomgosh, but he didn't tell him how he was supposed to take over for their dead friend. Besides the fact that he didn't need to wear his glasses anymore, Jason didn't know anything had changed.

But before the bird had abruptly disappeared, Raven had told him to listen. For right now, Jason felt he should follow the bird's advice.

Besides, there might be more coming. Raven had said there would be between two and five. That seemed like a pretty fuzzy description for a bird who claimed to know everything. So far, Jason saw only two.

Neither one of them was moving naturally. Instead, both of them jerked around, the movements of their arms and legs exaggerated, like puppets with invisible strings. Maybe, Jason thought, these two were being controlled by the others Raven talked about. But where were the others? Were they invisible?

Well, they could be, Jason thought. After all, if he was the Oomgosh, nothing was impossible.

It took Mills a minute to focus on the other man. Every time he thought he had the hang of this multiple-personality thing, it shifted on him all over again. It was as if the three of them that had somehow magically crowded into his body—Mills, Rox, and Zachs—couldn't help but clash, even when they were trying to cooperate.

The way Nunn was shaking, it made Mills feel like a pillar of health. It was hard to judge the wizard's exact condition. Nunn's skin held no color at any time; his flesh had the tone and texture of bleached parchment, looking as though it might crack away at any moment to show the like-colored bone beneath. If Nunn had always looked like death before, he now looked more like a corpse returned from a freshly dug grave.

The wizard took a deep breath, as if air was all he needed to give him strength. He glared at Mills.

"Where are we?" Nunn demanded.

"I thought you'd know," Mills replied in a much quieter voice. "This is your island."

Nunn shook his head in annoyance. "Why are we here, Mills?" he demanded.

Except he didn't look like the wizard anymore. Instead, he was wearing the face of another, as if Nunn, too, contained beings that struggled for control.

"Nunn?" As if to illustrate that struggle, the voice that issued from Mills's mouth was no longer his own. "You've changed," the second voice added.

The wizard inside Mills was trying to take control. But Mills wasn't ready to retreat. He knew the face now wearing Nunn's form, a face from back on Chestnut Circle. A drop of sweat rolled down his face as he opened his mouth to speak for himself.

"Carl?" Mills managed a second later. The single syllable came out more like a hoarse croak, as if Mills had lost the use of his own vocal cords to the other beings inside him.

"Kill him!" another, higher voice issued from Mills's throat. "Kill him now!" For an instant Mills's face felt as though it were on fire. Mills shuddered. Both of the other beings were pushing to take charge of his physical form. Mills felt dizzy, disoriented. It was an effort simply to stand.

"Yeah," said the voice of Carl Jackson, speaking from Nunn's body. "That old magician was a real weakling—he needed somebody to take over his—" Mr. Jackson froze, his shoulders drooping, fingers curling to make his hands look like claws.

"No," another voice whispered, a voice in pain, Nunn's voice, "you don't know—you can't control—"

Mills was startled to hear the voice from his chest laugh at the pain he/they heard in Nunn. The wizard Rox had taken control again. "You're in worse shape than I am. But I think Nunn's right, my dear—Carl, is it? Somebody should take those jewels away from you before you hurt yourself. How lucky for you that I brought you to a quiet place for the exchange."

Nunn straightened up at that, somehow looking both broader and taller than before. "Don't touch me!" Jackson's voice demanded. "Take one more step, and I'll flatten you!"

Whoever was occupying Nunn's form took a step of his own toward Mills, balling a hand into a fist. But when he tried to swing his arm, Nunn/Jackson stumbled and almost fell.

Mills shook his head, or rather, Rox shook it for him. "Muscular control *is* a problem when you've got more than one consciousness. I tend to avoid quick movements of any kind. But slow, steady action is fine." He grabbed the wizard's sleeve. "So give me a minute while I work these dragon's eyes out of your hands."

"Nunn!" Now Jackson's voice sounded like it was in pain, too, as he looked down at his hands. "Let me use these things!" The jewels embedded in both his palms—the dragon's eyes, source of the wizard's power—started to glow a sickly green.

"Yeah!" Jackson laughed, the pain forgotten. "Let's see if I can make a fist with magic behind it!"

He tried to yank his sleeve away from Mills's grasp, and almost lost his balance a second time.

"You really are pitiful." Rox chuckled. "So I'll have to take what I need."

"Nunn will trick us!" Mills's face burned again as the third being within tried to take control. "Let Zachs fly!"

"Zachs!" came Nunn's whispered response. "Remember who made you!"

The burning sensation only got worse. "Zachs remembers who hurt him!"

Carl Jackson's face flickered across Nunn's features as he looked down at his glowing palms. "We got two of these things, right, Nunn? We should be able to overpower them!"

He lurched forward, wrapping his hands around Mills's throat.

The jewel! Mills thought—we have to use—

Give me control! Rox called back.

"Let me burn!" Zachs interupted out loud. "I will destroy Nunn's hands!"

The world was consumed by fire.

Something new was wrong here.

Jason stared at the place where the two men had disappeared.

Their argument had lasted only for a moment. But neither one of the men was what he first appeared to be.

Jason saw it first in their faces. They kept *changing*. It was like their features, eyes, noses, mouths, chins, were made out of a soft clay, constantly remolded by some invisible hand. Their argument—which never seemed to make any sense—only became increasingly loud. With jerking movements they both lunged forward, as if they would strangle each other. Then, as if they were two puppets controlled by a single string, both Mills and Nunn threw their heads back and screamed.

The scream ended with a flash of brilliant light. Jason had to look away.

When he turned back, both men were gone, with nothing to show they had been here but a small patch of singed grass.

Raven had been right, Jason thought. There had been both two and five here, people inside people. And he had been able to see all of them, too. He wondered if that had something to do with being the Oomgosh.

But, beyond being able to see all the different people, Jason had no idea what had happened.

"What did I tell you?" Raven called as he flew down from his hiding place. "What do wizards know?"

At the moment Jason wasn't sure what he knew, either.

◯ Three

Constance Smith was sure the dragon was testing them.

The power was flowing back into her gem, but slowly, like a great kettle full of water forever approaching the boiling point. She could float now for short distances. Their new arrival, Sala, had been so shocked the first time Constance had drifted by, a couple of feet above the ground. It was amazing how quickly Mrs. Smith had learned to take her powers for granted. And that could be deadly.

They really knew so little about this place. This power of the dragon's threatened to lull her into an odd sort of complacency, when, at any instant, the dragon might find some new way to kill them all.

The wizards were all sham. They claimed to know the secrets of the dragon's eyes, but theirs was a power bought through trial and error—not true understanding. There could be no true passage of knowledge between wizards. She had woken during Obar's instruction of Todd and Mary Lou, and seen the explosive results. Each person used their gem differently; or perhaps, Constance realized, each gem used one of them. The more she directed her dragon's eye, the less she realized she truly knew. Surely, the others with the eyes must suspect the same. And yet none of them—especially the great wizards Obar and Nunn—would ever admit such a thing. How could they defeat anything, much less an all-powerful dragon, when they couldn't even look at themselves?

Obar himself had told them early on that wizards were not to be trusted. She wondered if anything here was as it first appeared. The way the so-called dragon's eyes had fluctuated in power, going from great instruments of magic to near powerlessness, only to now have the magic slowly return; perhaps the dragon simply wanted to play with them before it destroyed them. Maybe everything here—the Anno, the tall trees and thick vines of the forest, the tentacled creatures from beneath the sea, perhaps even the gem in her hand—were claws of the dragon, ready to turn on them at the serpent's whim.

It didn't matter. She had to do her best. Constance shook herself and, with the aid of her gem, willed herself to stand. She had to believe she was brought here for a reason, that she and all the rest of them mattered. What other choice did she have?

And the others found a way to persevere, no matter what happened. Mary Lou had stepped away after Todd's magic had torn the corpse apart. Todd had run from the clearing—not that she should worry about him, she'd never seen anyone have such a powerful connection with his eye. And the Newton Free Volunteers had simply taken the teenagers' places and started stacking bodies on their own.

Obar had frowned at that, tucking his hands deep within his soiled white robes, as if the Volunteers were somehow challenging his magic. Which Constance guessed they were. Sometimes, magic wasn't the best way to get the job done.

Eventually, Obar had bowed to the inevitable, and used his magic to burn the pile of corpses. The rest of them had gathered on the far side of the clearing, farthest from the thick black smoke, but they could still smell the odor, a smell both sweet and bitter, like when you left a roast in the oven too long.

On the far side of the smoke she heard a woman scream.

She quickly glanced at those around her. The neighbor women, Joan, Rebecca, Mary Lou and Rose, even crazy Margaret, were all here. It had to be Sala.

Constance squeezed the gem and wished herself to the other side of the clearing. She was there almost too fast, between one blink of an eye and the next, rushing toward the first of the great trees. Stop! she called, and was suddenly impossibly still, a change so sudden that she almost lost the contents of her stomach. She put a hand to her throat and forced her breathing back under control. The gem's power, so slow to return before, seemed to be coming back now all in an overwhelming rush. It felt as if the dragon's eye was using her, as if she was not so much filled with its power as in danger of being consumed by it. She had to regain some control.

Another set of noises pulled her from her thoughts. Before, there had been screams; now she heard laughter. But the laughter sounded every bit as desperate as the screams that had come before.

She looked between the trees, and the scene to which the magic had brought her. She could see Nick and Sala, both some twenty yards away, both relatively still, but around them the whole forest was moving. It was the vines, Constance realized, those thick blue-green creepers that seemed to grow over everything at the forest's edge, and that made strange, almost animal sounds when they were cut. Now the vines had risen from the ground, dropped down from overhanging branches, freed themselves from the boles of trees. They were swirling in the air, dancing to some unheard music, whipping about in an ever-more-ecstatic frenzy.

It looked to Constance as though the forest was a single being with a thousand tentacles. The way the vines swung, not always in unison but always with a common rhythm, reminded her of those strange multilimbed creatures you saw in documentaries about the bottom of the ocean, or the bottom of a telescope.

Nick and Sala were at the exact center of the commotion. For all their movement, the vines were not attacking the two of them directly. They seemed more intent on keeping them prisoner, twisting about their ankles and wrists to keep them in place, whipping before their faces if they tried to run.

Sala pulled on the vines that wrapped around her body. Nick was more successful in cutting them away. He laughed constantly, but there was no joy in it. It sounded more like some hysterical fatigue. A dark, viscous fluid spurted from the many places he had severed the tendrils. But his movements were slowing, his balance not always sure. The sap from the vines didn't seem to give him the same energy as blood. Still he stood his ground, slashing vine after groping vine, the constant laughter hoarse in his throat.

Constance stared at the hundreds of vines waving before her. So much was happening, what could she do about it? The vast number of moving vines was almost overwhelming. She remembered the trip she and some of the others had taken across the ocean, and the tentacles from beneath the deep that came to sink their ship. They had needed Todd's youthful power to overcome that menace. She wished now that Todd had stayed so that he could burn these vines in the same way he had destroyed the tentacles at sea.

Mrs. Smith had a different magic, and she would use it as best she could. She looked at the dozen vines closest to her and thought of scarves she had knitted on winter nights, the intricate dance of knitting needles that had joined disparate threads into a whole. Over, under, left then right.

The vines tugged this way and that, fighting her control, but her magic was stronger. Over, under, left then right.

The vines twirled about each other, joining in an ever-tighter pattern. Over, under, left then right.

The mass of creepers she had concentrated on were completely entangled, pulling against each other in ever-tighter knots. They would threaten no one. So her magic worked, in small, concrete ways. But could she braid the entire forest?

She looked out to the commotion that still encircled the two adolescents and, for the first time, noticed something beyond them.

Past the swirling vines were a ring of the Anno, the naked, bald, wizened little creatures that still looked almost human. Their large eyes seemed to flicker in the darkness, as if the vines were only an extension of their thoughts. Beyond that they were utterly still, watching silently, as if waiting for the proper moment to make their entrance.

And above them, almost lost in the shadows of the trees, was Mary Lou. She hung suspended some three feet above the heads of the little creatures. She must have flown through the air to this spot just like Constance, but the sight of the Anno beneath her seemed to freeze her.

Or perhaps she had stopped the Anno.

Nick staggered as a vine encircled his waist from behind. Sala's arms were so wrapped by the vines that she could no longer move. Mary Lou stared back at Mrs. Smith with a gaze that didn't seem to focus on anything.

For an instant everyone was still.

"Mary Lou!" Mrs. Smith called. "I need your help!"

And she heard Mary Lou's reply in her head. *The Anno say*

that this comes from the dragon. He is displeased with the way we have used our eyes.

So this was the dragon's doing? Certainly, Constance had never seen anything of this magnitude before. Nick turned around and hacked at the vine that had grabbed his waist. Four other vines reached for his arms, his chest, his head.

The Anno say that the dragon requires sacrifices, the girl's voice continued in her head. *These two would do nicely.*

These tiny near-humans liked to eat people. They had come close to eating Mary Lou. Constance wondered how the teenager could report so dispassionately on what the Anno demanded.

Somehow, Nick had managed to free himself from the latest attack and was struggling toward Sala. The island girl had vines twining around most of her lower body now. A single strand reached up to caress her face. Eventually, Mrs. Smith thought, the vines would suffocate her.

If this came from the dragon, it looked like this was where Constance and the dragon firmly parted company.

"We are in this together," Constance said aloud, even though her voice wouldn't carry through the chaos of the clearing. "If I can help it, I don't want to lose any of us."

I do not entirely believe the Anno, was Mary Lou's reply.

"I believe in the power of our eyes," Constance whispered. She was quite sure Mary Lou heard.

But what could they do with their dragon's eyes? As if in answer to her question, Constance felt her head flood with images. She was one of many small things, running through the forest. She saw a great wing, blotting out the sky. She was facing up to a great wall of fire. She heard a great rumble, a noise so deep that it might crack open the ground beneath her feet.

Constance realized these images came from the Anno. They spoke of fear and frantic activity, things the Anno must perform so that the fire would leave their home, rising into the heavens until it became no larger than any other star. The Anno believed they were doing the dragon's bidding. They were driven to it by the threat—or promise—of destruction.

I am the vessel, Mary Lou called out to her in the midst of this riot of images. *You must be the source.*

Mrs. Smith frowned. Those certainly didn't sound like the

sort of words Mary Lou would use—at least the Mary Lou she had known back on Chestnut Circle. But then, that Mary Lou had changed every bit as much as Constance.

She had said she was the vessel, but for what? Those pictures appearing in Mrs. Smith's mind? Mary Lou was certainly feeding them to her, and the images seemed to come from the Anno. Was Mary Lou saying she was acting to transmit those messages? Perhaps she had found a way to use her magic sort of like a radio tower. She could send and receive messages. She transported those messages. She was the vessel.

But she needed someone else to be the source.

The Anno were acting on messages that they thought came from the dragon. The only way they might stop their extreme behavior was to give them new messages, show the small but vicious creatures that there was another option.

It was up to Constance, then, to create new pictures, new images.

But what?

Nick shouted. Sala screamed. Constance stopped herself from breaking her mental link with Mary Lou. There was no way her magic could free the others in time.

But Mary Lou had told Constance that there was a way to defeat the vines. If they worked quickly, and together.

Mrs. Smith pictured a peaceful clearing, full of the neighbors and those they had met in this place. Into this clearing walked three of the Anno. And everyone was smiling.

Why were they smiling? There had to be a reason. Mrs. Smith imagined herself stepping forward. She had something in her hand, something to give to the Anno. She couldn't picture exactly what it was. She knew that Anno had certain objects they valued highly; things that they used in their rituals. Mrs. Smith had never paid much attention to that sort of detail. Perhaps Mary Lou could give details to that part of the vision.

One of the Anno accepted her gift. And suddenly Constance could sense the dragon, as if the great serpent had forced itself into her vision. But the dragon was very far away, and there was something—the way all those in the clearing stood, the fact that they were all together, the presentation of the gift, *something*—that kept the dragon from coming nearer.

Mrs. Smith heard a low moaning noise outside her vision. She opened her eyes and saw that the vines had stopped moving, and were falling away from Nick and Sala. The moaning came from the Anno. They still stood on the far side of the clearing, but they looked to Mrs. Smith now and, in unison, bowed their heads. Then the sound from their throats was gone, and they vanished in the shadows.

Mrs. Smith realized something important had happened here, something larger than simply saving two of their party. That scene in the clearing was only something she imagined. Why did she feel that it held a deeper truth?

"Stop it!" Nick cried. Constance looked back to where Nick, free now of the vines, was rushing toward Sala. Or, rather, he was being dragged toward Sala, for his feet fought his forward momentum. But the sword that he held at arm's length seemed to be stronger, forcing him on.

Sala lay huddled on the ground, her breathing shallow. The vines had nearly overwhelmed her before they had retreated. Now Nick's sword was seeking her blood.

"No!" Mrs. Smith thought herself there, and she was at Sala's side. She held her gem tight and imagined a great, invisible hand, held palm out, that would stop Nick and his sword where they stood.

"Never!" Nick said between clenched teeth. He raised his sword above his head and brought it down in a slicing motion, cleaving the magic in two.

Constance gasped. She had felt an instant of pain, a dull pain, like banging against a desk, but pain nonetheless. Somehow, Nick had broken her magic. She had thought this sort of thing impossible.

She formed two hands this time and made them fly above and behind Nick, swooping in to grab him by the shoulders.

Nick jerked away as the hands descended, spinning and skewering first one and then the other. Mrs. Smith felt the distant sword's point twice—bee stings, this time.

"No way to stop it," Nick groaned, and ran toward them. Mrs. Smith stepped in front of Sala. If she couldn't stop Nick, she would be the one to accept his sword.

But Nick stumbled. The sword fell from his hand. He stared down at it for an instant, then he, too, fell forward, his last energy fled.

"A bit too close, wouldn't you say?" Obar said from Constance's side.

She frowned. She hadn't heard him arrive, but that wasn't surprising for a wizard. What was strange was how Obar had been able to stop Nick where Mrs. Smith had failed.

Obar had given Nick that sword in the first place. He had claimed he hadn't known the sword's dark secret, and that it would be dangerous to take the sword from Nick now.

Mrs. Smith thought that Obar wasn't telling everything he knew about the sword's power.

Never trust a wizard.

○ Around the Circle:
Bobby's Perfect Summer

The screen door slammed behind him. Bobby Furlong knew what his mother was going to say even before the words were out of her mouth.

"You be back here in time for dinner, young man!"

As if Bobby was ever not home in time for dinner. It was the one time the whole family was together. They sat down around the kitchen table—the dining room was only for special occasions—all in their regular seats, at 5:35 every weekday. His father would mumble a few words about work while his mother brought out the food. Then his mother would complain about the high price of something, or maybe mention that she thought one of the neighbors was snubbing them, and who did they think they were, anyway? Her nightly conversation out of the way, she sat down and his father turned to Bobby and asked him the question.

"So how was school today?"

It was always the same question, and it always demanded a different answer. Bobby had learned that saying "good" or "boring" or "nothing much happened" just wasn't enough. He had to come up with some story about something—and the more positive the better—like the hard questions he had gotten right on a test, or winning at soccer, or at least what happened at this week's assembly. His parents didn't want to hear any problems. They'd say things like "Chin up!" and "You'll get over it!" and then change the subject. And his father would start to tease him if he ever mentioned girls.

But dinner wasn't for hours yet. Bobby's best friend Jason had shown up at the door, with the kind of smile that said he had a secret.

Bobby smiled back at his best friend. They didn't have to talk much. They already knew what mattered.

"What's up?" Bobby asked.

But Jason only grinned. "C'mon," he called as he leaped off the Furlongs' front steps.

"What?" Bobby demanded. He had to tell his parents something about where he was going.

Jason looked so excited he could barely wait to run to this thing, whether Bobby was with him or not.

"Wait'll you see."

"Yeah?" Bobby looked back from the screen door. His father wouldn't come home from work until a few minutes before dinner; his mother was in the kitchen with the radio. They'd barely know he was gone.

He frowned back at Jason. "Better be good."

"Better than that!"

"Going to Jason's!" he called before his mother could call the question after him. He and Jason always said they were going to the other's house. Their parents never checked.

"C'mon," Jason said again, and headed out into the woods.

Their whole street bordered the woods. The man who sold Bobby's parents their house had said there would be other streets just like Chestnut Circle springing up here, but that hadn't happened yet. Instead, there were trees to one side and overgrown farmland to the other. Bobby often thought that the best thing about his street was what stuff was around it.

Jason led them down one of the regular paths, past the rotten log, around the wild grapes, over the narrow part of the crik, the water moving pretty good over the shale. But then Jason kept on walking, up another path over the hill on the far side. They were going farther into the woods than Bobby had ever been.

"Hey, Jas—" Bobby began.

His friend didn't even turn back to look at him. "Wait," was all he said. He led Bobby down through a gully and up along another ridge. That's where Jason stopped, pointing ahead.

"There," he announced.

Bobby looked ahead and saw the old, half-fallen-down shack in the middle of the trees. But Bobby knew it was a lot more than a shack.

"This is our fort," Jason said.

Bobby had thought the exact same thing, the minute he had seen it.

School had ended for the summer a week later, and Bobby and Jason had begun to really get the fort together. It wasn't much to begin with, just a dirt floor, a roof with a good-sized hole, and four walls, with two of the walls half fallen down.

But Jason's father had some scrap lumber that he let the boys use. They managed to prop up the walls, and even built a rough ladder to let them look out of their spy hole in the roof. That way, they could see for miles.

In the distance, somebody really was building something. When the wind was blowing the right way, Bobby and Jason could hear the sounds of hammers and big earth-moving machines. Mostly they saw clouds of dust. The two of them decided that the enemy was out there, beyond those clouds.

The noises grew louder as the summer went on. The builders were moving toward them. They were going to build streets close to Chestnut Circle after all.

By the end of July, they could see the trucks and earth-movers. From within the safety of the fort, the big machines sounded like tanks rumbling through the desert. The enemy was getting closer. They had to defend their position. Bobby and Jason took turns climbing up to the spy hole and shooting the invaders with the invisible guns they had in their hands, always careful to make just the right rat-tat-tat sounds.

Nobody particularly wanted to know what the boys were doing with their time. Bobby's parents seemed happier with him out of the way, so long as he was back home in time for dinner; Jason's parents spent all their time worrying about his two older sisters. So the boys read comics and traded baseball cards and listened to Jason's transistor radio.

August ended, and their world was shrinking. The big machines looked a lot more like trucks and bulldozers than enemy tanks now that they were only a couple hundred feet away. The woods that had seemed to stretch forever beyond their fort was now nothing but dirt. Jason couldn't come every day anymore; his mother kept dragging him and his sisters on never-ending back-to-school errands. Bobby kept showing up, though, just to have a place of his own to go.

One day ran into another. The machines were quiet, so it

had to be the weekend. The heat felt more like summer's middle than its end. Bobby lay back against the packed dirt of the fort's floor. It was cooler here when you didn't move.

But he was moving. He looked up at the spy hole in the roof, and rose up through it without using the ladder.

The world outside was different. The machines were not just quiet, they were gone. The forest had returned. But now it went on forever, green on top of green, a jungle as far as he could see.

He could tell other things had changed as well. There were things greater than trucks and tanks out there—wild monsters that they would slay, not with a gun or a sword but with a glance. They could be great cats roaming the wild, hawk-billed birds of prey, or giants who could crush the forest below like so much kindling. He couldn't wait for Jason to join him. The world was full of light and noise and possibilities.

Somewhere out there he heard a voice. It came from the beasts on the ground, echoed by the parrots in the trees, picked up by the rumble of distant thunder. It was a single word, said over and over. His name. Bobby.

Jason was calling him.

He heard his friend's voice, close by his ear. The forest was gone. He was no longer floating over the world. He opened his eyes.

Jason smiled down at him and said, "Boy, are you in trouble."

Bobby stood quickly. What had he done this time?

"It's after six o'clock," Jason explained. "They went down to look for you around the school. I told them that's where you had to be."

Bobby nodded, impressed by his friend's quick thinking. At least the fort was still theirs, for now.

"I lost them for a minute, but you'd better get home."

Bobby ran all the way home, even though it hardly made a difference. He knew exactly what was going to happen.

Bobby had slept through dinnertime. He'd broken the only rule that mattered. His father yelled, his mother cried. This was the way he repaid their trust. He was grounded until Christmas. They wouldn't let him out of their sight.

Except that they didn't want him underfoot, either. Bobby spent most of his time in his room. He was grateful now that school was only a couple days away; it would give him something to do, away from his parents' disapproval.

His mother still demanded he come home right after school was over. And stay in his room, no back talk, they didn't want to see him until dinner.

He snuck out anyways, three days into the new school year, when his mother had to leave to go to the store. He had to see everything one more time, peek through the spy hole, lie back on the cool dirt floor, maybe even think again about that different world outside.

The bulldozers had been there already.

The fort and everything around it was gone, with no sign of the old rotting shack or any of the trees and bushes. The gulleys and hills were gone, too. It was all flat, all brown, all dry and dusty. The great trucks roared back and forth across the place that used to be woods, dumping and pushing the dirt to fill in the crik. The whole place was empty, waiting for homes just like those on Chestnut Circle.

He was too old to cry, but he wanted to anyways. He wanted to go see Jason, but was afraid his parents would find out. Their place was gone.

But Bobby had to go, too.

Dinner was waiting.

O Four

Todd didn't even know why he was running.

When he had used the magic back in the clearing, it had hit at something deep down inside. It felt like the same thing that had torn the corpse apart wanted to tear him apart, too; something so strong that it still kept him moving.

What scared him the most was that it wasn't something new. He had carried it with him from back on Chestnut Circle. It was why he had always had to be tough, why he had led a gang at school, why it was always safer to sneer and laugh at others than let your true feelings show. He had done his best to keep it hidden, sometimes even from himself.

But it was always there, like if he turned fast enough he could see it, standing just behind him. Somehow, his having a dragon's eye just made it more real. In a place like this it could be real, fit right in with the giant trees around him. The more he thought about it, the more he knew how it would look—big and dark and overwhelming.

And its face would look like his father. His drunken, angry father, hitting Todd when he was younger and smaller, hitting his mother all the time.

He had spent a long time running from that face. Running, just like he was doing now.

Todd forced his feet to stop. He wasn't going anywhere, only running away. He had been racing down a wide path cut through the forest; probably the same path his father had used as part of Nunn's army. But that army had been turned back, at least for now, and Todd's father had disappeared.

He opened his palm and looked at the small, green gem he held there, the dragon's eye. It seemed to glow gently in the dim forest light. He couldn't help but feel that there was a reason behind his getting this gem, and not for any of the reasons he used to win back in that other world; because he was stronger or meaner, or had a smarter tongue or a gang behind him. He had gotten this gem—and it was clear that it was meant for him—because of what was inside him, the same force that had used the dragon's eyes to burn a sea monster to ashes and tear a corpse to bloody bits of flesh. He might have a terrible power, but somehow, that was what the dragon wanted.

There was no running away from the dragon's eye. Standing here alone in the dark woods, he knew the dragon's eye was leading him somewhere, maybe to face his father, and all the things inside himself, maybe all at the same time.

What would he do with his father once he found him? He wished he could make his father change. "But nobody ever made Carl Jackson do anything!" Todd's father shouted that sort of thing even when he was sober. What would he do, now that he had the gem, if his father tried to hurt him or any of his friends?

Maybe he would have to crush his father, the same way his father had tried to crush him.

The gem in his hand flashed for an instant and there was something else inside his head besides his thoughts. He saw a series of very clear pictures, as if someone had popped a television inside his brain.

He saw a battle, between Nick and Sala and a hundred moving vines. Sala! He had been so full of himself, he had left her behind. He hoped he could save her. He hoped she would forgive him.

Mary Lou was there, and Mrs. Smith. Obar stood off to one side, watching. All three of them had dragon's eyes—is that how he was getting these pictures, from the dragon?

Did the eyes connect all the people who held the stones?

Maybe he would have time to think about all that later. He was already running back the way he had come. If anything happened to Sala, he would never forgive himself.

And he would kill anything that touched her.

Nick didn't know what to do. His hand no longer held a sword.

He had needed blood. His sword had needed it, really; the enchanted blade had used up all of its own power and Nick's energy as well. He knew he needed blood or he would die. And he would get it from whoever was most convenient. They had all ceased to be people; they were only vessels to be drained.

He and the sword had become one being, a being with great needs, but a creature who also could not be stopped. Obar had taken that away. He had said something, and the life that passed between Nick and the sword had died. Nick's fingers had gone numb. The sword had fallen away.

Nick fell to his knees. He had no strength, and he no longer had the sword. He had nothing.

He was vaguely aware of hands picking him up, carrying him back into the clearing. Of other hands forcing him to drink. His mouth chewing some sweet, pulpy fruit. How long had it been since he had eaten, or had anything to drink? The sword had given him another kind of nourishment.

His vision, nothing but a blur since he had lost the sword, began to clear. He recognized some of his neighbors; old Mrs. Smith, Bobby Furlong, who used to live across the street, and Stanley, one of the Newton Free Volunteers. For an instant Nick wondered what had happened to Maggie. Something had started between Nick and her, before the sword had taken over.

Next to Bobby sat Charlie, Nick's dog. But the dog had been changing ever since they'd come to this strange place. A ridge of bone had formed over the dog's eyes, his shoulders had become even larger and more muscular, and his canines now were so large that the dog's mouth could no longer contain them; two needlelike points hung over Charlie's lower lip. Charlie now looked like nothing so much as some strange ornamental statue; some ancient representation of a dog from the netherworld.

"Hey, Charlie," Nick managed, his voice not more than a whisper.

Charlie simply looked back at him, no barking, no wagging tail. Maybe, Nick thought, Charlie wasn't his dog anymore. Maybe Nick had changed, too—changed so much that the dog no longer recognized him.

"Nick?"

He glanced up at the sound of his mother's voice. At least

some things hadn't changed. The look of concern on her face
was no different from what he'd seen back on Chestnut Circle.

"Hey, Mom." He did his best to smile. He didn't want her
any more worried than she was already.

A man stepped up next to his mother.

"Good to see you're awake."

Nick frowned. That's right. Somehow his father had gotten
here, too. Nick felt he should remember more of this. What
else had the sword done to him?

They gave him some baked meat. His mother told him it
was a kind of rabbit. Somebody named the Captain had caught
it.

Things blurred again after that. He must have fallen asleep.
He saw all the neighbors around him, a dozen of them, parents
and kids both. And all of them were bleeding. Obar staggered
up to him, his white suit marred by a crimson stain that spread
as Nick watched.

"What have you done?" the wizard moaned.

"No," Nick replied with a shake of his head. "What have
you done?"

The wizard started to cry, and his tears were blood as well,
red-brown streaks staining his corpulent cheeks. Nick turned
away. What did it matter? No matter what he did, he couldn't
stop the bleeding.

He opened his eyes and he was walking. It took him a minute to realize that he was awake now, that somehow he had
begun to walk in his sleep. His feet kept moving still, as if
they had a purpose they weren't sharing with the rest of him.

It was dark and quiet around him. He must have slept for
hours. Despite that, he was still exhausted. With that thought,
he knew where his feet were taking him. There was only one
thing that could give him strength.

Nick looked around. There was a fire built in the middle of
the clearing, and a man standing beyond it. But the man had
his back turned toward Nick. Nick had difficulty telling—his
eyes still weren't quite working right—but the man looked like
his father.

But Nick had more immediate needs to deal with. His feet
had led him to Obar's tent.

Obar had used his magic to construct an elaborate mass of
filmy white canvas, with five separate levels each decreasing

in size, as if his command of sorcery might still give him some status among the others. Nick stepped past the front flap. He had half expected the magician to construct some sort of mystical barrier that Nick couldn't pass. Instead, the front of the tent was wide-open. Nick could hear Obar softly snoring as he stepped inside.

As elaborate as the tent looked from without, it was almost featureless within. Obar lay at the exact center of the open space, deep asleep. Directly above him, hovering about four feet in the air with nothing to support it but Obar's magic, was the sword.

Nick moved quickly to the weapon. Something in the back of his brain, something perhaps not quite fully awake, asked if this might not all be too easy; that perhaps Obar wanted Nick to take the sword again.

But that voice was far too small to argue against Nick's need. A shudder went through him as he touched the sword hilt. Without effort, the sword and scabbard swung about and attached themselves to Nick's belt. He shuddered again. It was a feeling of pure joy. He was complete again.

And, as soon as the sword had touched his hand, he was sure that this was exactly what Obar wanted. Nick dependent upon the sword. Nick under Obar's control.

Nick could feel the anger grow inside him. This magician's trick would be Obar's last. Nick needed strength. The sword needed blood. The sleeping figure before them would make the perfect sacrifice.

Nick's elation increased as he drew the sword from the scabbard. He would plunge the sword point into Obar's heart, and everything would be his.

He swung the sword down toward the magician in white. The sword point bounced away, his weapon leaping up like a rubber ball, the motion so violent that Nick almost lost his grip.

This was where Obar had placed his protection. He had woven some sort of barrier around his sleeping form.

But Nick had a magic sword. He gripped the hilt in both hands this time, using all his strength to drive the point straight down into the magician's back.

Blood! Nick thought. I must have blood!

The sword jerked wildly as it descended toward the magician, the point burying itself three inches into the soft dirt by Obar's side.

"No!" Nick wailed, the one syllable going on forever, beginning as a moan and ending as a scream. He had drawn the sword. They had to have blood now.

The magician had foiled him. But there were others nearby, others who slept without the aid of magic, others the sword could take easily. Nick rushed from the tent.

He lived for the sword. The sword lived for blood. There was nothing else beyond that.

○ Five

Evan Mills was afraid he was lost.

He knew it as soon as he opened his eyes. The place he found himself was full of rocks and mist, a different part of the island, or perhaps some other island entirely.

But he had known he was lost before his eyes were even open. He was lost within his own body. Only one of three entities currently occupying his physical form, he had managed to become a minority within his own flesh.

He was on his hands and knees, his head close to the ground, as if he had been bowing toward something in the mist. Could this be the doing of one of the others inside him? He could still feel the others, somewhere deep within, but they felt distant, removed, as though they had been even more shaken than he was by recent events.

Mills pushed himself away from the ground, using a sharp outcropping by his side to pull himself to his feet. He felt a little light-headed, not surprising after what had happened. The ground sloped upward just ahead, showing half a dozen more thin, tall slabs stretched out before him, before both rocks and ground were lost in the surrounding gloom. Perhaps the mist would clear at the top of the hill, and he could get some idea of his surroundings. Using the rocks by his side to help maintain his balance, he started up the hill.

He almost fell after half a dozen steps. He grabbed the stones by his side, afraid it was some problem with his balance. It was only with the rock's support that he realized that the rock he leaned against, and the ground beneath him, were doing the moving.

It must be some sort of tremor. He hoped he wasn't walking

up the side of an active volcano. He suddenly wished the wizard would wake up inside him, just to let Mills know where they were.

Mills stared ahead into the fog. The line of rocks grew progressively larger, each one slightly bigger than the one before, as if they had been placed there by some ancient Druids following some great design. Well, why not? Mills thought. If the dragon had brought his neighbors here, he could have brought Druids as well.

The earth moved again, shifting violently beneath Mills's feet. He was beginning to wonder if he could walk anywhere.

His mouth opened, and a deep voice said, "I know where we are."

It was Rox's voice. Hearing it—and speaking it—brought Mills an odd mixture of despair and relief.

"We have been called here," Rox continued. "Before the dragon." The wizard paused, than chuckled dryly. "Actually, we are *on* the dragon. No doubt such a position keeps the creature from accidentally crushing us."

Mills looked down at the stone slab he still held. But it wasn't a rock. It was a part of the dragon.

"What does it want?" Zachs cried out for all of them.

"We are still aware," the wizard replied. "It is my guess that the dragon will let us live. Perhaps it just wants to—say hello."

"It will hurt!" their third, high voice added. "Hurt Zachs! Hurt us—"

Mills's head was filled with light.

He thought for an instant that the brightness was before him and instinctively moved to shield his eyes. But he had no sense of where his hands might be, or his eyes, no sense of his physical form. There was nothing but light, as if his body had been tossed aside so that his inner self might be examined under this overwhelming glare.

His three inner selves, Mills realized.

The light was gone. There was an instant of blackness so intense Mills wondered if he might ever see again.

"Are you still here?" Rox asked, although Mills couldn't quite tell if the wizard was using his voice or speaking inside his head. "Am I?"

Mills blinked, and the world came back into focus. They

were no longer on the back of the dragon. Instead, they were surrounded by trees. Mills had never thought the towering trunks could be so reassuring.

"I am here," Mills said with his own voice.

"And I am with you," Rox replied from within.

"Zachs hurts!" the third voice cried. "What have you done? What have you done?"

Mills realized the third voice—Zachs's voice—was no longer inside him.

There was a flash of fire, high above them in the trees. "Zachs hurts! Zachs will burn!" A circle of flame appeared in the branches fifty feet overhead.

The fire stopped suddenly, coalescing into a single point of light.

"What are you doing down there?" Zachs demanded. "Why aren't you with Zachs?"

This, Mills realized, was the dragon's doing.

"Zachs is free!" the high voice cried. "Zachs is gone!"

A wall of flame rushed away from them, burning toward the horizon.

The dragon didn't want Zachs to be a part of us, then, Mills thought, or maybe said.

"It is done," the wizard replied, "and there is nothing the two of us can do about it. Now it is just us two. Perhaps we can learn to work together."

Perhaps, Mills thought, you can also learn to tell the truth. Still, Mills had to admit he was glad to be rid of the mercurial Zachs, one part fire, another part vengeful child. And the dragon had simply plucked the creature out of them. How could they hope to survive, if the dragon toyed with them so easily?

And what would Zachs do now that he was free?

After the strength of that explosion, Nunn was astonished to see he was still alive. He managed another breath. The pain in his rib cage—so overwhelming only a moment ago—was subsiding. He looked down at his hands. He could feel his fingers again. Distantly, he could also feel the cool power of the gems in his palms. And, somewhere deep inside him, he could feel the spirit of Carl Jackson.

Nunn had to get off his knees. He might need to defend

himself—either from outside, or from within. He would be able to do it in a minute, surely, as soon as he gained a little strength. He decided to concentrate for a moment on his breathing.

At least the confrontation with Rox had allowed the wizard to regain control of his own body. Jackson had been dislodged—or he had fled—from Nunn's conscious mind when the world had exploded around them.

But, besides whatever lurked within, Nunn seemed to be quite alone now. That explosion had thrown the wizard somewhere else, in another part of the forest, with no sign of Rox and the other creatures who had joined him. Nunn looked up from the spot where the wizard and the spirit within him had landed, scanning the trees and the sky for something familiar.

The sky suddenly appeared too vast, the trees swaying crazily as if they might topple and crush Nunn beneath their bulk. Nunn doubled over, his head touching the ground as he was overwhelmed by a new wave of nausea.

No. This was too much. He would not let this happen.

Nunn closed his eyes. This was all the dragon's doing. He had sworn long ago that the dragon would never get the better of Nunn. Nunn had become the master of the world the dragon left behind. He had conquered or killed all who stood in his way—all but his brother Obar. But Obar had changed with his confrontation with the dragon. He'd become indecisive, disoriented, a little addled, really. While Obar was still capable of using his own dragon's eye, Nunn had never seen his brother as much of a threat.

Perhaps, Nunn thought, this was another mistake. He seemed to have underestimated so many of his foes of late.

The wizard opened his eyes wide and took a deep breath of the forest air. He had become too immersed in his own magic and had lost connection with the world around him, the very place from where the magic sprang. How long since he had truly noted the thousand different shades of green and brown, the mingled odors of life and decay? In the stillness, he could hear small creatures scurry through the dying leaves nearby, and birds call back and forth high overhead, and beyond it all, a sound fainter still, like a great wind in the distance.

Nunn did not care for this last sound. Something was coming, something alien to the wood around him. Nunn did not

trust the power of his dragon's eyes, or his own physical re-
action to it, enough to conjure some notion of what this new
thing was. The disturbance was still very faint, only noticeable
because of the quiet of the rest of the wood. Whatever it was,
it seemed too far away to be a danger—yet.

Nunn took a step forward and was pleased to feel his vertigo
and nausea were gone. Perhaps the eyes were taking care of
that problem first, and would soon glow with enough energy
to be of real use. He could—cautiously, this time, begin his
final plans.

He thought how this world had changed as he walked along.
Before the so-called neighbors had arrived, he had been master
here for so long he hadn't even considered the possibility of
failure. But—in these last few days—time and again, he had
underestimated those around him. He should have realized that
at least some of those the dragon had brought would be worthy
of the challenge. And he should also have realized Obar would
do his best to ally himself with the newly powerful.

This was all the dragon's doing. Nunn was more clever than
this. But the dragon changed the rules, just as it had the time
before. Nunn could feel the anger rise in him as he thought
about the creature. He wished he could take his own gems,
and the five other eyes as well, and turn them on their creator,
annihilating him in fire. He wished—

Nunn stopped, and listened. The distant noise had grown
closer, more of a roar of air now than a rush of wind. Nunn
looked overhead, and saw a flicker of fire. *The dragon,* he
thought for an instant, but the flames were too small, too subtle
for that being's grand gestures. There was another sound behind the roar; the laughter and shouts of an excited child.

Zachs. The creature Nunn had created was setting fire to the
treetops.

Nunn cursed the dragon all over again. He couldn't let his
creature find him when he had so little power. Zachs hated his
creator and had no mercy, two attributes Nunn had found quite
useful in the past. Now his creation could kill him.

Nunn's anger burned inside him as he climbed within a
particularly thick tangle of vine. How could he prevail if he
had to hide from his own creation?

But already he could feel the power creeping back to those
stones embedded in his palms. Even now, in this most vul-

nerable of moments, he had certain advantages he could not forget.

There were only two here still alive who had survived the last visit of the dragon. And only one of those two was fully in control of his own mind.

The endgame was near. This world would change again. And Nunn would let no one, or no thing, stand in his way.

Nunn huddled beneath the leafy growth, the pain within him fading from memory. He raised his hands before his face, each gem glowing green—faint still, but far stronger than before. Soon they would be full of power, ready for use. Soon he would no longer have to hide from Zachs or Rox or Obar. He would challenge everything on this world. He would kill anyone who stepped in his path. But he would reserve his greatest anger for the dragon. He would use these instruments of power to humble, perhaps even destroy, the beast. The others would die by Nunn's whim, or in dragon fire.

When the dragon arrived, anything was possible.

And Nunn had to use the possibilities; like Carl Jackson, cowering so deep inside. Perhaps it was time to call on Carl and see if the new addition to Nunn's being could be made useful. Nunn had used many creatures—human and otherwise—before. Most had been consumed and forgotten. Only a few, like Zachs, were ever missed.

The roaring had stopped. Nunn pushed free of his hiding place. Zachs had moved on. And the gems in Nunn's hands glowed even more brightly than before.

Nunn really smiled for the first time in ever so long. Simply because Carl Jackson began as a human didn't mean he should remain that way. This was a real possibility.

There was more than one way to handle a creature like Zachs.

No doubt Carl Jackson could be taught to burn.

○ Around the Circle:
The Oomgosh Remembers Spring

The tall man strode into town. Even though he had never been here before, he was a stranger to no one, for even if you had never seen him before, you would know him instantly. He was a large fellow, but his face was that of a friend. His skin was the color of new bark on sapling, that same green that speaks of spring and the warm days to follow. What grew on top of his head looked not so much like curling hair as tiny leaves, and his strong arms looked not so much like muscled flesh as strong branches that might hold up the sky.

The townspeople peered at this newcomer through the cracks of their shutters, huddled indoors with their sweaters and coats, staying close by their pitifully small fires. For that year winter had refused to end, cold rains alternating with freezing winds, as if the elements wished to sponsor a never-ending fight between ice and mud.

Of all the village, only one small child ventured forth, too curious about the tall man, and too bored by the unending winter, to remain indoors. The child marched right up to the newcomer.

"Who are you?" the small one demanded.

The tall man returned the slightest of smiles. "Who might you think I am?"

The child considered that and answered with the sort of honesty that had not yet been educated out of him (or her).

"I have not seen your face before, so you are new here. In fact, I have never seen anything like you before. You are like all the things around us, but mixed up and made new."

"Then you are not frightened of me?"

The child shook his head.

The tall man's smile grew the slightest bit broader. "Good. Why don't you show me your village?"

So the child did just that. And the tall man was not in the least surprised, for it was a village, much like yours or mine, where people walked and talked and went to market and found special places to gather for one reason or another; where people were born and raised families and tended crops and marched off to war and died. All in all, it was a quite unremarkable place, except that winter refused to leave. And, of course, there was one curious child who had come to talk to the stranger.

The tall man nodded to the child as they reached the bank of the swift-moving stream that showed where the village ended. The stranger knelt, and placed one green finger in the water, then brought that finger to his lips. He repeated the action, this time thrusting his finger into the mud at the water's edge, and bringing that dirt to his lips as well. When he was done with this, he stared into the eyes of the child and said, "Thank you."

The tall man stood at that, and added, "As long as there is one to greet me, I shall welcome them in return. Tell me, is there something I might do for you?"

And the child, who knew no better, replied, "I do wish this winter would end."

The tall man nodded at that, and his smile grew broader still. "The very reason I am here." He pointed to the stream before him. "The water is good, and the soil is ready. It is time, then, to call the sun. He has had all of winter to rest. He is ready, too; he simply needs to be reminded."

With that, the tall man's smile grew as broad as any smile the child had ever seen. And, just as the great smile broke across his face, so did the sun suddenly appear, as the clouds parted to reveal the blazing ball of fire in the midst of a clear spring sky.

And with that, the people in their houses all ran away from their peepholes and pitiful fires and rushed from their houses to meet the miraculous stranger.

But the tall man was gone, and all the villagers could see was one very happy child playing in the sun.

O Six

"Hey, Charlie," Bobby Furlong whispered. "We've got to take care of each other."

He rubbed the new ridges that had formed on the dog's head, fresh masses of bone and cartilage beneath the fur that had made Charlie's skull swell to half again its original size. The dog didn't seem to notice that anything was different. He looked up at the boy. As much as Charlie's head and body had changed, the dog's deep brown eyes were still the same.

Bobby grinned down at him. "So what do you say, huh, boy?"

Charlie licked the back of Bobby's hand, all the answer Bobby would ever need.

"Bobby?" his mother called. She had woken up at last. "Why are you bothering with that dog?"

He turned to look at where his mother still sat, leaning her back against one of the great trees. She had been wandering around the great clearing for most of the afternoon, a large, uneven space, like a huge hand with half a dozen fingers that pushed on into the woods. His mother seemed intent on exploring the edges of every one, with Bobby obediently following, so they might be out of sight of the tents and bonfires of the rest of the neighbors as often as possible.

She frowned back at him, wrinkling her face in disgust. "Smelly animal."

His mother had never liked animals. They tracked up the house, got up on the furniture, shed hair all over the new carpet. Bobby never would have dared to ask for a dog back on Chestnut Circle. But since Nick couldn't take care of his pet anymore, Bobby was overjoyed to take the responsibility.

"Don't you dare bring that dog inside the house," his mother continued as she struggled to her feet. "What are we doing out here, anyway?"

In the pair of days they had been in this strange new place, his mother had seemed to become more and more withdrawn and confused, until she no longer accepted anything around her. Now his mother simply refused to believe that they were anywhere but Chestnut Circle. In her head, she was safe at home.

Bobby had hoped that some sleep would help to shake her out of it, get her to see what was really happening, but there still wasn't any change. She continued to stare at him like she expected an answer. Maybe, Bobby thought, he could calm her down if he played along.

"Uh—you remember, Mom," Bobby answered, just to say something. "We're going to have a picnic."

"Picnic?" She snorted. "Your father's idea. Not only do I have to make the food, but now I have to cart it outside, too." She turned away from Bobby and started walking toward the line of trees at clearing's edge.

"Mom!" Bobby called after her. "You'll get lost in the woods!" He looked around, and saw that once again there was not another neighbor in sight. He patted Charlie a final time and stood up. If she didn't stop soon, he'd have to run after her.

"Don't tell me what I'm going to do, young man," his mother replied without looking around.

His mother was going to get herself into real trouble. The neighbors had started to talk about the problem after the battle. Mrs. Smith had thought that Margaret Furlong was going to hurt herself. A couple of the Volunteers thought it might be better if they tied her up. Mrs. Blake had said that sounded inhuman. Bobby had felt like he was going to cry.

While they all argued his mother had curled up against a tree and fallen deep asleep. That stopped the debate about what to do with her, at least for the moment. There were other decisions to be made first. The rest of the neighbors had moved over to the far side of the clearing to deal with the bodies.

And his mother had woken again and started walking. At first, Bobby was content to follow. The whole great clearing seemed like one huge haven, safe from the rest of this strange world. Now the space, with its never-ending nooks and pathways, seemed to go on forever.

His mother stopped walking and turned to look from the trees back to her son. Before she had fallen asleep, she had been smiling, happy to be in what her mind told her was home; now her frown seemed to have become a permanent feature of her face.

"Your father's bound to be around here somewhere. When I find him, I'm going to give him a piece of my mind."

"Mom?" How could he remind her his father had been swallowed by Nunn?

She turned again and marched with remarkable speed into the forest.

Bobby started to run after her. "Mom! You have to stop now!"

She didn't even look back at him.

"Don't talk back to me, young man." Her voice softened a bit as she added, "I know once we find Leo, everything will be fine. It would be just like him to wander off into the park."

She pushed past the first of the trees. His mother wasn't very strong. Maybe he'd have to knock her down. He hadn't touched his mother in years—she "didn't like to be handled," was the way she put it. Was there any other way to stop her? Bobby didn't even think his father was alive anymore. What could he say? Oh, how he wished she'd just turn around and go back to sleep!

He looked down and saw that Charlie trotted by his side. Charlie's head bobbed up and down as he looked at Bobby, as if the dog was agreeing to be a part of all this. There was a real bond between them. Bobby felt like Charlie really knew what Bobby needed, without him having to say anything. It was so different from his mother and father. His parents had never listened to him, even when they were all back on Chestnut Circle. It figured that the only person he could really talk to was a dog.

His mother stopped again. "I'm tired," she announced, frowning at her surroundings. "Where's Leo? Weren't we just home a minute ago?"

Bobby could hear something happening back at some other corner of the clearing—a great deal of yelling and carrying on. Maybe it was good they were away from there after all.

His mother didn't react to the sounds at all. Bobby guessed they weren't what she wanted to hear.

He hurried forward, but she started to move again before he could close much of the distance. She pushed herself through the great tangle of vines, on into the place below the great trees where it was so dark no vine would grow.

"Mom!" Bobby called again. Nothing would stop her. Maybe they should have tied her up after all.

Bobby ripped aside a tangle of vines to follow her.

Watch out!

Bobby jumped back as a spear embedded itself in a tree inches away from his face. Bobby recognized the markings—a poison stick, used by some of Nunn's creatures, the same thing that had killed the Oomgosh.

But the warning—it hadn't been in words exactly, at least not the kind you heard. It was more like Bobby suddenly got the feeling of danger; the feeling that came behind the words.

Bobby had no time to wonder where the warning came from. His mother had stopped. She was staring at something ahead, a shadow moving between the trees.

"Leo?" she called.

The shadow shrieked and rushed to meet them. The ape-thing leaped out of the shadows, badly wounded and frantic to survive. All Bobby could see at first were claws and teeth. He realized he was also running, straight to his mother's side.

His mother screamed as the ape lunged forward. Bobby had no weapons. How could he defeat something like that with his bare hands?

Charlie leaped in front of Bobby, his weight landing full on the ape-thing's chest. The dog latched onto the thing's throat before the ape could get its claws into the dog. Dog and ape were carried backward by the force of Charlie's attack.

Charlie stepped away. Blood pumped from a gaping neck wound. The ape-thing spasmed, then was still.

The dog panted up at Bobby. Charlie's muzzle was covered with blood.

Bobby stared back at the dog. That warning that had come into his head; it had to come from Charlie. Somehow, the dog had warned him about the danger.

Bobby turned to his mother. She stared somewhere out beyond him, as if she was looking for something far away, deep in the forest.

"Mom?" he asked softly.

"Not home . . ." she whispered. ". . . home . . . home . . ."
She began to cry.

"I'm sorry, Mom," Bobby said. He reached out to take her hand. Charlie barked once.

Take her back.

Bobby heard it, or felt it, inside his head again, an urgent message to get out of the woods. The dog was quite still, staring out at the trees. Charlie was telling him there were other ape-things—or something worse—in the forest. Bobby turned back toward the clearing, still holding his mother's hand. He gently tugged her forward. She let him lead her that way, her eyes shut tight, as if she was unwilling to see anything. It was slow going, his mother stumbling over the rough ground she couldn't see. Bobby was glad they were moving at all.

Bobby felt a little safer as soon as he had led his mother past the vines. They had left the shadows behind and were back in that slightly green-tinged sunlight of this place. The dog barked again, a happier sound than before. Charlie was once again at Bobby's side. Bobby shook his head.

"So what's goin' on? Huh, fella?"

But no new warnings, or feelings, or strange thoughts of any kind jumped into Bobby's head. Charlie looked up at him, tongue hanging from his mouth, as if he was no different from any other dog.

Carl Jackson didn't know exactly what had happened back there between him and that creature that looked like Evan Mills. He didn't even know where the hell he was. All he knew was that he wasn't going to take this anymore.

There was no light here. The only sound came from his shoes as he dragged them across some hard surface. Carl put his hands in front of him as he moved, but he hadn't brushed up against anything in over thirty paces. What could be this big and this dark? He felt like he was in an underground foot-ball stadium.

"Hello, Carl."

He froze. The voice had been soft, and close to his ear. It was a voice much too gentle to be Nunn's.

"Don't you know me?" the voice asked.

What was this, Carl thought, some kind of goddamned quiz? But he had to keep his anger under control, at least until he knew what he was facing.

"Should I know you?" he asked instead.

"We've been neighbors for seven years."

Those goddamned neighbors again. But Carl would know that whiny voice anywhere. "Leo? You're still alive?"

The air was filled with a lingering sigh. "It's not much of a life. I'm here by myself most of the time. It's easy to lose track of time. I sort of fade away when there's nothing to do. Still, I'm glad to have your company."

"Company?" Carl almost laughed. "So what are we going to do? Just sit around here in the dark?"

Leo laughed instead. "Oh, you don't know how to see? Just a minute."

Carl heard a sharp scratch, like someone lighting a kitchen match. A flame danced before him. Beneath that flame, Carl saw a hand. Leo's hand, he guessed. Except the hand wasn't holding a match. Actually, it looked like the end of Leo's finger was on fire.

"Your finger!" Carl yelled.

"It doesn't hurt," Leo replied calmly. "Nothing hurts in here. Give me a second to adjust the light."

"In *here*?" Carl asked as the flame somehow both dimmed and managed to illuminate an area about six feet square. Leo Furlong smiled back at him. Besides the burning finger, he looked like the same short, skinny, bald-headed guy Carl had ignored for years.

"Oh, we're both inside Nunn," Leo explained casually, as if what he was saying might actually make sense. "Where, exactly, I'm not too sure. His brain, perhaps. Or maybe we're trapped inside his spirit. Not that the spirit has much physical form. But then, we don't have much in the way of the physical here, either."

"What are you talking about?" Carl wanted to slap Leo in the face, to stop all this nonsense pouring out of his mouth. "I'm right here in front of you!"

"That's because you expect yourself to be here," Leo continued with the slightest maddening hint of a smile. "That's one of the lessons I've learned about this place. If you can expect something here, it's yours."

"*What?*" Carl wondered if he might strangle Leo instead.

"Oh, here," Leo said, his slight smile turning to a frown of concentration. "Let me show you."

The light flickered and shifted. Carl shouted and jumped back. Leo towered above him. Carl's former neighbor was suddenly twenty feet high.

Leo smiled down at him. The tiny grin was much larger than it had been before. "It's a trick, Carl. Of course, who's to say what's real when you're stuck inside a wizard?"

Carl took a deep breath. No matter how large he was, Carl refused to be frightened of Leo Furlong. "What did you do?"

"We haven't moved. I've just adjusted my expectations. I always wanted to be bigger than everybody else."

"So, you can use this to do whatever you want?" Maybe, Carl thought, all this trickery was a little bit like that globe Nunn had given him.

Leo nodded happily. "You can fulfill your every fantasy."

Carl Jackson saw real possibilities here. Of course, his fantasies had a lot less to do with a giant Leo Furlong and a lot more to do with blond European starlets. Still, even starlets might get tiresome if he was stuck here with Leo.

Carl stared out at the never-ending darkness. "Is there any way to get out of here?"

The light flickered again and Leo was back to normal size. "There were others here before. I was afraid to leave with them."

"Mills was here!" Carl replied, suddenly understanding. "He made it out all right!"

Leo hesitated before he answered. "You might say that." He smiled back at Carl. "It's nice to have someone to talk to again."

Did Leo want to keep him around as a constant companion? Carl shivered, despite the fact it wasn't cold or warm or much of anything here. He had to get out of this place, too. Trapped for all of eternity with Leo Furlong; what a thought. What *had* happened to his globe, after all?

Carl looked down at the weight he felt in his hands. He was still holding the globe. Or maybe Leo was right, and Carl was only holding it now because he had just thought about it.

Frankly, Carl Jackson didn't care, so long as the damned globe worked.

Leo sighed. "There is another disadvantage to this place."

"Which is?"

"Nunn's coming. I can feel it. He must have work for me to do. He comes and fetches me outside, see—" Leo hesitated. He examined Carl with a frown. "Unless he's coming for you."

So Nunn could just reach in here and pull them out? Carl liked this place even less than he had before. He looked down at the object in his hands, still full of strange lights and swirling mists.

Carl guessed he would find out whether or not the globe worked right about now.

At first, Jason had thought it was the vines. The Anno had done something to them, somewhere else in the forest. He could feel how the vines were forced to pull themselves from their resting places, to writhe and grasp for—what? Something living, certainly. But before Jason could guess at the location of the disturbance—much less how and why the Anno were causing this, or even how he knew the Anno were the cause— the trouble with the vines was past.

The forest was quiet again, but the feeling was the same. No, this went far beyond any simple act of the Anno. The way Jason felt now, the whole forest was *restless*.

That was the word that came to Jason first. Something was here that didn't belong. He could feel it through the soles of his bare feet. He couldn't remember when he had lost his sneakers. Sometime, when he rested, he must have taken them off. There had been no reason to put them on again. His feet were always warm where they touched the earth. His sneakers were a part of his old life, the life on Chestnut Circle. And, like the glasses before them, they were gone.

He thought about the messages he received from his contact with the island. The tree man had shown him how to do this, before he died, how to listen to the dirt and the plants and the running water. Something grew from beneath his toes, fine hairs that sank into the ground like roots whenever he stood still.

In those few brief moments Jason had had time to think about what was happening around him, and to him, he wondered why he wasn't more upset with these changes to his body, and to his whole life. But—in those same moments—Jason had never felt so calm, or so full of life. He knew the feelings of plants and the moods of birds, how to read the clouds in the sky, and what messages were carried by the wind. It was as if everything on the island was a part of him, and he gave something of himself to all around him. Maybe that's why he knew about the Anno; whether he liked it or not, he and those creepy bald guys were related now.

That was a part of the restlessness around him, Jason realized. The island—and all the living things upon it who now spoke to Jason—was used to the slow rhythms of the sun and the wind and the rain. But those rhythms were changing. New things were being added to this place; Jason among them, along with all the neighbors. But the uneasiness he felt around him spoke of more than that. The island was waiting for something to return.

No, not just "something." Jason knew it was true as soon as the thought entered his head. The island was waiting for the dragon.

What did that mean? Somehow, Jason felt, if he could just reach deep enough into the mass of roots that made up this island, he would find an answer.

He was surprised when he moaned, as if someone else had been using his voice. The sound came from his throat, but it came from the forest. Somewhere, the forest was burning.

He wondered for an instant if the dragon had come. But this fire was much too small for the dragon. When that creature came, the forest whispered, the devastation would be complete.

The forest was burning. His forest. The fires were small now, but they would spread if not tended. His forest was in pain.

Something runs through the trees! the forest exclaimed. Something made of fire, leaving nothing but ash.

"My Oomgosh!" Raven was suddenly there, flying directly above him.

Jason frowned up at the hovering bird. "There is something wrong, isn't there, Raven? The forest is burning."

The Raven cawed in reply. "I can see the fire from the sky. It is a job for the Oomgosh."

And so it was, Jason supposed.

"I have come in case you need to be shown the way," Raven called.

Jason shook his head. The forest had already told him that. "I know where it is," he said to the bird. "I know what I have to do."

The large black bird rose with a great beating of wings. "Raven never doubted. Come, my Oomgosh! We must fly!"

○ Seven

Zachs was free! No one could hold Zachs, not Nunn, not Rox, not even the dragon. Zachs would fly, Zachs would burn, Zachs would destroy all those who trapped him or hurt him!

But first Zachs was hungry.

Nunn had shown him how to eat the energy of others. It was the reason Zachs was born. While trapped inside the weakling Mills, Zachs had been living off the energy of the dragon's eye. It was enough to stay alive. But it was nowhere near as satisfying as killing for your food.

Zachs flew, and Zachs fed. He burned the leaves from the tops of the trees, snatching small animals and birds startled by his speed. Nothing was as fast as Zachs. Plant, animal, bird; all were reduced to ash to fill Zachs's need. But as he fed, his hunger only seemed to grow.

The screams of the tree dwellers were pitiful. He wanted something larger to feed that hole at the center of his fire, something more intelligent, something that would really show fear before it died.

"I would stop that." The words caused Zachs to stumble in his progress, leaping from tree to tree, leaving nothing but a trail of smoke and ash. He ignored the branches burning around him and stared down at the forest floor.

"What?" he replied.

A small, round face looked up at him from far below. The four words had come from the voice of a child turning into a man, a voice not quite sure of its tone, or even its pitch, yet Zachs had heard it clearly.

"You must stop that," the voice continued, "or you will be stopped."

Zachs jumped down to a lower branch to get a better view. It was indeed a boy, not much larger than Zachs. And he wanted to challenge Zachs's fire?

"And who are you, young man?" Zachs leaped to a branch that was lower still, careful now to keep his fire close to his skin. What need had he to burn common leaves when he could soon savor the sweet taste of a child?

The boy, who wore ragged clothes but no shoes, looked back at Zachs. "Jason," was his answer.

"At least," another, harsher voice added as a great black bird swept past Zachs to land at the boy's side.

Zachs found this newcomer annoying. He was so looking forward to playing with this child who would become his dinner. This new creature looked to be nowhere near so innocent. And, if the bird's flesh were as harsh as its voice, it would be bitter to the taste as well. Still, the bird was no more than a morsel. Sweet Jason would be sweet enough to cover any aftertaste. Zachs set the branches to burning on his either side so that he might be framed in fire.

"Zachs will stop nothing!" he called down to the pair on the ground.

The bird cawed at that. "Some fire beings can be so unreasonable."

The boy nodded at that. "Then Raven and I will make you stop."

Zachs was already tiring of this game. "Zachs is free! Zachs will burn! Zachs has no time to talk!" He clapped his hands and flame shot forth, rushing in a circle around the boy as the bird cried in alarm and took to the air.

Then Zachs wouldn't bother with the bird now. Not until after he had killed and fed upon young Jason.

"Enough!" he called, hoping the child would manage a final cry of fear. "Zachs's fire will consume you."

But Zachs's dinner shook his head. "No—No. I'm the Oomgosh, now."

What was this Oomgosh? Zachs laughed. "Nothing can stop Zachs! Zachs will kill everything!"

"Now, my Oomgosh!" the bird cried.

The boy stared up at the bird. "But how do I stop fire?"

The large black bird replied, "You already know every answer, my Oomgosh. I am only here in case you need reminding. How have you put out fires before?''

"Of course," the boy said sadly.

Zachs clapped his hands again. This was very good. The boy had started to cry. Oh, how Zachs would enjoy this meal!

Zachs glanced down at his arm. A drop of water had landed there; a second one soon followed. Where did the rain come from? The sky had been clear only a moment before.

The drops made sizzling sounds where they hit his skin. They itched at first. Surely it was only a passing shower. If he was caught in a full rainstorm, the pain would be unbearable.

"Much better," remarked the bird below. "Do I have to tell you everything, my Oomgosh?''

The boy wiped a tear from his cheek. "Since you know everything, Raven, it would be a shame not to share it. But give me a minute so I can remember my dead friend.''

The tears came faster now, and so did the rain. The circle of fire was nothing but smoke and dying embers. And where the rain hit his skin, Zachs burned.

"You are truly the Oomgosh," the large bird called, "with wisdom like that." He flew up high with that, his wings almost brushing Zachs, his birdcall sounding far too much like a laugh.

And the rain came faster and harder. Zachs howled. He would have to flee, and seek shelter, so that the rain did not extinguish him in the same way it was dousing all the surrounding fires. The bird glided down to join the boy again, its wings spread wide as if it didn't have a care in the world.

"Zachs will get you!" he screamed down at the two below as he crouched for an instant beneath a great branch.

"Raven looks forward to it.''

The bird *was* laughing at him! And now the boy joined in! Zachs screamed as he ran from the rain; screamed in pain and anger. No one laughed at Zachs. No one would stop Zachs ever again. The boy and his bird were safe for now, but Zachs would remember. Zachs would teach them to be afraid. It was a shame they would be dead so soon after their lesson.

Zachs would burn down the whole world, if that was what it took to destroy them.

●　●　●

After that confrontation, Evan Mills never wanted to move again.

He knelt upon the forest floor, somewhere on the island, no doubt, in whatever place the dragon had chosen to deposit them when it was done. It was easier to stare at the ground, with its mixture of dead bark and rotting leaves. It hurt to look up toward the sun.

He was sure he had a fever. His joints ached, his skin felt as if it were on fire. And the nausea he had once felt when he first held the jewel had returned, this time to consume his entire body.

He had thought before that his discomfort had come from the three beings, with their three different energies, trying to inhabit the same form. Now that Zachs had fled, shouldn't the agony be over?

"You assumed the dragon was helping us," the wizard said inside his head; the wizard who could also apparently read his thoughts. Evan Mills remembered how he once worried about his privacy. Now he felt too sick for any of that to matter.

"Perhaps," Rox continued, "in taking Zachs, the dragon was wounding us instead."

Mills tried to gather his thoughts, hoping it would distract him from his fever. "You mean . . ." he said aloud, "the dragon wants us to die? Why?"

The wizard chuckled inside Evan's head. "Who can say? Perhaps the dragon wants all of us to die. Except—I wonder— if the dragon removed Zachs because it was afraid of the three of us—together."

If Mills had felt any better at all, he would have laughed, too. "Afraid? Of the—three of us? Afraid of three beings who—could barely walk?" His stomach convulsed again, despite the fact that he had felt no need for food or water since he had gained the dragon's eye.

"Three beings who perhaps were never meant to be united," Rox prattled on.

Apparently, Mills thought, one thing they weren't united in was his misery. Maybe, it occurred to him, his stomach was convulsing from the lack of food and water. Perhaps the removal of Zachs had done something to the jewel—

He clutched at his stomach and groaned. He was too sick to think about maybes.

"That means we—the three of us—are a challenge to the dragon," Rox continued. "That means that there is some way, however remote, that we can win."

"How—" Mills began before he realized he felt too sick to speak aloud.

How, he thought instead, can you think about winning when I feel like I'd almost rather die?

"Another obstacle the dragon has placed in our path," Rox replied dismissively. "I still wish we could gain more of the eyes."

We seem to have enough trouble with the one we've got, Mills silently replied. He didn't even want to think how Rox had taken over his form, and how the wizard had tried to rip the jewels away from Todd and Nunn.

From all the stories, Mills thought instead, the dragon is all-powerful.

He waited for another spasm to pass before he continued.

It destroys everything it touches. How can a creature like that fear anything?

"All things have rules by which they live. The dragon is not chaos. He is only a more powerful form of order. We are a part of that dragon's order as well."

The pain swept over him again, so debilitating that Mills could barely listen. Would this being inside his head go on forever? His tone reminded Mills of some droning college professor, forever lecturing. Mills was in no mood for lectures. Maybe, if he groaned loudly enough, he could drown the wizard out.

But the wizard's tone, if anything, seemed to grow louder and more animated as he rushed to his conclusion. "There is a reason the dragon doesn't simply destroy us. When the dragon last came, some were destroyed, but some were allowed to live. Only the wizards survived in this place. But there are other islands which the dragon barely seems to have touched.

"We fit into the dragon's plan. There is a logic, a direction, that we can't understand—at least not yet. Maybe we could consider it a challenge. This never-ending cycle—I believe the dragon wishes to end it, too."

Perhaps it was his fever, but Mills could recognize a certain logic in Rox's thoughts. If only he could do more than squat upon the ground—

"There is no need to kneel, Evan."

It took Mills an instant to realize this new voice was actually talking to him outside his head. Mills opened his eyes. There before him was a figure outlined in blinding green light. Mills squinted at the newcomer, trying to make out something recognizable in the glare.

"Who?" he asked weakly.

"I may be a being of almost unlimited power," the newcomer said softly, "but I'm also your neighbor."

Mills tried to ignore the pain and concentrate on the newcomer; short, with a bulge around his middle and shoulders that sloped, a posture that said he was incredibly angry and totally defeated at the same time. Mills remembered that body. If you took away the blinding illumination, the thing in front of Mills would look just like Hyram Sayre.

"Hyram?"

"Long time, no talk, huh?" the glowing green figure agreed. "I've seen a lot of the other neighbors, but this is the first time I've run into you."

Mills managed a grunt for a reply. Once they'd gotten to the island, Rox had kept them away from the other neighbors so they might better be able to steal another dragon's eye.

"But you're squinting. Sorry. I'll turn down the illumination." Now he only looked slightly green. Besides that, and the large hole in the middle of his chest, he could be the Hyram Sayre from back on Chestnut Circle.

But what do you say to a glowing neighbor? You've turned green?

Hyram laughed as he glanced down at his dully glowing form. "The color suits me, don't you think?" He looked back to Mills. "We've all changed, haven't we?"

Was it that obvious, then? Mills had never wondered if there was some physical manifestation of what was going on inside him. He could have sprung horns or wings or a three-day growth of beard and be none the wiser. He had spent so much of his time joined to Rox and Zachs in abject misery that he hadn't had much energy for anything else.

But Hyram was staring at Mills as though he expected an answer. "I've had some—additions to what was here before,"

Mills managed. "It's a little difficult to explain—"

"After what I've been through, I'll believe just about anything." Sayre laughed as he said that, too. Mills didn't think he had ever seen his neighbor so happy. "Let me take a look."

Before Mills could move, Hyram had leaned forward and placed his glowing green hand on the top of Mills's head. The way his head felt—electrified almost—he half wondered if Hyram had stuck his hand inside.

"Oh, dear. This is all rather complicated, isn't it?" Hyram laughed again. Maybe, Mills thought, he was being a little too cheerful. The nausea, shocked out of him for an instant by the green man's appearance, seemed to be creeping back.

"You can't see." Mills heard impatience slide into his voice. "There's things inside me—"

"No," the green man interrupted. "I see things quite differently. You're just a little mixed up, is all."

Suddenly Sayre's other hand was inside Mills's stomach. Mills could see the wrist disappear right through both the cloth of his torn shirt and the grayish flesh beneath. Worse than that, he could feel the fingers moving around inside. Perhaps he'd throw up after all.

Hyram smiled apologetically as he pulled his hands free. Mills was relieved to see that the hands were both still green and clean; he couldn't have handled it if they had been covered with blood or bile.

"That should help," Sayre said softly, "at least for a little while."

Now that the shock was wearing off, Mills realized that the stomach pain was gone.

"Just straightened out some of the lines." Hyram wriggled his fingers by way of demonstration. "There's somebody else in there, isn't there? I just did my best to let you live side by side. There seems to be—something else missing, though. Sorry I can't be more specific." He shrugged in apology. "I'm afraid there aren't any guidebooks for godhood. It's sort of a learn-as-you-go proposition."

Godhood? Mills almost laughed. If Hyram Sayre was a deity—well—Mills had acquired magical powers, and his stomach now felt just fine; nothing was impossible.

"Thank you," Mills said instead. It never hurt to be polite.

"Whatever you did. I wonder if there's any way either one of us can explain any of this."

Hyram frowned for the first time since he had arrived. "I have the feeling I'm needed elsewhere. I'm much better now at trusting my feelings." He looked up and began to rise from the ground. "This floating above the world can get a little lonely, though." He gave Mills a final glance. "Maybe, when this quiets down a little, we can get together for lunch or something."

Mills couldn't think of an answer to that. He waved goodbye as Sayre ascended toward the heavens.

"It pays to have friends in high places," the wizard said inside him.

"But he said we had a hole inside us?" Mills was asking himself as much as the wizard. "We have to ask Zachs to return."

"No," Rox replied firmly. "Zachs will never agree willingly. We'll have to force him back inside."

Mills wondered if even that would work. He shook his head. Only now, with the pain gone, could the doubt rush in. "Do you have any idea if my friend is right? Will that cure us the rest of the way?"

Rox's next answer was even more dismissive. "I think it's too late to talk about cures for any of us. But I think it will prepare us for the dragon."

His sword was leading him to a great quantity of blood.

Nick realized it as the sword twitched when they surprised some small creature in the underbrush at the forest's edge. The sword had pointed at the thing an instant before it moved. The creature was gone by the time Nick could react, only the rustling of bushes and vines said it had ever been there. But, for an instant, the sword had detected the thing's warmth, its point gravitating toward the warm fluid pumping through its veins the same way a divining rod found water. The sword had veered toward blood before, but it was blood close by, a warm body an arm's length away. The point turned away from the now still leaves and led Nick forward, toward somewhere else, someplace, Nick thought, where there would be a lot of fresh, flowing blood, oceans of blood, enough for both of them.

The sword began to tremble as he walked, urging him forward. For an instant Nick had a vision of his former life; the day he went to the circus with his dad. He remembered the way he held his father's hand, dragging his slow parent forward, feeling as if it would take forever. What had happened to that excited child?

He had gotten a sword.

For an instant Nick was afraid the sword would shake itself free of his grip. Except his grip was so strong, so necessary, he could never let go of the sword. Blood! the sword told him. Blood was very near! As exhausted as he was, he had to run. The blood would save them both!

The trees opened up before him. His goal was waiting for him in another clearing. He stumbled into the open, his sword swinging back and forth, confused by all the waiting blood.

He was met by a chorus of growls.

He was surrounded by wolves. There were a dozen or more, all staring up at him. He had faced wolves before. They hadn't attacked yet. Perhaps they remembered.

The closest of the wolves took a single, tentative step in Nick's direction.

Maybe, just maybe, he and his sword, exhausted as they were, could outwit a dozen animals.

"Ah," a man said as he stood up behind the wolves. Nick recognized the former Captain of Nunn's Guard.

"Friends," the Captain said with a broad grin. "It appears we have a new volunteer."

○ Eight

George Blake saw the way his wife looked at him, the way her eyebrows rose in disapproval and the corners of her mouth turned down in anger. He supposed he was lucky she looked at him at all.

He had barely gotten back here, rescued from his kidnapping by Nunn by that strange Captain and those wolves. He had barely gotten back, and already Nick was gone; gone and in trouble. That was obvious despite the fact that Blake could never quite believe the explanations for what had happened to his son. So what was George supposed to do now? Talk Nick out of swinging that sword? His son had never listened to him when Nick still had his head on straight!

Not that something like that would make any difference to Joan. He had no idea what she wanted him to do; he just knew, from all those years of marriage, that she most certainly wanted *something,* and he was expected to know what it was, usually without being told.

Blake sighed. He wasn't being fair. Here he was, close to Joan and Nick again, and the first thing he did was to replay the worst moments of his marriage. It was thinking like that that had gotten both Joan and him into trouble, back when they had had a marriage. He could probably never make up for all those things he'd done so long ago, on another world. He remembered all those nights he spent alone, wishing for another chance with his wife and child.

Now he had been given that chance. He looked again at his wife, her returning glare daring him to speak. It had been so long since they had talked they were out of practice.

"Look, Joan—" he began.

"I have to go after him," she replied before he could even form a coherent sentence.

Blake frowned at that. "Do you think that's wise?" He didn't want to lose both of them again. "I don't know if he can control that sword."

His wife made a sound half laugh, half sigh. "Don't you even care about him? He's your son, too."

Blake had to keep his eyes from rolling up toward heaven. This was the way every conversation with Joan seemed to spin out of control, with him regretting every other word that came out of his mouth, then getting angry because he didn't know what else to do.

"Look, Joan," he said again. "I'm here. I'll do what I can." He made a slashing motion with his hand as he spoke. He wasn't quite sure why. Maybe he wanted to cut through the bullshit.

But the hand seemed to set Joan off. "Just like all you did for us back on Chestnut Circle!" she shot back.

He shook his head. "It was a lot more complicated than that."

"So is this." Her words were growing short and sharp, as if she were honing them for that fatal thrust.

But Blake had had enough. "Joan, would you just shut up for a minute! I did some piss-poor stupid things to the whole family before. I know that. But for some reason we're all back here together. Maybe we can never be a family again, but maybe we can find some way to save our son!"

For once, she didn't have any immediate reply. He could still see the anger in her face, but there was something else in her expression now; shock, perhaps, or sorrow. He hoped she wasn't going to cry.

"So," he added after he'd taken a deep breath. "How the hell are we going to do this?"

"Excuse me." The female Volunteer, Maggie, stepped close to them. "You're going to need some help."

It was Blake's turn to be startled. Before he could think of a way to reply to her statement, they were joined by the two remaining Volunteers, the husky, bearded Wilbert and the thin and balding Stanley.

"Nick has taken to the forest," Wilbert added. "We know the forest."

"We've *survived* the forest since we've come here, hey?" Stanley ventured, his deep voice making his every utterance sound like a pronouncement of doom. "Without us, you may never see your son."

"Something big is going to happen soon." Wilbert smiled and shook his head. "We get the feeling that it's important for all of us to stick together. And maybe fetch back those of us who tend to stray."

"Thomas died so that we could get this far," Maggie added. "We need to see this through the rest of the way."

Blake found himself overwhelmed by this offer of help from virtual strangers. Here he was, barely able to talk to his own wife, and these people were willing to lay down their own lives to help both of them. How could he even begin to thank them? He was never very good at this sort of thing.

"Thank you," Joan said simply before Blake could make more of a fool of himself. "I think there's somebody else we need to talk to."

"The wizard," Maggie added.

Of course. The wizard had given Nick the sword. This was something Blake could do.

"I'll find him," he announced as he stepped beyond their little group to survey the rest of the clearing. The space was larger than it first appeared, with cul-de-sacs and hidden paths that led back into the trees. There was no way Blake could see the whole of it from here. The chubby fellow in his ragged white suit seemed to have wandered off somewhere. There didn't seem to be much of anybody else left around either.

Mrs. Smith glanced up at him, squinting her eyes as if she'd just woken up. Mary Lou sulked under the shade of a nearby tree. Sala sat on the grass, looking forlorn. Only Rose Dafoe appeared busy, dumping dead leaves and branches into a great pile at the clearing's center. He wondered for a moment what she was doing. It could be anything from building a shelter to starting another bonfire.

"Excuse me, George." Harold Dafoe walked by him, carrying another load of branches. Rebecca Jackson followed close behind, her arms filled with more of the same. Rose waved the two of them forward, pointing to the spots where each of them should place their loads. She had no doubt organized this project for the remaining adults from Chestnut Circle. Back in the old neighborhood, Rose always liked to be in the center of things.

"Has anybody seen Obar?" Blake asked the industrious trio.

"He suggested this," Rose said brightly.

"We're going to build a bonfire," Harold added quickly, "to keep things away at night." If Rose always made all the decisions in their household, it was left to Harold to do all the explaining.

But why couldn't Obar simply create a bonfire tonight, the same way he had to burn the corpses? George was sure Harold had an explanation for that, too. He just didn't particularly want to hear it.

Instead, he asked, "So is Obar helping out?"

Harold shook his head. "No, he excused himself for a while. You know Obar."

No, George thought, he didn't. He doubted that any of these other people really knew Obar the way they thought they did.

"George?" Mrs. Smith interjected, fully awake at last. "I can't sense Obar anywhere. He's nowhere nearby."

"Or he's doing something to keep us from seeing him," Mary Lou added. She stood by the old woman's side. She looked directly at Blake for the first time, as if she only wanted to participate if Mrs. Smith was there as well.

Mrs. Smith nodded at that. "He's had a lot more time to get used to his jewel than we have."

So both these women had their own questions about Obar. Maybe it was because of what had happened to his boy, but George realized he wanted to see the worst in this wizard. "So he can use his experience to hide things from you?"

"Yeah." Mary Lou showed the slightest of smiles. "But we can do things he can't even dream of."

"Each jewel reacts differently, depending upon the one who holds it." Constance Smith's stone glittered in the sun as she held it out for all to see.

George shifted impatiently from one foot to the other. All this business with the jewels didn't matter. Nothing mattered except rescuing Nick. And now the man who had caused these things to happen had disappeared.

Blake was surprised how furious this made him feel. He wanted to hurt Obar, to make him talk. But how could you

hurt someone who could kill you with a single glance? He'd
have to hold on to his anger for now. He walked back over to
the Volunteers.

Wilbert nodded at him as George approached. "He's gone,
isn't he? It was getting a little tough around here for wizards."

Stanley spat into the leaves. "Is anyone surprised?"

"Wait!" Maggie called. "Someone's coming out of the
woods."

Blake turned quickly, hoping they were wrong about Obar,
there would be simple answers, they'd find Nick, they'd get
rid of the sword, he and his wife and son could be happy again.

But that sort of thing only happened in stories.

"Sala!"

She knew it was Todd before she even looked up. He
walked out of the forest like he owned the world. When he
looked straight at her and smiled, she thought she had never
seen anyone so handsome. If she had ever been angry with
him, she forgot about it in that instant. She was so happy he
wasn't angry with her.

She stood as he ran across the clearing to meet her.

"Something happened to you," he announced with a frown
as he took her in his arms.

That whole horrible moment with the vines came flooding
back. "How—"

"I could see it through the other eyes. This jewel I have
lets me witness things through the others who hold them. Mary
Lou, Mrs. Smith, Obar—I had three images crowding in on
me at the same time." He laughed bitterly. "And I couldn't
do a thing. It just made everything more confusing—more upsetting." He hugged her even more tightly than before. "I
shouldn't have run off like that. I'm not alone anymore. I
needed to be here. You needed help."

Sala hugged him back. She wished somehow she could help
Todd, to let him know that, so long as they were together,
things would be all right.

"The others helped," she said softly. "Nick slashed through
the vines. Obar and Mrs. Smith tried to help, too. But it was
Mary Lou who really made them stop."

Todd shook his head so violently it made his whole body
shake. "I should never have left you."

She didn't want to hear Todd beat up on himself anymore. She held on to him for a long moment in silence. "I'm so glad you're back," she said at last.

"But who did this to you?" Todd insisted. "Why did it happen?"

Sala hadn't really thought about that. The vines were just one of those things that *happened* in this crazy place. But one person had stayed calm through the whole thing; one person had stopped it from happening.

"I have a feeling Mary Lou knows more about this than anyone," she answered.

"Fine." Todd pulled away from his embrace and took Sala's hand. "Come on. Let's find Mary Lou."

He turned to Mrs. Smith.

"She's gone, Todd. Just now. I didn't realize it until you mentioned her name." She stared at the stone she still held in her hand. It didn't seem to be glowing in the same way it had before, but perhaps a cloud had covered the sun. "These jewels still never quite work the way you want them to. She's somewhere nearby, but I'm not exactly sure where. I do know what she's doing."

Where would someone as self-important as Mary Lou go? Right into the middle of the action. As far as Sala was concerned, that didn't take a dragon's eye.

"She's looking for Obar," Sala said.

"By herself?" Todd demanded.

"She has her reasons," Mrs. Smith counseled. "Or maybe the dragon has them."

Sala shook her head. She thought the others looked confused, too.

Mrs. Smith went on as if she didn't notice. "Of course, simply because she's gone off by herself this way doesn't mean she has to stay by herself."

Todd showed the older woman a strained half smile. "Time for another heroic rescue, huh?"

The wizards were going to have to leave again? Sala squeezed Todd's hand.

"You've got to go find Mary Lou?"

Todd looked at Sala for a long moment. "Yes. But not alone. I've spent too much time as a loner. Let's do this together."

So she was going with Todd, to find Obar, and maybe fight the dragon? Sala wasn't sure whether she should be overjoyed or petrified.

"The three of us will go, then." Mrs. Smith shook her head as she looked at the two of them. "I was a fool to sleep. The dragon gathers its strength and we must gather ours. There will be no more rest until this is over."

Obar knew when his time was up.

He didn't want to hurt anyone he didn't have to. He had promised to help the others whenever he could. And a part of him had sincerely meant that. He had thought certain things could be accomplished if they all worked together. And that had worked, to a point.

But it was too close to the final moves. His final plans were showing through. He had to survive the coming of the dragon. And if one or two of the newcomers had to die to ensure that survival, that, too, was unfortunate, but necessary.

He walked through the deepest part of the forest, the heavy leaf cover above turning the world around him to perpetual evening. He could have transported himself directly to the Anno's camp; but he preferred a few moments by himself to gather his thoughts. Before the neighbors had arrived, he had spent most of his time alone, perfecting his magic, studying what he could find about the dragon, and those others who had come before him, preparing for that moment that was very close at hand. He had become used to a solitary life. These last few days had been quite unsettling.

He looked up at the towering trees. He walked beneath giants. Even after he became a wizard, he had always considered himself a part of the natural order of things and tried to live within them.

He was different from his brother, Nunn. Obar made a real effort not to harm others unnecessarily. He remembered how, while pretending to cooperate with Nunn, he had kept Garo from dying, more or less, keeping his spirit alive, guarded by the Anno. At first, Obar had thought he had done this simply because of an aversion to murder. Later he realized the ghost of Garo could be useful, especially if the ghost were made to forget exactly who was controlling him. Sometimes, good deeds were rewarded.

Obar caused a swirl of leaves to rise before him. The leaves took the shape of brash, young Garo before his death. A simple spell, but one Obar wouldn't have been able to manage even hours ago.

Obar had made good use of Garo before the dragon had taken him. And he needed Nick for certain things that were to come. Only Obar, the true owner of the sword, could save Nick. In time, the young man would come to realize this. Obar just hoped the sword wouldn't kill Nick first.

Now he had to call in some favors of his own. After all, he hadn't told the neighbors everything he knew about the dragon.

The leaves swirled before Obar again, changing into the lovely silhouette of Mary Lou for an instant, then sprouting wings as they transformed into a brown and rustling dragon. Obar smiled. It felt good to have the magic flowing into him once again.

Obar snapped his fingers and the dragon exploded outward, now nothing but leaves falling to the ground. A slightly greater use of power, and still Obar felt none of the fatigue that had dogged him these past days. At last, the gems were returning to full strength.

The trees around him grew close together, the branches above so close that the ground beneath was always in shadow. He was below the great mass of trees in which the Anno made their home. He made a complicated motion with his hands and said three words, and he was rising toward the platform above. He wanted to make the proper entrance. First appearances were so important.

He studied the trees to either side as he made his journey aloft. These were the oldest trees on the island, their bark scarred by innumerable storms, and perhaps as many visits from the dragon. How did the trees survive when so much else perished?

There were so many questions, with so few answers. It was no wonder he had to take preventive measures. He was a bit sorry it had to come to this. He was as fond of the Anno as he was of anything on this island. But he needed some very special magic, and perhaps a small sacrifice of a life or two to the dragon.

With the Anno's assistance, he had tried to begin this spell using Mary Lou, soon after the neighbors first arrived. That had almost undone everything. How was Obar to know the dragon had other plans for the girl?

The early failure meant he had to be more careful in his next attempt. The aftermath of battle seemed the ideal time, with all the other gem bearers either fled or exhausted. Obar had enlisted the Anno's help again, animating the vines to spirit away both Sala for the sacrifice and Nick for future use. But Nick had resisted. The spell had not culminated quickly enough. The Anno had failed him again.

In a way, Obar mused, what would happen next was the Anno's own fault.

Obar had risen to the level of the Anno's camp, spread out upon the great platform they had built between the trees. The wizard muttered one more word, and he was surrounded by a halo of light.

A great cry went up among the small folk as they fell prostrate on the rough wooden planks. Obar always found this particularly satisfying. He felt it was such a shame, when he was in the presence of others visiting these little folk, and had to prevent the Anno from showing their respect. He much preferred being treated as a god.

The Anno began to sing to him in their strange, high voices. The hymn had a soothing effect. He realized how much he had been overreacting to recent events. He was a magician. He was in control. Perhaps he shouldn't write off the newcomers yet. They were frightened. They wanted to believe. Even though some of them held dragon's eyes, they knew very little about their use. It shouldn't be too difficult for Obar to fabricate some explanation for the neighbors. Maybe he could use them again, too.

He would use whatever he had to to survive.

But it was time, at last, for Obar to perform his special magic, the culmination of all his study, all his practice, all his waking hours, since the last time he had seen the dragon.

He might find a small problem or two with this new situation. He had perfected this spell using human blood, after all. But he should be enough of a magician to make adjustments.

The spell worked best with the blood of young females. For that, he had to let the Anno do the choosing. He could never tell the difference between one small, balding creature and the next.

More than a dozen of the Anno rose and stepped forward at his request. He quickly chose three of the healthier-looking ones. He motioned the first of them to kneel before the wooden bowl that the village elders had so thoughtfully provided.

The knife materialized in his hand as he smiled down at the first of the volunteers. She looked up at him and smiled back as if this was the happiest day of her life.

◯ Around the Circle:
Owl and Mouse Discuss Dinnertime

So there was a certain evening in the forest, no different from any other evening, perhaps, unless you were a certain unfortunate mouse.

The mouse busied himself in the usual way, scurrying from shadow to shadow, looking for a scrap of this or a bit of that to feed himself and his family. But, with a horrible chill, the mouse realized one of the shadows above him was moving. Before the mouse could duck for cover, or even look to the sky, much less cry out to the gods of mice, he found himself pinned to the ground by a great, taloned claw.

In that instant the mouse was sure that this evening would be his last. But the great talon that imprisoned him had not yet drawn blood. Perhaps, the mouse thought, he had been captured for some other purpose. He dared to look up at his captor then, who was a great, gray owl.

"Who?" Owl inquired in a voice that was half the chill of winter and half the dark of night.

"I am a mouse," the rodent replied, "as you can plainly see. What do you wish of me?"

Owl regarded him for a long moment with her unblinking eyes before she replied, "Dinner."

"A bad idea, that," the mouse quickly replied, for as long as he was talking in the open air, he was not being digested in some owl's stomach. "Surely, you want to find someone else to satisfy your appetite."

"Who?" Owl asked again.

"Well. Certainly not an industrious mouse such as myself. Think of how I get rid of tiny bits of food and other things

86

that might clutter the woods. It is mice like myself who keep the forest clean.''

''I seldom waste words,'' was Owl's reply.

But words were all that were left to the mouse, and he was determined to use as many as possible. ''It is mice like myself who dance beneath the stars; mice who bring life to the land of night. Do you wish to deny me my place in this world?''

This time Owl did not wait quite so long before replying. ''All things have a place in this world. Unfortunately for you, your place is inside my stomach.''

At this, the mouse became frantic. ''Think of my family! Think of all the nights a young mouse has yet to live! Is death more important than these? Do you only wish to toy with me before you gobble me down? Have you no mercy?''

''Who?'' Owl replied again, and any further protestations upon the part of the mouse were lost with a single swallow.

Owl stood upon the ground for a long moment, her great dark eyes staring into the night. Perhaps she savored the entertainment she received from the mouse before she made him her meal. Perhaps she savored the silence after so much frantic noise. Or perhaps she was merely digesting.

For a long moment there was no other noise in the forest. The insects had stopped their constant noise, sensing danger nearby. Small creatures froze, certain they would be next. Even the night wind had paused, stilled perhaps in silent reproach for the cruelty one being can impose upon another.

''Who?'' Owl replied.

Then the bird spread her great grey wings and flew, ready for evenings yet to come.

For there would always be dinner. And there would always be owls.

O Nine

"Snake! There's something in the woods!"

It was about time.

Snake turned away from the ocean. He and his two cohorts had waited here for hours without a word from Nunn.

"Think it's the wizard?" the Claw asked. He stroked the silver hook that gave him his name, a sure sign he was as impatient as Snake.

"Maybe it's food," One-Eye said with his usual whine. "Begging your pardon, Snake, but we could have been better provided for on this trip."

Snake grunted back at his men. He didn't need to be reminded how badly planned this whole adventure had been. The wizard had demanded their help back on the island Snake and his compatriots called home—had it only been the day before? In the past, Nunn had done Snake a favor or two, using his magic to kill the occasional officer of the law, not to mention that competitor Nunn caused to vanish. Snake had known that sooner or later he would have to pay.

At first, Nunn's request had seemed simple enough. But what started out as a simple robbery and murder turned to an ambush at Snake's tavern, which ended in a full-scale battle. It was bad enough that the fight destroyed his tavern; Snake's livelihood, or at least the honest part of it. But because of that battle, Snake had developed dangerous enemies—others with dragon's eyes just like Nunn. He was quite sure these new adversaries—one of whom had made off with Snake's own daughter!—would kill him at their first opportunity. He could do nothing now but stick by the wizard's side.

Which was no doubt what Nunn had planned all along. As

much as he hated the wizard, Snake couldn't help but admire Nunn's devious mind. But now the wizard had brought them to a strange place only to abandon them. That made no sense, unless something had happened to Nunn.

A great rustling came through the undergrowth nearby, as if whoever approached was tearing apart whole bushes in their way.

"Wizards don't make that kind of noise," the Claw remarked.

Snake scowled as the clamor in the woods grew louder. Whoever was coming through the vine-covered trees was making no attempt to be quiet. It was more the sound of panic, where speed was far more important than stealth. Snake wondered if they'd missed another battle inland.

"It's those damned animals," announced the Claw as three apelike things broke free of the undergrowth.

"Nunn's toadies," One-Eye added.

"Filthy creatures," Snake agreed. He wasn't at all happy to see these things outside of Nunn's close control. These apes were as hotheaded as the red fur that covered their lice-ridden bodies. "We may have do to some killing."

But the Claw laughed. "No, Snake, look!" And Snake saw that the red-haired apes had stopped to stare at the men on the shore. Then, rather than fleeing or attacking, the three animals bowed.

"They recognize us!" Claw added.

"Who would have thought they had the brains?" One-Eye asked. "Wish they could tell us what happened to the wizard."

At that, the three apes all began to speak at once, first with some soft, cooing noises, but getting louder, as if each of the creatures wanted to be heard over the others.

The Claw laughed. "I think they are trying to tell us."

"And damned annoying it is, too." Snake spat into the vines curling at his feet. He'd had just about enough of this island, with its chattering apes and strange shadows that covered the sky. He'd had about enough of the wizard Nunn, too. "Is there any way we can shut them up?"

But hearing the men's voices only seemed to excite the apes more. Their coos and hoots turned into shrieks and screams as the three red-furred things jumped and waved their arms.

"Maybe they're trying to say something important," One-Eye ventured.

"Damned if there's any way we can tell," the Claw replied.

Snake decided that it didn't matter. "Kill them."

The men both turned to stare at their leader. One-Eye said it first. "But they're the wizard's creatures."

"With something this damned annoying, who cares?" He waved his men toward the advancing apes. "Kill them anyway. And make it quick."

Claw and One-Eye knew better than to question Snake twice. Each leaped on one of the three creatures, One-Eye stabbing his in the heart, the Claw using his hook to rip out his creature's throat. The first ape died silently, the second had time for only a single, gurgling scream.

The third ape almost had a chance to run. It managed to turn enough so that Snake's dagger lodged in its back. The ape fell, and the island was mercifully quiet.

"More to my liking," Snake agreed.

His men stood over the dead beasts. "You think we could eat these things?" One-Eye asked.

"We may have to." Snake laughed at the Claw's less-than-pleased expression at the suggestion. "I think we can find better pickings farther inland. The people on that other ship all came from this island. There's got to be a town, a camp, something around here. I think it's time to go exploring."

One-Eye retrieved Snake's dagger and returned it to its owner. Neither One-Eye nor the Claw had any objection to the new plan. They both knew what happened to those who voiced too many objections. Snake was leader once again.

He could start to make plans. Recent circumstances had kept him from a couple things he considered necessary, like killing a couple of people who had gotten too close to his daughter. And not even a wizard was going to stand in the way of that.

Snake used his shirttail to clean the knife as he led the others into the woods. The blade shone in the afternoon sun. He'd been neglecting it lately; it felt good to get a little practice. Snake started to whistle a song he'd heard back in his tavern.

It was just that kind of day.

Nick was surrounded by a dozen wolves.

"Ah. We have a visitor."

Nick looked beyond the wolves at the man who stood on the far edge of the gathering, and recognized the self-satisfied smile and the strange scars that adorned his cheeks. He was the man who had killed one of the neighbors early on, the man who had rebelled against Nunn, the one they called the Captain.

"The wolves hear the howls of their fellows," the Captain said, his voice so cheerful Nick half expected him to break into a little dance. "More join us every day."

"Frresh meat," one of the wolves agreed as he stared at Nick. All the wolves stared at Nick, but none of them attacked. What did this Captain want from him? His mind was hazy. All he could think about was blood.

"They have left their mantraps behind for fresher kills," the Captain continued. "Kills that I will give them."

Nick wondered if that was a threat. He had killed wolves before. His sword swung back and forth, as if deciding which wolf would make the choicest victim.

"They are not so different from you and me. We are all looking for blood, aren't we?" The Captain looked down at the wolves gathered before him. "But you are just in time for a little sport. I think it's time we released one of our tender morsels from its cage."

The wolves parted before Nick, and in their midst he saw a cage of sorts made out of woven vines, a loose basketlike contraption perhaps three feet high and twice that across. The cage was filled with a great many brown-furred creatures, each about the size of a fist. From what Nick could see from a dozen feet away, they appeared to be some sort of local rodent with long tails and long ears, something halfway between a rat and a rabbit.

The Captain made a great, sweeping gesture with both his hands, including all who stood before him. "So who shall be first?"

One of the wolves growled, as if calling for the meat.

"Please!" the Captain chided. He waved toward Nick. "Be polite. Let the visitor have the first kill."

Another of the wolves grabbed a corner of the vine basket with its teeth and lifted it for a second. One of the rodents scurried free, running down the only open space in the clearing, straight toward Nick.

"These little creatures are so obliging, aren't they?" the Captain continued. "Quick now! I'm sure we'd all like a demonstration of your skill."

Nick's sword moved faster than his brain. It pulled him forward with a step as it swept his hand down to skewer the rodent midbody, the force of the stab almost cutting the small animal in half.

The dying creature managed only half a squeal before the sound was replaced by the great sucking sound the sword made as it drained the small body of blood. The corpse rattled to the ground, now only a tiny fur sack of bones.

Nick took a breath as the warmth brushed against his veins. It was only a taste of what he needed, like trying to warm frostbitten fingers near a fire. Still, it was something. He pulled his sword close to his chest. He could control himself for now.

The Captain nodded his approval. "The wolves tend to play with them a bit before they eat. Your method is almost merciful."

"We rremember the sword," remarked the wolf who had raised the cage.

"Enough!" growled the wolf who had demanded the first kill. "Otherrrs need to eat!"

The Captain nodded again, and the wolf by the cage once again took the vines between its teeth. Another rodent ran free, down that open space that led to Nick.

The other wolf was quickly after the small thing. But the rodent showed remarkable speed, rushing straight for Nick and the forest beyond. Nick took a step to the side, hoping to get out of the way of the wolf-and-mouse game.

His sword moved quickly and violently, so surprising Nick that he barely managed to maintain his grip. The blade jerked down to skewer the second rodent as the wolf was about to pounce on top of it, sweeping the small body up beyond the lupine's snapping jaws.

Blood ran from the tiny carcass, but only for an instant before it was absorbed by the enchanted metal. The wolf howled as the sword drained its latest kill.

The Captain frowned. "That was most impolite. We have rules around here."

The angry wolf jumped for Nick. His sword whirled about, flinging the not-quite-drained rodent away as the blade took the wolf in the chest. The beast's forward momentum knocked Nick from his feet. They rolled across the ground together as the sword sank ever deeper into the wolf, its snapping jaws turned into death throes. The two lay still at last as the sword finished its noisy work.

"Of course"—the Captain's voice filled the stillness—"with a sword like that, who needs to be polite? Our first rule is that only the strong survive. You had already gained the wolves' attention. Now you have their respect."

The sword had finished its work. The wolf's body, now drained of blood, seemed to weigh nothing on the far end of the blade. But Nick was shaking so hard that he almost lost hold of the sword; almost but not quite.

The spasm passed, and Nick looked up to see the wolves tearing apart a dozen or more of the rodent things. The cage must have tipped over while Nick and the wolf were fighting. Nick was glad the wolves had something to do besides stare at him.

The Captain smiled from where he stood at the far side of the wolves. "Truly, you have found your brothers. Welcome to the pack."

A couple of the wolves growled at that, but none seemed upset enough to disturb their meals. The Captain walked toward Nick, carefully stepping around his charges.

"I have lost my human lieutenants—your neighbors." The Captain sighed. Nick remembered that his father had been one of those with the Captain. "I sometimes felt they were performing under duress. Our interests were different. They are probably better off with the others—your neighbors, as I understand. On the other hand, your interests are very apparent. I believe we can work to each other's advantage."

Nick stared up at the Captain. This man still wanted to work with him, after what had happened with the sword?

"Hey." The Captain's smirk was back. "Wolves have got to eat. And so do you. My wolves need meat, I give them meat. With you, it will be blood."

Nick managed to push himself to a sitting position. He felt flushed, as if he had a fever. His voice sounded hoarse as he asked, "What do you want from me?"

"I have certain things I need from this world. Let me tell you my plan." He stopped a few feet short of Nick. As he

spoke, his hand played with the hilt of a dagger he wore at
his belt. "We will kill Nunn at the very least. And that little
freak of his, Zachs. Perhaps then we will kill Obar as a favor
to you." He chuckled. "Maybe, if we kill all of them, the
dragon won't have to come, after all. What do you say?"

Nick didn't feel capable of making any decisions, especially
with someone like this. "I don't know."

The Captain continued to stare down at him.

"I haven't had time to think," Nick added, mostly to fill
the silence. "Things haven't been very good."

"Things are always bound to get worse," the Captain
agreed, "unless they get far, far better. Here." He took a step
forward and extended his hand. "I'll help you up."

"One minute." Nick rose to his knees and thrust the sword
back into its scabbard. "It's safer now."

Nick let the Captain help him to his feet. He didn't want to
agree to anything, and yet he didn't want to run from here just
yet, either. Maybe this was a place where he could take some
time and figure out what was happening to him. Not that this
company would be among the safest. He'd want to keep his
sword close by. But, with his sword, he wasn't among the
safest to be around, either.

"You look like you could use some rest," the Captain said.

That Nick could agree with.

The Captain pointed to Nick's right. "There's a good spot
under those rocks, in a nice patch of shade, out of the wind.
We'll watch out for you. We will, you know."

Nick realized he believed him. The Captain had plans for
him. He could rest, and be fed just like the wolves, and maybe
leave those worries behind long enough to figure out how he
got into this, and how he could get himself free. The Captain
would use him, but he would use the Captain, too.

It made as much sense as anything. Nick stumbled over to
the dirt in front of the rocks. He curled up in a natural hollow,
the rocks behind him.

This time, he had no trouble finding sleep.

Mary Lou recognized this spot in the forest, even though
she didn't know exactly why she was here. Once again, she
had acted on a decision before she even realized she had made
it. Here she was, on her own again.

It was hard for her even to remember the events that brought her here. As the other neighbors talked about Nick and his sword, she had realized she had to do something about Obar. But then, she had simply—left, without a word, without even a further thought. Mary Lou wondered why she couldn't talk about it with the others. Well, she knew why she wouldn't talk to her parents about it, but what about telling Bobby, or Jason, or Mrs. Smith? Heck, she wasn't even talking about it with herself.

She'd remembered the feeling she had sometimes gotten when she had used her magic before, as if others were controlling her, like she was some puppet jerked by invisible strings. But even if that were true, who could be the puppeteer? It certainly wasn't Obar.

"About time you got here."

The voice was a whisper close by her ear. She knew the voice, even though it couldn't be here.

"Garo?" she called back.

"None other," the whisper replied.

She took a deep breath as she felt her heart pound heavily in her chest. Having Garo back made her both happy and frightened at the same time. In the past, Garo had both lied to her and sacrificed himself for her. She wondered what his plans were this time around.

Of course, she couldn't see him. He was only a voice, with no physical manifestation at all. Typical Garo.

"I thought you were eaten by the dragon." She couldn't keep the accusation out of her voice.

"Well, maybe," Garo answered, "but that's no reason to stop speaking to me."

Her next thought was chilling, not so much for what it meant for Garo as what it meant for what might be controlling her.

"Then the dragon brought me here?"

"Come now, Mary Lou!" Garo laughed. "You can't blame everything on the dragon, can you?"

And what did that mean?

Maybe, Mary Lou reflected, she wasn't so happy to see Garo after all.

○ Around the Circle:
An Evening with the Smiths

Constance Smith stared down at the telephone. Now she knew there was somebody else.

The signs had been everywhere. Kevin's late nights at work; his lack of energy; the phone calls—always "from work" when he answered the phone, the hang-ups when she answered. All those excuses that didn't quite work. It would have been obvious to anybody else. She had just gotten so good at looking the other way.

She looked out into the living room, the curtains that needed cleaning, the old, comfortable couch that could really use re-upholstering, the knickknacks that lined the mantel, bought on trips to Florida and Mexico when they were first married. The house was full of things that reminded her of Kevin, things that gave her comfort. She had built her life surrounded by this security. This was truly home, or it had been home until that phone call. Now that security seemed empty, as if the world had cracked in two to show its hollow inside.

The curtains, the couch, the knickknacks; none of it looked right anymore. Twenty-three years of marriage, twelve spent living in this house. Kevin and Constance, everything in this house said, together forever. Everything in this house lied.

She heard the scrape of the key in the front door. Kevin? She had never expected to see him again, after what that woman—that bitch—had said on the phone. How dare he show his face here after what he had done, the way he had lied? She would throw him right back out of here, change the locks, sell the house, move far away.

She felt the tears start down her cheeks as the door opened. Kevin stood in the doorway, his glad-to-be-home grin fading as he saw her face. "She called you, didn't she?"

She could only stand there, beyond answering, her head full of other days, and other words from Kevin.

"Connie, nothing's more important than the two of us together."

Only Kevin called her Connie.

"Connie, if you think it's important, you can do just about anything you put your mind to."

Kevin would smile, making some little thing she had done seem like a triumph.

"There's nothing I want to do more than come home at night."

She could feel the way her cheek brushed his sweater as they sat side by side in front of the fire.

"Connie, as soon as this project is over, I swear—"

And then he'd be out the door.

Kevin had walked up to her then, in the here and now, and tried to take her in his arms. She stood stiff and distant, not yielding to his pressure on her shoulders.

"I left her, Connie. That's why she called. She was lashing out, trying to hurt you. But I couldn't leave you."

So she let him talk while she allowed herself tears.

As angry as she was, she still wanted him here. He was too big a part of her life—Kevin, the curtains, and the couch. They had been together too long, depended on each other too long. Even now, she half believed all these words of tenderness and apology. But when he held her she felt a cold place between them that hadn't been there before. She had tried never to lie to him. How could she forgive his lies so quickly?

"Nothing's changed," he whispered.

She turned away then, glancing at the mantel, the couch, the curtains. Everything was different here.

"Connie?" he asked after a moment's silence. "What do you say?"

She looked up at him. A day ago she would have said she knew his every wrinkle.

"Nothing's changed," she replied.

The cold would never go away.

O Ten

"Quiet!" Mrs. Smith called. "Quiet please!"

Her voice cut through the cacophony around her, bringing on a sudden silence. The others, both neighbors and Volunteers, all seemed to have their own ideas of what they should do next. Now they all turned to look at her, waiting for her leadership.

That silence was a symbol of the trust they held in her, both as a neighbor and the first of those neighbors to gain a dragon's eye. At least she hoped they all still trusted her. Sometimes she even wondered if she trusted herself. It was only here, in this new world, that she had become a leader.

She smiled at her audience. No matter what she might feel, this was no time to show doubt. She let her calm voice fill the stillness. "We are all someplace we don't want to be, presented with difficult choices. I don't think there is any way all of us can be happy, but at least we can hear each other out."

George Blake stepped forward to the front of the crowd. "We have to find Nick!" he insisted. "The longer we wait—"

Rose Dafoe looked at him skeptically. "The more forest creatures will be drained of blood? Nick can probably protect himself as well as anybody here."

George Blake frowned back at her. "That's not the point. We have to free him from that sword."

His ex-wife Joan turned to him then. "And how do you propose to do that?"

"I don't know." George threw his hands in the air, as if ready to surrender at the first sign of opposition. His voice rose close to a shout. "I'm the new guy here, right? How should I know about anything?"

They wouldn't get anywhere if they started to argue. "Magic got him hooked to that sword," Mrs. Smith interjected. "Magic can free him." She didn't know quite how Obar had connected the boy to that sword, but given time, she was sure she could undo any spell of Obar's.

"Nick can take care of himself," Rose's husband Harold chimed in, once again following his wife's lead. "We should be looking for Mary Lou."

"And what's happened to Jason?" Rose added quickly. It was interesting, Mrs. Smith thought, how the Dafoes always brought up their girl before they even mentioned their son. She supposed that was one advantage to her never having children; you never had to pick favorites.

"Jason can take care of himself," Bobby piped up from the edge of the crowd. The boy didn't look at the others, instead petting the oddly deformed dog who was always by his side. "Besides, he's got Raven."

"I wish somebody would shoot that bird."

Margaret had spoken. Mrs. Smith glanced at the disheveled woman sitting in the dirt, then looked up to see that everyone else in the clearing also watched Margaret. Was the woman actually relating to something in this world? This was the first time since well before the battle that she had even acknowledged a conversation around her, much less joined in.

Now even Bobby tried to make eye contact. "Mom?" he asked softly.

She shook her head, refusing to look back at any of them. "Birds nesting in the eaves!" she said bitterly. "Getting their dirt all over the gutters!"

Was she still talking about their Raven? Maybe she thought the bird was in the old neighborhood. Mrs. Smith still hoped this outburst might be a sign that Margaret was breaking free of her delusions.

But Margaret's outburst had also stopped the growing argument. The neighbors looked at each other as if no one quite knew what to say. Mrs. Smith jumped into the silence before someone else could.

"I agree that it's important to stay together," she said, careful to keep her even tone. "Whatever power we have, it is strengthened by unity. I think it would be far better to have the children with us, especially if we can determine speedy ways to rescue them.''

"How can any of us leave if we're waiting for the dragon?'' Joan asked.

"That's what I wanted to talk about—'' Mrs. Smith began. She had a growing sense that the dragon was near. But, if it was as all-powerful as the legends said, why hadn't it already overwhelmed them? Something was keeping it away. Maybe something hadn't happened yet, maybe too much was happening. The dragon's arrival could depend on so many things, the actions of the neighbors, the wizards, the Volunteers. After all, wasn't it the dragon that had brought them here? Couldn't they all be part of the dragon's plan?

"How do we know the wizards and the dragon aren't working together?'' demanded Rebecca Jackson.

Mrs. Smith frowned at that. The question sounded so different from what she had come to understand. She had been so busy learning about her new powers, she hadn't bothered to explain any of it to the neighbors. If, like Rebecca, you were only on the sidelines observing this strange new world, it must be truly frightening.

She nodded back at Rebecca, careful to give her an answer they all could understand. "You've seen how much the wizards hate each other. You think they'd hate each other any less with the dragon around?''

Rose interrupted her with a braying laugh. "So you say, Constance.''

"Now, Rose,'' Mrs. Smith replied gently. "Someone's got to take the lead.''

"And it has to be you?'' Rose turned to the others. "Who made her so important, anyway?''

Wilbert stepped forward. "Now I think your Mrs. Smith needs to be heard. We've been here a lot longer than you folks, but everything she says sounds like just common sense.''

"Rose has a point, too,'' her husband insisted. "All this planning—the way our children disappear. How do we know this isn't all some kind of trap?''

"We don't,'' Constance agreed. "I don't think it's as simple as the dragon wanting to steal the children. We're in a complicated place, and we're now all a part of that place. For all I know we're all a part of the dragon's plan.''

She stopped and looked at the confused faces around her. Her musings made even less sense when she said them aloud.

"You have to trust me." She held up her dragon's eye. It truly seemed to glow again for the first time since the dragon had let its presence be known. "Because of this, I can see some things the rest of you can't."

"So you're as crazy as this crazy world?" Rose asked.

"Why don't you go after Mary Lou?" her husband echoed. "Do you just want to leave her to die?"

Mrs. Smith frowned. This gathering was slipping out of control. She remembered, when they first moved to the suburbs, how her husband and she used to go to town meetings, until they could no longer stand the bickering. This felt like more of the same, except instead of sewers and schools they were fighting over life and death.

She decided to try again. "No, Mary Lou is important. I think she might not be in control of her actions—"

"And the rest of us are?" Rebecca asked.

"I've had enough of this." Rose laughed again. "Why should I listen to any of you?"

Harold put his hands on his wife's shoulders. "Now, Rose—"

Mrs. Smith had been waiting for another crisis. She should have realized it would be here. The neighbors were no more than that—just neighbors. Their abduction and the battle that followed had forced them to work together. Nothing could force them to like each other.

This had all happened so fast, she realized, there hadn't been time to reach a consensus on anything.

Rose and Harold and George and Rebecca started to shout at each other about who should do what when, content to ignore Constance entirely. Mrs. Smith could barely stand still amid all this arguing. Whatever they did, they would have to work together when the dragon came. How could she make them see this had to be done?

They needed action.

"Nick can't have gotten too far," she interjected. "He was exhausted when he left here."

That shut the neighbors up. They turned back to look at her.

"I bet I can find him without any trouble," Todd chimed

in. He had been watching the others so quietly she barely remembered he was there.

"I think I might be able to find Mary Lou quite quickly—" she continued, hoping she wouldn't have the same kind of trouble she had had the time before, when the girl was hidden by the dragon. It was the only time her eye had failed her.

"So one of you lucky folks with those stones looks for Nick, and the other one hunts for Mary Lou?" Rose demanded. "What about the rest of us?"

Mrs. Smith didn't blame Rose or George or any of the others who objected. They were all frightened out of their minds, but only she could do something about it. How powerless the rest of the neighbors must feel without any dragon's eyes of their own.

"I think we're all safe," she answered, "at least for the moment. In a place like this, what else can we know?"

"Why won't anybody let me go home?" Margaret Furlong wailed.

Another of the Volunteers stepped forward. "We know the island," Maggie said with a nod to Mrs. Smith. "One of us should go with each of the parties. I can track Nick easily enough."

Wilbert smiled at that. "You'll volunteer for Nick, I guess I'm going for Mary Lou."

"So everyone's leaving—" Rose interrupted.

"We can take care of ourselves." Bobby's voice cut her off, stronger than before. He glared straight at Mrs. Smith now, as if daring her to tell him he was wrong.

Rose looked like she was going to object until she looked at the dog at Bobby's side.

"Somebody's gotta stay behind," Stanley agreed. "I'm gettin' tired of all this marchin' around anyway."

"Bobby, Charlie, and one volunteer," Rose drawled. "That should take care of just about anything."

"Now, Rose—" Harold cautioned again.

It was Rose's turn to stare at Mrs. Smith. "I don't see why she should get that magic stone anyway!"

Joan Blake put a hand on Rose's shoulder. "That's not for us to say. That comes from the dragon."

Rose pulled away. "The dragon this—the dragon that. If I had that eye, I'd make sure all these things wouldn't happen!"

"Sure, Rose," her husband said softly. He turned back to Mrs. Smith, as if he had to make some sort of truce between his wife and reality. "A lot of what's happened doesn't make any sense."

"It doesn't have to make sense," said Stanley with a shake of his head. "We just want to come out of this alive."

That was one of many things Mrs. Smith couldn't guarantee.

One of Snake's men cried out as he tripped over a root hidden in shadow. They were making far too much noise. How could they sneak up on anyone if they couldn't even get through this forest?

One-Eye groaned where he lay on the ground.

Snake waved toward the fallen man with his knife. "Pick him up, you idiots!"

Snake wished he didn't need all his men so badly. Otherwise, he could just kill the clumsy fool.

When they had first reached the island, he had divided his men into three parties, one to watch over the boat, another to guard the rowboats, a third to accompany Nunn. Nunn, of course, had promptly vanished when his party had only marched a few minutes from shore, informing Snake and his fellows to wait for his return.

As soon as Snake had decided to act on his own, he had gone back and added the rowboat party to his own, hiding the boats farther up in the trees. Then they had marched inland, looking for food, water, and a little sport.

At first Snake had felt quite happy about it, freed from Nunn's yoke, ready to return to that lowlife of theft and mayhem he knew best. After all, what trouble could a barely inhabited island pose to half a dozen seasoned fighting men?

It took him only a few minutes to learn the truth.

Two of his other men, the Beast and Pete, had rushed to rescue their comrade from where he'd fallen among the roots and bushes. The forest had closed in around them, the trees so thick overhead that the floor was lost in a perpetual evening gloom. His men were constantly stumbling and cursing as roots and sinkholes seemed to appear from nowhere.

Snake half imagined the roots would rise up to snag their toes when they weren't looking. For you could not spend all your time watching the ground. There were creatures spying on them from high in the trees, the sudden rustle of leaves above them where there was no wind, strange, high-pitched cries that Snake had never heard from any animal or bird. And twice things had fallen from above, each time narrowly missing some member of his party. The first time it had been a branch, the second a rock. The branch he could understand. But even in this strange forest, he didn't think rocks grew on trees.

He had no advantage here. He was used to the familiar alleys of the port town, or the open vistas of the sea. By the time he realized his mistake, they had gone too far to turn around.

"Hurry it up!" he called to the others. "Better we find someplace out from under these trees. From what Nunn said, there should be people somewhere nearby, people not used to fighting."

"Good for a meal and some entertainment, eh, Snake?" One-Eye called.

"At the very least," he replied. The others laughed. It was best they kept their spirits up until they saw some action.

"Snake!" Pete called from where he led the party. "Voices!"

All movement stopped as Snake motioned for silence. There were indeed voices up ahead, arguing in some foreign tongue, but definitely human, so much better than those high-pitched things hiding in the trees. Humans you could deal with. Humans you could kill.

"All right," Snake whispered to the others. "Now's the time for quiet and caution. Let's move a little closer and see what we're up against."

The great trees were spreading apart before them. Maybe they were finally approaching a clearing. Not that the way was totally clear in their path, for, as the trees started to open up, great, thick vines replaced them, growing between the great boles in a last attempt to rob the forest of light.

"Seven people I can see," Pete called softly from his position in the lead. "Most of them are women, too."

"Any weapons?" Snake asked in the same low tones.

"There's one skinny guy with a bow," Pete answered. "There's a boy and a dog, too."

Another ripple of laughter went through the men around

him. A little too loud, maybe, but what did they have to worry with a defenseless camp like that?

"Is Sala there?" Snake demanded.

"Could be," Pete answered after a moment. "I'm not sure I see everyone."

Good. He could make Sala pay in front of all the others. It almost made it worth marching across this damned island.

Snake raised his arm to motion the others ahead, and looked in astonishment as a vine twisted around the arm.

"What?" Pete cried. Snake looked ahead and saw another vine winding around Pete's waist.

"The vines!" One-Eye called behind them. "They're alive!"

"Well, cut them!" Snake already had the knife in his hand. "Cut them deep!"

The vines started to wail. Any chance of secrecy was lost. Snake couldn't believe it. The whole damn island was alive.

He would slash every vine and tree in this goddamned forest. He just didn't care anymore, about secrecy, or noise, or even wizards.

He just wanted to survive.

"The island is ours, my Oomgosh!" Raven called as he flew between the trees. "You control the elements, and Raven is creator of all things!"

He wished right now that Raven wouldn't call him that. Sometimes he wanted to be the Oomgosh, but sometimes he wanted to just be Jason.

He had felt great for a while after he'd beaten Zachs. He'd saved the trees, too. The tall tree man—he wanted to say the real Oomgosh—would have been proud. Jason had learned from his elder, and now he learned from the island, and all the things around him, from air to wind to rain to roots. With all the world helping him, how could he help but follow the Oomgosh's footsteps?

But something was still missing. Sure, all of the island was telling him what to do. But nobody was talking to him, not in the way they used to. He'd run away from his parents and the rest of the neighbors. Now he started to miss them, thinking fondly of talking over breakfast with Mary Lou, of shooting the breeze with Bobby, even listening to his father give him advice that never fit the situation.

He found himself scuffing his bare feet on the forest floor as he walked.

Raven fluttered down from the sky to rest on Jason's shoulder. Jason remembered how, when he had first drawn the bird's attention, he had been surprised; now he had come to expect it.

"Where now, my Oomgosh?"

Jason winced at the sound of his new name. "Don't call me that, Raven."

Raven squawked and fluffed his wings.

"What does the master of the forest desire?"

"You may think this is silly, Raven. I need to see my family."

Raven's caw was softer now, almost a chuckle. "You still have one foot in the old world, and one foot in the new. I would never tell the Oomgosh what to do."

But Jason had felt something when he paused for a moment. "There is someone else at the camp, Raven. Someone that shouldn't be there." Someone watched from the protection of the woods, but more than that he couldn't say. The vines were so agitated, their messages were confused.

"Time for Raven to make an inspection!" The bird launched himself from Jason's shoulder.

He had to get closer, too, in case something went wrong. Jason started to run.

Strangers at the edge of camp, the vines said. *Six of them watching, standing on our stems, tromping on our roots.*

He sent a message through the ground. But the vines were already acting on their own; vines unhappy for the way they had been used by others. Jason could feel them tighten around the newcomers. They snared the humans' arms and legs, pulled them to the ground, squeezed the air from their bodies.

Jason paused to better feel the messages, carried root to root. The strangers were fighting back. They were slicing at the vines with their knives. Pain. The vines were in pain.

Jason could feel it, too.

Tighten, the vines called to each other. *Crush them.*

Wait! Jason thought.

Kill before we are killed!

Stop! Jason called through the roots at his feet.

Nothing. No change. More vines stretched out to overwhelm the newcomers.

Jason had to concentrate.

Stop! The Oomgosh commands!

All tension left the vines at the mention of his name.

That wasn't what he wanted. Their prisoners were free.

Hold them! he thought. But it was Jason's thought, not a command of the Oomgosh. The roots told him the strangers had fled into the clearing, beyond the reach of the vines.

The vines had obeyed. The Oomgosh truly was their master. But Jason was not truly in control of his power. He had wanted to hold these newcomers, keep them away from the others. Instead of killing the strangers, he had set them free to enter, maybe even attack the camp.

He heard a harsh call above him. Raven had returned. "They are truly strangers, my Oomgosh," the black bird called as he circled down from the sky. "They come from some other island. Raven feels they are Nunn's men."

Jason's worst fears had just come to life.

"Hurry!" he called to the bird as he set off running. "We have to make sure they don't hurt anyone!"

Raven flew above him, matching his stride. "No one will stand before us, my Oomgosh!"

This time, he really wanted to believe what Raven said.

○ Eleven

Nick woke a second before the stranger spoke.

"So who is this, heh? Somebody else to believe our Captain's lies?"

He opened his eyes. Somebody Nick didn't know stared down at him, a man dressed in the dark clothes and odd armor of Nunn's troops. Nick stiffened, rolling onto his back on the ground. He saw a flash of grey at the edge of his vision. The wolves were still nearby. They were watching over him, making sure nobody harmed him. So the Captain had told him, the same Captain this man spoke of, the Captain who lied.

Nick tried to reclaim his thoughts from sleep and dreams of death and his sword. Perhaps there was a purpose for this man to be here. Perhaps Nick didn't need to kill him just yet. He let his hand brush casually against his belt. His sword was still at his side, still in its sheath. He didn't need to draw it yet, not for a moment or two. His dreams of blood and conquest would nourish him for now.

"The Captain feeds us well," the nearest of the wolves called to the man standing over Nick. "Bewarre, humans. Do not go against us. Wolves are always hungry."

Nick had had his fill of this mystery man, too. "Who are you?"

The other man looked surprised, as if this was something Nick should have already known. "Why, I am Pator, of course. And these are the Captain's troops. He hasn't told you about us?"

Nick raised himself to his elbows. There were other men behind this first one, all dressed like Pator. A group of them spread across one side of the clearing while the wolves con-

108

gregated on the opposite side. Neither group appeared overly fond of the other.

"I thought the other humans were gone," Nick said.

"What?" Pator replied. "Oh, we lost a couple of fellows who didn't come from Nunn's army. Ran back to their wives in that clearing. They weren't really the Captain's type, if you catch my drift."

He waved to include his fellows. "Nine of us have joined him for good. We had all of us had enough of Nunn, but there seemed no alternative but death, at least until your arrival shook up the island. Now, who knows?" He laughed very softly, as if the joke was meant only for him. "The Captain may be crazy enough to win."

Nick pushed himself to a sitting position.

"Let me give you a hand." Pator reached for Nick's right hand. Nick offered the soldier his left. His sword hand free, he allowed Pator to help him to his feet.

Nick took a minute to look at the others. A couple had swords, one a bow. The rest were outfitted with knives and spears. None of them seemed about to attack. Rather they held back at the far corner of the clearing, all staring at Nick as if afraid of him.

Pator nodded before Nick could say a word. "We have heard of your sword—yes. And how, when it takes you over, you show no mercy." The soldier laughed. "Nick. A good name for a man with a blade. You'll fit right in. Let me introduce you to the other men. First we have Umar—"

He paused as the wolves growled in unison behind them. The soldiers cried out a second thereafter.

"Hey, Nick!" a new voice called out; Todd's voice. "See, what did I tell you?"

Nick turned around to look at the kid from across the street. Todd wasn't alone. He had brought two women with him, that girl he'd picked up on that other island, and Maggie, the Volunteer whom Nick had almost shared a bed with, until his sword had taken him over, demanding Maggie's blood.

But he couldn't even smile at Maggie, for Todd had brought Nick's father, too.

His father tried to smile. He failed at that the same way he flopped at everything else. How could Todd have done this?

If there was one person on this world that Nick didn't want to see—

"Nick," his father began, "your mother's worried about you."

Nick almost groaned. So he'd try to weasel his way into Nick's affections using Mom. "I worry about her, too," he said instead. "How about you, Dad? Do *you* care about me one way or the other?"

His father's attempted smile failed miserably. "Sure," he stumbled. "Of course. I've always—"

"Listen, Nick," Todd quickly interrupted Nick's father's ramblings. "They sent me here to ask you to come back. The dragon's coming. Mrs. Smith thinks it's better if we fight this thing together." Todd paused a second before he added, "And I'd like you with us, too."

This was the first time Nick had ever heard Todd actually ask for something from someone else. Todd sounded like he really needed Nick around. Hell, if Nick's father hadn't been here, he might have actually considered going.

"You want him to leave us?" Pator stepped forward. "What do we matter? Our Captain is working with you. We're all on the same side."

"Surely," Nick's father hurriedly said. "We should all work together. But it's important for Nick to come back to his family." He reached out a hand as if he might actually touch his son. "Why don't you come, Nick? We'll work everything out."

Nick came close to laughing. His father would never change. Always good for promises, bad for results. He'd promised to stick by Nick forever, work out whatever problems he'd had with Nick's mom. And then he had disappeared.

Nick didn't know how to answer his father without hurting his whole family more. He turned away instead.

"Nick?" It was Maggie's voice this time. "You know, we could use you."

When his father spoke again, the friendly tone was gone, replaced by a familiar edge. "Nick, you will answer me. I'm your father!"

Todd turned on the old man before Nick could say a word. "Hey, we brought you along because you were worried about your son, not to fight with him."

"I think this is between Nick and me." His father spoke to Todd without even looking at him. Once his dad got started, he could be good and mad at everyone. Todd's hands balled into fists. Nick and his mother expected his father's attitude. With other people, Nick was surprised his father had never gotten his lights punched out.

"If we're going to do anything," Todd said evenly, "we have to work together."

"Who are you to tell me what to do?" Nick's father demanded.

"I'll show you just who I am." Todd was ready to take a swing.

"Todd, come on, cool it!" Nick called. If anyone was going to fight with his father, it had better be Nick.

He slapped the scabbard at his side. "This sword—right now it's who I am. I have to be able to use it someplace away from my family. Someplace where people understand what I have to do."

Todd nodded. That was enough for him. He looked to the soldiers who stood beyond Nick. "What about the rest of you?" Todd asked. "Do you want to join us back at the clearing?"

"We never ask for wizards," Pator said. "We want to manage for ourselves. If we are to die before the dragon, we trust the death will be swift and glorious." The soldier allowed himself the slightest of grins. "Maybe the time will come when we can watch each other's backs."

"Nick," Todd added. "If it gets bad, we may ask again."

Nick actually found himself smiling at that. "If it gets bad, I may come." He shook his head. "I don't trust Obar." He glanced at his father. "I don't trust many people right now."

Todd laughed at that. "I won't trust anybody—period."

Nick realized he would be well advised to feel the same.

Sala spoke for the first time: "Listen, I am not new to this place like these others. When the dragon comes, we're not even going to have time to think about trust!"

"This island is not so big," Pator said softly. "I think we will meet again."

Nick's father turned to Todd. "That's it? You're not going to force him to come back?"

"I don't think we're going to change his mind," Maggie interjected.

"And I don't force anybody to do anything," Todd added. "I had a bit too much of that from my own father."

"Nick!" his father demanded. "We still have to talk!"

When would his father ever learn? "When could we ever talk to each other?"

"But we can't—" Nick's father looked back and forth between Nick and Todd. "I won't let—" He looked like it was his turn to hit someone.

Todd simply held up his glowing green eye.

"Nick, if you need us, we'll be around, okay?"

The four of them vanished in a flash of light. Nick stood there silent for a long moment, empty, as if the sword sucked emotion from him as readily as it drew blood from others. But it wasn't the sword this time. If he let himself open up, he knew he would cry.

Nunn felt like a stranger in his own head.

He had created this place, this home for the energies he had consumed. Before, he had thought of them as ghosts, mere echoes of the personalities that had once existed, to be used at Nunn's whim. But then Mills had escaped, taking the spirits of the wizard Rox and the fire being Zachs, ripping all of them free of Nunn's consciousness.

The power given to Nunn by the dragon's eyes was a wonderful thing. If you could believe in something strongly enough, the eyes would create it. It would exist. When he and Obar had first learned from Rox, then cooperated to open the magic world around them, they had created the spells to conform to certain patterns, creating rituals that would bring a regularity to the magic. Looking back on that early spellcasting, Nunn believed all that mumbo jumbo was more for the magician's benefit than for the resulting magic. The lure of near-limitless power was also an invitation to chaos. The establishment of ritual was necessary so that the magician would not go mad.

But the escape of Mills and the others had been a reminder. Other wills could undo your magics. The power was not absolute. A necessary lesson, Nunn imagined, with the dragon so near.

Once, he had kept his spirits filed away for future use. He had been able to reach in here and pull out whomever he wished. Now he could barely recognize the place. He had imagined a great house here, much like the castle his magic had built in the world outside. Now there were new walls, new doors, new windows to views he had never seen before. His vision of this place was unraveling before him, to be replaced by—what?

He heard a scraping sound behind him, like someone dragging chains across a cold stone floor.

He turned. A man, half-transparent, as if too apologetic to fully materialize, stood before him.

"Leo," Nunn said.

"Hello, Nunn." Even Leo seemed much bolder than he ever had before. He actually was smiling, and stared Nunn straight in the eye. "You're looking for Carl. I wouldn't if I were you."

Now this weakling would tell him what to do? This had gone too far. He would bring this whole illusion crashing down around them. "Who are you to tell me—"

"Oh, you could destroy me with a single glance," Leo said with a nod. "But so could Carl." There was that smile again. "It puts me in a difficult position, let me tell you."

So Carl was challenging Nunn's power even here. He might have to eliminate this Jackson sooner than he had thought. But his anger had given Nunn a plan of action. This place was his illusion, and only he could destroy it, room by room, brick by brick, if he had to, until Carl Jackson's hiding place was revealed.

It was Nunn's turn to smile. "Excuse me, Leo."

He raised one eyebrow. The wall behind Leo turned to dust. No Carl there. Yet Nunn thought he would be somewhere nearby.

Leo's eyes widened as the dust blew past his feet. The smile was gone.

"I'll just get out of your way now," he said softly.

"Yes, why don't you?" Nunn agreed casually. Leo vanished, not beyond Nunn's reach, but no longer in his face.

He concentrated on the next barrier beyond the one he just destroyed. When this one evaporated, it disturbed some of the spirits that hovered in this place. They did indeed resemble ghosts, mere shadows of their former selves.

"Nunn," they whispered. "Not you."

"Why?" they called. "Why me?"

"Not me," they pleaded. "Not me."

They had been trapped in this place for too long, so long that they could do nothing more than repeat their last pitiful words and deeds before Nunn consumed their souls. Even their spirits were old now, their remaining identities paper-thin, like a memory that barely brushes against your consciousness, there for an instant and then gone forever. There seemed to be a dozen or more of these faint echoes of men confined in this tiny space; so many people who had existed so long ago, before an earlier incarnation of the dragon. Nunn could not even recall their names. He had consumed hundreds, maybe thousands, just like them, after all.

These creatures from his past did not concern him. He would not get lost in history. He destroyed a third wall and a fourth, a whole corner of this little kingdom Nunn had created so long ago. More spirits screamed away, hundreds of them now, seeking escape, perhaps, or the oblivion that had been denied to them for so long.

He heard a different sound then, both faint yet very near. For an instant he thought it might be someone more newly dead, or a trick of Carl's, until it came again.

Nunn.

He heard his name repeated a dozen times or more. But not by voices, by sounds from anything resembling human or animal. If these things were whispers, they were whispers found in the marrow of his bones.

It is time, Nunn.

You cannot turn us away.

We come for what belongs to us.

Nunn.

Nunn knew these whispers. They came from those dark things that fed on light and warmth; shadow creatures he had used before who always wished to use him more. Perhaps the fleeing spirits had drawn them here, allowing the shapes to feed on something that was almost Nunn; something that only increased their hunger more.

Nunn.

Give us what is ours.

They would absorb all the energies within the wizard in a single gluttonous rush. They had almost taken him once before, when the dragon's eye had failed him, and he had only been rescued by Carl Jackson and the magic globe. The dark shapes needed his magic like other life needed the sun. Now the things were back again, to collect a debt he had thought he would always be too strong to forfeit.

Nunn.

Open to us, Nunn.

We will take it, one way or another. Do not make it difficult.

But Nunn was strong again, his dragon's eyes burning in the palms of his hands. He would blast the dark things for their presumption. But he could do nothing while he was lost in his inner world.

"Having fun destroying things?" a far more human voice asked. "I always do."

Carl Jackson stood before him. In his hand he held the globe. Nunn's globe, full of his earlier power, which Jackson had dared to use against him.

"Time for a little one-on-one?" Carl said with a smile.

Carl Jackson was nothing but a fool. He had no idea how dangerous Nunn could be with his power restored. He should be far more afraid. He would be far more afraid, after Nunn dealt with certain other unpleasant things.

Nunn allowed his image to gain sufficient definition so that Jackson might see the gems glowing in his palms. "I think you have no idea what it would be like to battle with me."

"Really?" That only seemed to make Jackson's grin grow wider. "I don't fight fair."

That was one thing the two of them had in common. Fair? Nunn didn't know the meaning of the word.

Nunn. Give us what we need or we will take it.

He had no time to waste on someone who was simply mortal. He had to return to the actual world, and fight the darkness where his gems held the most power.

"We're not fighting at all," he said as he extended a hand to Carl. He would bring Jackson with him, no matter what the consequences.

Jackson's grin was gone. "What are you trying to pull?"

We will take it now.

"We have larger problems at the moment," Nunn replied.
We need warmth. We need life.
Carl was going with him.
Nunn.
He had a debt to repay, after all.

The girl's voice startled Obar, but it was gentle compared with what came next.

"I'd stop that now."

Obar looked up from his work to see Mary Lou. She stood above him, as if she had simply appeared there by magic.

The knife dropped from his hand, his mind numb with the force of the Anno's mental shout. Mary Lou had returned to them, and their collective being rushed out to embrace her. To the Anno, Obar was merely a god. Mary Lou was something special.

Obar hid his trembling hands within the folds of his soiled white robes. He did not want her to see how shaken he was. One of the small creatures lay before him, the blood pumping rapidly from the large gash in her throat. But it was nowhere near enough, and he hadn't even begun to cut either of the others. He stood and smiled pleasantly at her, as if using a knife was the last thing on his mind.

"How nice to see you back among the Anno."

"Before, I had no idea what you were trying to do. How you were using these poor creatures to increase your power." She held up her dragon's eye. "Now I can respond."

How much did she know? For those who held the dragon's eyes, anything was possible. Still, she had only held her eye for a matter of hours.

"You don't have the experience," he said, hoping that it was so.

He did not expect to see her smile. "I may not have the experience, but I do have help."

Obar frowned, looking past Mary Lou, then turning around to survey the rest of the Anno's platform. As soon as she had said it, he realized it was true. There was someone else here. Not on this physical plane; there was no one else in sight. But his eye gave him access to other places, other realities. He reached out beyond Mary Lou's voice, beyond the mental cries of the Anno. Someone waited with Mary Lou, someone watched him, just beyond the real.

As soon as he touched this other place, it was filled with laughter.

"Garo?" Obar asked.

The laughter continued.

"This gets more interesting with every passing minute." Obar did not mention it also grew ever more disturbing. When Garo had been in Obar's service, he had learned things Obar did not wish to be known. He had thought—he had hoped—that Garo had been lost to the dragon.

"Interesting enough for us to have a little talk?" Garo replied.

"That's all you can do, isn't it? Talk?" Obar could ignore Garo then, and concentrate on the girl. Perhaps he could get rid of Mary Lou before any real damage was done.

"I'm here to stop you," Mary Lou announced abruptly. "The Anno have a role to play in this, but it is not the role you have chosen."

Obar was amazed at the youngster's audacity. "Who are you to tell me this?"

"Someone more honest than you," Garo interjected. "Honest in motive, honest in feeling. I get giddy just thinking about it."

"We are evenly matched now," Mary Lou said as she held up her gem.

"An eye for an eye," Garo agreed.

Obar shook his head. "You do not begin to fathom the depths of my power—"

"You going to bring that boy out to cut her up?" Garo asked.

"Nick?" Mary Lou asked. "Is he around here somewhere?"

The Anno, quiet until now, began a mental song as they danced around them, as if even they had lost respect for Obar. This was not going at all well.

"Nick's gone, too?" Garo mused. "Poor Obar. This world's going to be filled with disgruntled ex-employees."

"Nick and I still have a connection," Obar admitted. He tried to ignore the giddy Anno. He wanted to destroy this laughing fool. But how did you crush a ghost?

Perhaps it would come down to a test of their magics. He tried to center himself, to prepare for the task ahead. He spoke in his most superior tone: "There are certain rules I have learned in my years as a magician, rules you could not possibly comprehend."

"Don't you know that the old rules no longer apply?"

"Really?" Obar replied. He could barely believe the gall of this girl. "How could you possibly—"

Mary Lou nodded cheerfully. "The dragon told me."

Obar couldn't help himself. "The dragon—told you?" he replied, the authority gone from his voice.

"Well, with Garo's help," Mary Lou admitted. "But how do you think I got Garo's help, after all?"

So Garo *had* been taken by the dragon? Obar did not feel at all well. How could one approach the dragon when others had already rushed into its confidence?

"Then you know the dragon's plan?" he asked.

But the girl frowned at that. "The dragon doesn't tell me everything," Mary Lou admitted.

"An uneasy alliance at best," Garo whispered in Obar's ear. "But then, around here, are there any other kind?"

They were interrupted by a flash of light. Obar turned around to face the newcomers. There were just too many people around here with a dragon's eye.

Mrs. Smith stood amidst the cowering Anno, one of the Volunteers to her right, Mary Lou's father to her left.

"Mary Lou," Mrs. Smith began. "Thank goodness I've found you. We have to—"

"I don't need you now." Mary Lou interrupted without even looking around.

"Mary Lou!" her father called. "We were worried—"

"Not now, Daddy," was her reply.

"But, dear—" Mrs. Smith sputtered.

"I know you mean well," Mary Lou answered evenly, "but you have to go away."

And the three of them were gone. Mrs. Smith, whom Obar had thought was the most powerful of the newcomers with a dragon's eye, banished by Mary Lou without a glance.

Mary Lou was still staring at him. "Now, Obar, it is time we got down to business."

Obar looked around. The Anno had paused in their dance

to watch him as well. And he felt as if Garo had almost popped right inside his head. His plan seemed to have unraveled completely.

Obar was finding this all most upsetting.

O Twelve

Joan knew that someone was near. They had all heard those all-too-familiar sounds from outside the clearing, the same thrashing and the screams they had heard during the attack on Nick and Sala. The vines were claiming new victims.

There were only male voices shouting and screaming this time, speaking an unfamiliar tongue when the words weren't too hoarse to even be heard.

Stanley had held the neighbors back from investigating. "Wait a minute," he'd said in a voice just loud enough for those around him to hear. "Those are strangers. Maybe this is for the best."

"If they're strangers, they must be the enemy?" Even after their recent battle, there was a part of Joan that didn't want to agree with that.

"We must assume that we are under attack," Stanley replied. "This time, the vines are protecting us."

Charlie stared at that spot in the woods from where the noise was coming. He growled in agreement.

"We have no idea how large a force is against us," Stanley continued. "Perhaps we should adjourn into the trees upon the clearing's other side until some of our more powerful allies return."

"But what's to keep the vines from attacking us over there?" Joan pointed out.

Stanley stared at Joan before answering, "Nothing whatsoever." He shook his head. "Take one thing for granted around here, and you're dead." He waved his bow toward the commotion outside camp. "As long as they're being attacked by the vines, those people aren't attacking us. If we can't go anywhere, at least we have a minute to prepare. Retrieve your weapons.''

He pointed to a spot on the edge of the clearing just shy of the trees. ''We'll gather in a circle, me on one side, Bobby and Charlie on the other. If need be, we can give them a fight.''

They were in for another battle? Joan hadn't really recovered from the first one. Rebecca and Rose were already heading for the tree where they had piled the knives and bows they had used before. Harold, Bobby, and the dog all moved over to the spot Stanley had set for their stand. All of them, except for Joan, getting ready for the fight.

''Wait!'' Stanley quickly pulled an arrow from his quiver.

The cries in the forest had stopped. They stood in an instant of total silence, like the world had forgotten how to make noise.

Joan didn't even see them come into the clearing. She was grabbed by the shoulders from behind. She felt something sharp at her throat.

''It's a knife, dearie,'' a deep voice said close by her ear. ''I wouldn't make any quick moves, you or any of the others.''

''Let her go!'' Stanley replied. He nodded at the arrow already fitted into his bow. ''Or you'll be wearing this, heh?''

''You can shoot one of us,'' a new voice drawled lazily, as if its owner had all the time in the world, ''but the other five will take care of you.'' The voice of their leader came from somewhere to Joan's left. With the knife at her throat, she didn't dare turn her head.

A man swaggered in front of her, walking in a small circle so that he might look at all the neighbors. His pants and shirt were ragged and torn, caked with the same mud that adorned his face and hands. From the smell coming from him, she wondered if he had ever washed in his life.

She was not surprised that his grin was missing a few teeth. ''My name is Snake. We've come for my daughter, Sala, a little something to eat, and''—his smile broadened as he glanced at Joan—''a bit of female companionship.''

He nodded to Rebecca and Rose, who now both carried knives. ''Put those down now, ladies, and we'll have a much better time.''

The other newcomers, as well dressed and groomed as their leader, strolled among the neighbors. Harold folded his arms before him as if that might protect him. "Sala isn't here."

Snake nodded pleasantly at that, too, as if nothing in this clearing could possibly upset him. "Ah, but I can tell by your tone that she'll be back. Perhaps we'll wait, then. There seems plenty to go around."

A bird cawed high overhead.

The grip tightened on Joan's shoulder. "What was that?" the man who held her called.

Snake shrugged. "A crow or something. Nothing to be concerned about."

"You're not listening to me, hey?" Stanley interjected. As far as Joan could tell, the arrow in his bow was aimed straight toward her. "Let go of the woman. Then we'll talk."

Snake sighed with that. "And this gentleman is talking back? I guess we have to kill him as an example." The knife in his hand made the slightest twitch in Stanley's direction. Two of Snake's men turned and approached the Volunteer.

Margaret had gotten to her feet again. She wandered over to stare at Snake.

"Leo?" she asked.

"Come, my Oomgosh!" Raven called from the trees.

Somewhere, out of Joan's sight, Charlie barked, then growled. A man screamed.

"Hell!" Snake called, all trace of a smile gone. "Kill the dog!"

All of Snake's men whom Joan could see looked at something behind her. Joan realized that Stanley had released his arrow. She felt a rush of air by her ear, heard a grunt behind her. The hard grip on her shoulder was gone, and she was spinning, falling to the ground.

She looked up from where she hit the earth and saw Raven diving for one of the newcomers, the bird's claws raking across the man's eyes. Another man ran toward Jason, knife in hand. Jason simply watched him come, until, the man almost upon him, Jason's arms reached out so quickly that Joan's gaze could not follow them. Somehow, the man with the knife was flying through the air past Jason's shoulder, tumbling twenty feet or more to hit the base of one of the great trees with a sickening crunch.

"Leo!" Joan heard Margaret scream one final time. She realized her neck was wet. Joan looked at the fingers she had used to touch the dampness and saw that she had been cut by the knife. She was bleeding.

"Do you need help, hey?" Stanley was squatting by her side. "They came in fast behind me. Guess I'm out of practice." He frowned at her wound. "He cut you as he died. We may need to put something on this, but I think you'll heal."

"Oh, God," Joan whispered. She started to shake.

"Breathe deep," Stanley instructed. "You've been through a lot, but you'll be fine." He called to the others. "Can I get some help over here?"

"I need to stand up." She shook her head when the Volunteer offered to help. It was important for her to have a sense of independence. Maybe, she thought, it was more a sense of control.

She got to her knees first, then to her feet. The wound at her neck made her a little light-headed, but her balance was fine. All she could think of was how Nick's dog had been attacked and wounded, and how the dog had begun to change, to mutate into something half dog, half monster. Before she was whole, but now she also had a wound. Now she was open to this world's infection. Would she grow spikes and ridges of bone like Charlie?

Joan closed her eyes. Mostly, she was feeling sorry for herself. Everyone here had to change if they wanted to survive. She thought about those others with the gems—the dragon's eyes—powerful stones that half the time seemed to control their supposed masters. She thought of Mr. Mills, once the quiet vice-principal who lived across the street, who seemed possessed by the spirits of others. And she thought—as she had with her every waking minute since he had gotten that sword—about Nick, and how that damned piece of metal had taken over his life.

She wished she could pull that sword from her son's hands and break it across her knee. She remembered the last time she saw him, after the first attack of the vines. He had been covered with sweat, but the way the moisture matted his hair and glistened on his pale flesh, it looked less like exertion and more the result of some wasting disease. His eyes were sunken, his cheeks hollow. He was beginning to look like death.

She had felt totally powerless. With that sword in his hand, her son was beyond reason. So what had she done? She had sent her husband to do what she was too afraid to do; to do the impossible, and rescue Nick from himself.

George's quest was doubly hopeless, for she knew Nick blamed George more than her for the breakup of their marriage. If only things had been as simple as that! Joan and George had been together for twenty years, but they had never really found a way to talk. Even now, she didn't know what she really wanted from George, or Nick. Or herself. Maybe she was going to die, not knowing anything.

She opened her eyes. She wasn't dead yet, and she had coped with change before. This wound was her own fault. She had become a target because she had been the only one not preparing for a fight.

What chance would her son have if she gave up, too? She tried to take a deep breath, but her neck flared with pain. She let the air out slowly, carefully. For now, she would take small, measured breaths instead.

Joan looked around the clearing. There were three bodies, three of the men who attacked them. One had had his throat ripped out by Charlie, a second lay broken at the base of a tree. And another had an arrow that entered his brain through his eye. Joan could still feel his hands on her body, his knife at her throat.

All the bodies belonged to the enemy. Somehow, the neighbors had survived again.

One of their attackers was still alive. He moaned on the ground, clutching at his face where his eyes had been, blood streaming down his cheeks like tears. Rose and Rebecca both stood nearby, knives in their hands. If he wanted to put up a fight, they'd be more than happy to kill him.

Stanley frowned at Joan from the middle of the clearing. "Two of them got away. Snake ran at the first sign of trouble. They took Margaret."

"Mom?" Bobby called. He looked up from where he had been studying Charlie's wounds. The dog licked at them—two on its right foreleg, one more on its front left paw. They were nothing more than scratches, really.

"Mom?" Bobby called again, louder this time. He stood, jumping from one leg to the other, his head whipping about to look at every corner of the clearing, ready to run someplace, anyplace, if he only knew where.

He looked down to the dog. "Charlie! You can smell her, can't you? We've got to get her!"

But Stanley grabbed Bobby's shoulder. "Wait a moment there, hey? All our troubles seem to start every time we split up."

"Wait a minute." Jason held up a hand that looked green in the forest light. "They haven't gotten very far. I can find them whenever you want."

Jason didn't seem very happy with that information. He looked miserable as he glanced furtively from one neighbor to another.

Raven fluttered down to perch on Jason's shoulder. "What does the lord of the forest desire?"

"This is all my fault!" Jason pounded his chest with his fist. "I let them in here."

Raven cawed softly in reply. "You were learning, my Oomgosh. No one learns without mistakes."

"Mistakes that end in death." Jason looked at the body at the base of the tree, as if seeing it for the first time. "I killed someone."

Raven tilted his head quizzically, as if surprised that Jason would even mention this. "The Oomgosh kills when he must. But he is here for the living."

"But Bobby's mother—" Jason insisted.

"It was strange," Harold said with a shake of his head, "the way she went up to Snake."

"No stranger than anything else Margaret does," Rose added.

"Maybe," Rebecca suggested, "she wants to be missing."

"Couldn't we have stopped—" Jason began again.

"Raven controls no destiny but his own," the bird replied with a shake of his wings. "No one has that power—Raven, Oomgosh, or dragon." The bird tilted his shiny beak up so that it reflected the sun. "Of course, Raven's influence is everywhere."

"I'm going to run things for a minute here," Stanley interrupted. He turned back to Joan and walked toward her. She had trouble focusing on him. Her eyes kept wanting to close. "And we're going to put something on that neck to stop the bleeding." His hands guided her shoulders, so much more gentle than the hands that had grabbed her before. "Why don't you rest against this tree? I know a thing or two about healing poultices. One of those handy things you pick up from a life in the woods.''

Joan let herself be guided until she was sitting against the tree. She was surprised at how pleased she was to be told what to do.

"Is there something I can do?'' another man's voice asked.

Joan frowned. There was a green haze in front of her eyes. Stanley let out a little yelp.

"Glowing green men!'' Stanley shouted. "Showing up out of nowhere, just like everything else around here. I will never get used to this godforsaken place!''

"Sorry,'' the green haze replied apologetically. "When you float from place to place, you don't make much noise.''

"Hyram?'' Joan asked. Why did her voice sound like it was very far away?

"Hi, uh, Joan,'' the green-glowing Hyram Sayre answered. "I thought maybe I could be of some help.'' He laughed, a high-pitched, nervous sound. "While my powers aren't as great as I once imagined, I should be able to help with a simple neck wound. That is, if that's all right with you.''

"You're offering to help,'' Joan replied, more to get the concept clear in her own foggy head than to answer her glowing neighbor. "Sure. Why not? The more the merrier.''

"Good. This will only take a moment.''

She saw a flash of green light. Joan closed her eyes. Her neck felt like it was burning. She tried to pull away but found she was frozen in place. The burning grew less, going from pain to irritation to a general warmth that was actually rather pleasant.

"I know what all of you are thinking,'' Hyram said as he worked on her neck. "Why would I come back to a place where they had no respect for my lawn? Not that you—uh, Joan—would have run across my grass. But your son, and those other boys . . .'' Sayre paused to take a deep breath. "But that was a different place, and I am a different person. If indeed I am still a person.'' Joan opened her eyes and saw Hyram's face, glowing faintly green but finally in focus, poised a foot above her own. He frowned down at her neck as he continued. "But even a special fellow like me can get lonely. I would like to help you all to survive.'' He glanced quickly at the other neighbors. "Even children and dogs." He laughed again, somewhat incredulously this time, as if even he couldn't believe what he was saying.

"There." Hyram pulled back his hand and took a step away. "All done."

Stanley took Hyram's place, examining Joan's neck. "Whatever you did, it seems to have knitted the wound nicely. Think I might still put a poultice on it for safety's sake."

"Todd's back!" Rebecca called.

Joan forced her eyes back open. She had barely realized they had closed. "Nick?" she asked.

George was in front of her. "Joan! What happened?"

"She's been cut but she'll be all right," Stanley answered for her. "We had a little unpleasantness here right after you left."

"Nunn's men," Maggie called from above one of the bodies.

"My father's men," Sala added.

"We've got one of 'em who's still alive." Stanley spat. "Don't know if he's going to be alive for long."

But no one was answering Joan's question. "Did you get Nick?"

"He wouldn't come back, Joan," George said. "He wouldn't even listen—"

"I think he's going to be all right, Mrs. Blake." Todd stepped up next to her husband. "At least we should give him a chance. There are some things he's going to have to work out."

"I tried," George added weakly.

Joan Blake attempted a smile. "Somehow—we'll all get through this."

"They get any of us?" Maggie asked Stanley.

"Nobody dead, but they kidnapped Mrs. Furlong."

"We've got to go get her, then," Maggie replied.

"Maybe," Stanley allowed. "Maybe not. If we're going to go out rescuing anybody, we got to plan it more sensibly. Look at what happened here. Moment the folks with the jewels— and two of the best with weapons, too—run off, bang!—we get attacked. May be coincidence. May be a hell of a lot of other things, too."

"You think somebody's conspiring against us?" George asked.

Stanley pushed a shaking finger in George's face. "I think this whole damned world is conspiring against us, and we're gonna have to start acting that way. This 'excuse me while I go off and be a hero' business is gonna get us all killed!"

Maggie stared back at her fellow Volunteer for a long moment. "Stanley, I have never heard you talk so much in all the years I have known you."

Stanley thought about that a moment before replying. "Neither have I." He nodded at George. "Sorry about the finger. Just found it a little too annoying, hey?"

"So we should go after Margaret, shouldn't we?" George insisted.

"Probably," Stanley allowed. "Just have to go about it in a calmer fashion. First, we figure out which way they've taken her—"

"They've gone that way." Jason pointed through the trees. "They haven't made it very far. Mrs. Furlong isn't walking very quickly."

Stanley nodded. "Then we figure the safest and quickest way to get her back. No heroes—"

"I can find her!" Hyram Sayre seemed to glow twice as brightly as he leaped into the air. "I'm a changed man. I'll do anything for a neighbor!"

Stanley sighed. "This is gonna take a while to get straight, isn't it?"

Joan found that very funny. But she couldn't laugh any more than she could keep her eyes open. Her neck still felt very warm. It was a peaceful feeling. She knew for a single moment that everything really would work out after all. But then that feeling was gone, too, as fleeting as everything else on this world.

There was nothing left to do but sleep.

○ Thirteen

Snake was beginning to think this was a mistake.

"Leo!" the woman carped, each word harsher than the one before. "Are you mad at me? Why don't you let me rest? I always said you didn't listen enough to me, Leo. If we don't stop this minute, you'll never hear the end of this."

The woman wouldn't shut up. He was feeling more sorry for this Leo with every passing minute. One-Eye pulled her stumbling along after them. Despite her thin frame and pallid complexion, she seemed perfectly capable of keeping up with the two men, just so long as they let her keep on talking.

Snake had found out, through one of her rambling complaints, that the woman's name was Margaret. Beyond that, any real communication seemed impossible. She didn't respond to threats. She would look straight at Snake when he spoke to her, even make a face or two when he called her by name, but he didn't think she understood a single other thing he said.

"Leo," she yelled from where One-Eye brought up the rear. "I'm getting really angry—"

Snake either wanted to laugh or kill somebody. Under normal circumstances, his reasoning had been sound in what they'd done. Better to have a hostage; it made the enemy think twice about attacks and ambushes, and raised the possibility of a trade for his dear daughter Sala. But this particular hostage? Before Nunn had left them, the wizard had managed to give Snake and his men the ability to converse with these newcomers, just so Snake could find the one person with whom it wouldn't work.

Not that she'd ever stop conversing! "You think that just

by not talking to me, you can shut me up, don't you, Leo? I haven't even begun to talk. I never really told you how I felt about your mother—''

Now he'd hear about the woman's entire family! Snake wished he could just knock her out and carry her. The only thing that kept him from doing so was the slight chance they might kill her in the process. For purposes of negotiation, it was much better if you kept your hostages alive.

"Begging your pardon, Snake," One-Eye said. "But I could do with some rest myself." He seemed to be wheezing a bit; the result, no doubt, of dragging this Margaret woman behind him.

Snake had had enough of both of them. "So we should stop here and just let them catch us? She's been making so much noise, even those people back in the clearing could follow us!''

Shouting at One-Eye wouldn't solve their problems. Snake had to admit he hadn't thought this through. He cursed Nunn for bringing him to this foreign territory, in a place where good, reliable men could be killed by boys and dogs and birds. Now here they were, Snake and the only man he had left, a cripple besides, in a place where the trees grew so high Snake couldn't even follow the direction of the sun.

He had to find someplace to hide; someplace where they might eventually make a stand. Maybe they should go back to the boats, if he had any idea where the boats were. He was used to open seas and nice, orderly towns. Maybe the best thing to do was to kill anyone who got in his way and take the skeleton crew left on the boat and get out of here. If Margaret kept complaining, a quick knife to the belly. If One-Eye wanted to rest, Snake would let him rest, with a nice slit across his throat.

The thoughts of murder calmed Snake down, the way they always did. But Snake still needed Margaret for insurance, One-Eye for the dirty work. Somehow, life always fell short of his dreams.

"Snake!" One-Eye called to him.

Snake looked up from his musings. There was a man waiting for them, leaning against a tree just ahead.

"I'd stop right there." The man gave Snake a shark's grin, all teeth and no humor; an expression that appeared even more bizarre thanks to the three scar lines the man sported on either cheek. He was wearing dark clothing that seemed to blend with the shadows in the forest. Snake wondered if it was some kind of uniform.

Snake still held his knife in his hand. He judged the distance to his newcomer—certainly not more than twenty paces. He might be able to kill the man with a single throw. Still, this fellow seemed awfully confident for someone alone in the woods. There would be a fair chance he'd have a few friends hidden in the area. That was the way Snake would do it, after all.

"Sorry." Snake held his knife before him, just so the other man would know it was an option. "We don't have time to talk." He wondered if it was worth it to just start running. This was an island, after all. If he hit the shoreline, he'd be able to find his ship eventually.

"Perhaps." The man pushed himself away from the tree and sauntered in Snake's direction. "It looks like you have something that doesn't belong to you." He pulled a sword from his belt and waved it at Margaret. "It would be better if you gave her back."

One-Eye and the woman had stopped by Snake's side. Margaret squinted at the newcomer through the forest gloom.

"Leo?" she asked.

The scarred man shook his head. "This doesn't have to come to blows, you know. You work for Nunn, don't you? At least you did recently. Don't be surprised. This is a small island—nothing's a secret. I worked for Nunn, too. Used to be his captain. That was before I went freelance, started a little army of my own. Things are changing here. Nunn's days of glory are at an end."

One-Eye took a couple of steps back as Margaret sank to her knees. She moaned softly but for a change had nothing to say.

Snake waited for movement, or some noise from the surrounding forest, but all was still for now. Perhaps they weren't going to die just yet.

"What do you want from us?"

"Join me"—Nunn's former captain pointed his sword at himself—"and give up the woman. You get the benefit of my fighting forces, and a chance to survive what's to come. Without me, the two of you are dead already."

Snake had expected to be surrounded by this Captain's fellows by now. Instead, all the man did was talk. Maybe he really was working alone.

"Sorry." Snake walked casually away from One-Eye and Margaret. That way, this Captain could be attacked from two directions. "My days of working for other people are over."

The Captain, instead of backing away from the potential attack, actually walked closer to all three of them. "A pity. We're talking about survival. And, of course, you'll be giving up that woman—"

One-Eye hit the Captain hard on the back of the head.

He groaned and fell to his knees.

"You're dead," the Captain began before One-Eye hit him again.

The Captain fell face-first on the forest floor.

Snake paused for a long moment, still waiting for an attack from some other quarter. But there was nothing. This time, he had guessed right. He let out a long sigh. "I do hate people who talk too much."

One-Eye smiled down at his victim. "What say we finish him off and proceed on our way?"

"What are you doing to Leo?" Margaret was on her feet again. She rushed forward, pushing herself between One-Eye and the body.

"What now?" Snake groaned. What was going on in this woman's head? How did the Captain become Leo, anyway? Snake had thought that honor was reserved for him!

"You know," One-Eye said wistfully, "for an older wench, her body's not half-bad."

Snake saw that Margaret was pressing her whole body against his lieutenant, pushing him away from the fallen Captain.

One-Eye leered at Snake. "You did promise us some recreation, you know."

"Stop what you're doing to Leo!" the woman pleaded. "I'll do anything!"

"We don't have time for that now!" Snake snapped. The thought of making love to a woman constantly shrieking about her Leo didn't appeal to him in the least. Maybe he would just have trouble getting used to a weathered woman like Margaret after the pert breasts and smooth skin of his little Sala.

"I've got to save Leo!"

"Maybe it'll shut her up!" his lieutenant called.

One-Eye did have a way of finding the best possible outcome. But it was folly even to talk about something like this, exposed as they were out in the open. If this Captain could find them, others would follow.

Margaret screamed.

One-Eye had grabbed the shoulders of the woman's dress, as if ready to tear it off. "Why not? She won't have any idea of what's happening to her. The best of both worlds, as I see it."

Margaret slapped One-Eye in the face. Maybe she had some idea of what was going on after all. Maybe she was a better con artist than Snake gave her credit for. She screamed again. Just what they needed—more noise.

"Not now!" Margaret said in a hoarse voice. "Can't you see it?"

"One-Eye!" Snake barked. "We've got to get out of here."

"But Snake," One-Eye whined, "once I get started—"

"Come now," a voice called from overhead. "I'm appalled by what's going on, and I'm not even human."

Snake swore. You stayed in one place for more than a moment and this is what happened. Was this what the crazy lady meant when she asked if they could see it? He looked up, and saw someone, or something, floating gently down from the sky.

The creature in the sky sort of looked human, except for the glowing green color of his skin and that hole in his stomach that showed the woods beyond. Snake doubly cursed the day he ever let Nunn talk him into anything.

The green man landed as softly as a leaf falling from a tree. He smiled at Snake. His teeth were green, too.

"Hyram Sayre was my name, back when I was a human. Now I'm more of a deity, I guess. Please back away from poor Margaret, and I won't have to hurt you."

Not again. Snake triply cursed the moment he was inspired to take a hostage. But Margaret was still his only bargaining point. Just because somebody was glowing green didn't make him dangerous.

"Prove it," Snake demanded. He still held the knife in his

hand. He was betting it would cut through green flesh as easily as it would through the regular kind.

The smile vanished from the strange man's face. "Now I'm getting annoyed. No one takes Hyram Sayre for granted."

The green man jumped forward, fists flying. A green fist passed right through Snake's chin. And Snake's knife flew through the space where Hyram's chest should be, almost throwing Snake off balance.

The green man was horrified. "Oh, dear. That didn't work at all. I'm rather insubstantial."

Snake started to laugh.

One-Eye tugged at Margaret's sleeve. She shrieked again, as if she now preferred that to talking. "No, can't you see it?" she called, staring out into the forest. "Watching us?"

"There are other ways to defend this woman." The green man was at Margaret's side in the blink of an eye. "Excuse me, Margaret."

"It's so beautiful," she replied. "And so cold."

"This will only take a minute," the thing called Sayre added. And the glowing green man actually disappeared inside the woman's form.

Margaret jerked away from One-Eye's probing hands. Her head yanked one way, then another, her right hand flying up, then her left. She looked like some Punch-and-Judy marionette with tangled strings. Her next words were slurred and halting. "This will—have to—Leo?—do."

One-Eye made a grab for her.

"I—Leo?—just need to borrow your body for—is that you, Leo?—a moment." Her words grew more distinct the more she spoke. "I'll do my best not to disturb anything. Where have you been? Leo? Can you see it? In the woods?"

One-Eye finally got a hand on her elbow. She punched his jaw so hard he spun around before falling to the ground. Snake had made a mistake with this woman. She wasn't frail, she was wiry.

One-Eye lay very still where he had fallen. He was out cold, maybe hurt. Maybe dead.

Margaret glanced down at the fallen man, then across the clearing to her one opponent left standing. "Now, Mr. Snake, it is time for you."

Snake did what he should have done a long time ago. He turned and ran.

"Can you see it, Leo?" the woman called after him.

Constance was somewhere she didn't want to be. She hated when this happened, when something wrenched the magic out of her control. When it had happened before, this loss of control, it had been the dragon's doing. This time, to her surprise, she had been banished by Mary Lou, but she wondered if the dragon was still behind it.

She looked around her. Last time this had happened, she had visited some realm controlled by the dragon, perhaps someplace even within the dragon itself. Her surroundings now were more mundane, in the midst of large trees that blocked out the sun, another part of the never-ending forest that covered this island. Wilbert was still with her; the protector she'd been convinced to bring along in case the danger came from the ordinary world. She was glad she had talked Rose out of sending Harold along as well. At least Wilbert knew how to take care of himself. Having to protect someone from the neighborhood would be far too much.

She heard panicked cries from somewhere nearby. That was something else about this island. Someone always seemed to be screaming.

"We've been sent somewhere?" Wilbert looked around. "You have no idea how that just happened, do you?"

Mrs. Smith shook her head.

"Well," Wilbert continued, "at least we're on equal footing there." The screams started again. "I suppose we should investigate—cautiously, I think."

Constance frowned, trying to judge the distance to the noise. "Should I get us closer?"

Wilbert shook his head. "I think there is already too much magic about. To prevent any further surprises, why don't we walk there?"

Not that Mrs. Smith could exactly walk. The fatigue from her use of the dragon's eye seemed to take a toll on her physical form, making her casual movements more unsteady than ever before, even as the magic within her grew. If this continued, she wondered if it would be possible for her to embrace the magic entirely, and leave her physical form behind.

Still, she glided close above the ground, using the least noticeable amount of magic possible, as she followed Wilbert
toward the commotion ahead.

Wilbert led them to a tree ten feet across at its base, a good
shield against whatever was happening on the other side. He
held up a hand for Mrs. Smith to wait, then crept around the
great bole to the right. He poked his head around the edge of
their cover, then quickly pulled it back.

"There's two of them," Wilbert called softly to her, "and
they're being attacked by something we've seen before." He
glanced about again. "From his clothes, I'd say one of them
is Nunn. Can't tell about the other. They're so deeply involved,
I think we can get a little closer."

They moved silently around the edge of the tree, Wilbert
still in the lead. Constance could see the melee before them
now, Nunn and one other male being attacked by those dark
shapes that had ambushed the neighbors in the clearing the
other day; ambushed them and stolen George Blake. They
were shapes that seemed to eat light, devouring all color and
illumination from the world around them. She remembered, in
her brush with them, that their touch was as cold as they were
dark, as if they took the heat from the world as well.

From the way the two fighters were screaming, the dark
things were quite capable of inflicting pain as well.

Her distance vision was quite good, one of the so-called
advantages of age. She recognized the second fighter.

"That's Carl," she whispered. "Carl Jackson. Todd's father."

"Wondered where he'd gotten to," Wilbert replied. "From
talking to Todd, I think I sort of wish he'd stayed lost."

Wilbert tried to wave her back out of the open, but she
walked past him, fascinated by the battle. Nunn managed an
occasional shot of energy at the flying things, but half a dozen
of the shapes hovered above him, as if waiting for the proper
moment to surround and smother him.

"Oh, Lord," she said softly. She would not like to die like
that.

Wilbert stepped up by her side. "I don't think we should
get involved," he whispered. "Think about who's out there,
Mrs. Smith. Shouldn't we just let the things kill them?"

Wilbert was far more practical than she. She wasn't sure

she could watch anything die when she could prevent it.

The battle before them was almost already lost. Nunn and Carl Jackson seemed to have already lost part of their beings to the darkness. As they screamed and dodged the flying shapes she could see other parts of the forest through the fighters.

She wondered how the things were draining away the mortals. Wilbert had warned her against using too much magic. But she had worked without her physical body before. Perhaps if she projected her aura forward, she might be able to get a better view.

"Watch out!" Wilbert called.

She was so intent on the battle, she was not watching the forest immediately around them. A dark thing like an obsidian manta ray floated toward them. As it descended it made the slightest of sounds, the rustle of dead leaves exploding into flame.

"Bad move," she murmured. She lifted the stone from where she clutched it in her palm, staring through the translucent green facets at the shape above. The obsidian blob disappeared in a blaze of light.

"That'll show 'em." Wilbert chuckled.

But the light seemed to draw the attention of the others. A number of the things lifted away from their attack on Nunn and Jackson to float in their direction.

"It appears that our choice has been made for us!" she called to Wilbert.

Wilbert nodded back to her, notching a shaft against his bow. "Let's see what a few old-fashioned arrows will do."

A dozen or more of the dark things floated their way. They appeared to drift on the breeze, as if they were attacking you by chance, so certain they could kill you that they were in no hurry to finish their task.

Mrs. Smith hated anyone or anything that made assumptions. That sort of thinking had almost ended her marriage years ago; marriage to a man she would most likely never see again. But that experience had caused her to examine everything around her, become more open to new events, perhaps even led her to be the first of the neighbors worthy of a dragon's eye.

Now she was giving human motivation to blobs from another world. Funny, she mused, the thoughts that go through your head when you're waiting to die.

The shapes drifted closer. No sound came from them at this distance, just the shapes, bobbing up and down on the wind in a silent dance.

"Let's see what this does." Wilbert shot an arrow right through the very center of the dark patch in the lead. The arrow sped on through the darkness as if the thing wasn't there, but the creature spun away from the others, a hole showing in its very middle for an instant before it was sealed to make the darkness whole again.

Wilbert grunted at that. "I may not be able to kill them, but maybe I can misdirect one or two."

"Do it, then. If we can keep them from attacking in force, maybe I can kill them one by one." Constance was hoping that would be enough. She was sure there were limits to the power of these dragon's eyes, but she thought that—should the other shapes leave Nunn to attack Wilbert and her—her strength would go first.

Another of the dark shapes came within range. She blasted it easily.

The other shapes danced closer. There really was a pattern, a rhythm to their movements. The sounds they made were so soft that most of the battle seemed accompanied by an eerie silence, which somehow made their dance all the more fascinating.

Wilbert began to sing.

"When Johnny comes marching home again, hurrah, hurrah."

He shot an arrow. Constance blinked. She had to be ready to turn away the next of these creatures.

Wilbert went on: "We'll give him a hearty welcome then, hurrah, hurrah."

Another arrow spun into the sky. She pulled her eyes from the dancing darkness and followed the trajectory of the arrow as it pierced a single shape and fell down to the woods beyond.

"The men will cheer, the boys will shout, the ladies they will all turn out—"

A third arrow flew aloft to hit its mark. Constance saw what Wilbert was doing. His hoarse song gave them something to focus on, a rhythm to break the hypnotic silence. Watching the dark things dance had almost thrown her into a trance.

She blasted the next shape to come floating too close, smiling and nodding at Wilbert's continued song. She wanted him to keep on singing, but she would spare him by not joining in. As bad as Wilbert's voice was, hers was even worse.

She destroyed a second shape, and a third. She risked a glance to see how the original battle was faring, and was pleased to see the two men standing their ground. Not that the shapes had given up on them. Nunn sent a blast of green fire to engulf one. And Carl Jackson sent a line of flame to destroy another.

Where would Carl get power like that?

"Constance!" Wilbert called. "Look out!"

She pulled her attention back to the closer battle and saw three of the dark things swooping toward her with surprising speed. She sighted the first one with her gem, then the second, both shapes disintegrating in grand bursts of fire. The third one spun about, disturbed by one of Wilbert's arrows, but it would still swing much too close. She turned quickly, but too late. One edge of it glanced across her shoulder. There was an instant of cold unlike any she had ever felt before. She groaned, lifting the gem before her eyes. The third shape was gone, the flash driving her back a half-dozen paces.

"They've disappeared!" Wilbert called.

"What?" Constance opened her eyes after closing them against the glare. She looked above them, then over by Nunn and Carl. There was not a single dark shape in the sky.

There seemed to have been dozens of them only a moment before. Where had they gone? Somehow, she felt like they had vanished not just from the forest but from the world as well.

"They're just plain gone!" Wilbert said with a whoop. "I think you've saved us all."

"Let's hope I don't live to regret it," Constance agreed. She looked over at the others. Jackson was on his knees, while Nunn appeared to have passed out entirely.

Now that she thought of it, a rest was not a bad idea.

Nunn looked up from where he lay upon the forest floor.

His flesh appeared whole again, the eyes glowing dully from their homes in his palms. He was fatigued, but he was alive.

They had destroyed the things, or more likely driven them

away. With those creatures, there always seemed to be more. But the victory didn't belong to Carl and himself. They had had help, help he was too exhausted to acknowledge or even to recognize. One minute they were beaten, the cold so deep in Nunn's bones he could barely raise an eye to defend himself. Then others had come to fight, the shapes had found new targets, and Nunn had found the strength to keep on fighting.

The shapes were gone. He had been spared, and he had no idea who he had to thank. Certainly it was one of the others with a dragon's eye. But he would never expect mercy from most of those! His rival wizards would never help, and Todd would have gladly seen his father destroyed. It had to have been one of the women, Mrs. Smith or Mary Lou, full of misplaced kindness, the sort of weakling who couldn't stand to see another die.

Mrs. Smith or Mary Lou; a dear, sweet soul. She would no doubt be over shortly to check on his condition. He should strike her down immediately, of course, when she least expected it and was the most vulnerable. But he was uncertain of his powers. What if he couldn't kill her quickly? And, hard as it was for him to admit it, he actually felt a degree of gratitude toward the woman for the rescue. Nunn was startled by the thought. There was no place for that sort of feeling now. Even considering things like gratitude and good feeling in passing would probably get him killed.

No doubt this was his exhaustion speaking. Once he had allowed his eyes to spread their power back through his form, he would show no further signs of weakness. But his recovery would take a few minutes more.

He felt the vibration, then, from deep beneath him. It was subtle. He would not have noticed it save for the way his senses were augmented by the dragon's eyes. It was a rumbling he had called for once, and looked for in his service; like so many other things Nunn had used and thrown away. It came from things that lived beneath the earth, great hulks that had no eyes, and gained their nourishment from molten rock.

The rock dwellers were strong, but loud and clumsy. They were undependable at best. He had rid himself of those things long ago, certain that, with their primitive senses, if he no longer called them, they had no way to find him.

The rumbling was constant. If driven to it, the hulks could

eat solid stone as well. If their desire were great enough, if they had a claim above, they could eat their way to the surface, to devour anything they chose.

Nunn felt a darkness inside him as deep as the cold those lightless shapes had given him. He had been foolish to promise his power to so many, foolish to believe he would never have to pay.

Slowly, very slowly, the rumbling grew louder, the vibrations more intense, as though, deep below the spot where he lay, there was a great chasm being eaten into the earth. If what he suspected were true, the next few hours would be very trying indeed.

It was not simply that the dark things had found him. Soon he would hear the stirring of great creatures from the sea, and the whistling of wings of those small beings who looked like angels, but could kill with a touch. All of his past alliances were returning, all certain they would collect upon those promises he had made so long ago. They knew it was a day of reckoning, the day of the dragon.

Nunn felt very tired, as if he was overcome by the weight of every spell he had ever performed.

He heard footsteps approaching through the dead leaves and dust of the forest floor. Had his savior finally arrived to take her due?

But when he turned his head, he saw a man.

"Time to pay the piper, Nunn."

Carl Jackson was feeling better, too. And the globe he held was full of power.

○ Fourteen

If everyone had a place in this new world, Mills thought, he was the running joke.

"Why must you be so negative?" Rox asked from somewhere deep within. "We had the potential to be the most powerful of all, you and Zachs and I, a mixture of knowledge and magic and raw energy. But with power comes problems. If we could find balance, we could rule them all."

The wizard's seriousness only made it worse. They were a joke, and Mills had to laugh. "So we need to find balance, besides finding Zachs?"

"Perhaps . . ." Even the unflappable Rox paused, waiting for the all-too-familiar pain to wash over them again, pain that moved from lungs to stomach to intestines, like every organ in Mills's racked body was being ground into tiny pieces.

But there was only a twinge, and the pain was gone. Whatever Hyram Sayre had done for them was still holding, at least for now. But Mills had no illusions about the permanence of the cure. If they did not do something soon, the pain would once again become so bad that they could no longer move.

Yet according to Rox, their dilemma was simple. "So," Mills summarized for them both, "if we regain Zachs, we might become masters of the world, but if we can't find him, we will surely die?"

It was Rox's turn to chuckle. "A clear choice, don't you think, Mills?"

Mills noted Rox's sarcasm without particularly wishing to acknowledge it. "So you say. But how do we find Zachs?"

"Well, we do have a dragon's eye, even though it hurts us when we use it on ourselves. And I have a certain amount of sorcerous knowledge independent of the gem. Zachs is not a subtle creature. He shouts his thoughts, broadcasts his power. Even without the eye, I should be able to locate that kind of magic.''

"And then?''

"Using our dragon's eye on something in the outside world eased our pain when we were three in one. I imagine it will still have some of the same effect. We need to track down Zachs and explore our options while there is still time.''

So it would be a grand adventure, this pursuit of Zachs, so long as the pain stayed away. But there were other things the grand wizard Rox wasn't talking about.

"Is there—time, that is?" Mills asked.

Deep within Mills's head, Rox let out a sigh. "Who can say?"

Mary Lou was surprised at first at how easy it was.

Obar started with a simple bolt of energy, the sort of thing she could deflect with a simple thought.

"Come on now, Obar," Garo's ghost voice taunted. "Mary Lou might not have much experience, but she does have a certain talent. We expected better from you! Subterfuge, hidden magic, dastardly sneak attacks!''

Obar did not look happy. "If you weren't incorporeal, I would kill you.''

Garo chuckled. "That would be redundant. You killed me once already, after all.''

"You know, Obar," Mary Lou offered, "we don't have to fight about this. We could talk, maybe come to some sort of an agreement.''

The wizard paused and looked at Mary Lou for a long moment. "I wish that I could. I might, if you didn't work for the dragon.''

"Work for the dragon?" Mary Lou was startled. She hadn't thought of what she was doing in that way. But she was working with information she had gained from—somewhere. It had to come from the dragon, or Garo, who worked for the dragon. She had been so certain of her mission here, she hadn't even thought about what might be behind it.

"Think why you want to stop me," Obar continued. "Just because the dragon doesn't want something doesn't mean it isn't the proper thing to do. Even the dragon must obey certain rules. I am simply trying to bind the dragon to certain . . . behaviors that I would find beneficial.''

"Ah, Obar," Garo replied. "I admired your reasoning even before you killed me. Those behaviors you speak of would of course include sparing yourself when the dragon arrives?''

Obar's face screwed up into a distracted frown, as if the question was barely worth answering. "Well, of course. Without that, the rest of my actions would be pretty pointless.''

"And those binding spells you use will of course involve the blood sacrifice of others," Garo added.

Obar shook his head. "I do not relish these things I do, but when they are necessary for survival, I do not back away from them, either.'' He stared straight at Mary Lou. "Let us forget this parrot for the dragon for a minute, shall we? As I said, I do not back away from challenges. If you had more knowledge of the power in the dragon's eye, I imagine you would do the same. Once I have saved myself, I will attempt to save the rest of what we know, including as many of the others as possible.''

"It would be a dull world if only Obar were left," Garo agreed. "Obar with a world full of those subservient to him is another matter entirely.''

"You will both stop it!" Mary Lou demanded. When she had come to this place, she realized, she had two visions that had been placed in her head. One was of Obar, and blood; the wizard reaching out to slice at anything he could reach—animals and birds, the Anno, the neighbors, Mary Lou. Blood spouted out in geysers. It flowed everywhere, rivers of dark red brown that robbed the world of color and led to darkness everywhere. Mary Lou didn't want to see that vision again; she flinched at the thought of it.

How much warmer was the other picture given to her, in which she saw before her a great winged creature so huge and mighty that it should have been beyond human comprehension. Yet somehow she was privileged enough to see it all, its scales like a million glittering jewels, its breath a golden warmth that would rival the sun. The glorious creature approached, bringing nothing but light.

She realized how quiet she had gotten, listening to the wizards. Both of them had yammered at her, and she hadn't been able to do any more than listen. This was no different from her parents telling her what to do, saying they trusted her, respected her, until something happened—like the morning they sent her older sister away—and they turned and told Mary Lou it was none of her business. These people were just the same. Do this! Do that! Don't ask questions!

Wizards lied. Obar had tried to kill her before. And Garo had been in on the sacrifice with the Anno. Even these visions she found in her head—one full of horror, the other of joy— they were deep, they were compelling, but were they true?

Mary Lou found she was getting angry. The dragon's eye burned in her pocket; she could even feel it through the fabric of her jeans. She wondered if this was how Todd felt before he released his own angry sorcery.

She reached into the pocket and touched the stone, and was filled again with the vision of light. If only she could be surrounded by that now! But no, she couldn't wait for some creature who fed her visions that she had never really asked for. Whatever light there was in this place would have to come from her.

"I have power now," she said to Obar, "and whatever experience I may lack, I have gained knowledge that you may never hope to possess. If you wish a contest, stone to stone, I'm ready."

Obar closed his dragon's eye within his fist. "What do you want me to do? You are an agent of the dragon, whether you acknowledge it or not. Garo's presence is proof enough of that." He paused to look back at the Anno, who had stopped their frantic activity to stand silently and gaze worshipfully at Mary Lou. "The net result of the spell you interrupted would be to have the dragon pass me by; me, and a few others I would have carefully chosen. But, in fighting you, I not only gain the dragon's attention, but its anger as well."

"Watch out for Obar's golden words," Garo cautioned. "He would still kill you if he could."

"And why should I believe you?" Mary Lou shot back. "You fascinated me when we first met. I imagined you were a handsome prince, sent to take me to a castle far away from here. And what did you do? You almost got me killed!"

"I'm sorry for that. But I went to the dragon in your place." She remembered how he had made that sacrifice. In that one

moment, she had really cared about him. She wondered now
how naive she had been, a high-school girl in a strange new
world. How naive was she being now?

She laughed, a bitter taste at the back of her throat. "And
now the dragon will use me for something else, before it kills
me and everyone else I know!"

Garo did not respond. Did that mean she was right? Why
didn't she feel better about guessing the truth? If she could
find any truth with a wizard or a ghost.

"Garo?" she asked. "Why did you come back? Did you
have any say in the matter?"

"Actually," he said in a voice softer than before, "I wanted
to be with you again."

And she wanted to believe him, too. But she didn't know
who to believe—Garo, Obar, dragon, or none of them. She
wished Todd or Mrs. Smith were here so she could have another dragon's eye at her side, and another brain to help sort
all this out. She felt frozen, unable to act in any way.

There was no floor beneath her.

She shrieked as she started to fall. Part of her was calm,
though, and caught her with the magic in her hand, and
brought her back up to the platform, to set herself down on
the plank next to the board that ceased to exist.

"Forgive me," Obar murmured. "I had to try."

But she could barely even hear the wizard speak. She was
filled again with visions. They came to her every time she used
the gem.

The great creature looked down at her—the dragon, his mas-
sive head staring at her tiny face, but acknowledging her as
one who was worthy. The smoke from its nostrils sparkled as
if it was made of gold, and the great eyes shone with an inner
light warmer than anything Mary Lou had ever seen.

This was a different aspect of the creature from those she
had seen before, as if the dragon could bring light as well as
fire.

She shook off the vision, full of hypnotic, golden light.
What if the stories weren't true? What if, instead of burning
everything before it, the dragon would bring everything to a
better place?

What if, what if, what if?

Mary Lou wished she could burn the vision out of her head.

Why was she here? What did the dragon want with her? The dragon was not simply showing her these things. It was trying to bend her to its will.

The anger was growing inside her. She was angry at the dragon, too. She felt the eye vibrate like a rumble in the dragon's throat.

There was a promise hidden in these visions. The dragon would give her power unknown by any of the others who held the eyes. If she used her eye to destroy Obar, she would let out the fire—the true dragon's fire. If she went any farther, she would be afraid of losing herself. The dragon would use her. And she would, in some way, become the dragon.

It was a bargain, or it was a trap.

And the dragon's only true purpose was to destroy.

She couldn't trust the visions, the thoughts, anything going on in her head. If only someone would tell her what to do!

"Garo," she began, "if I use the gem—"

"There are certain things I can't tell you," the ghost cautioned. "Perhaps, when the dragon is done, some part of us can be together."

So it was a foregone conclusion, from Garo, at least, that the dragon would overwhelm them all.

"Garo—" she began, and even she was surprised to hear the despair in her voice.

"Mary Lou," Garo replied quickly. "You know this before I even tell you, because this is the way you've done things before. Think about what you do, Mary Lou. Decide for yourself what you need, before you listen to—"

Garo's voice was gone, silenced between one word and the next. Gone in a moment, like a twig caught in a roaring flame. Gone, she imagined, because he was trying to tell her the truth.

It was not safe to use her magic. Soon, the dragon's eyes might not be safe for any of them to use.

"Garo is gone, isn't he?" Obar asked. He held up his gem. "Is it time for the two of us to finish this?"

"No! Our fight only serves to strengthen the dragon!" That much she knew was true.

Obar paused to stare at her thoughtfully. "The words from your mouth never cease to surprise me."

She looked back at the wizard, not knowing what to do. She felt she had pushed the dragon away, but only for a moment.

And when it came back, it could destroy them all.

"Oh, the dragon will not destroy us that easily!" Obar protested, as if he could read her thoughts from the lost look on her face. "It has to be a challenge. From everything I've learned about the dragon—and I've devoted myself to the study of the matter—it is a game the creature plays. That is why he brings us all here. That is why he allows some of us to survive, no matter what the legends say. And—if it is truly a game—someday, someone else will win."

He looked at her for a long moment. "Perhaps we will work together, at some point, if we do not need to challenge each other again to survive. But know this. If I survive, I plan to be master."

Mary Lou stood there, half watching Obar for some new casual treachery. But her thoughts were drawn inward, trying to remember the details of those visions, so strong only a moment before. Now they seemed no more than distant memories, something that had happened to someone else, something she had only heard about in passing.

It had taken Garo first. The dragon would try to leave her with nothing at all.

But she still had her anger. That she wouldn't forget.

There was another flash. She thought at first it was Obar, trying again to gain some advantage, until she heard the older wizard curse, and a second voice shout back words that were even worse.

The dragon was gone. The eye was hers again. Mary Lou blinked, and got ready for a fight.

Mills would not cry out at the pain.

Rox had found some likely magic, and together they had decided to pursue it. They had used magic to leap to the likely spot, a leap that had brought back the pain. It was still over in only a moment, not lingering the way it had before. But the agony was real this time, far more than the warning twinge they had felt before. If they continued to use the magic on themselves, Sayre's remedy would break down completely. Still, if they could regain the fire creature and become whole once more, it might all be worth it.

Mills opened his eyes to look at the place to which Rox had brought them. They were standing on a platform built high in the trees, surrounded by those small, wizened creatures that used to attack the soldiers when they'd first come here.

"The Anno," Rox informed Mills. "That's their name."

Very nice, Mills thought, but Zachs was nowhere to be seen. Instead, he could see Obar and Mary Lou, each holding a sparkling green dragon's eye.

"This is it?" Mills demanded. "This is the magic you've found?"

"Hold on," Rox replied aloud. "It's not what we were looking for, but perhaps we can work with this."

Obar saw the two of them together in Mills's body, and cursed. Rox shouted back some words in kind. Even now, Mills thought, this was all like some great game to these people, a game in which he would never know the rules.

"These two eye holders seem to be having a bit of an argument," Rox said to Mills alone. "Perhaps we should throw our weight to one side or the other. After all, an extra eye on our side wouldn't hurt."

Mills didn't quite know what the wizard meant by that, either. Maybe he should just give up trying.

"Once more into the fray, dear Mills!" Rox shouted merrily.

Mills found his feet shuffling forward over the rough wooden planks, one foot, then the other, rather like those lumbering monsters in old black-and-white movies. Rox was taking him to meet the others.

"Zachs will triumph!" the fire being cried. "Zachs will win!"

After the rain, Zachs had been so angry that he had flown around the whole island three times, so fast that he was no more than a streak in the sky. Trees and wizards and humans and even a certain boy and his bird (Zachs would kill them!) became no more than blurs as Zachs outraced the wind. Zachs was faster than anything! Zachs was better than anyone!

And, as fast as he went, Zachs was clever enough to still see things below.

Zachs saw others that were now what he once was, before he became the king of fire. Nunn had taught Zachs how to count. There were close to two dozen of them, huddled in a cave by the water. Nunn had brought these creatures, too, these red-furred monkeys with a language all their own. He had brought hundreds of them to be Nunn's ape army.

But one of these apes he had pulled aside, a young one, not quite fully grown. And Nunn had changed this ape with pain and fire. Zachs had been like these apes once, but now he was so much more.

Zachs came back to the cave when he was done with his flying. For he had come from these apes, although it seemed like very long ago. These apes who had struggled for Nunn, died for Nunn, so that now nine out of every ten of them were gone. They had worked for Nunn. Now they would work for Zachs.

Nunn had taught Zachs how to count, and how to rule.

Nunn had had an army of hundreds of these things, and armed them with poison sticks, which could take life when you gave the enemy but a single scratch. So many of them, so well armed, and so many of them dead.

There were twenty of them left now. Quite recently, there had been twenty-one. Zachs had had to demonstrate what would happen if one of his new soldiers ran.

Perhaps Zachs could not do everything himself. Why would he have to do everything, when he had these others to die in his service? But they would die in glory, and those who lived would serve beneath him, ape princes to the fire king.

They understood him, after all, in a way beyond stupid human words. Zachs was once like these creatures. He once had red fur, could once talk to these creatures in their primitive tongue.

Red-furred apes were not afraid of the rain. Zachs would use them in those rare moments when he could not act alone. Zachs would use them to find the boy. They would tear at his young skin, his rich blood rushing from him through a dozen wounds. But they would not kill him, oh no.

That final honor was reserved for Zachs, and Zachs alone.

○ Around the Circle:
Raven Finds a Place for Fire

It is well known how Raven first obtained fire, how the bird first flew up through the sky to the house of the sun and there stole the flame. And how the owner of fire chased Raven back to the world, so that the bird had to pass this new thing along to his friends, from Raven to Owl to Sparrow to Otter to Mule Deer. And how the owner of fire grew so close to Mule Deer that he singed the deer's tail, which was why the tails of such deer are short and black to this day. And how fire at last passed to Turtle, who dived into the river to escape the fire's owner, and rubbed the fire on the roots of the trees that grew out into the water until the fire went out. So it is that fire is hiding in all trees and bushes and plants, and only awaits the proper coaxing to emerge again.

Fire, though, can have a mind of its own, and can become a creature far too large to control, almost as hot as the house from which it came. So it was in the early days, when the animals were still learning the nature of things. So they had started a fire for warmth, but in that particular time it had not rained in months, and the fire quickly leaped from its beginnings to consume all the trees and bushes around.

At this, the animals cried, for it looked like fire might destroy their whole land. "This beast is just too great!" they shouted. "He cannot be stopped!"

But Raven had an idea. For, as powerful as the great fire was, it did not sound happy. In fact, it roared with frustration. Even though it reached for the sky, it was trapped by the trees and bushes it burned, for all of these were rooted to the ground.

"I crave the open air!" fire cried with its deep, rumbling

voice. "I leap higher and higher! I will be free!"

So Raven took to the air, for there was but one way to save this land and give fire what it desired. So Raven flew fast and true in a circle about the blaze, so quickly that the flames that grabbed at him could not catch him. Raven sliced at the edges of fire with the sharp edge of his wings, loosening the great blaze from its earthly bonds. And soon fire was free.

"Fly away now," Raven called, "to somewhere you may burn in peace!"

Fire roared its approval and took to the air. And thus was born the creature who would become the dragon. And Raven, in his way, could be called the dragon's father.

But Raven says there is a lesson to be learned from this:

It does not matter where something begins, or who first brought it into this world. It matters, rather, who ends up with it.

Or so the story goes when Raven tells it.

○ Fifteen

Bobby was glad to be running. When you ran, you didn't have very much time to think. And now he ran with Jason and Raven, Charlie and Maggie, all of them after his mother.

Besides a few words of shouted conversation, a "this way!" from Jason or a "the trees are thinner over here!" from Raven to guide them, there hadn't been time for questions. Bobby kept waiting for someone to ask, "Why weren't you watching your mother?" or "Why couldn't you stop them from taking her?" Nobody did, they had all been together back there, it happened so fast, nobody was to blame. But Bobby still felt he was responsible. She was his *mother,* after all.

But he was even more ashamed of something else, something that stayed with him no matter how fast he went.

Part of him was happy when his mother disappeared.

Not that he wanted anything bad to happen to her. But he had grown so tired of looking after her. With her mind lost back in Chestnut Circle, she had no idea where her body was wandering. Except for this business of strolling up to total strangers and asking them if they were Bobby's father. Sometimes, it just seemed like she was looking for trouble.

Bobby's mother had changed so much!

She had always spent a lot of time on her appearance back in the world they'd come from, clothes nicely tailored, hair done once a week at the beauty salon. An orderly house had been very important to her, too. They always had dinner at the exact same time. There had been plastic slipcovers over the furniture in the living room, which were only taken off when company came. And they hardly ever had company. Things were orderly but simple, and his mother was in charge.

Life was so much different here than it had been on Chestnut Circle. His mother had been afraid at first, holding on to her family, the only thing she knew. But Bobby had run away from Nunn's army with the help of Raven and the Oomgosh. Then Nunn had taken away her husband, Bobby's father. And his mother simply couldn't handle it. Her family was gone. It had been too much for her, and she had left them.

But her body was still here, on this island with Bobby and the others, even though her mind was not. She believed this place was her old home and wandered about as if she were safe on Chestnut Circle. She couldn't recognize danger or safety, night or day.

And because of that, she had become a danger to everyone around her.

"The place where Margaret is?" Mr. Blake called. "Will we come to it soon?"

"We're almost there!" Jason called. They had been trotting quickly through the woods for less than five minutes. Mr. Blake seemed to have the most trouble breathing, puffing heavily at the rear of the group.

"Would you like to rest?" Maggie called over her shoulder.

Blake shook his head. "No. Let's get there. I'm glad to be moving in this crazy place."

So other people felt the same way Bobby did.

"I just don't understand this," Blake went on. "What are we doing here, really? We're making plans in a place where plans don't make sense."

"You mean, maybe the stories are true," Maggie called, "and we are all just controlled by the dragon?"

Raven cawed harshly and swooped about to join the conversation. "Simply because the dragon says it is so, does not make it so." He spread his wings to land on Jason's shoulder. "No one knows about such things as well as Raven."

Jason smiled at that. He slowed to let Raven find a proper grip. "You are an expert then in what's real, and what is not?"

Raven fluffed his feathers self-importantly. "I know what is, and what is only a boast."

Jason nodded at that. "And you make frequent use of both."

Raven cawed loudly. "You understand me better every day, my Oomgosh!"

Jason looked ahead, squinting a bit, as if he could see past all the trees to their destination. "Come, we have people to rescue."

"You are correct, my Oomgosh." The bird spread his wings and flew. "Raven scouts ahead!"

They would find Bobby's mother in a moment, then. Jason seemed very sure of that, very sure and calm. Bobby hoped his old friend was right. Most of him hoped desperately that she hadn't been hurt.

But a very small part of him wished he would never see her again.

The Captain rubbed his head as he sat up. He was getting too used to having wolves back him up. Here he was, off on his own for a change, and he had almost gotten himself killed.

The woman sat next to him. She rocked gently back and forth, humming to herself.

He wondered if it was worth it, talking to a crazy lady. Hell, he wasn't too normal himself. He turned to her and grinned. She kept on rocking.

"I think you saved my life," he said. "I was trying to save yours."

"Leo?" she said at first. And then, her voice oddly lower, "No. I know you, Captain. I'm sure Margaret would thank you, too, if she could."

"Who?" the Captain asked. But he already knew. Perhaps it was the voice, or the strange, green light in the woman's eyes. "You're the zombie guy."

Margaret laughed. "I *was* dead the last time we were together, wasn't I? A little too close for comfort, as I recall, thanks to our dear friend Nunn."

Too close? The Captain shivered. As he recalled, they had both been sharing the same body—his.

"Well," Margaret continued cheerily, "I'm feeling much better now. I wish I could say the same for Margaret here."

As if waiting for her cue, the woman started to rock and hum again. "Leo?" she sang softly. "Leo, Leo, Leo."

The Captain rubbed at the tender place on the back of his skull. They had really whacked him one. But the guy who had snuck up on him was out cold in front of them.

"I chased away the Snake fellow," the man inside Margaret

explained, "and knocked out this other one. I was here to rescue Margaret mostly. But, with all that we've been through, I couldn't help but feel close to you. Figured I had to stick around to make sure you're all right."

The Captain nudged the fallen man with his toe. He got no response. "Is he dead?"

Margaret considered that for a moment. "No, I think he'll come around."

The Captain shook his head. "Maybe I'll enlist him in my army after all. He's sneaky enough."

"After what he did to you?" Margaret asked as she rocked. "Leo," she whispered.

The Captain shrugged. "Either that, or I'll kill him. My standards vary according to the needs of the moment."

It was Margaret's turn to nod. "Probably wise, considering what goes on around here."

The Captain stood and stretched. "Well, this certainly has been pleasant. But what the hell are you doing talking out of the mouth of a crazy woman?"

Margaret chuckled. "I've been able to help a number of people with their ills. With my new powers I've been able to actually jump inside of them, mess around a bit, and make them better. It's been very satisfying. Much better than what I used to do, spending all my time tending—well, enough about my own life." Her face grew far more serious. "I have a couple problems here, though. I don't seem to be doing Margaret much good. And I can't seem to get out again."

"You mean, you're stuck in there?" The Captain couldn't help but smile at that.

Margaret nodded. "As I see it now, that is, everybody's a sort of mixture, part physical, part mental—body and spirit, I guess. I've been able, in a couple of cases, to deal with physical difficulties and make them better. Margaret's difficulties are—different."

The Captain nodded. He'd been there and back. "It's her head, right?"

She sighed in frustration. "It's so convoluted. Fascinating, and a little frightening." Her voice grew lower still, as if talking in the strictest confidence. "My guess is that, even when we used to live across the street from each other back on Chestnut Circle, she wasn't quite right."

"Really?" The Captain looked wistfully at the surrounding forest. Being grateful was one thing, but he was beginning to wonder if this fellow would talk his ear off forever.

The man in Margaret shook her head. "I keep thinking I've found my way out, but there's always another corner, another turn. She won't let me leave." She laughed ruefully. "And when I let *her* go, well—you've heard her talk about Leo, of course. When I really let myself fade back, give myself a moment to relax, you know, I can feel her taking over. I may not get out at all. I could get lost in here—forever."

"I wish I could help you," the Captain said, deciding that, no matter how dizzy he still might feel, it was time for a change of scene. He glanced once more at the still-unconscious man at their feet. As screwed up as this character next to him was, she looked like she could take care of herself.

Margaret wasn't about to stop. "But there's this other thing, too," she added urgently. "She keeps watching this owl. Or maybe the owl is watching her."

The Captain stared back at the crazy woman with the crazy man inside her. In all his years surviving in this forest, he had never seen an owl. Perhaps this was another sign of change. The Captain wondered if there was some way to use it to his advantage.

"Ahead! Up ahead!" a raucous cry came from above.

The Captain stood. "I think we're about to have company."

Four people came trotting out of the trees, accompanied by the dog and that big, talking bird. The neighbors were here: two of the boys, his former lieutenant George, and Maggie.

Looking at Maggie, the Captain actually felt a bit of regret, something he'd thought was far behind him. Who knew how long it had been? Time here seemed to pass by like a dream. Once, before he'd had these scars on his face, Maggie and he had meant something to each other.

She actually smiled when she looked at him. "So we have something to thank you for, Douglas?"

The Captain shook his head, then nodded to Margaret. "It's all her doing. Of course, she's not exactly what she seems."

"None of us are, are we?" Maggie agreed.

One of the kids ran forward. "Mom? Are you all right?"

"Yeah, yeah, she's fine," the guy inside the kid's mother

replied. And Hyram Sayre began to explain his troubles to a brand-new audience.

The Captain felt himself relax a bit. He was working with these newcomers now, and they accepted him, no matter what else had happened in the past. It was actually sort of nice not having to kill people at every single opportunity.

George Blake stepped up to him, looking a bit hangdog. "Captain. I guess I ran away—"

The Captain waved away his apology. "The current arrangement is fine. We're allies, after all. I've got the feeling we'll be fighting side by side again soon enough."

Blake turned pale, as if more fighting was the last thing he wanted. He nodded curtly and shuffled away. Some things didn't change. The Captain still enjoyed making George Blake feel uncomfortable.

He was glad they were on the same side for now. All these folks, neighbors and Volunteers both, had interesting possibilities. And that dog alone—it sure got uglier with every passing moment. Looking at its growing teeth and claws, the Captain bet that dog could take down three or four of his wolves easy.

"Mom?" the kid called out. "Are you in there at all?"

"Oh, she's in here all right," his mother's voice said in a tone that was probably supposed to be reassuring. "Whether or not she'll ever talk to anyone again is another matter entirely."

She frowned, then added, "Leo? Leo?"

"Douglas?" Maggie had come over by his side. "So you've added that boy, Nick, to your ranks?"

The Captain raised an eyebrow at that. "You're well informed."

Maggie shrugged, as though information was the least of her worries. "Watch out for Nick," she said. She bit her lip as she studied the man she used to know so well. "I mean that two different ways. Part of him is just an innocent child—"

"—and part of him would kill you without a second thought," he finished the sentence for her. "It's contradictions like that which make life interesting. He'll get some practice with me. He may even learn something from that sword." He paused a second to try on a smile. "And maybe we can find a way for him to live without it."

She stared at him, her face opened up by surprise. "You'd actually try to help him?"

"Sure, Maggie," he whispered back. "For you."

She frowned at that. "That was a long time ago."

"Was it?" he asked, but she'd already turned away, back to the new people in her life. The Captain laughed at himself. If he could be one tenth as good at talking to a woman as he was at killing people—then what? The dragon would never come? They'd all live happily ever after?

The others were all clustered around Margaret. It looked like Sayre had an audience for as long as he wanted.

No one turned around as the Captain walked away. It was time for him to get back to his wolves, and a life he could understand.

Her voice startled Carl Jackson, snapping his concentration.

"Not yet," she said.

His eyes had only drifted away from the globe for an instant. Who would dare?

"There are other ways," she added.

And he saw that meddling Mrs. Smith, standing twenty feet away from them. Well, she wouldn't stop him. No one would!

"Shit!" The word tore from Carl's throat as soon as he turned back to Nunn. Carl was no longer holding the globe! The sphere was floating in the air, a few inches above his palm. He grabbed for it, but it bobbed out of reach, tiny points of light dancing deep beneath the blue smoke within, so close, yet completely untouchable.

Nunn smiled as he got to his feet.

"Shit, indeed." He nodded to where Mrs. Smith stood to his right. "I do thank the dear lady for that timely intervention. It just took me a moment to collect myself."

"I don't like to see people killing each other," Mrs. Smith said quietly.

Carl couldn't believe this was happening. "Even a piece of fucking scum like this?" He glanced quickly at Mrs. Smith, then back to Nunn. Now that his globe was gone, he expected an attack from one of them any second now. "I know how rotten this man is, I've been inside him. You've ruined my best chance—"

"Your only chance, dear Carl," Nunn interrupted. He made

a soft, tsking sound that Carl found infuriating. "I did think you'd be most useful. It was a shame that you got ambitious. Killing me with my own power would have been a nice touch. It's a shame—for you—that you let me meddle with that globe again."

Carl couldn't stand to see Nunn win like this. He'd find some way to push that attitude back in the wizard's face. He might not have the globe, but he'd go down fighting.

He glared back at Nunn. "I'm not dead yet."

"Really?" Nunn chuckled. "Well, give me a minute and I'll see what I can do."

"Wait a moment." It was that pain-in-the-ass meddling Mrs. Smith again. "Does this really have to happen this way?"

Nunn turned his sneer in her direction. "What do you expect me to be—grateful? What do you want, some starry-eyed alliance, a treaty where we lie to each other about how much we'll cooperate? Even our brief time together should allow you to know me better than that. Why should I work with anybody else when I can have it all myself?"

Nunn stopped himself and looked down at his gems.

"I do feel the slightest bit of gratitude toward you, stopping poor Carl from completing his messy murder." He looked back to Mrs. Smith. "Not that you'll stay alive to repeat my words to anyone. I wouldn't want this to ruin my reputation, after all. But I will let you watch while I consume Carl. I hope you'll find it quite instructive." He paused just a second to shake his head. "After that, I'm afraid you'll have to go as well."

Carl wished he could find some opening, anything that would allow him to stuff that smugness down the wizard's throat. A sharp rock, a fallen tree branch, something you could thrust or throw past the wizard's defenses and startle the smile from his face. After that, he wouldn't care if Nunn killed him. That moment would be worth it.

Mrs. Smith could only shake her head. "You're amazing, Nunn. Don't you think I'd have something to say about all this, too?"

She nodded into darkness.

"Wilbert?"

Somewhere, out in the woods beyond her, Carl heard the twang of a bow. Mrs. Smith had brought one of the Volunteers with her and magically hidden him. An arrow went screaming toward Nunn.

"Pitiful!" Nunn cried in a voice that sounded as startled as it was angry. "You won't hit me with another—" His power burned the arrow out of the air.

But Mrs. Smith was doing something with her gem. A swirling ball of golden light was arcing toward the wizard.

"Oh, come now," Nunn replied, his voice already calmer and more confident. He held up his hands so everyone could see the twin gems in his palms. "This is why I have two of these, so that I can deal with both of you."

Two beams of green pulsated from the wizard's hands, one pointed toward Mrs. Smith, the other headed for the invisible archer.

Something fell out of the golden globe and knocked Nunn's sphere back into Carl's hands. This, Carl realized, was what she had been planning to do all along.

Mrs. Smith and the archer screamed as they were each hit by bolts of energy.

But then Nunn screamed in turn as Carl unleashed the power of the sphere.

There were flashes of light everywhere, as if so much power used so quickly was too much even for a place like this. The forest seemed to be gone. Other objects blurred around them, just out of focus.

Nunn kept on screaming. Carl couldn't stop laughing. Nunn didn't sound so superior now. Carl had hurt him.

And whatever could be hurt, could also be killed. Carl's laughter filled the air, echoing back to him as if he was surrounded by a dozen more just like him, all equally triumphant. How quickly things could turn around. He'd kill Nunn, climb to the top, take over this place.

Yeah, he'd be the master of everyone, as soon as he figured out where they were.

◯ Sixteen

Sala could feel no pity for the man. She hated her father that much, her father and what he had let this man do to her.

Back in the port town, the man who groaned in agony in front of Todd and Sala had been called the Beast. He had done special things for Snake, and Snake had given him special rewards. Those hands, groping for a release from pain, had once ripped the clothes from her body. That hoarse voice, moaning now in agony, once laughed as she tried to get away.

But now the Beast was busy dying. He wasn't important anymore, except for what he could give them.

Todd squeezed Sala's shoulder. He would get the answers.

"Where is he?" he demanded.

The Beast answered slowly. "I don't—we came from the boat—no—I can't see anything!"

"Maybe I can help you with that," Todd said with a frown. He pulled his dragon's eye from his shirt pocket and held the gem a few inches away from the Beast's bloody face. The dragon gem glowed, throwing out a halo of light around the wounded man's face.

"I can find Snake with this, anyway," Todd murmured to Sala. "Even I know that much about the eye."

"A glow!" the Beast cried. "Yeah! I can see a glow!"

The neighbor women who had gathered as their audience whispered about that. The Beast licked his blood-flecked lips and smiled.

"I need answers from you now," Todd called. "Now, about Snake! What was he here for?"

The Beast paused a moment before he answered. "Well, to get us a meal. Yeah. And to find his daughter, Sala!"

So her father had actually followed her from another island? "He won't let me get away!" she whispered. "I'll never be free."

A couple of the women took a step forward, as though they might comfort her. But Sala didn't want comfort.

Todd touched her shoulder and smiled. "Your father might be stubborn. But your father has never met anybody like me."

With that, his dragon's eye flashed bright green for an instant, as if confirming Todd's power.

"Where would Snake go from here, Beast?"

It took the wounded man an even longer moment to answer, as if he had to pull himself out of a deepening trance. "He might go back to the ship. Yeah. Snake feels better on water. Except we got turned around on our way here. Don't know where the ship is."

"He's probably lost out there in the forest," Todd said to Sala. He turned back to the Beast. "And you were working under direct orders of the wizard Nunn?"

"Yeah. We were, yeah. Except Snake got tired of waiting for him. Yeah. I don't think Nunn'll like that."

Todd looked up at Sala. "He may not have any help, either. We should be able to track him down. Then you can do whatever you want with him."

Whatever she wanted to do with him. Sala wasn't sure what that would be. Part of her wanted to kill him. But another part of her wanted him to suffer for a long time first.

"The glow," the Beast said. "Yeah, the glow." A spasm shook his whole body. "Yeah!" he shouted, raising his head a few inches from the ground on which he lay. Then his head fell back, and the rest of his body went limp.

"I think he's dead," Todd said.

Sala was glad.

Zachs was so happy he had found the cave!

He and the red furs were like family. It had given Zachs an idea the first time he had seen them. Since Zachs had so much more to offer, he would be the father. And all the apes would be his children, and would do whatever their father wanted. That was the way that families worked.

The cave was close by the sea, and the entranceway would fill with water when it was high tide. This was the place where

Nunn had the apes brought when he first prepared for his great battle. Zachs knew about this because some of the apes were quite good artists and had drawn pictures on the walls of the cave, pictures of huge boats full of apes. The boats were gone now. Nunn never thought about letting the red furs go home. But that was all right now, because all the red furs had a new father, and a new family.

This was the place where the ships had left food, and weapons. It was why all the apes had come back here after the battle had failed and Nunn's army was destroyed. It gave them a place to be fed and be safe, although by now most of the food had either rotted or been eaten. There were more poison sticks here than they all could carry together, far more than a hundred of them, far higher than Zachs could count. Poison sticks never rotted, after all.

Zachs felt sorry for his new family. They were trapped in this damp and smelly place, with nothing to do and nowhere to go. While he wouldn't kill any more of them—they were family, after all, Zachs was very strict with his discipline, as any father had to be. A little singed fur here, a little slap of fire there, and Zachs's family was very well behaved. Even though Zachs had lost the red furs' language when he had been reborn in flame, they talked well enough; his children with pictures, and Zachs with fire.

Now Zachs had plans. Children needed things to do. And Zachs needed worlds to conquer. So he would take little trips every day at high tide, looking for adventures. Early the first morning he took his family and showed them how to surround and capture and slaughter and eat a family of wild pigs. Oh, how much fun they all had had! But Zachs knew they needed a bigger challenge.

So Zachs set out again, looking for a real battle, perhaps with those humans. There would be a chance to use the poison sticks on a few, and keep the others for food.

But Zachs would keep away from wizards! Wizards hurt. Wizards killed. Clever Zachs would learn with his new family, and after he had killed the boy and the bird, he might find a way to kill Nunn, too. But not now, not yet. Zachs was smarter than that.

So Zachs looked and looked. And what Zachs found was perfect! A little party of men, a little party of wolves, and no wizards at all; a fine first step for Zachs's army.

Did Zachs say army? He meant family. He and the red furs would come closer through action, show their ties of blood by letting the blood of others. Their family would always stay together. Their blood would win.

Zachs burned with family pride.

"What?" Hyram Sayre demanded to know. "What did you say?"

"I just wanted you to be careful where you walked," Margaret's son Bobby replied, a hurt tone in his voice. "That's all."

"Sorry," Hyram said back with Margaret's voice. "Didn't mean to snap."

It was his fault. He was having a hard time paying attention. He kept drifting off. Margaret's head would turn when he wasn't paying attention, and both of them would be staring at that owl. That damned owl. What did it mean? Why was it always near them?

Bobby held one of Margaret's arms while the Volunteer Maggie held the other. They were leading her back to the clearing. All of them had been so helpful before as Hyram had talked about his problems. They talked about how the dragon's eyes might help, and how he wouldn't be trapped at all. He had felt so good about being able to talk to his old neighbors in ways that just hadn't been possible back on the Circle.

He forced Margaret's eyes to look at her surroundings. George and Jason carried the man Margaret had knocked unconscious between them. George huffed and puffed, while Jason didn't even seem to notice the extra weight.

But it was so hard to concentrate on the world around them. The woods seemed to go on forever. And the others seemed so intent on their travel, on getting back to their camp and keeping Margaret from tripping over some root or stone or log, they didn't have much time for Hyram. After being so involved, their voices and actions seemed farther away now, fainter, like a radio playing in the other room.

But there were compensations. Hyram was becoming more familiar with his new surroundings, as if he just had to settle in a bit and get comfortable. Now that he had paused in his rushing about, he found Margaret's mind opening up before him. And in that opening, central to her thoughts, was Chestnut Circle.

Suddenly Hyram could see it all, the seven houses, the Jacksons, Dafoes, Furlongs, Smiths, Blakes, the one belonging to Mr. Mills, and Sayre's old place. It was a beautiful day on the Circle. The sun was out. Birds sang. And everything was green.

The real Chestnut Circle had never been that perfect, although Hyram had always wanted it to be.

There was really only one thing he wanted to look at. His lawn. If only he could visit that lawn now, with his new powers of growth, of regeneration.

It looked beautiful in Margaret's dream. Perfect, not a blade of crabgrass or a single dandelion. He took a step forward, and he was walking across the street to stand on the edge of his beautiful green expanse. But why should he expect anything less? Even in here, Hyram Sayre was the lawn god.

His shoes, newly shined and in much better repair than the last time he'd looked, were a wonderful contrast, deep brown against rich green. Sayre was surprised how restful it felt just to look at this. Here he was, a creature of power in one place, viewing his most perfect lawn in another. At that moment it seemed like the best of both worlds.

Somewhere, he heard voices.

"Hyram?"

What did they want with him now?

"Hyram? Hyram, are you there?"

The voices were too far away. The lawn went on forever. He couldn't be bothered with anything now.

The wolf closest to Nick had its ears pinned back, its snout raised.

"Therre is something out therre," it said deep in its throat.

"Something not wolf," another of the animals agreed. "Something not human."

"Rrred furrs," a third wolf added. "Rrred furrs."

The warning had everyone moving, both humans and wolves. Pator stepped up to the first of the wolves. "They're coming for us, aren't they?"

Nick stroked the sword still in its sheath. The hilt felt warm against his palm. "Should we attack them first?"

"Shouldn't we wait for the Captain?" asked Umar, the other man who spoke English.

"But the Captain isn't back," Nick argued, "and we have no idea when he will be. Should we just sit here and let ourselves be surrounded?"

"Watch out!" Pator shouted.

Nick looked up to see something falling from overhead. Animals and men scrambled away to avoid the flight of poison sticks, maybe a dozen or more, thrown into the clearing. One shaft pierced the side of a wolf. The animal howled and crumbled to the ground.

"Damn the Captain!" Nick shouted. "We can't let somebody get away with this." He looked around. The animals were standing, the men were on their feet with weapons ready. There was really no reason for him not to draw his own sword, too.

"Fresh meat!" he called to the wolves.

"Frresh meat!" the wolves called back.

"Let's go out and get them!" he shouted, drawing his sword and raising it above his head.

The wolves seemed ready, but some of the men frowned and muttered.

"Come on now!" Nick called. They had to be united in this. And Nick needed blood. He had been far too long without it. "Come on!" They had to go. "Whoever doesn't follow me feels my sword!"

Pator raised his sword then, too. "We attack!"

Nick led the rush, running from the clearing, his sword swinging overhead. He could hear the others follow, wolves barking, men shouting, all of them rushing to glorious blood and battle.

○ Seventeen

It had been a long time since Evan Mills had known what he really felt. As soon as he—or the wizard inside him—and Obar had seen each other, it was inevitable that they were going to have a fight. Life decisions seemed so much simpler for these wizards. If Evan wasn't so busy doing Rox's bidding, he would have laughed.

Mills was a little surprised that Rox could perform his magic, even with the dragon's eye in Mills's hand. The pain had been palpable when they had first arrived in this new place. Mills didn't think Rox's magic could be very effective with his host's body bent over double in agony. The wizard inside him, however, had no such second thoughts.

"We must protect ourselves!" was Rox's explanation, although when the fight began, Mills wasn't sure who fired the first sorcerous shot. There was an exchange of lines of fire, two beams of green light that exploded where they met midway between the combatants. These battles always started something like this. Mills suspected the wizards did it for show. Rox followed that with a flaming spear, which Obar caught in a flaming shield. They exchanged three or four more kinds of magical firepower, without either one gaining the upper hand.

Rox was making full use of the dragon's eye, but to Mills's astonishment, the pain did not return. The use of magic projected outward seemed to help his physical form. Before, they had used their magic to help others. Now Rox was trying to destroy Obar in any way possible. Helping people, hurting people, it didn't seem to matter. So long as they were using the magic on somebody else, the pain went away.

Mary Lou seemed reluctant to join in at first. She stood off to one side of the conflict, surrounded by those weird little creatures that looked like nothing so much as a group of ancient, hairless dwarfs. From the way the Anno watched her every move, it was obvious they were on her side.

She flinched when a bolt of energy came too close, sending half a dozen of the Anno scattering away. "I will defend myself if I have to. But if we only use our magic in this way, we only serve the dragon."

Obar paused in his attack long enough to laugh. "This is the woman who stopped my spell of protection against the dragon!"

"We only get stronger!" Rox cried back. "If anyone survives the dragon, it will be us!"

They might share the same body, but Mills had no idea where that wizard got his reasoning.

Mary Lou shook her head. "The dragon is hungry. He will take us one by one." She looked first to Mills, then to Obar, her gaze totally without emotion. "You know the creature comes to consume the world. We are the little morsels he nibbles on before the main course."

Rox shot another bolt of energy into the sky, so drunk with laughter and power that he couldn't hear anything, but Mills wanted to listen. He didn't want to be anybody's appetizer.

What Mary Lou said made sense. The dragon wanted this sort of unthinking battle from them. It was leading them into certain courses of action that kept them apart, making them weak by fighting among themselves. Evan Mills wondered why. Perhaps the creature also wanted a show before the main course.

"Who cares about dragons?" Rox called. "I feel wonderful!"

"And I will feel much better," Obar retorted, "when I have put both of you away for good!"

Mills managed to grab motor control of his body long enough to glance up into the sky. Perhaps his eyes had been dazzled by the sorcerous light show, but the world around them seemed far darker than it had before.

"It's getting dark!" he called.

"Evening comes at last," Rox replied.

"No," Mary Lou cautioned. "He's right. Evening's falling

much too quickly. Give the sky another moment, and it will be night.''

This world was never that natural in the first place, but Mills really hated it when the physical laws just got tossed out entirely.

''Is this the dragon?'' he asked. ''Maybe we've called the creature here with our fight.''

''Do you think the dragon cares that much about us?'' Obar called back. But Mills noticed that both he and Rox had paused in their battle.

''It gives us these eyes,'' was Mills's answer.

The others were silent for a long moment. Mills spoke again, confessing quickly to all those things he had been thinking about since he had first found himself inside Nunn.

''I've always wondered about that aspect of this place. Those eyes seem awfully central to this whole struggle. What purpose do we serve to the dragon? Why doesn't the fire-breathing lizard just come and take them back? Is there something greater than the dragon that watches out for us, too?''

''There is always the possibility of something greater,'' Mary Lou agreed.

Even Obar frowned thoughtfully at that. ''Are you a religious man, Mr. Mills? I certainly was—once.''

''I think the dragon is still busy elsewhere,'' Rox objected. ''We'll see him soon enough.''

But the sky kept growing darker, and there were no stars.

Mrs. Smith had been in her share of strange surroundings. And they seemed to grow stranger every time she grew close to the dragon, like the creature existed in a separate time and place, where the laws of the world did not apply.

From the looks of their current location, Mrs. Smith thought, the dragon must be very near.

The first thing she was aware of, after realizing she had been brought somewhere else, was that she still held her dragon's eye. The proximity of that eye always gave her a sense of well-being, even in a place as strange as this. But even with the eye as her center, it took her a moment to orient herself.

There seemed to be no real up or down here, no floor and no sky. She was spinning slowly about in the too bright void, and as she looked about she could see the others doing the same. Nunn looked grimly determined, as if even being transported to a place such as this would not turn him from his goals. Carl clutched the smoke-filled globe with both hands and laughed like a madman. They all seemed to be drifting apart, spinning away from each other like they were caught in a slow-motion gale, or the aftermath of a silent explosion.

There was light here, too. If anything, it was far too bright, with strobing flashes from time to time that made her shut her eyes. It felt as though this place was filled with so much power that it could barely be contained. Had their use of power brought them here?

And where was Wilbert?

She heard a whimper behind her. She let the force spin her about, until she caught her first glimpse of the large Volunteer, curled into a ball against the void.

"Wilbert!" she called.

He did not respond to her, but she could hear him speak, talking very quickly under his breath, as if he was reciting Hail Marys or multiplication tables or baseball scores or anything to keep him sane.

He opened his eyes and took a ragged breath that could easily have turned into a scream. When he saw Mrs. Smith, he tried to smile. It didn't work.

"Well," he managed in a hoarse voice, "if I'm in hell, at least I've got company."

"I don't think this is hell," Mrs. Smith replied, "but it may be pretty close."

Wilbert closed his eyes. "Oh God. Oh Lord. I thought I was dead. Maybe we're all dead."

"Not quite yet, I don't think," Mrs. Smith said, trying to reassure him with the sound of her voice. Maybe she was trying to reassure herself, too. "Although death could be very much a possibility."

She decided this was a good time to see if her dragon's eye still worked.

Reach out, she called to the gem. Reach out and bring him to me.

The gem in her hand flared green once, and then a second time. Then at last, as if the stone had to make some adjustment for their new surroundings, it sent out a green strand toward Wilbert, a magic rope to snare him and pull him in.

Wilbert snagged the rope when it reached him, and pulled himself forward, hand over hand, to speed up the process.

He shook his head when he reached Constance's side. "Things don't make sense. Time is not right here."

"From what I understand," she replied, "time is never right around the dragon."

"Yeah. The dragon." Wilbert nodded his head. "I knew I'd end up in one of these places sooner or later. Well. If you're going to die, at least you get interesting surroundings."

Mrs. Smith didn't like to hear that kind of talk. "No one's going to die here if I can help it. Especially not you or I."

Wilbert rewarded her with his first real smile. "Lord, woman. I am glad I met you. You're always so reassuring." He sighed. "I've got an odd thing to say, but I can't imagine a better place to say it. My mother died when I was twelve, and I've always felt a bit lost, until you came along. Is it all right, in these last few minutes I have, if I pretend you're my mother come back?"

"These last few minutes?"

"It's a feeling I have. One thing I learned in this world, it's to trust your gut."

What a strange thing to ask. She had never been a mother, had none of the skills, none of the experience. Still, if this would calm Wilbert down, what harm could it be?

"Of course," she answered softly.

His grin widened at that. "It's a bit childish, I suppose. But, when you're about to die, they say your whole life flashes by. That includes the child parts, too, I imagine. Maybe that's what's going on."

They were interrupted by a flash of green.

"Would you pay attention, Mrs. Smith?"

She looked away from Wilbert to see Nunn staring at them from perhaps a dozen feet away.

The wizard grinned unpleasantly. "This is what happens when I try to show a little mercy. The universe falls apart. Rest assured, Mrs. Smith, that I will kill you at the first reasonable opportunity."

"I would expect no less." She knew she could fight Nunn if she had to. Somehow, even a reliable evil seemed preferable to the chaos that now surrounded them.

''We are far too close to the dragon now,'' Nunn said. ''For us to leave, someone has to stay behind.''

''Someone?'' Mrs. Smith asked. Was this another call to battle?

''Not just anyone. The dragon gets the one with the worst defenses.'' Nunn opened his hands to reveal his gems. ''Voilà.''

The light shifted from bright white to green.

She heard Carl Jackson scream. And then Nunn joined in. There were three people screaming, and the third one was her.

Three people screaming. Only three.

Wilbert, Constance thought.

They were back to the real world, but it had changed.

The trees around them had been crushed. While the forest was still tall and strong a hundred feet away, this place was a ruin.

As if it was brushed by the dragon's claw, Constance thought.

She heard two men cry out, and Carl's crazed laughter. The two would never stop fighting.

She turned and saw Nunn enveloped in a blaze of green fire. He screamed in agony and vanished, consumed in an instant.

''At last,'' Carl Jackson said. ''I knew I could get Nunn if I really tried.'' He turned to Mrs. Smith with a grin. ''And now it's time for you.''

Carl opened his hands. In the very center of each palm was a dragon's eye.

○ Eighteen

The dragon wasn't here, exactly.

Mary Lou had been in the presence of the dragon before, but she had never felt the dragon so near. Obar and Mills had not only stopped their fight; they ignored each other now, as all three looked up to the strangely discolored sky. The Anno cowered on the platform around them, overwhelmed by this new presence, but the bravest of them lifted their heads for an instant to gain a peek above.

She didn't know how long they all looked into the gathering darkness. Time was suspended; she stared for what might have been an hour, or simply the space between one heartbeat and the next. The silence around them was total. Not only were there no sounds from the Anno, but the forest was silent as well, not a noise from insects, small animals, or birds. Mary Lou realized there was no wind or breeze. It was as if the whole world was holding its breath.

Time and space were terms without meaning. The only meaning was the dragon. Even though they waited to see it, it was already here. Even though they feared its coming, it was already in their thoughts, their hearts, the marrow of their bones.

The whole world paused.

Mary Lou blinked.

The world shifted again, and the darkness was gone.

Obar let out a low groan. Mills whistled with relief.

Jewel in hand, Mary Lou let her mind reach out, exploring for the inevitable presence. But there was none of the smothering mass, none of the stifling heat that she had felt before. The world had returned to a simpler state.

"The dragon has gone elsewhere," she said simply. "We're spared for the moment."

Obar and Mills turned to look at each other, their hands raised in defense, as if this reprieve was nothing more than an excuse to resume battle.

"We should end this fight," Obar said with the slightest of smiles. "Why don't you surrender to someone with far more experience?"

"You killed me once," Rox's voice shouted with Mills's mouth. "The least I can do is return the favor."

"No, wait!" Mills's more temperate voice interrupted the other occupant of his body. "We all know that we were very close to death a moment ago. We need to work together, to use reason, rather than force."

Mary Lou's own eye flashed, protecting her from some invisible spell. The Anno shrieked in alarm, using their real voices rather than their mental ones. She looked quickly at each of the wizards. Obar, so superior a moment before, looked as surprised as she felt. Mills looked confused, but his arms were opened toward Mary Lou, as though Rox had thrown the energy at her while Mills was still speaking.

"You are quicker than I thought, Mary Lou." Rox laughed as if this was nothing more than some great game.

"Now you attack the girl?" Mills called with almost the same breath. "Have you no reason?"

"I would be far more reasonable," Rox replied smoothly, "with another dragon's eye or two."

"This fighting leads us nowhere!" Mary Lou called. But neither of the others was paying attention.

"We can only survive by gaining power," Obar added as he looked again at his adversary. "Power, and the knowledge to use it. The dragon spared us last time through luck. That won't happen again!"

"Then give it up, old man," Rox called.

This time, Mary Lou saw the blinding bolt from the sky, appearing from nowhere and aimed at Obar. But the wizard was surrounded by a halo of soft green, and the killing energy could not reach its goal.

Mary Lou realized there was a group of the Anno moving around her. Like a guard, she thought. A second party of the small creatures, maybe fifty or more, glided across the platform toward the other wizards.

"No!" Mills called, but he looked up in the air above the platform. A ball of light flashed in the sky, but no bolt of lightning followed. Mills twisted and stumbled, his arms flailing out of control, as if he were trying to hold back the wizard inside him.

Obar raised his hand, and a great tongue of green fire leaped to engulf the struggling Mills.

"No!" Mills called again, but this time the word seemed shouted by two voices. The fire vanished from around Mills's body. He had not been burned.

"You are still unsure," Obar remarked very softly, as if he spoke more to himself than to the others. "When you slip, I'll have you."

The two wizards glared at each other for a long moment as the Anno moved silently to surround them. The men took no notice of the smaller creatures; all their attention was reserved for each other. Mary Lou watched the two combatants, as if she had once again been forced to the sidelines. If this went on, one of the wizards would find a way to destroy the other.

She knew a single gesture from her could throw the battle to one side or the other, but she didn't want to see winners and losers. She just wanted it to stop.

"Mary Lou!"

The Anno wanted her attention. She looked from Obar and Mills to those who now surrounded them. The small creatures had joined together, linked arm in arm to form a circle around each of the wizards. It made Mary Lou think about ring-around-a-rosy. The collected Anno started singing—in voices so high she wasn't quite sure if she heard them with her ears or her mind. She had seen the Anno do this trance thing before, first when they had almost sacrificed her to the dragon, later when they had controlled the vines.

They looked so much like children, although their intent could be so deadly. The Anno's cries rose and fell as they circled the two taller men.

Ring around a rosy, Mary Lou thought.

Obar looked annoyed at the new activity around him, like one would look at pets who disobeyed. The Anno's singing grew higher still.

A pocket full of posies.

Rox used the distraction to shoot a ball of flame, but Obar recovered quickly to meet the attack with some fire of his own. The two forces exploded on impact twenty feet above the platform, midway between the wizards.

Ashes, ashes, we all fall down.

"Mary Lou!" the Anno called again mentally, as if this was all a show for her benefit.

The Anno stopped their singsong chant. But their high cries were now answered by a thousand other cries in the air.

Hundreds of small birds hurtled down from the sky. Some flew close to Obar, swooping close by his head and outstretched arms, seemingly not so much to harm him as to discourage him from interfering. Most of the birds seemed headed for Mills. They pecked at his clothes, flew in his face, clawed at hands and hair.

In the Anno's universe, Mary Lou had to be protected, Obar had to be contained, and Rox had to be destroyed.

But the wizard's magic was greater than any forest-spun spell the Anno could devise. After a moment of disorientation, Obar had lifted himself from the ground, alarming the birds and giving himself a temporary reprieve. Mills had followed the other's example, surrounding himself with a halo of green that caused the birds to bounce away.

The wizards were each a half-dozen feet above the platform now. They would leave her and carry the battle somewhere else. She didn't want them to kill each other, and she didn't want to take any more time following them. The dragon had picked both of them for some reason she didn't think she would ever figure out, but they would be important, maybe necessary, to the fight that was to come.

Green fire exploded between the two wizards as they both rose higher still. Maybe, Mary Lou realized, there was another way to end this. She could not defeat their power, could do no more in battle than merely counter their magic with her own. But what if she could add to their power instead? If she could heighten their actions, take them out of their control, she could manage them as easily as if she were to snatch away their eyes. If Rox and Obar wanted to rise above the fray, she'd make sure that they flew farther and faster than they ever imagined. They wanted magic, they'd get magic. She would make sure the two of them were truly lost in the power of the dragon.

"What?" Rox called as he shot skyward.

"Who?" Obar echoed as he spun about in ever widening circles. He flew full speed into the forest, the protective field around him causing him to bounce between the trees like a silver ball in a pinball machine. His spells would protect him from bodily harm while ensuring that he was totally out of control. Mary Lou almost laughed.

The element of surprise was with her. Now she had to follow these two hyperactive wizards and get them to listen to reason.

"Mary Lou!" the Anno called after her as she levitated above the platform. She could feel their longing for her in her head, know the loss that would come to them when she was gone. But she could no more fulfill the Anno's wishes than she could the wishes of her parents. She would follow no one's plan, even if that plan came from the dragon—no one's plan but her own.

All three of them rose above the trees as the two wizards tried and failed to stop their cartwheeling progress across the sky. She was afraid to feed any more of her own magic into their increasingly frantic spells for fear the wizards might be crushed by their own magic aura or explode with some sorcerous overload. Obar was shouting something, while the creature that mixed Rox and Mills seemed to spend half the time cursing, the rest laughing. The dragon's eyes were making them crazy. Maybe, she thought, they grew crazier as they used the dragon's power. Would she be any different?

But she couldn't let the wizards go, not now. She had seen as much of the dragon and its plans as she wanted. She had stood on the sidelines too long. Now it was time to fight back.

She did her best to give the wizards direction, all three of them together, spinning madly about in a vortex of magic. But their flight had a destination. They would spin all the way back to the clearing, where, with any luck, she could get both Todd and Mrs. Smith to help contain these two, reason with them, get them all to work together.

Maybe they could even find a way for the craziness to end.

○ Around the Circle:
The Day of the Dragon

They say the dragon has but one purpose, and that is to destroy.

But listen carefully to the tale tellers, for even something as great and fearsome as the dragon cannot destroy it all. There must be some seed, some beginning that can grow again, something, indeed, that has escaped annihilation. For otherwise—with nothing to destroy—the dragon will have no purpose.

Not that these fine points matter for all those who will be destroyed. Those who have truly seen the dragon never live to tell about their tale.

So it was that with a casual exhalation of flame, the dragon destroyed a city. All the great monuments of mortals, all their hopes and dreams and fears, the memories of ancestors and the children yet to be born, gone in an instant, with barely a thought.

The dragon glanced behind and was pleased to see where once there had been tower and street, forest and stream, there was nothing left but deep black ash.

But the dragon is so great, its vision encompassing all, that sometimes it misses the little things.

Life was still buried within the ashes; life that will rise again. Black feathers the color of the ash flutter, a black beak emerges to test the air. Raven shakes away the debris, hops to the top of the ashen pile, and calls out to the sky.

"Still alive!"

On rare occasions, even something as great as the dragon will hear about the little things, like a black bird hiding in the dragon's shadow, always free.

So the dragon's time came again, and the dragon laid waste to another great city, and all the countryside around, a whole nation consumed by flame. And all of this was particularly satisfying to the great creature, for the dragon loved to burn.

But there was still something left alive, still always just out of the range of its fires.

The dragon would not be defeated. The great flying reptile would burn ever more to catch that miserable bird. So the dragon destroyed a whole country, and then a continent, but still Raven flew ahead.

Great was the dragon's anger. The dragon would destroy it all. There would be nowhere for even a bird to escape.

And so the dragon burned the world.

With that, the dragon was exhausted. It had done all that it could, and it had to rest.

The dragon was gone.

And there was a stirring in the ashes. A bird with feathers the same color as the destruction around him popped his head out and looked around. The dragon had left at last, defeated once again.

So it was that Raven flew away to begin the world anew, the quiet air broken open by his cry.

"Still alive!"

What is true and what is not? It is for you to decide. That, after all, is the nature of tales. But think of this.

The dragon burns the world, but Raven tells the tale.

Who, then, is the stronger?

BOOK TWO

Dragon Burning

○ Nineteen

Carl Jackson looked down at the hands of the most powerful man in the world; his hands, each one sporting a bright green jewel embedded in its palm. When he first saw the jewels set deep within his flesh, he thought they would burn him with dragon's fire, or cut him with their sharp edges, but they didn't hurt at all. If he felt anything in his hands at all, it was a wonderful warmth, a warmth that spread to his entire body to make him feel better than he had in years. It was a little like that first high you got from a good Scotch, but this high wasn't just for a moment. No, he knew this feeling would last forever.

Carl Jackson had always known it would happen this way, even if he would never be sure exactly how it had happened. He remembered that he'd been trying to beat Nunn before the wizard got him, and that Mrs. Smith had tipped the balance in his favor. Why she would do that was almost beyond him. Just helping an old neighbor, he guessed. Not that they'd ever talked, back on Chestnut Circle. He'd always thought of her as that uppity bitch two houses down.

Well, even Carl Jackson could be wrong. She saved his butt, and he would return the favor. He wouldn't kill her the way he had planned, wouldn't even kill her at all, so long as she agreed to do what he wanted. And what he wanted was her gem.

"Carl?" the old woman called tentatively. Sweet-old-lady Smith, the woman everybody in the neighborhood loved. She looked like she didn't trust him, like she was about to start some magic of her own. Jackson would be ready. He'd spent his entire life being double-crossed by others, his unbending boss, his good-for-nothing family, even the army, who threw him out on his ear. Now at last he had a chance to get even. With these gems in his hands, he could stop her before she tried anything.

"I never knew I could feel this good." He smiled. "But I could feel better."

Mrs. Smith spoke quickly. "Carl, we have to think about what we're going to do. The dragon just took one of us, and he's probably going to get the rest of us unless we do something about it."

He chuckled at that. She sounded even more worried than before. He liked it when he could make people really uncomfortable. He'd always known he was better than all those assholes who'd put him down. It just took coming to a brand-new world to prove it.

"Do you understand what I'm saying, Carl?" Her voice was rising now, just the way schoolteachers and principals and drill sergeants and bosses and his worthless excuse for a father used to yell at him when he decided he wouldn't pay attention; as if any of them were worth his time.

She kept on talking: "Whenever the dragon wants, it can take one of us."

This really was getting under his skin. What did all that crap the Smith broad was spouting mean, anyway? That guy with a bow was gone? So one of the crazy locals bought it. What did that have to do with him?

Mrs. Smith floated toward him. Man, that was creepy the way she moved without flexing a muscle. Couldn't she walk or something? Carl used the fingers of both hands to rub the jewels in his palms.

"We have to prepare for this," she said sternly. "You're coming with me, Carl Jackson, if it's the last thing I do."

What was that, a threat? The gems felt warm to his touch. This old bag didn't know who she was dealing with. Carl would never be threatened again.

He opened his arms wide so she could see the glowing gems in his hands, gems all ready to be used. "I'd stay right there, lady."

She frowned at him, but kept on floating. "Carl!" she chided. "Think for a minute. We were neighbors."

Neighbors? As if that meant anything! Time for a little demonstration. Carl had spent enough time around Nunn—and inside the wizard, too—to get some idea how this all worked. He concentrated, picking his spots. Green light shot from his hands, and trees exploded on either side of her.

Whoa. That was not bad at all; two of those huge trees reduced to splinters, and he hadn't even broken a sweat. Before, when he had just held the globe, there had been limits to what he could do. Now he could probably blow up the whole damn world.

But he was getting ahead of himself here. First he'd handle Mrs. Smith, take her jewel, maybe teach her a little lesson after all. With his two dragon's eyes to her one, he should be able to do it in no time.

It wasn't until the dust cleared from the explosion that he realized she was gone.

Jackson cursed under his breath. Why'd she want to go and do that for? He was going to grab her eye and get it over with. If she was going to make it difficult for him, maybe he'd have to make her suffer a little more, too. Hell, he was pissed now. Maybe he'd make her suffer a lot.

The jewels burned in his palms now, but it was a fire he never wanted to go away. He'd already beaten Nunn, and incinerated that old bag of bones where he stood. He'd get Mrs. Smith, and anything else he wanted, sooner or later. It was only a question of when.

At first, Mrs. Smith thought that Carl had followed her. There was something wrong when she used her eye; she felt unbalanced, as if she carried extra baggage. Had Carl Jackson, in his inexperience with these gems, somehow managed to sabotage her dragon's eyes as well?

Wilbert was gone, vanished with the visit from the dragon. Since she no longer had to worry about transporting him, she was able to use a simple removal spell when Carl attacked her, transporting herself from one known place to another. Oh she had thought it was simple, until her magic threatened to spin wildly out of control.

She flew now through that limbo that existed between here and there, one of the many magic domains of the dragon she had been able to access with her eye. She looked again at her dragon's eye, both with her own eyes and with the link she had formed between the gem and her mind. She had planned to rematerialize in the middle of the clearing among the neighbors, but if there was danger here, she would much rather face it alone. The dragon's eye shifted in her vision, as if it pulsated before her, adding and discarding glittering facets as it breathed in and out. Her mind reached out toward the stone, and heard something new, like a whispered conversation just too far away to be understood.

The eye had never spoken before, and she didn't think it was speaking now. There was someone or something else here, some extra intelligence trying to communicate with her. But who or what? This sort of thing was too subtle to be Carl, and if the dragon had a voice, it would not waste time whispering.

Still, having identified this strange new presence, she was confident she could cope with it. She materialized just outside the clearing where the neighbors waited. Until she understood the true nature of this thing, she didn't want to expose any of the others.

"I know you're here," she called softly.

"I never doubted that you would," replied a voice somewhere nearby. "Excuse me while I make myself a bit more presentable."

A disturbance like a tiny whirlwind rose from the forest floor before her. Leaves and dust and rotting branches swirled about until they had solidified into the image of a man with robes of night and a face the color of bone.

"Nunn," she acknowledged.

"At least what's left of me." The apparition held up his hands to show two dark pits where the jewels used to be. There was no blood; no sign, really, that the thing before her was in any way a living being.

"I owe you an explanation at least—in return for the transportation," the ghost-Nunn continued. "When I realized Jackson had the upper hand, and the eyes were being pulled away from me, I managed to set up a decoy. Well, it was a part of my physical form, really; there wasn't time for anything else. That's what you saw burn. A very nice effect, I must say. Then I had to find a way to put some distance between myself and my problems. You provided that." He looked down at his pale, empty hands. "I've got a few spells left. But, without the eyes, they take a great deal out of me."

Mrs. Smith allowed herself a shallow breath. Somehow, she

or her gem had picked up a passenger; Nunn was at least telling the truth in that. Nunn, like Obar, always liked to talk, and perhaps she could learn more from him if he kept his distance. Without his dragon's eyes, she could destroy him with a glance. And yet, it was no doubt the nature of Nunn that a small bit of worry clung to the back of her thoughts.

Not that Nunn was done speaking. "I should have destroyed Jackson from a distance, rather than trying to take his energy. My greed has always been my undoing." Nunn sighed. "I tried to use the confusion to get rid of him once and for all. Instead, he turned the tables on me."

Was he presenting all this information to gain her sympathy? Mrs. Smith was not impressed by this performance. "What do you want from me?"

The apparition attempted a smile. The illusion was hollow. Within the curling lips, she saw nothing but darkness.

"My needs are simple," the thing with Nunn's voice said. "I am addicted to the power of the eye. If I am not near it, I will die."

So she was supposed to show charity for this ghost, this madman, this sadist? She remembered how Nunn had tried to trick her before.

"Die, then," she replied.

Nunn began to fall apart, as if his spell could not stand up to her dismissal. Dust swirled away from his fingertips, leaves flew away on the wind, leaving the edge of his robes in tatters, his features even more sunken than before.

Even as he disintegrated he remained calm. "Without my gems, I will soon have no physical form. I can be no threat to you at all. To survive what is to come, each of us will need an edge. My experience will be most helpful if you wish to survive."

She thought about Wilbert, and the dragon. The Volunteer had been snatched away in a way she was powerless to understand, much less fight against. All of them might follow in Wilbert's footsteps. She had to use every resource available to her. How could she say no?

She stared at the fading figure before her. "You only need to stay nearby?"

"Only within a few feet of the eye." As his form grew

indistinct his voice seemed to fade as well. "Without physical form, I cannot steal the gem away."

Not right now, perhaps, Mrs. Smith thought. After all, what was the disintegrating form before her now if not a physical manifestation of the wizard? Part of what Nunn spoke was certainly a lie; he knew no other way to talk. Still, Mrs. Smith could use his knowledge. She just had to guess when his lies became truly dangerous.

She knew she would regret this, but it was what she had to do.

"You may accompany me for now."

"You will not destroy me, then?" The apparition fell back to rot and dust, leaving nothing but a vague haze in the air, like a bit of smoke or the last patch of morning fog, fragile, then gone.

She felt a coldness graze her palm as Nunn brushed against her jewel.

"If you have a flaw," the voice added, now little more than a whisper, "it is mercy."

The honesty in Nunn's voice frightened her more than the possibility of his lies. Perhaps now, Nunn would hide nothing from her at all.

She felt a moment of panic, as if Nunn might overwhelm her with some hideous truth. She took a deep breath, felt the warmth of the dragon's eye where it rested in her palm. The gem was still firmly a part of her. He had no power over this eye as long as it was in her possession. She could crush him at any moment.

But so long as the wizard was near, she couldn't rest. Nunn had knowledge. But Nunn had no mercy of his own.

"Rest assured, Mrs. Smith, I will do anything to survive the dragon," came the wizard's whisper, close by her ear. "And no doubt you, too, will find you will do the same."

No, Mrs. Smith didn't imagine she would rest at all.

She could still feel that spot on her hand where Nunn's magic had touched her. It was the same cold she still felt in her shoulder. Not the touch of a living thing at all. It felt more like the touch of the dragon.

She instructed the stone in her hand to complete the spell. It was time to rejoin the others, and see what they intended to do to survive.

○ Twenty

Todd watched Sala pace back and forth in front of him. She hadn't been able to stand still since she discovered her father had followed her to the island. Todd was impatient to be gone, too, but he couldn't leave until Mrs. Smith had returned. No matter what he or Sala wanted to do, he knew someone with a dragon's eye had to remain with the neighbors for protection.

And this strange place was getting even stranger. Without warning, evening had almost turned to night, all the light and sound draining from the world around them. And then, just as quickly, the strange darkness was gone, and the sky had gone back to evening again. Todd didn't even want to guess what that meant. For all he knew about this world, a moment from now the sun could rise where it had just set and the day might go in reverse.

Sala stopped and stood in front of him, her feet wide apart, her arms folded defiantly before her, as if she had been pacing all this time just so she could end up in front of Todd.

"My father's getting away." She made the four words sound like an accusation.

But Snake's escape was one of the few things Todd wasn't worried about. He tried on a smile as he said, "We're on an island. Where could he go?"

"Oh, he'll think of something," she replied bitterly. "They've got a ship hidden somewhere. My father's working with Nunn." She blurted out a short, barking laugh. "My father's a very clever man. He's going to come up with some way to make me pay."

The other neighbors had gathered around to listen. Todd guessed it was easier for everyone to focus on somebody else's troubles than it was to worry about what was going to happen to them.

"Pay?" Todd's mother Rebecca asked. "What have you done?"

Sala's voice grew hoarse as she answered: "I tried to escape." She began to shake as if the warm summer air had turned to ice.

His mother didn't reply to that, but Todd could see the sad, lost look in her eyes. Todd and she both knew about no-escape situations, too.

Sala held her arms tight across her chest, but her shivering only got worse. Todd couldn't stand to see her this way. He tried to take her shoulders, but she jumped back like she didn't want to be touched.

Todd found himself yelling. "Look! Don't take it out on me! I didn't make your father or any of this crazy place!"

He was sorry as soon as the words were out of his mouth. He didn't want to snap at her. He wasn't really angry with any of the people here.

But he was very angry. He was very mad at Sala's father, and what he had done to her. He wanted to make sure he'd never do that sort of thing to anyone again.

And after he was done with Snake, Todd would like to handle his own father, too. He wanted to act, and act now.

Todd nearly laughed at how eager he was to get out of here. Acting was easy. Sometimes, it was more painful if you were given time to think.

He saw how much Sala hurt, and how much his mother hurt, too. And—seeing it in others—he realized how much he hurt as well. Before now, he had never wanted to look at that. It had been easier, back in his old life, to turn that hurt around, quickly, without thinking.

Mostly, he had used his gang members to hurt others. Even then, he didn't want to do the damage himself. He could bully the dorks and nerds in the schoolyard as long as he didn't have to look in their faces.

Of course he beat his own gang around himself. That was a different matter. He had every right to push *them* around. They were punks just like him. They deserved any grief they got.

His father had been so good at hurting those who didn't

deserve it. Without thinking, he had started to walk right in his father's footsteps.

No. Todd looked away from the others, staring up at the tall trees, their leaves etched black against the fading light. It was no use blaming himself for what was past; that other world was gone. Somehow, he had to use his power here, to make things better for him and Sala and his mother and all the others around him. Here, it wasn't making up for lost time; it was making a whole new life.

Todd looked back to the others. Mrs. Smith was here. He sensed her arrival an instant before she appeared in the clearing; her and somebody else.

"Where's Wilbert?" Stanley asked as soon as it was apparent to the others that she was alone. But she wasn't. Todd could sense—something.

"I'm sorry," Mrs. Smith said, and Todd didn't think he had ever seen her look so sad. "Wilbert's gone with the dragon."

The other neighbors all seemed to talk at once.

"Gone?"

"You mean dead."

"Did the dragon eat him?"

Mrs. Smith shook her head. For the first time she looked a little bit like a helpless old lady. "The dragon was so close. It had been drawn by the power we'd used in our battle—I think. We needed a sacrifice. It had us. It let all of us go—but one."

Stanley's face lost what little color it usually had. "First Thomas and now—" he whispered. "Damn all these wizards and dragons. Wilbert would never listen."

He turned and walked away from the gathering. Maggie ran to follow him.

"Wilbert's gone." Todd kept looking at Mrs. Smith. "But you're not alone."

She looked first at Todd, then at the other neighbors grouped around him. "You would know that." She didn't seem as sure of herself as she had before. "No, I am not alone. But listen carefully to what I have to say."

Everybody shut up at that. Mrs. Smith certainly knew how to get attention.

"I have Nunn with me," she announced.

Silence turned to shouting as, once again, the neighbors all tried to talk at once.

Mrs. Smith raised a hand for silence. "I only brought him here once I was sure we would all be safe."

Mrs. Dafoe started to speak at that, but stopped with a glance from Mrs. Smith.

"Basically," the older woman continued, "he's my prisoner. He has to do what I say, or I can take away what he needs to live."

Rose Dafoe could be still no longer. "But where is he, exactly?"

Mrs. Smith shook her head. "Since he doesn't exactly have a physical form, he's tough to pinpoint. He is close by my dragon's eye. He needs to be there to survive. But I'm not the only one who is aware of him. Todd could sense the wizard's presence as soon as we arrived."

"That's why I asked," Todd agreed.

"And he's still here?" Mrs. Blake asked.

Todd nodded. He could still sense the second presence near Mrs. Smith. He took a step toward the old woman and felt the strange force flutter away, as if it wanted to keep its distance. Could Nunn be afraid of him?

"It's good to have confirmation, especially where Nunn was concerned," Mrs. Smith added. "He's totally vulnerable. Maybe that's why I let him stay. I could kill him easily—at any minute."

"Do it," Stanley said. Todd hadn't even seen him rejoin the group.

"But we may need Nunn's experience to save us from the dragon—" Mrs. Smith began.

"Nunn is worse than the dragon," Stanley replied. "He kills with malice."

Mrs. Smith sighed. Todd didn't think he had ever seen her look less happy than she did at that instant. When she spoke again, her words came out slowly, as if she was carefully choosing every one.

"Nunn is my responsibility. If anything happens because of what I've done, I will find him and—if I have to—destroy him. Until then, we may have a use for him. These are desperate times, and they deserve desperate measures."

Mrs. Smith lifted the hand that didn't hold her gem and

rubbed her eyes. She looked old and tired and barely in control. Todd could see that the others noticed the change in her, too—the others who had believed that Mrs. Smith was going to save them all.

The neighbors exchanged glances, the looks on their faces all saying the same thing. If even Mrs. Smith would lose her cool, how could any of them survive?

"That's what he'd be counting on," Stanley retorted. He spat at Mrs. Smith's feet, a projectile no doubt aimed at the invisible Nunn. "Our desperation keeps him alive, and later that desperation will make us slip up so he can gain control, eh?"

Todd felt uneasy about this, too. Even if he accepted Mrs. Smith's judgment, there were still parts of her explanation that didn't make sense. "If Nunn is with you, depending upon your gems to stay alive, what happened to his dragon's eyes?"

She looked up at him for a moment before she answered, staring at him with her pale blue eyes.

"Carl's taken them now."

His father? His father had the gems? Todd's hand squeezed his dragon's eye so hard it hurt.

"I've got to get out of here—now." Todd had to stop his father before he truly figured out how to use those things.

"No!" Mrs. Smith replied, a new firmness in her voice. "The dragon's almost on top of us! Your father will never learn enough about them in time. The rest of us have to join together from now on."

Mrs. Smith didn't really know Todd's father, didn't know what he was capable of. She hadn't lived with him for years, always afraid of making the wrong move, saying the wrong thing, crossing his father in some way that only the old man understood, passing judgment with a bottle at his side. The things Carl Jackson had done were bad enough when he could only inflict pain with his fists. What sort of a monster would he become when he was given real power?

Todd saw the worried look on Sala's face. She knew how upset he was. He had to calm down, think about this. Maybe Mrs. Smith was right. Maybe.

He felt like the world was closing in around him. The dragon's eye in his hand was no longer enough. With his father, anything was possible.

• • •

Nick could feel his heart pounding in his ears, a singing in his veins. He was only an extension of his blade, metal and flesh, together keening for warm, red blood. The only time he was truly alive was when he and the sword were searching for sustenance.

Wolves ran to his either side. Pator and the other soldiers were close behind. He would not be stopped. None of them would be stopped. Nick thought of the Vikings: the berserkers, who lived only for battle, so fierce and single-minded that they appeared to have the strength of ten. He was like one of those berserkers now. Nothing could stop him and his sword.

More poison sticks flew through the air, but Nick and his party were a moving target now, and the projectiles seemed to be tossed quickly at them, without much effort to aim, as if they already had their enemy on the run. The deadly spears fell harmlessly to either side of their charge. Nick saw short, reddish figures between the trees ahead.

"We're getting close!" he called to those behind him. "Fresh meat!" He ran even more quickly, doing his best to keep up with the wolves.

There were other figures, at a much greater distance, disappearing into the darkness of the forest. But half a dozen of the creatures seemed to have lagged behind. Nick recognized the red-furred ape-things that Nunn had brought to this place. Nick's sword had tasted their blood before, and found it almost as nourishing as the blood of humans.

The apes looked confused as Nick and the others rushed to meet them. A couple turned to run, two others shrieked and stood their ground, while the remaining pair took a couple of steps back, as if torn between fighting and fleeing.

Nick chose one of the apes who stood and fought as his first target. If he could get his sword into one of the brave ones, it would take the fight right out of the others.

Nick rushed the ape, his sword held before him. The ape feinted with the spear stick, but Nick knocked it easily aside with the side of his blade. His foe tried to lower the spear, to thrust it below Nick's sword arm, but before the ape could make a further move, the sword caught it in the neck, the force of Nick's blow driving the metal so deep into flesh that the sword tip touched the creature's spine.

The ape stiffened for an instant as its blood poured into the magic sword, then went slack, its diminishing weight hanging from Nick's weapon. Then, at last, its body began to shrink into an emaciated husk as the last fluids were drained from the corpse. Nick had seen this transformation dozens of times before, but he always found it exhilarating.

Pator had stabbed a second ape in the chest while two of the wolves had felled a third, tearing pieces from the creature until its screaming stopped. Nick wanted to shout with the power streaming from his sword. The battle would be over in a minute, their victory assured.

A high-pitched voice screamed above the sounds of battle. "No! It will not happen this way! You are dead! They are Zachs's family!"

"What the—" Pator called as a ball of fire leaped down from overhead.

"Zachs's family!" the fire shouted. "You will not kill Zachs's family! Zachs decides who lives and who dies!"

The fire stood upon the ground, showing burning arms and legs and head, a flaming creature much the same size as the apes.

"Stand firm, my children!" the fiery creature called. "Zachs will protect you!"

The three apes still standing against the attack gathered close together, poison sticks at the ready. From the way they had cowered when this Zachs had first appeared, they seemed to obey him more from fear than from any family devotion.

A wolf launched itself into the air, its jaws opening for this Zachs's throat. But the burning thing pointed at the wolf, and a great tongue of fire burst from its fingers to envelop the animal. The wolf screamed for an instant as it burned.

The presence of their leader seemed to distract the remaining apes more than anything else. One of the three stepped back, trying to hide behind the others, unsure, no doubt, whether it preferred to die by sword or by fire.

The ape that stood at the right front of the little group barely looked at Nick as he plunged the sword into its chest.

"Zachs will not forget this!" the fire creature screamed as the sword did its work. "You will die! Everyone who fights Zachs will die!"

Nick's attack had propelled his fellows into action. Umar

and a pair of wolves brought down a second creature. The ape that had hid behind its fellows stumbled back, suddenly exposed. The poison stick twisted about in its awkward hands.

The creature cringed as the other wolves drew near, then moaned with sudden agony. It had poked itself in the side with its own weapon. It looked down dully as the fur about the wound turned from red to black.

"No! No! No! Zachs will kill you all!"

Zachs clapped his hands, and a great shaft of fire rushed toward Nick and the others. Nick turned toward the onrushing blaze, either through instinct or guided by his blade. Nick found that he was screaming, as if urging the fire forward to take them all.

The fire consumed the withering body on the end of Nick's blade, but then went no farther, as if the great inferno was all being drawn within the sword as well. Nick felt a great heat, as if both he and the sword were in the grip of a great fever, but he didn't dare let go of the blade.

"Noooooo!" the fire creature wailed. "Zachs will find a way to kill you yet!" He leaped back up into the trees overhead. "Kill you! Over and over and over again!"

Nick was shaking. He and the sword had taken the fire and survived. But the battle had used up all their strength. They needed fresh blood now.

The last dying ape whimpered on its knees nearby. The sword spun about, guiding Nick's hands, and plunged deep between the creature's shoulder blades.

Nick shivered again, but this time it was a spasm of pleasure. He was beginning to feel the first inklings of returning strength as the blood cooled his sword.

But then the spasm increased, Nick's arms shaking so violently he would lose his grip on his weapon. There was something wrong with the blood. Why hadn't he thought of this? It was tainted.

It was poison.

Nick screamed with a white flash of pain.

Then darkness.

○ Twenty-one

Evan Mills found himself spinning in the middle of nowhere.

At first, the calm now surrounding him had startled him far beyond the violent battle that had gone before. Somehow, Mary Lou had managed to overcome both of the wizards by their own magic. Mills had watched, first in amazement, then in amusement while Rox had been overwhelmed as his every spell grew too large for him to control. From the odd yelps and mutterings that had come out of Obar, he appeared to fare the same. Their spells out of control, the two combatants had to stop their duel. Rox, in fact, appeared to have disappeared altogether. And Mills suddenly found himself with a moment's peace.

The three bodies containing four souls, Obar and Mary Lou, along with Mills and his visiting wizard, spun through one of those places Mills could never quite understand, some other reality that led between the spaces on the dragon's world. It was a place that had no source of light, and yet he could see the others with perfect clarity, a place without color or form or points of reference, yet Mills felt they were moving at tremendous speed.

Even though his was one of the bodies using magic in this place, all this power was still a great mystery to him. Heaven knew Rox wouldn't explain anything if he could help it. It seemed to Mills as though the magicians could do almost anything, except that which the neighbors wished to do most. After all, if the dragon would let them use their magic to travel through a place like this, a place separate from the world of the seven islands, why couldn't they just magically march back to Chestnut Circle and leave all this behind?

The ending of *The Wizard of Oz* came back to him. "You could *always* go home, Dorothy!" the good witch Glinda had announced with her smarmy cheer, as if Dorothy's life was always under her own control. As if any of their lives were ever under their own control, even for a moment. Mills thought about the world he'd left behind; a world full of botched personal relationships, fights with the schoolboard, endless phone calls listening to the angry parents of children he disciplined.

"There's no place like home."

He had just been marking time in that other place. Here, well, he was likely to die at any moment, but it sure as hell was a lot more interesting than what he'd left behind. Mills smiled out at the void. As much as he could, he'd sit back and enjoy the ride.

It was a little like being on a merry-go-round, the three of them bouncing up and down as they whirled about. Obar looked a little glazed. Perhaps Mills looked the same. Mary Lou's frown of concentration was intense enough for all three of them.

Mary Lou was a far different girl than she had been a week ago, before the dragon had brought them to this place. He couldn't help but look at the kids on Chestnut Circle with a teacher's eye. He had thought she would go places, if not for her parents. Now she was in a place where her parents had no control and her power had no limits.

After all, Mary Lou was *the* wizard, the one among them all most favored by the dragon. That was one thing Mills was quite sure of. Of course, he had no idea whether that was a good thing for her, or a bad thing.

He suspected, though, that they would all find out very shortly.

Obar was the ice-cream man.

He remembered how this cycle had begun, how the eye had told him that the dragon had chosen, and opened the portal to bring the chosen from the other world.

Obar had always known this would happen, and yet he had never sufficiently planned for it. The chosen were always the most important. After all, Obar had once been one of the chosen himself; was still one of the chosen, with the dragon's eye clutched in his hand. So Obar had arrived to greet the neighbors and win their trust.

He had picked an image out of the subconscious of one of them. Mrs. Smith, he thought. Even then, she had seemed very important. He had taken that ice-cream wagon out of her thoughts, reproduced it, and rode out among them to dispense frozen treats. It had seemed like a good way to earn their confidence.

Now it was his turn to be frozen. These newcomers had turned this world around. The first time Obar had survived the dragon's fire, he had only to worry about the dragon. Now these neighbors were everywhere, old ladies performing tricks it had taken him years to master, and youngsters making magic he had never even dreamed of.

He was frozen, but the dragon's eye was a part of him. He could use it without thinking. He had had the luxury to explore its limits, and see what else there was available to him in the strangest of worlds. Surely that should give him some advantage still.

He was frozen, and filled with thoughts of his past. He had sought and dismissed the aid of other creatures, the last remnants of other cycles long past. The dragon had brought them here, too. But nonhuman allies proved far too fickle. Their needs were such that they might disappear in the midst of battle, yet they wanted far too much in return. Obar had given up on most of them far before his brother Nunn, preferring to enlist the nearly human Anno or the once human Garo rather than those dark shapes Nunn trafficked with. So he had hoped to enlist the neighbors, but on his own very special terms. But there was never enough time.

He was frozen. So many things were coming to an end. He had never planned it this way. He had hoped at the very least to bring all the children under his sway. He had only time to half prepare Nick, who was to be his assassin, and the secret he had hidden inside Charlie when he had healed the dog back after that first battle. To do more than that would have alerted the neighbors to his designs long before he was ready. It was a subtle business, in a place where there was no longer time for subtlety.

He was frozen. Overwhelmed by his powers, he had stopped

using magic for fear it might destroy him. Mary Lou had done him a service of sorts. It was far easier to rage in battle than to plan for what was to come. Now he had time to think. Battle was a waste of time. Obar was clever enough to find other directions to victory.

Mary Lou could not hold two wizards prisoner forever. As great as her powers were, he or Rox would find a way to break her spell. Never again would they ignore her, or underestimate her abilities.

Her actions would cause quite the opposite. At their first moment of freedom, perhaps Rox and he would have to join together to destroy the greater threat.

Rox was surrounded by darkness.

He realized he must be deep within Mills's consciousness, burrowing into his new host in the same way he had learned to inhabit the out-of-the-way corners of Nunn's mind.

He had no idea how he had gotten here, or indeed how exactly to resurface in Mills's conscious mind. But this was a trap of his own devising. When things had gone out of control, he had rushed here for his own protection. Unthinking, he had panicked and retreated to the dark, those closed-in places where he might never be found.

He was too unused to being free.

Now that he was here in the closed, safe dark, he knew his panic had not begun with this. Rox had been trapped from the first. He had panicked from the moment he had been freed from the safety of Nunn; panicked and tried to gain power— or use power—all to keep himself from looking at his fear.

Now it was different. Only when he felt safe could he think. Only now did he realize what he had to do.

He had learned how to hide within wizards; hide within them and use them to his advantage. That was his strength. He would use Mills so long as he survived. Should Obar win, Rox could exist inside the other wizard just as easily, like a worm gnawing away at Obar's insides. Let Obar and Nunn and this Mary Lou have their great spells, their grand gestures. Of all of them, only Rox was clever enough to survive.

The dragon had allowed him to survive for a reason. The only thing that mattered was revenge. When the dragon burned, it burned for him.

He had acted rashly before and almost lost it all. Obar would most surely die, one way or the other, and Nunn would follow. And Rox would watch it all.

Images swirled through Mary Lou's head.

She could barely believe what she had accomplished. She controlled the others around her, juggling them with her will. The spell she had woven of the three separate magics bound them together, propelling them forward. She was fed by the power of three dragon's eyes, and they opened up her mind.

She didn't see the others merely as figures swirling before her in the mist. She saw images within each of them, as if she perhaps could read their thoughts as well. And when she looked away from them, she saw flashes of the whole world, as if every secret of this place had been spread open before her.

Obar was still the wizard in soiled white, but a second picture overlapped his face, and in that vision, Obar was a spider with a great web, a web that had snared a few but had space for so many more.

Rox's face was hidden from her, but his image was strong. He looked like a snake, burrowed in the ground, but his eyes were ever watchful, his coils gathered and ready to strike.

The image that hovered about Mills was more difficult to decipher at first. She saw a core of light in the middle of darkness; like an ember that still glowed deep in a pile of ashes, but an ember that would not easily be extinguished, and would someday burn anew.

Her mind went searching, her new sight trying to make sense out of the other things new to her life. The Anno were still gathered in the spot where she had left them, watching the spot in their midst where she last had stood.

They wanted to hide her from the world. She saw herself reflected in their eyes. And her vision of the Anno? They looked like mother and children at the same time, wanting both to nurture her and depend on her nurturing in return, forming a closed circle of their own. But their needs were not hers. She had gone beyond sacrifice, to her family or anyone else.

There was one more she could not help but see. The dragon was a fire that burned around them, drawing them all into an ever-tightening circle of flame. Once she had found it, she could not turn away from the creature. It was everywhere.

Her new sight ranged over the whole world. She could see the neighbors, the other wizards, humans and creatures she had met since she had come here. They were not as clear in her sight, but should she grow closer, she was sure she could see into their inner selves as well. In all this world, there was only one she could not look inside.

And that one was Mary Lou.

Mills realized they had to be going home. No, not to Chestnut Circle, but rather to that place at island's center they had claimed for their own. A safe place, if there was such a thing here.

Safety. Security. Mills wouldn't mind a bit of those himself. Ever since Mills and his cohabitants had obtained their eye, they had had nothing but obstacles thrown in their way, as if they were the least favored of all those who held the eyes. Mills had never asked for any of this. All he wanted to do was survive.

On and on they spun through the void. While embarrassing to the wizards, at least the current situation wasn't immediately life-threatening. The stasis was even keeping the pain away; another gift from the dragon, no doubt, although he imagined the gift had been intended for Mary Lou.

His mind was miraculously free of Rox's thoughts. As the battle had grown, Rox's feelings had become almost as disconcerting as sharing his body with another being. Rox's hatred was overwhelming and totally unreasoning. Mills could feel the man's emotions as clearly as his own. Rox still seemed an enigma, a combination of great wisdom and great madness. Mills knew that some of the madness had come from the dragon's eye.

Mary Lou said a single word. Mills thought it was "Now!" but it really didn't matter. The swirling void fragmented around them as if it was as fragile as the mist, dissolving beneath the strength of reality. Mills and the others stood in the middle of the clearing where the neighbors had made their camp.

"Wow, Mary Lou!" Todd called. "You sure know how to make an entrance!"

Obar materialized at Mary Lou's side and fell in a dead

faint. Mills was feeling a little woozy himself. He sensed a warmth in his right hand, a strength that spread up his arm to the rest of his body. He opened his fist and stared at the glowing dragon's eye.

He was tempted for an instant to throw the stone away. But even he—levelheaded Mr. Mills—could not willingly give up that much power. Maybe, if Rox had really gone, he could use the stone along with the other neighbors to help them all survive.

His gaze returned to the stone in his hand, glowing faintly in the last light of evening. It really was quite beautiful.

○ Twenty-two

Hyram Sayre was feeling far too human. The world inside Margaret was both totally irrational and totally familiar; far too comfortable and far too upsetting.

He could not just remember the world of Chestnut Circle, he was there. Margaret must have wanted it so much that she rebuilt the whole neighborhood in her head. Every detail was perfect—the springtime sun, the gentle breeze, the distant sounds of children laughing. He could feel the blades of grass between his toes.

But it was an idealized Chestnut Circle. Never had the houses been so bright, the street so clean and new, the lawns so perfectly green.

Ah, green, wonderful green. To live his life in this one, perfect moment—this moment of green.

Sayre had to get out of here—now. Not since he was married had he felt this combination of bliss and entrapment.

Hyram had to stay calm. He still had godlike powers, after all; no matter how compromised they might be at the moment. There had to be some way to get beyond this. Perhaps, if he reached out beyond Margaret, used her eyes and ears to look at what was really around him, he might regain his bearings.

New people had entered the clearing while he had been exploring Margaret's mind. Mary Lou Dafoe and Evan Mills had joined the other neighbors; all of Chestnut Circle was getting back together.

No one seemed to be paying any attention to him now where he sat, watching the others from the interior of Margaret Furlong's skull. Maybe, for the moment, that was best, giving him a calm place from which he could study his options.

George Blake was talking to Evan Mills.

"I'm new here," Blake was saying. "I don't know what to do."

"We're all new here," Mills replied. "My guess is we'll know what to do, when the time comes."

The neighbors were talking, the way they did back on the Circle.

"Mary Lou!" her mother called to her. "Thank heavens you're back! I don't want you worrying me like that!"

"Rose, I don't think that's such a good idea," Joan Blake said gently.

Rose looked sharply back at her. "What I do with Mary Lou is my business."

Joan shook her head. "Back in the other world, your experience might have helped your kids adjust to the world. But what good is any of our life experience in this place?"

Rose turned on the other woman and started to shout. "What do you know? Your son's become a killer!"

Joan Blake seemed at a loss for words.

"Rose!" Rebecca Jackson leaped in. "That was uncalled for. I've had enough of cruel words in my life. We have to work together, not snap at each other."

Rose Dafoe turned away from both of them. "Raising my family is nobody's business but my own. Isn't that right, Mary Lou?"

Mary Lou didn't respond. Instead, she just stared. Hyram recognized that look. That was the way it was with kids, wasn't it? Sullen and angry, it was no wonder they went out of their way to ruin your lawn.

The conversation swirled around him, just like it would back on Chestnut Circle. Neighbors getting together. Talking about things at a distance, not that they'd ever invite Hyram Sayre to join in. There, George Blake laughed at something Evan Mills said, the two men standing off to one side, ignoring the women. And Rose Dafoe was talking very intently with her husband. He kept shaking his head and looking past her, as if he might find some way to escape.

It was just like life before they came here. The place might be different, but the people were the same.

But even this spot was not that different from the neighborhood. Margaret's vision of the Circle seemed to overlay his own. The patchy grass and bare earth of the clearing was transformed into the manicured green lawn and neat pavement of the neighborhood. The white-board-and-brick houses were just behind him. It was at times like this he was glad he'd come to Chestnut Circle, even if he couldn't fix his lawn. Another peaceful day was coming to a close. He could smell the backyard barbecue.

But the neighbors were getting together. Why didn't they invite him? Sure, he had slammed the door in George's face. And he had threatened Joan with a lawsuit if she couldn't keep her kid off his lawn. She protested that it wouldn't have been Nick, he wasn't that kind of boy. Hah! He knew all the kids were doing it. After all, they were all the same.

But that had all happened on a different world. Why didn't they invite him now?

Except, the more he looked at the others, the more it looked like the same world all over again, the women in their bright spring colors, the men ready to find an excuse to run off to play a round of golf. If George Blake would turn around, Hyram was sure his apron would read DAD'S THE CHEF!

No! This was Margaret's vision. Could he help it if it appealed to a part of him as well? The house, the yard, the total devotion to the lawn; it was always inside him, and it longed to come out, to wrap him in the warm tendrils of suburbia. But he had to keep reminding himself that he had found a greater purpose here.

"Excuse me, mister?"

He looked up at one of the younger boys. Bobby. Bobby Furlong. That was his name.

"Do you think I could talk to my mother?" he asked. Of course! Bobby was Margaret's son. He had been asking Hyram questions before. Where *was* his mind wandering?

For now, he needed to concentrate on this young man in front of him. What would be the best way to answer?

"You could talk to her," Hyram ventured after a moment's thought, "and she might be able to hear you, but I don't think she'll answer back. I'm right here and she hasn't tried to talk to me. I don't think she wants to speak to anyone."

Bobby nodded and tried to smile.

"Mom? If you can hear me, I'd like you to come out from wherever you are. I wish you were here—we all do. There's a lot we have to do. But you have to be a real person in a real world. With Dad gone . . .'' He looked away.

Hyram thought Bobby might start to cry, but instead he looked back in his mother's eyes.

"I don't want to lose you, too,'' he added, his voice cracking halfway through.

"Leo?'' Margaret replied softly.

Bobby looked at the ground. "I don't know what else to say.'' He glanced up. "Thanks for letting me talk.''

Hyram didn't know what to say, either. He was afraid that most of Margaret's thoughts were elsewhere, lost in that Chestnut Circle that never was. Maybe a little part of her heard, though. He hoped her son could get through to her in a way that Hyram couldn't.

"No problem,'' Hyram blurted out at last. Bobby nodded and turned away, that ugly dog of his trailing behind him.

Kids and dogs. For once Hyram didn't feel like shouting at them.

He glanced around the clearing. No one had taken much notice of Bobby and Hyram's little talk. But what else could he expect? No one paid attention to him because he sat quietly in their midst, his personality hidden inside a woman whose own utterances made no sense. If he wanted their recognition, he would have to earn it.

"Pardon me,'' Hyram announced.

"Margaret, you wanted to say something?'' Rebecca Jackson asked.

It was a first step. But he didn't feel comfortable, staring up at everyone. He willed the woman's body to stand. Somewhat awkwardly, the body complied.

"No,'' he answered simply, "not Margaret.''

"Hyram?'' Joan Blake asked. "You're still in there?''

Hyram felt a flare of anger. Of course he was still in here! Where else would he go? But then he realized, unless he spoke out, there was no way for the others to know that.

"Hyram Sayre?'' Mrs. Smith called from the other side of the clearing. "Where?''

Three of the neighbors all answered before Hyram got the chance, all talking about how Sayre had somehow gotten trapped inside Margaret while trying to help her. Some of the details were a little off, but the gist of it was fine.

He found himself flattered by all the attention.

Mrs. Smith floated through the crowd to Hyram's side. "I'm sorry, with Nunn here, I'm afraid I've neglected our other problems. Perhaps I can help to disentangle the two of you."

She stared at him for a long moment. Sayre felt a vague stirring deep inside. It felt a bit like an upset stomach.

Mrs. Smith frowned and shook her head. "I'm afraid I can't get a handle on this," she admitted. "Maybe if I got help from Todd and Mary Lou."

She called to the two youngsters, and they were soon both by her side. Not that either one of them looked like they wanted to be there. Todd looked impatient, like he'd rather be off someplace in his hot rod, while Mary Lou looked like she barely even knew this place existed.

"I want to surround Hyram Sayre's spirit and free it from Margaret's body. I'm going to try to lift him upward and forward, out of Margaret Furlong entirely. I'd like you to do this with me."

Todd shrugged. "I can try."

Mary Lou only nodded.

The three of them all held their jewels forward in their fists and stared at him. Perhaps, Hyram thought, there was such a thing as too much attention.

Margaret screamed.

"Stop!" he shouted with her voice.

He had only felt the pressure for a second, but it had been greater than the agony that came from his death at the hands of the Captain, not so much the feeling of being gutted as being turned inside out, flipflopping his internal organs for his skin.

It took Sayre a moment to catch his breath. When he did, he managed a halting explanation. "I feel—both of us feel—like we're being torn apart."

Mrs. Smith frowned. "This is all wrong. We might end up killing both of them."

Mary Lou shook her head. "It's something about Margaret. It's like she doesn't want to let him go."

Mrs. Smith considered that for a moment before replying. "All of us have special powers. Margaret's seems to be the ability to repel our magic."

"Mrs. Furlong is stronger than all of us?" Todd asked in disbelief.

"Only in this one very special way," Mrs. Smith agreed. "Apparently, all of us here have very special strengths. Margaret's strength strikes me as almost—hysterical in its intensity."

"She always was an opinionated woman," Rose Dafoe added flatly, as if that might explain everything.

Hyram realized that meant that none of the neighbors could help him. He would have to find the answer within himself. But to do that, he thought it best to get away from reminders of old houses, lives, and lawns.

"I have to leave," he said to the others.

"Margaret," Rose called with alarm, "you're glowing!"

"What do you mean, Leo?"

He almost put a hand over Margaret's mouth. He hadn't meant to call Rose that.

"Well," Rose replied, "you've turned green."

Hyram suddenly felt very defensive. "Stranger things have happened." That just meant his own power was manifesting itself throughout Margaret now, something that might actually be a positive sign. His new power had always helped him as well as others in the past.

"But why do you have to go?" Joan asked.

Hyram shrugged. Since the change, he had worked much more by intuition. He just knew it was time to go. He simply needed to go somewhere quiet, where he could think of a way to cure them both.

With that, Hyram rose into the sky. His new body came along easily, its green glow illuminating the upturned faces of the neighbors below.

He remembered sometimes, back in the old world, when his stubborn lawn was getting the best of him, he would look up into the sky and wish he could just fly away. And now he could. He could fly until his troubles were frozen away by the depths of space, or burned to cinders in the sun. He could fly forever, and fulfill his every dream.

He just never realized he was going to bring Margaret Furlong along.

• • •

Snake was truly lost. He had seen nothing but trees behind trees that looked exactly like other trees since he had begun his hurried flight; hundreds, maybe thousands of the huge things, always in his way, so he had to dodge around them, tripping on hidden roots and stones, but always stumbling forward to run some more.

He had to stop at last. He didn't know what hurt worse, his lungs or the muscles in his legs. At least there was no sign of pursuit. And not much sign of anything else, either. With luck like this, he could starve to death all by himself.

To top it off, night was falling. Whatever sunlight managed to get in from overhead was fading fast, the greens and browns of the forest turning to grey. Snake looked at the nearest of the surrounding trees, dark, looming shapes that he'd be unable to see at all in a minute.

Just because he hadn't met any animals yet who were likely to rip out his throat didn't mean there wouldn't be some around when the place got good and dark and he could no longer run. The bloody trees were far too big around to climb. There wasn't a sign of a cave or some other place where he might hole up and defend himself. And if he built a fire, it would lead the others right to him.

But if there was one thing Snake had going for him, it was his anger. His attitude, and everything he'd done about it in this place, was so fucking negative that it was even beginning to piss *him* off.

"Hell, Snake," he murmured. "What's got into you? There isn't a thing in this world can get the better of you."

The sound of his own voice cheered him. At least it was a noise he knew in this godforsaken wilderness. This wasn't the first time he'd seen a setback in his plans, and probably wouldn't be the last.

"Snake's slippery enough to come out on top!" He chuckled. That's where he'd gotten his name, after all. To return the favor, of course, he'd slit the throat of the jackass who named him. The thought of slitting throats cheered him even more.

"A little blood'll set things right!" By all rights, he should be slitting a few more people's throats at this very minute, and then teaching his daughter a lesson or two besides.

"A little blood, a little boff, and Snake's in his glory!" he shouted to the gathering gloom. It was all this damn island's

fault. And that damned wizard Nunn. Wizards! When they
threatened you with magic, all sense went out the window.
Otherwise, Snake would never have come to a place like this
without a couple of dozen men to back him up.

"A pox on wizards!" Snake called to the night. "Catch
'em by surprise, they'll bleed as well as anyone!"

There. He was already breathing easier. Now, if he could
only find something to drink, he could make a night of it.
Failing that, though, he'd better find a good tree to put at his
back before the light was completely gone.

A shadow fell over his face, blocking out what little light
was left in the day.

"What we got here?" some new voice asked.

Snake froze. He stopped for a second and *bang!* They found
him. So much for Snake the escape artist.

Well, he still had his knife. He put his hand around the hilt,
but kept the thing stuck in his belt for now.

"Just some poor fool who's lost his way in the woods."
He smiled like an idiot, still not looking straight at his accuser.
That sort of thing always put the other guy off his guard.
"Don't want to be in the woods at night."

The other man chuckled at that. "Man, I can agree with you
there. Who would want to live in a place like this?"

That wasn't quite the reply Snake was expecting. He turned
to see a figure standing close behind him. It was difficult to
see the fellow in the gathering gloom, but at first glance he
didn't look like anything special, maybe an inch or two taller
than Snake, maybe a little thinner. And he didn't look like any
of the folks Snake had left behind when he started running.
Maybe, if this character was as lost as he was, Snake could
get the drop on him. Maybe he could cut the stranger's throat
just for sport.

"Name's Carl," the newcomer said. "And I wouldn't try
anything."

Snake slipped his hand from his knife and pretended he was
scratching his belly. "What d'you mean?"

Carl laughed at that. "I can see the knife. If someone surprised me in the middle of nowhere, I know just what I'd do."

Snake would have to be a little more careful. He decided
he'd let Carl make the next move.

"You were making a bit of noise, my friend," Carl said.

"Decided I'd come over and see what all the shouting was about." Carl shook his head. "I'm new here. Too bad you don't know your way around. I need somebody who knows this place."

Was this Carl going to up and *dismiss* him? Snake had had enough of the stranger's lip. "I can show you a lot more interesting things than this bloody island."

"Really? That's the first interesting thing I've heard. This place is so big, it's almost overwhelming. All these possibilities." He turned away from Snake to survey the forest.

It was the opening Snake had been waiting for. He took a single step behind Carl. In an instant Snake's knife was at the other man's throat. "I can talk just as fancy as you." Snake grinned at the gathering gloom. "Now we'll see who gives the orders."

"I don't think there's any doubt about that." Carl lifted his fist where Snake could see it. He slowly opened his hand. There, set in the middle of his palm, was a glowing green stone.

That took the smile right off Snake's face. "Oh, Lord. You're one of them. Save me from wizards evermore."

Carl laughed and turned back toward him as Snake dropped the knife. Carl opened both his hands so that Snake could get a good look at the two dragon's eyes, set in Carl's palms the same way they had been with Nunn. Like any wizard, Carl wanted to flaunt his magic. Snake expected a demonstration. He hoped he could stand the pain.

A lance of green fire missed his nose by an inch. Whatever was left of Snake's fighting spirit just went out to sea.

He sank to his knees. "Oh, hell," he said with a groan. "Do what you will with me. If you kill me now, at least I'll get a rest."

"Oh, I don't kill people. I let them suffer first." Carl chuckled. "Why not?"

Snake wouldn't give him any more satisfaction. He'd groveled enough. Instead, he merely shook his head.

"What?" Carl demanded. "What are you talking about?"

"But . . ." Snake looked up at the other man. Was this some sort of game the magician was playing? Snake hadn't said a word.

"What are you doing inside me anyway?" Carl put his

hands up to either side of his skull. "Leo, I want you out of my head!"

Leo? Who was Leo? This wizard was even crazier than Nunn.

Snake stood again. Carl didn't even seem to notice.

"I don't want to talk about it!" Carl shouted. "I'm in control now!"

Snake took a step away. A line of green fire burned the dead leaves before him.

Carl was looking straight at him. "You're not going anywhere! I just have to have a little discussion. . . ." He paused and frowned. "Well, why do you have to know my business anyway?"

Carl shouted a string of words, sometimes making it halfway through a sentence before starting again. Snake could make no sense of it. As far as he could tell, Carl was arguing with himself. Occasionally, fire would erupt from one or the other of his gems, shot off in no particular direction.

It had been so quiet when he was lost in the woods. Maybe, Snake thought, there were things far worse than being alone.

Jason had slipped away from the clearing to stand in the woods. He had wanted so badly to rejoin his parents, and be with his old friends and neighbors again.

It had been all right as long as he was moving, helping them to find Mrs. Furlong. But after that, the others didn't need him anymore. They just treated him like Jason, the kid from back on Chestnut Circle.

And he wasn't Jason anymore. Well, that wasn't exactly true. There was still a lot of Jason in him. But there were new parts of him, too.

It got worse still after they had brought Mrs. Furlong back to the clearing. The neighbors started arguing about this and that, things that as far as Jason was concerned weren't important at all. Why couldn't they stop for a minute to listen to the song of the wind, the whisper of water flowing underground, the quietly reassuring chatter of the roots that held the island together?

They couldn't hear, because they weren't the Oomgosh.

It was somewhat better here, just outside the clearing. Jason felt that he could breathe again. The forest sounds were no longer masked by human speech, but he could still hear the neighbors talking and arguing and laughing, faintly in the distance, to remind him where he had come from.

Raven flew down to him out of the trees.

"Ah, my Oomgosh!" the bird called. "So we are on our own again?"

"I guess so," Jason agreed. "My home's out here now."

"Raven always knew that you would see the light. But come! We have work to do!"

"We do?"

"Important times are coming!" Raven cawed.

"And the Oomgosh has important things to do?" Jason asked.

The bird chuckled as it wheeled about in the air. "After Raven, my Oomgosh, you are the most important of all!"

◯ Twenty-three

Nunn was never worried, until now.

He had kept himself alive by shifting his being largely into that other plane of existence that occurred here, side by side with reality. Mastery of that other plane, that second reality, was a key to working magic here. Nunn had often thought of it as the dragon's plane.

Or the dragon's reality.

He had no other option but to escape here when he had been attacked by Carl. But he felt especially vulnerable in this place, with the dragon so close.

He had, of course, managed to keep a window open to the more normal world, a window that allowed him some proximity to another dragon's eye, and also a chance to stay, invisible, in the middle of all those the dragon had chosen for this cycle, waiting for an opportunity to gain back the power he had lost.

But there were problems with this existence. The laws of this place were different. Sometimes the world he viewed through the window sped on by as if everyone was in a race. At others, no one moved at all, frozen like statues in an eternal moment. Far worse, though, were the times he simply lost sight of things, a blank spot between one view of the world and the next.

It frightened him when he wasn't able to concentrate. His thoughts would become as invisible as the rest of him. He would vanish like the mist. The great and powerful Nunn would fade away like a whisper on the wind.

He would have to return to a physical state soon. Ideally, he would find a dragon's eye he could steal to give him an advantage. He imagined that Mrs. Smith would expect no less from him.

So he watched and waited, observing the drama that went on in the clearing as all those innocent fools tried to prepare for what was to come. Now and then he would even feel a bit of sympathy for their plight. That worried him, too. Could his proximity to Mrs. Smith's stone cause her attitudes to bleed over to him as well?

All things were possible. That was what he was counting on. Once he had a dragon's eye in his hand, all would be right again.

And then an opportunity presented itself, as he surely knew it would.

"Well," Rose Dafoe said, "maybe now we'll get some peace around here."

Sometimes, Mary Lou wished her mother would just shut up. Margaret Furlong had flown up into the sky until she was no more than a tiny green speck, one more star among the multitude. The whole thing had really been quite beautiful, except maybe to her mother.

Night had taken over most of the sky, with only a thin band of red and yellow left on the horizon. Stanley had grabbed a couple of the neighbors as soon as Hyram and Margaret had made their exit, and he was instructing them on the building and lighting of fires.

"Well, they both did talk too much," Rose added defensively when nobody agreed with her.

"Another one of us is gone," Rebecca Jackson pointed out. "This place seems to take us, one by one."

"Margaret might be better off this way," Rebecca reasoned. "At least she's got Hyram to look after her."

"But what about Bobby?" Joan Blake asked. "Both his parents are gone now."

"We'll have to take care of him," Mrs. Smith said. "I think we all need to be family if we're going to survive."

Mary Lou wondered if there was some way she could help. She knew one thing. If they were going to be family, they'd have to do it in some new way where people were honest with each other and didn't hide their secrets from the world.

Mary Lou wished that Todd would open up about what was

troubling him. From the way he looked toward the forest, the way the corner of his mouth twitched, even the sad expression in his eyes when he looked at Sala, Todd looked as upset as any time she had ever seen him.

She looked around the clearing. Obar still lay where he had fallen. No one had made any attempt to move him.

Mr. Mills was all over the place, talking with everyone, offering to help with anything that came up, acting like it had been years rather than days since he'd last seen the neighbors. He had stuck his dragon's eye in his pocket and was quite cheerfully ignoring it.

Rox may have retreated, but Mary Lou was quite sure he was still with Mills, and would reemerge as soon as he saw an opportunity. And she could vaguely sense Nunn somewhere nearby Mrs. Smith. She realized that all but two of the dragon's eyes were in this clearing now, as well as all three of the old wizards who first held the dragon's eyes when they arrived. All three of the wizards had been deprived of their powers for now, but she did not think any of them were defeated.

Todd turned to Mrs. Smith. "It's quiet now. What if I were to just go and explore?"

Sala tugged at his sleeve. "I don't know. You only have one eye. He has two."

Todd shook his head. "We have to get your father, too."

Mrs. Smith answered, "If anyone knows, it will be Mary Lou." The older woman looked straight at her. "We were gathering here to fight the dragon. Do we still have time?"

Mary Lou was startled that Mrs. Smith would turn to her. She was almost as startled that she had an answer. "The dragon won't come until certain conditions are met." She searched her thoughts for the reason behind her answer, but could find nothing more. "I don't really know what the conditions are. I just know they aren't here yet."

That seemed to satisfy Todd. "So the sooner we get out and back, the better."

"But Sala is right," Mary Lou pointed out. "Even though your father has less experience than you, he is twice as powerful."

"So I'll need someone else to go with me," Todd agreed. "Will you come, Mary Lou?"

The answer appeared in her head with a frightening certainty. "No—I think my place is—here, with Mrs. Smith and the others."

"I'll go." Mr. Mills stepped forward. "I may not know much about the eyes, but I probably know as much as your father. I need some practice using the thing without the wizard around."

"Is there some way we can get Nick back here?" George Blake asked. "Now that we have Obar, maybe we can get rid of that sword."

Mrs. Smith frowned at that. "I don't know if we can control Obar. If we were to bring Nick here now, the magician might use him against us."

Rose gasped as if such a thing was unthinkable.

"I think—no one should leave here for too long," Mary Lou interjected. "We'll see Nick again—when the time is right." The words were pouring out of her mouth because she was supposed to say them. But even she didn't know what they meant.

Todd nodded. "Sala! Come with us!" He took the young woman's hand. It was obvious that the two really cared for each other.

Sometimes, Mary Lou wished Garo could have been real— in more ways than one.

"We'll stay in touch," Todd called to her, "and be back as soon as we finish our business."

Then the three of them were gone. For some reason, the dragon inside of her didn't object.

"Nunn!" an older man's voice called. "It's Nunn!"

Mary Lou looked across the clearing. Obar was awake.

"Nunn! Get away from me! He's after my jewel!"

Mary Lou thought her mother's hopes for peace were gone forever.

Nick was dying. Nick was burning.

He opened his eyes and his whole body, his arms, his legs, his torso, everything was encased in flame. He opened his mouth to scream, and fire rushed in to sear his mouth and throat, roasting him inside and out.

He opened his mouth, but there was no sound.

He opened his eyes. He was sitting up in the middle of

camp, surrounded by soldiers and wolves. There was no fire, but he could see his arms were shaking and covered with sweat.

He had been sure that Zachs had him, but the fire demon was only in his dreams.

His poisoned dreams.

Pator was at his side. "Good. You're awake." He knelt down next to Nick. "Drink this." He lifted a hollow gourd to Nick's lips. Nick did what he was told. Water had never tasted so wonderful.

He waved the gourd away when he started to choke. How long had it been since he had last had a drink of water?

Pator placed the half-full gourd on the ground by Nick's side. "We weren't sure you were going to recover."

"The poison," Nick managed. His throat did indeed feel as though it had been scorched by fire. There had been a great shock to both Nick and the blade when the tainted blood had been sucked into the sword. The poison had repelled his sword in a way even the fire could not do. But his sword had taken in some of the poison first, and passed it on to Nick.

Pator nodded.

"Because—of the sword," Nick said haltingly, "I don't think I was—poisoned in the same way as the others." He looked up at Pator, the question in his eyes, the only question that mattered. "Because of—the sword—"

"I wrapped the sword in a cloth," Pator explained. "I didn't want to touch it." He pointed to his right.

The sword lay against one of the trees, about a dozen feet away. Nick was too weak even to crawl to it. He wanted to ask one of the others to bring it to him—now.

"You were good—to keep your distance," Nick said instead. "Even now, I long to touch it."

"And have it do to me what it's done to you?" Pator laughed. "No offense, but we have enough madmen in our midst as it is."

Nick was having trouble listening. Now that he could see the sword, he was having difficulty thinking about anything else. He and the sword had to be together. The dozen-feet distance between them was beyond tolerance!

"Now this is a sweet scene."

"Our captain is back!" Umar called from the edge of the clearing.

"I see we have a visitor."

"Nick is no visitor!" Umar called with perhaps too much enthusiasm. "Nick is a hero!"

"We were under attack," Pator replied to the Captain's confused expression. "It was only through Nick's leadership that we repelled them. We lost a couple, but the others lost three times that many."

"Leadership?" He stood over Nick, staring down at him with an odd half smile. "You have hidden talents, then." He scuffed one of his boots on the ground close by Nick's leg. "A little quirk of mine I think you should know. When I pick someone to join my troops, I don't want them to usurp my authority. I've worked all my life to be a despot, after all." He laughed like it was all a joke, and turned to look at Pator. "But I wasn't talking about Nick at all. He's obviously been accepted into the company. In fact he's making you all into a bunch of nursemaids. No, I was talking about that damn bird."

"Bird?" Pator replied as he and all the others looked to where their captain pointed.

There, at the edge of the camp, on the lowest branch of one of the great trees, sat a great, white owl.

This wizard business was a piece of cake.

Well, there was that momentary problem with Leo. Carl had been quite surprised when *he* showed up. Leo seemed to have been part of the package with the stones; when you got one, the other came along. Carl guessed that as a wizard you still had to take the bad with the good. But Leo always had been a pantywaist. He crumbled easily under Carl's abuse, and went scurrying back to whatever hidey-hole he had just crawled out of. As soon as Carl got a real grip on using these dragon's eyes, he'd burn Leo right out of him.

But he had more important things to attend to right now. Carl would get an army all his own, even if he had to do it one person at a time.

Just look at this Snake character. Once he knew Carl was a wizard, he was ready to do just about anything.

"So what can you do for me?" Carl asked, his hands casually open, gems glowing in the gathering gloom. They could really use some light around here. And who better to bring light than a wizard? He raised his two hands and pointed them at the sky a few feet above his head. Twin lines of green met to produce a tiny ball of flame. Too small, really, the size of a Ping-Pong ball, it hardly gave out any light at all.

Well, Carl could fix that. He told his jewels to shoot again, and the fiery globe grew to the size of a tennis ball. That gave off a little light, but he could do better still.

Snake watched silently as Carl sent another burst of power to the globe. Not only was he producing light, he was impressing the hell out of this guy. Well, Carl would show him what kind of show he could put on.

The globe had grown to the size of a basketball, and it lit the whole area here beneath the trees.

"Nice, don't you think?" Carl asked, but Snake was still staring at the fiery globe above. Carl looked up and saw it had grown to the size of a beach ball, and it was growing still. How would he stop it? Carl had no idea how to take any of the magic back.

The fire kept on growing, the size of a medicine ball now. If anything, it seemed to be burning faster than before. Soon, it would probably burn the trees on either side, not to mention the ground on which Carl and Snake now stood. He had to do something, and quickly.

Well, he had made the thing. Couldn't he order it around?

"Get the hell out of here!" he called.

With that, the fireball rushed up past the trees into the night sky. If it kept expanding, he might add a new sun in the sky.

Carl took a deep breath. That may have been a bit too impressive even for him. Still, he wouldn't let Snake know that.

"That's only the beginning of what I can do," he said modestly.

"I can do things for you, too," Snake answered quickly. "I've got friends back at the ship. They'll help you, too."

A ship? Now that, Carl thought, was an idea. Maybe, instead of an army, he'd get a navy. At least he'd be able to get out of these damned woods.

It was too dark and close in this place. He'd seen the other wizards flying around. There wasn't any reason he couldn't do that, too. Of course, he'd have to bring his new assistant along,

too. Maybe they could find a place with a bit more light.
Maybe they could even find Snake's ship.

"Come on. I'm going to take you on a little trip."

"You're going to get us out of here?" Snake asked doubt-
fully.

"Yeah. You got a problem with that?"

"No!" Snake assured him. "Whatever you want." It was
too dark now for Carl to see the expression on the other man's
face. Carl hoped it was suitably fearful.

"Now!" Carl announced as he grabbed the other man's
arm. His feet left the ground, but it was hard to see where he
was going. Carl had wanted flying to be more fun than this.
But at least Snake's scream as they took off was really satisfying.

Leo Furlong didn't know a lot about what had happened to
him. He didn't really know if he was even still alive. But he
knew it was time to make a decision.

It had seemed safe inside Nunn; there were no choices to
be made then. The wizard's power had been so overwhelming,
it was like he had been defeated before he'd begun. So he had
amused himself by exploring this strange new world within
Nunn's magical brain. And when he found himself put to occasional use by the wizard, it was a small price to pay.

Now all that had changed. Through some trick of this place,
he found himself trapped within Carl Jackson, his know-
nothing neighbor. Sure, Carl had somehow gotten Nunn's
gems of power. But, you put a tuxedo on a mule, it was still
a mule.

The world Leo had created for himself here inside had
crumbled, his invented pastimes now no more than hollow
shells. Another minute attached to Carl Jackson? Even Leo
had his limits. And, if Carl Jackson could beat Nunn, anything
was possible.

Others had broken out of this magical prison before. Maybe
Leo still wasn't too late to help himself.

When he'd first discovered Carl, Leo had gotten a bit upset.
He'd confronted him in anger, and nothing more came of it
than a brief argument. Carl thought he had shouted him down.
Leo would let Carl go on thinking that, until he saw his chance.

In the meantime he experimented, subtly altering Carl's fire spell so that the blazing ball would not stop growing. Leo had thought that was hilarious. Better yet, it proved that he could influence anything Carl might do.

They were flying now. Leo had to admit that he rather liked it. He'd wait a bit before he made his next move. After all, if he was careful, maybe he could do more than just escape. Maybe he could take a dragon's eye or two along as well.

O Twenty-four

Nick couldn't walk. Nick had to walk. Nick would die if he couldn't walk.

The sword was calling him. Not that the piece of metal made any sound. Their need to be together was deeper than mere noise. Without Nick to guide it, the sword was nothing but a piece of metal. And without the sword, Nick was—

He was nothing more than a boy, growing up on Chestnut Circle, a boy with too much imagination, according to his father. He was a boy whose worst problem was that his father had left him and his mother; a boy whose biggest concern was whether or not his mom would let him borrow the car on a Saturday night. He was a boy who knew nothing at all.

How Nick wished he could be that boy again.

But that boy was gone, wiped out by Nick's need for the sword, a need he could feel in every muscle of his body, from the grinding in his stomach to the pounding in his head.

He managed to roll from his back to his stomach. If he lifted his head up, he could see the sword against the tree, half in shadow from the bonfire the others had built at the center of camp. His weapon was still wrapped in the rough cloth Pator had used to protect himself. And it was still twenty feet away.

He could manage twenty feet. If Nick couldn't walk there, he could crawl. He pushed himself up to his elbows and knees. His arms shook with the effort, but if he concentrated, he could do it. Right arm, right leg, left arm, left leg, then again, right arm, leg—

His left arm collapsed beneath him. His face fell in the dirt. He tried to push himself up again, but there was no strength left. He could barely lift his head.

The sword was hardly any closer at all; he hadn't managed to crawl more than a couple of feet. Maybe, if his hands and feet had enough strength left in them, he could drag himself there on his belly.

A boot stepped in front of his head.

"Can I help you with something?"

Nick tried to look up, but he could see no higher than the man's waist. The man squatted down to get closer to Nick. It was the Captain. His scars crinkled when he smiled.

"You need something, don't you?" the Captain asked.

He was taunting Nick. It must have been obvious to everyone what he needed. But Nick had no energy to fight back.

"S-sword," he managed.

"Your sword?" the Captain replied in mock surprise. "Well, I guess that could be arranged."

"Captain?" Pator asked from somewhere beyond Nick's limited field of vision. "Do you think that's wise?"

The Captain looked away from Nick and frowned. "Wise? What good is an unarmed soldier? Who am I to separate a man from his blade?"

Nick opened his mouth to tell the Captain to hurry, but he could no longer keep his head up. His mouth was filled with dirt.

"Oh dear," the Captain said above him. "We'd better get that sword for you now."

Nick could hear the Captain's boots move away over the hard-packed ground, then come back in his direction.

"Open your hand," the Captain said when he was directly above him. Nick did as he was told.

He felt the heavy weight of metal being pressed into his hand; his sword at last. But something kept his flesh from touching the metal. The sword was still wrapped in its cloth. What kind of joke was this? A sob welled out of his throat from somewhere deep inside.

But he had the sword. He gripped the cloth-wrapped hilt as hard as he could and dragged the blade across the ground close to his head so that he might see it. There! He had to stop for a moment and catch his breath, but the sword was very loosely wrapped by the cloth. If he pushed at the bottom edge of the wrapping with his thumb and moved it just a bit, he might actually be able to touch his weapon. He shifted his grip so that he could clearly see his thumb. The cloth was slippery against the hilt. He had to pause to rest twice more, but he was getting the rough material to move.

"Captain?" Pator asked from somewhere above. "Maybe we should—"

"Never come between a man and his weapon, Pator," the Captain said sternly. "I thought you would understand something like that."

No doubt everyone in the camp was staring at Nick now. Well, he would show them all what he could do. He pushed at the cloth one more time, and his thumb brushed against the leather of the hilt.

He felt the warmth immediately, the increase in energy a moment later. Even without blood, the sword gave him strength. A few seconds' contact with the blade, and he was able once again to rise to his elbows and his knees.

"There," the Captain commented. "What did I tell you? In no time at all, Nick will be back in action."

Nick pushed himself back so that he was upright on his knees. He shook the sword free of the cloth. The metal reflected the firelight. Flames seemed to dance along the blade.

He stood. But the warmth only went so far. His head still swam. He needed more.

"Blood," he whispered.

"Would you like mine?" the Captain asked. "Sorry, you can't have it. Let's see." He pointed to a wolf. "You there."

The wolf looked up from where it had been toying with a rodent about the size of a rabbit. The thing was wounded, but it was still alive.

"We need that," the Captain announced.

The wolf growled back at him.

"Would you rather volunteer your own blood to help Nick and his sword?"

The wolf clamped its jaws around one of the small creature's back paws and tossed it at the Captain.

"Excellent!" the Captain cried, throwing the squealing thing at Nick as soon as he had it in his hands. "Catch!"

Nick caught it on the end of his sword.

Blood flowed from the rodent, and warmth flowed into Nick. The sheer pleasure of it almost made him fall back to his knees. The rodent was reduced to a shriveled husk in an instant. But Nick could stand now without shaking. It was a beginning. But he needed more.

He looked around the clearing. Every eye, both human and wolf, looked back at him.

"More."

He took a step forward and almost stumbled. He still wasn't as sure on his feet as he would like. His sword required nourishment.

Pator stood at the Captain's side. Of all the faces that watched Nick, only he looked concerned.

"Captain, can't we help him?"

"I've never seen you so worried, Pator," the Captain said with his usual half smile. "Don't you think a good warrior should make it on his own?"

Nick had had about enough of the Captain. If he had to take somebody's blood, he knew exactly who he would choose. Sword raised before him, he took a step toward their leader.

"He's going through a lot," Pator replied. "He's still only a boy."

The Captain frowned at that. "Maybe then he doesn't deserve to survive."

"He's a good fighter when he's healthy," Pator added quickly. "We can use him."

The Captain grinned suddenly at Nick. "I daresay he's a better fighter than you, Pator. Why don't you give him a hand?"

With that, the Captain stepped behind Pator and pushed him straight toward Nick. Pator, surprised and off balance, stumbled forward. Nick froze, trying to control the blade before him and somehow turn it aside.

He didn't have the strength. The sword almost leaped from Nick's hands as it sank deep into Pator's stomach.

"Oh God," Pator managed before the death spasms overtook him. The one man who had tried to be Nick's friend, and the sword had taken his life. Nick wished there was something he could say, but his head was filled with flashes of light. His muscles shook with power. It didn't matter. Nothing mattered. Nick needed the blood.

The camp was silent as Pator shriveled on the sword, his blood sucked noisily within the enchanted metal. Nick could barely stand the power surging into him. His eyes rolled back in his head. His breathing came in short gasps. He was whole again; better than whole.

Then the sword was still.

"Well, Nick." The Captain cheerfully filled the silence. "You've killed my lieutenant. You know what that means?"

Nick had no idea. That he should die in turn? Even with this blade in his hand, he'd be no match for the group of humans and wolves against him. He shook his head as Pator's remains slid from the sword.

"It means you have to take his place," the Captain continued as if this were the most logical thing in the world. "It's an ancient rule of some sort, I think. I hope you're up to it."

Nick decided he would have to be; one word from the Captain, and the whole army was against him. But maybe, when the time was right, he and the Captain could have a little time alone.

Nick thought his sword would like that very much.

"There!" Snake called. He spotted the mostly dark shape floating in the water below. The crew had left only one torch burning on the main deck. Snake guessed they wisely didn't want to call undue attention to themselves in these strange waters.

"The ship?" Carl asked.

What else could it be? But Snake held his tongue. "Right below."

"Always wanted to be Captain of a ship," Carl the wizard agreed.

Snake nodded his head. Anything to stop this flying.

Carl whooped. "All right, there, matey! Coming in for a landing!"

He thought Carl was having a bit too much fun with the sailor talk. Still, you didn't argue with a wizard. At least when he could watch you. Sooner or later Carl had to sleep. Nunn had set up protections for that sort of an attack, but a low-grade wizard like Carl would never think of it. Snake, on the other hand, had thought a lot about it, every single minute they'd been in the air.

They started down toward the ship with a sickening lurch. This time, Snake managed not to scream.

"Closer, a little closer," Carl murmured. "Gently now."

Snake's feet hit the deck with a teeth-jarring thump.

"A little harder than I would have liked," Carl admitted. "I'll get better with practice."

"What the hell was that?" All three of the men Snake had left with the ship came running out at once. Patch came first, swinging his head quickly right and left to take in everything with his good eye. The Rat was second, short but quick, he quickly passed his fellows to reach the middle of the deck. Old Bill was last. Old Bill was always last. Slow and steady, his main talent seemed to be the ability to live forever. All three had been left behind for a reason; the Patch for his eyesight, the Rat for his height, Old Bill because no one could stand to wait for him.

Snake walked forward so that his face shone in the torchlight. "It's me."

All three of his men started talking at once, saying how good it was to see him and asking what the hell was going on. Snake raised a hand for silence.

"I brought someone with me," he added. He looked back at Carl and waved him forward.

"Four of you in all, hey?" Carl said with a grin. "A real fighting force. Don't worry. You'll like working for me."

"Work for you?" the Rat inquired. "Why should we?"

Snake sighed. "Take a look at his hands, boys."

Carl helpfully held them up.

"Just like Nunn," Old Bill added for anyone who couldn't notice the obvious.

"That's not so bad." Patch nodded. "With a wizard's help, we can sail away from here."

Why hadn't Snake thought of that? If he could get this wizard out on the high seas where he'd be far away from anything and anyone he knew, he might make it even easier to kill him. Then they could dig those stones out of his hands at their leisure. Even if their magic didn't work for the likes of Snake, he could always sell them to somebody when they got back to port.

"Just up and leave everybody behind?" Carl asked with a grin. "I sort of like that. Of course, there were a couple of people I was going to kill, but they can wait." He chuckled. "After all, maybe something else will kill them for me."

"Around here," Snake agreed, "that's almost a guarantee.

But Patch here's got the idea! You can sail with us back to our home port, an island with real civilization. Imagine what a wizard could do there!''

Carl strode across the deck, taking in the sights. "If I decide to do it, then we'll do it.''

Snake nodded to Patch that he should keep it going.

"But I didn't even mention the taverns!'' Patch said quickly. "And I didn't even mention the women, fine-looking women, and easy, too! Why, Snake's own—''

Patch stopped suddenly and grabbed at his throat.

"I told you I'd think about it,'' Carl said evenly. "That should have been enough.'' He grinned at Patch, who had fallen to his knees, grabbing at something invisible that was wrapped around his windpipe.

"When I want you to shut up, you'd better shut up,'' Carl continued. "Otherwise—well, why don't we let this guy show you what happens?''

Patch made a faint retching sound in the back of his throat as his hands fell limp at his sides. A moment later he fell face-first to the deck.

Carl looked at Snake and his fellows. "Yeah, he's dead. Now I've only got three men, but all three of you will know not to cross me. Something else goes wrong, though, and I won't be so easy on the next guy.''

He stopped next to Snake and slapped him on the shoulder. "Just because I'm new to this wizard business doesn't mean I'm stupid.''

Carl was smiling again, but there was a hardness in his eyes. Snake should have seen that before.

"What do you say to that?'' Carl asked.

"Uh—yes sir?'' Snake replied.

"That'll do for now.'' He turned away from Snake and looked at the others. "Someday I think it would be great to sail this boat and go to a whole town full of easy women. But there's a few things I have to take care of first—a few people I have to kill. You want to help me, you can stay alive. Any questions?''

"Sir,'' Old Bill said in that methodical way he had, "these people, are—''

"I'm going to start with my family,'' Carl replied, "and

finish up with a few other ingrates. Enough of that. There a place around here I can sleep?''

"Yessir," the Rat answered hurriedly. "There's some cabins downstairs, with a rather nice one for—"

"The man in charge," Carl finished for him. "That would be me. I'm gonna go down there and get some shut-eye. And I'm the only one going down there. Anybody follows me, I hear one sound outside of that cabin? Well, I guess I can do most everything I want with two men rather than three." He waved at Snake and the others and walked to the door that led below. "Good night."

He opened the door but paused, turning to look at the three one more time.

"Well?"

"Good night, sir!" the Rat shouted.

Carl nodded back. "You may stay alive for a while."

With that, he turned again and disappeared below.

"What do we do, Snake?" Old Bill asked when the wizard's footsteps became too faint to hear.

Snake's opinion hadn't changed. "We have to kill him. He's a little smarter than he first appeared. That's a bit of a problem. But, my boys, he's not as smart as all that."

Old Bill and the Rat both chuckled at that, just as they were supposed to. But Snake could find no humor in this situation at all.

"Boys?" Snake added. "Throw Patch overboard, would you?"

The other two moved to comply.

Kill or be killed, it was as simple as that. And Snake was an expert at murder.

The doorbell rang.

Hyram would have to get out of his chair to answer it.

No. There was no doorbell. There was no chair. There was only Margaret Furlong's mind, looking for images of comfort in a world so perfect it could never have existed.

Hyram Sayre had brought her aloft with his power, and tried to show her the beauty of this world, so much more green and unspoiled than that place of subdevelopments and shopping malls that they had come from. But what do you show to someone who will not see?

No matter what he did, Margaret stubbornly refused to change in any way. If something had to give, it was going to be Hyram's mind.

The doorbell rang. They were being awfully insistent. Couldn't a man wait a moment before he rushed off to answer—

Wait. Margaret's world was a fantasy. A complete and compelling place, but a fantasy nonetheless. And he was the lawn god, not just simple Hyram Sayre anymore, no, but a being who had been chosen to give life to the world. Being trapped with Margaret like this could only be a temporary setback. The lawn god had a destiny. Hyram might not be sure exactly what that destiny was, just yet, but with powers like his, it was bound to be great. Whatever it was, he was sure it was far beyond the limits of Chestnut Circle.

The doorbell rang. Whoever was out there was just going to lean on it until they got Hyram's attention.

No. They were flying, Margaret and he, floating, surrounded by the night sky, swinging about in ever-increasing circles so that they had left the island behind, and now flew high above a great, calm sea. Hyram could fly around here for hours in silent contemplation of the sea and the sky, if not for Margaret.

"Look!" he called to Margaret one more time. There, far below them, was a solitary sailing ship, a single torch burning above its deck.

The doorbell rang, and would ring forever. Maybe Hyram should march down into the basement and rip out the fuse that controlled that damned ding-dong, ding-dong!

No. There was no doorbell, and this was growing dangerous. This vision of Margaret's would not end. What could Hyram do?

The ship. It was just below. They could land there. Surely, he could speak to the merchants on board and explain their situation, perhaps get a few minutes' rest. How long had it been since he had slept, anyway? A couple of days at least. No doubt that was his problem. A little sleep, and he'd be able to handle these difficulties with Margaret with ease.

Yes, that was the answer, a peaceful rest on the ship below. Hyram let out a long breath and began his descent.

"We're going to visit a ship, Margaret," he said, more to help his own concentration than in any hope of getting an answer. "We'll meet some new people. Maybe we'll have a chance to rest."

"Leo," she whispered.

The doorbell rang. Sooner or later Hyram would have to answer it.

O Twenty-five

Dirt exploded at the middle of the clearing. A couple of the neighbors screamed. Stanley cursed and grabbed his bow. Mrs. Smith exchanged a glance with Mary Lou. Both held tight to their dragon's eyes.

Mrs. Smith was horrified. This was all her fault. She had allowed Nunn to sweet-talk her into taking him along, and now he was going to destroy them all.

She couldn't trust a word he said. Who knew what he was capable of? She was astonished that she had brought him here. She never imagined she would have done anything so foolish—what had she been thinking—

She thought suddenly of Mary Lou, and the things the younger woman had done for the dragon. Could the creature be manipulating the rest of them in the same way? If that were true, how could she trust anything?

"No!" Obar shouted. "I will not allow this to happen!"

"What's the matter, Obar?" Nunn's voice called out of the darkness. "Don't you have any feelings for your dear brother?"

Obar no longer held his dragon's eye. Instead, it appeared suspended in midair perhaps a dozen feet before him.

Something shimmered in the air on the far side of the eye, swirling about like a tight-knit flight of fireflies. It coalesced into a ghostly green outline of Nunn, with two points of green for the eyes and a thin line for the mouth. The mouth was curved, as if Nunn were smiling.

"Anyone who gets overwhelmed by his own magic," the ghost-Nunn said, "deserves to lose his dragon's eye."

234

"So you just waited for a moment of weakness—" Mrs. Smith began.

"Before I stole another eye?" Nunn taunted. "You know how desperately we need the eyes, Mrs. Smith. Do you think you could exist for one minute without yours?"

The eye had changed her, Mrs. Smith realized. But she would not be so foolish as to let hers go.

"Besides," Nunn added with a chuckle, "Obar would have done the same for me."

"He doesn't have it yet!" Obar called. He approached the floating gem cautiously, as if the eye might dart away at any moment.

The outline of Nunn made no move to follow his brother. "Obar and I, we both have an affinity for these eyes. You've seen that the gems tend to gravitate toward those who would be their masters. So this gem is suspended between two masters. Now we simply see whose affinity is stronger. Of course, someone who has kept a pair of dragon's eyes for all this time might have slightly more pull."

The eye was indeed starting to wobble toward the green outline of Nunn.

"I think I've spent too much time watching this," Mary Lou announced. She stared at the eye between the two wizards. It stopped its slow wobble toward Nunn and instead began to roll very slowly in the direction of Mary Lou.

"No!" Obar ran forward. His voice rose toward hysteria. "That's not for you—interloper! That stone belongs to one who practices the true magic!"

"There are some places my brother and I still agree," Nunn added, his voice still self-composed. "The true magic my brother and I have honed for—how long? It is very difficult to tell time around here, have you noticed?"

While Nunn's voice was calm and conversational, Mrs. Smith noticed that his vague shape had begun to drift after the gem as well.

"My brother and I do carry on certain traditions," Nunn added with a sigh. "Pity that Rox is nowhere around. He would complete the set."

"What is true magic?" Mary Lou countered. "Those spells you have stumbled upon and mastered? Or is true magic this whole world as it exists in the mind of the dragon?"

Obar lunged for the stone, but it danced away, just beyond his reach.

"This is no fair!" the wizard wailed. "We planned so long, worked so hard. And now we are reduced to fighting for a single stone." He paused in his advance, holding on to his side as if it pained him. Obar was beginning to look like a very old man.

Nunn's vaguely glowing shape was changing, his hand stretching out like a sort of tentacle uncurling to snatch the stone.

"Mary Lou!" Mrs. Smith cautioned.

"I see him," the girl agreed. "I always see him. I have been waiting for Nunn for a very long time."

The stone stopped rolling toward her, as if she dared Nunn to make his move.

"I don't know if I appreciate that remark. I don't think I even understand it." Nunn's fingers jumped forward to wrap around the gem, but instead of grasping the stone, his glowing green hand passed right through it.

His demeanor shattered at last. "What have you done to the stone?" Nunn cried. "What have you done to me?"

"Perhaps you're not as substantial as you once thought," Mary Lou replied.

Mrs. Smith was certainly glad that she and this young woman were fighting on the same side. Mary Lou could be frightening.

"There are other ways—" Nunn muttered.

The jewel disappeared.

"What?" Mary Lou called.

"Another of Nunn's tricks," Obar called. "Apparently, young lady, you still don't know everything."

Mrs. Smith realized that Nunn was gone, too.

"Did anybody see him?" she called to the neighbors who had gathered behind her. "What happened?"

Bobby stepped forward. "I know somebody who can find him." Charlie panted at his side.

"The dog?" Mrs. Smith asked. "How do you know?"

"Charlie told me so," Bobby replied with a grin. "He can do all sorts of things regular dogs can't." He turned to the dog. "So where's the wizard?"

Charlie barked and ambled forward, a frolicking monstrosity

of muscle with a head so misshapen it almost looked like a caricature of a real canine. He ran over to one of the trees at the edge of the clearing and looked up toward the branches. Charlie jumped up on his rear paws, his forepaws resting against the tree as he barked at what was above.

The side of the tree appeared to glow green, as though a neon fungus was growing there, throbbing in time with Charlie's barks.

"No, no!" Nunn called. "Get him away from me."

"I can do more than make sure you keep Nunn up a tree," Obar added, tugging at his tattered, disheveled robes, attempting, no doubt, to regain some dignity. "There is a little surprise I put inside Charlie."

"So you use these newcomers, too?" Nunn called. "Altering a helpless dog for your needs? Oh, I know about your plans for Nick, too. Shame you won't be able to use him."

That seemed to infuriate the wizard in white. "I don't care about Nick! This is my creation! The dog is mine to command." Obar shouted a string of those nonsense words he always used to control his magic.

And Charlie changed. He was no longer a dog becoming a monster. His body glowed, and grew. Even Bobby stepped back in alarm as the dog became twenty feet long and half as high, like some monstrous grizzly bear with a head that looked like nothing but horns and teeth. The monster was here, leaving the dog behind.

All the other members of the camp, save Bobby and the wizards, had gathered behind Mrs. Smith and Mary Lou. They were their protectors against this creature; Obar's creature.

The monster ripped at the side of the tree with its teeth, leaving a three-foot gap in the bark. The thing that once was Charlie roared.

"Kill him!" Obar shouted. "Kill Nunn now!"

But instead of rushing the tree, the huge creature spun about to stare at the others in the clearing.

"No!" Obar called again. "Kill Nunn! I created you! I command it!"

The Charlie-beast roared again, rising up on its hind legs to paw the air with its razor claws.

"Kill! Kill! Kill!" Obar screamed.

The creature charged.

• • •

Zachs was not happy with his family. He paced back and forth in front of them some twenty feet above the cavern floor. Walking in the air seemed to impress them so.

"Zachs knows you can win! There are more of us than them! They have nothing like our poison sticks! You must kill them! Kill them for Zachs!"

The apes cowered before him. More had shown up from the aftermath of battle with Nunn, another half a dozen stragglers returning to the closest thing they knew to home. Once there, they of course met their new father, so much more qualified than Nunn to lead them to victory.

Zachs was very happy the apes didn't talk. That meant they couldn't talk back. They couldn't tell him he became so excited in battle he did not lead his troops. They could not laugh at him for running when the sword ate his fire. As if any of that was Zachs's fault! Zachs screamed. He sent great gouts of fire up toward the ceiling of the cavern. The bright light showed the deep fear on his children's faces.

Obedient children made Zachs feel better.

He knew his children well. He was once one of them, after all, he knew what made them think, and what was the best thing of all to make them act. And that thing was fear.

The humans and wolves took unfair advantage of the disorganization of his troops, the newness of his command. This time Zachs and his family would learn from their mistakes. They would use stealth to surround the camp. There would be two apes against every wolf, three against every human. They would overwhelm those who dared to fight against them.

Then there was that one whose sword ate Zachs's fire. Zachs would make sure his family took that human's sword. Then Zachs would burn the human slowly, inch by inch.

Zachs's fire would not be beaten. Zachs's fire would rule the world.

"Damn it! This thing is useless!"

Todd wished he could just throw the dragon's eye away. He had thought it would be easy to find his father. But the signals made no sense. Todd was lost. And he'd dragged two other people out here with him.

It was all his fault. He hadn't practiced long enough, didn't know magic in the same way as Mrs. Smith and Mary Lou. His magic was good at reacting, like the time he burned that giant tentacle that rose out of the sea. He didn't seem much good at anything else, like disposing of bodies or finding other dragon's eyes. Mrs. Smith had told him what to do, but somehow, when he got out here, it had gotten all confused, and he had ended up bringing all three of them to someplace in the middle of these nowhere woods.

"Don't blame yourself, Todd," Mr. Mills said. He stared down at his own gem as if it might tell him the answer. "Something strange is going on here. The whole nature of this place is changing."

Sala hugged his arm and smiled at him. Todd guessed it was good he brought these two along. Between them, they made him feel like he wasn't a total screwup after all.

Todd frowned back at his own gem. "The way Mrs. Smith described it, this whole finding-people thing was a 'wish for it and there it is' deal. But—"

"You're getting to too many places," Mills finished for him.

"Yeah." Todd looked up and grinned. That was it exactly.

"Instead of one destination, the eyes try to give you three. My stone told me the same thing."

"What?" Sala asked, looking at both of them. "What are you talking about?"

"There's these three different places," Todd explained, "and the dragon's eye wants us to go to all three of them, all at the same time."

"I think the dragon's eyes are telling us something, like these three places are the most important here," Mills agreed. "Maybe they're the only places that are important. And I think your father's at one of them."

Yes! Todd thought the same. "I can feel him. He's so close! But where?"

Sala looked from Todd to Mills and back again. "I'm glad you two understand each other, but I'm just a poor girl from a tavern, and it looks to me like we're lost!"

"We are," Todd agreed, glancing around at the dark trees surrounding them.

"But maybe we can figure out where we should go," Mills added.

"So what can you tell me about these places?" Sala asked. "Anything?"

"I've seen glimpses—" Mills began.

"So have I!" Todd agreed. "One's full of fire."

"I think that's Zachs. Or it's to tell us that Zachs is there. There's something about that I recognize."

Todd decided he'd take a crack at describing one of the visions. "Another one shows a whole bunch of lights chasing each other around."

"Sounds like those wizards," Sala said, "always trying to beat each other up, and never getting anywhere. Could one of the places be where we just came from?"

Todd shook his head with a half grin. "Well, there's a lot going on back there."

"Then what's the third?" Sala asked.

"It's cold," Mr. Mills said. "Bright and cold."

"I think it's full of hate," Todd added. Far more than in the other visions, the feeling had been very strong.

"That sounds like your father," Sala replied. "My father, too."

Mills nodded, as though that made sense to him.

"I think that's where we should go." Todd sighed. "If I can get us there."

"You will," Sala said brightly. "You're still learning how to use that thing!"

"Even though Rox is hiding deep inside me," Mills added, "I still can feel some of his experience. I've got to learn from that. I'm a teacher, and somebody's even got to teach me."

Boy, he sure did sound like a teacher. But for a teacher, Mills was okay. Todd half smiled at the thought. "I've got to give myself a little credit, huh? I don't think I'm very good at that."

"With any luck," Mills added, "we'll all get better."

"I think you're going to do great," Sala said.

"You would," Todd said with a grin. "But that's why you're here."

Sala squeezed his hand. For one moment Todd wished they just had time to be an ordinary couple, talking to each other, holding each other, getting to know who they really were. But his father and the end of the world wouldn't wait.

"So we're going to one of the three important places, huh?"

he said with a cheerfulness he really didn't feel. "What say we go save the world?"

"Then that's where we go," Mills agreed. "I might want to pick up Zachs on our way back, though."

"That fire thing?" Todd asked. "Why?"

"Because I think it would bother the heck out of the dragon."

That sounded like a great reason to Todd.

○ Twenty-six

Someone was going to pay for this. Carl was just beginning to drift off to sleep, and all hell breaks loose on deck.

At least they had a little liquor down here. He'd found a half-filled jug on the table by the bed. First time he'd felt half-human since he'd come to this godforsaken place.

Whoa! He shouldn't have sat up quite so fast. He felt like half of his head was still back on the pillow.

"Take it easy, Carl."

Now he was hearing voices in his head. Hell, he wasn't that drunk. He had a voice in his head! Leo? Oh hell, what was he doing here?

"What are you," Carl shouted, "my conscience? Some fucking Jimmy Cricket?"

Jimmy Cricket? That wasn't right. But what did that matter? He was going to go up on that deck and kick some butt.

"Listen, Carl," Leo started in that lecturing tone of voice that Carl had heard all his life. "I've been thinking—"

"Shut up, Leo."

He pushed himself away from the bunk. He didn't have to listen to Leo or anybody. So what if he was a little unsteady on his feet? He could use his jewel to sober himself up in an instant. Or, better than that, he'd just float up there so he didn't need to keep his balance at all.

"Shut up, Leo," he said all over again, not because the guy had said anything else, but because Carl liked the sound of it. He was a wizard now. He had those goddamned eyes. He could kill people for the hell of it, and would, too. Carl didn't have to listen to anybody.

He floated out of the room and up the stairs toward the deck,

242

only bouncing against the walls a couple of times. He remembered how Nunn and those wizards would float right through walls. Someday he'd have to figure out how to do that, too.

There was a door in his way at the top of the stairs. Carl kicked it open.

"What the hell is going on out here?" he shouted as he shot out above the deck.

He stopped floating when he saw the glowing green woman. It wasn't so much that she was glowing, or was green; it was that he recognized her.

"Margaret?"

"Carl?" she replied. "Actually, it's Hyram. Hyram Sayre."

Hyram? That balding twerp that lived down the street? It sure didn't look like Hyram. Not that Margaret was any prize, but even in his present condition, Carl could tell the difference.

But nobody had answered his question, so he decided to ask it again.

"What the hell is going on here?"

"We just found them on deck," one of the sailors, the short one, quickly replied. "One minute, it's nice and quiet; the next, they come dancing down right next to us."

"Look, Carl," the glowing woman explained, "I'm glad I found somebody I know. You'll understand. We were tired. We were looking for a place to rest."

"Rest?" Damned straight he understood about that! "You woke me up out a sound sleep. I don't like to be woken up by *anybody*." Maybe it was time to play with his dragon's eye again, teach somebody a lesson, even if he still didn't understand what was going on.

He floated over to get a better look. "You sure look like Margaret."

The glowing green woman stared back at him.

"Leo?" she asked.

God, Carl thought, was Leo showing? This was getting stranger and stranger.

"Look, Carl," she continued, but her voice sounded different, more filled with authority. "Margaret's a little off. She thinks she's back at home, on Chestnut Circle—"

"It is Leo," she continued, her voice softer and higher-pitched, ". . . isn't it?"

Carl decided he still wanted an explanation before he started any demonstrations. "Okay, Hyram. But what the hell are *you* doing here?"

"I was trying to help her." Margaret pointed over at Snake. "She was wounded—by this fellow over here actually."

"You—hurt Margaret?"

Carl had said those words, but he hadn't meant to say them. It was like somebody else was using his voice.

Somebody else? Could Leo do that?

"Leo!" Margaret cried. "I've looked everywhere for you!"

"Come on, Margaret!" her voice shouted in frustration. "I'm trying to find us a place to rest!"

"No," Carl replied, pointing at his chest, "Leo's right here." May as well lay all his cards on the table. "Not that he's going anywhere."

Margaret's eyes grew wide. "I'm inside Margaret, and Leo's inside you? Boy, this is kind of a strange place, isn't it?"

Actually, Carl thought, if you looked at this the right way, it was a little funny. This whole thing could be a good test of his wizard skills. "Maybe I can get everybody out of everywhere."

"I'm coming out?" Leo said with Carl's voice. "Then I can kill this man."

Carl couldn't imagine Leo killing anyone.

"I've been taking lessons from you, Carl," Leo replied as if he could read Carl's thoughts.

"I don't know what's going on," Snake said softly to his two mates. "I'm getting out of here."

Carl glared at him. "You take a step, you're dead." It felt like both he and Leo had said the words at the same time.

"Carl? Would you let me take a look around?"

Oh boy, would he. He concentrated on the gems in his palms. *Let Leo out.*

And Leo was out, stepping from Carl's body like he was walking out of a door rather than another body. But Carl noticed he wasn't all there. He certainly looked like Leo, with his usual rumpled suit and geeky bow tie, but even in this dim light, you could see right through him. He wasn't all there. Not that Carl minded. No matter what Leo looked like, he was glad to be rid of him.

His wife frowned at the new apparition. "Leo, you've changed."

Leo smiled sadly at that. "Everybody has to change, Margaret."

Margaret shook her head violently. "No, no—can you really be Leo?"

"Just as certainly as you're Margaret. I'll have to find some way to become more substantial. I'm sure Carl could help with his eyes. Sort of a going-away present, huh? But then again, Margaret, you're glowing green and floating in the air."

"I'm afraid that's my fault," she replied, raising one of her hands. "Hyram, that is."

"Hyram Sayre," Leo said. "I don't think anyone's to blame. You brought Margaret back to me."

"Leo," Margaret said softly. "Can we go home?"

Leo smiled again. "Who knows?"

"I came in her to heal her wounds. I've done it before with other people. But once I got inside Margaret's system, somehow I got stuck. Leo, your wife can be a stubborn woman. Still, I've gotten rather used to her. You should see her memories of Chestnut Circle!"

Margaret shook her head. "I want to go with Leo."

"You're leaving me?" Hyram's deeper tones asked. "She hasn't been able to cope very well."

"Well, maybe she can with me."

Could this get any more sickeningly sweet? Carl couldn't take another minute of this.

"Enough!" he called, and blasted the three of them with dragon fire.

The three sailors shouted. The victims didn't have time. A pile of sail burst into flame beyond where the three of them had stood, as if his power had vaporized them instantly and gone to do other damage beyond.

He glanced at the three sailors, as if they might challenge his actions, but none of them looked him in the eye, instead content to study the fire or the deck beneath their feet.

"Well, put out the fire!" Carl called. "Do I have to think of everything?"

The sailors rushed to comply, tossing the burning sail over the side before it had a chance to spread.

"Did that feel satisfying?" a voice said inside his head. Leo's voice.

"What are you still doing here?" Carl demanded. "I thought you'd left!"

Leo laughed at that. "So I can let you kill me? I'll leave here when I know it's safe."

A glowing green figure rose through the boards of the deck, but it wasn't Margaret. It was Hyram Sayre.

"Somehow, we ended up below," Hyram said apologetically. "Margaret is safely asleep in a nice, dry corner. Meeting Leo and all seemed a bit too much for her."

Carl didn't like the way this was going at all.

"Margaret really helped me to appreciate some things I might have forgotten," Hyram continued in the most pleasant of tones. "Chestnut Circle really is a wonderful place. But I remember now, Carl. You never really cared about your lawn, did you?"

"What's that to you?"

"The time for peace is over," Hyram announced. "It is time for the lawn god's vengeance."

How dare he? Carl would blast him to hell.

Carl was almost thrown to deck as the boat started to shake violently, like the rattle in the hand of some enormous child.

Maybe Carl didn't want to mess with the lawn god after all. He leaned against a mast in order to stay upright and looked across the deck at his opponent. But Hyram looked no happier than he did.

"Did you do this?" Carl demanded.

But Hyram shook his head and pointed over Carl's shoulder. Carl turned around to look.

"Oh, shit," he whispered. Now this was serious.

○ Twenty-seven

A wolf howled in the woods.

"That means they're coming back again," Nick explained. "Pator posted sentries."

The Captain nodded sadly. "He always was a thorough man. You will have large shoes to fill."

Everything he said only served to make Nick more enraged. The others were careful not to show their feelings, a matter of survival. Nick could take the Captain easily.

"But he was also questioning my authority," the Captain added. "We can't have that. We are at war with the powers of darkness. If you don't want to follow my orders, say so, and I will let you leave."

"You didn't give Pator that chance."

"Pator was an army man, through and through. He wouldn't have stood a chance in the outside world. Besides, I was making a point."

"A point?"

"And I will keep on doing so, until someone makes a point with me." The man was grinning again. "These are extreme times, Nick, they call for extreme measures. Now, what say we work together? It gives us both a better chance to survive."

The Captain could do the most amazing turnarounds, killing without remorse in one instant, then urging his troops to work together the next. It was a special kind of madness that grew here. Maybe you needed it to survive.

But even Nick realized the Captain had a point. The Captain and his troops took him in when no one else would dare. Nick was no less a monster in his own way. It was his sword that killed Pator, after all.

The Captain turned to his troops. "Let's not give them a chance to surround us, hey? We will split into four groups." He quickly divided the remaining men and wolves into small parties, and instructed the first three to each position themselves two hundred paces away from the clearing at three different points.

"Keep well hidden!" the Captain called as the three groups left the clearing for the trees. When the groups were gone, there were only three left in the clearing, Nick, the Captain, and a single wolf.

Nick had started to learn how to differentiate some of the wolves from each other. He looked down at the wolf that remained. Its grey hair was streaked with white, and its right fang was broken from some ancient battle. Nick recognized it as one of the three that generally spoke up in the pack.

The wolf glanced up at Nick and licked its chops. "It has been too long since we have had a trrrue fight. Kill the apes and feast. Frrresh meat."

"So now we wait," the Captain said. "We are the bait." He waved at the carcasses and rough blankets that littered the site. "Perhaps we can arrange some of these supplies to look like sleeping bodies. The more this looks like a camp full of unprepared soldiers, the more my plan will succeed."

He turned and looked at Nick. "You could kill me now. Who would know? We're the only two humans here. Fang here could no doubt be bribed to your way of thinking with an extra ape carcass or two."

Nick patted the hilt of his sword, which he had sheathed right after the death of Pator. It was best not to give his weapon too many opportunities. "I think there'll be a better time for that than now. Do you really want to die so much?"

That made the Captain grin. "Part of me really does. I've seen too much, done too many things in the name of survival, for me to do much else than what I do now. And I'm getting tired." He shook his head. "It was wonderful to tear into Nunn's forces, destroy his attempt to control us all. But when that is done, what is left? I've changed too much to rejoin the volunteers. Maybe get vengeance against the dragon for screwing up my life?" The Captain laughed. "If only I knew how."

He nodded to Nick. "So kill me when this is over, if you want. It'll make for an interesting death."

Nick could think of many words for dying by his cursed sword. Interesting had never been one of them.

"Let's get this camp looking slept in," the Captain said. Nick followed his lead, stringing out stones, extra helmets and animal carcasses so that they looked vaguely like sleeping bodies. Even the wolf helped, dragging blankets with its teeth to cover their creations.

When they were done, the Captain looked back out to the woods.

"We wait for action, for something we pretend is glory. This place can give you that until you're sick of it."

Nick stroked the hilt of his sword. "All I know is that I need blood. I can't live without it."

"Oh, I can guarantee you that, Nick," the Captain said with a laugh. "That and more. Who knows? Maybe we'll even do something here to change the world."

Obar had planned for this moment ever since he had come to this place. To deprive his brother, the brother who had almost murdered him, of the one thing he longed for in life. And then to snuff his brother out of existence in front of an audience. Oh, he knew that Mrs. Smith and the others now suspected his motives. But the death of Nunn would go a long ways toward putting them back in his camp.

The dog was magnificent. Obar truly had created a monster, a thing that could bite and tear you to shreds in an instant. How his defenseless brother must be dreading his last moments!

The great brute seemed confused, however. Perhaps its new shape was disorienting; a change of that magnitude would probably be troubling, even to a dog like Charlie. The dumb animal had never suspected that it had a spell cast over it at the same time that Obar healed its wounds.

The gem was gone, of course. But without the presence of the gem, the spell should simply work because Obar had made it; he had woven that into the magic. Obar had planned for every eventuality.

The great beast roared. But he had turned the wrong way. It ran, growling, halfway toward Mrs. Smith and the neighbors.

"Nunn!" Obar called. "You must kill Nunn!"

The beast skidded to a halt. Obar's commands had gotten

through to it at last. It turned to regard the aged wizard.

"Nunn!" Obar screamed at the monster. Was its head too thick even to understand simple commands? "You found him before, back in the tree! Kill him! Kill Nunn!"

The beast lowered its head and growled. Obar was finding this all too much.

"Kill!" he screamed again. "Kill! Kill! Kill!"

The beast raised its head and charged again, this time straight for Obar.

"No!" Obar shouted. "Not me! I'm the one who made you!"

The monster roared in response.

"No!" Obar screamed. "This can't be happening!" He quickly chanted the most important part of the spell again. Surely, that would get the monster to obey.

If anything, the spell seemed to make the monster speed his charge!

How could he protect himself? Was there some warding spell he could still use with the small magics he had left? He had so much left he wanted to do.

"No!" he shrieked as the great dog fell upon him.

Obar felt one instant of pain. Then his body was torn far beyond that as well.

For the moment even Hyram Sayre forgot about vengeance. And even Carl Jackson screamed when the giant tentacle crashed down on the deck.

"What the hell is that?" Jackson demanded.

No one had a chance to answer. They were all too busy running away themselves.

The tentacle slammed along the deck, breaking a mast, punching a hole in the quarterdeck. It was ignoring the sailors and moving toward the one man who stood alone.

"What the hell does it want?" Carl screamed.

Hyram launched himself into the air to get a better view of the proceedings. The tentacle meant nothing to him. As the lawn god, he could easily get out of the creature's way.

"At my first guess, my dear Carl," Hyram ventured, "I would say it wants you."

Jackson started to shake.

"You can handle this, Carl," he said.

"Of course I can!" he added.

"Use your gems—my gems!" came out of his mouth a moment later. Both the beings inside the wizard were speaking at once, rather like some of those odd conversations Hyram had had with Margaret. Viewed from the outside, it was certainly disconcerting.

Jackson raised his hands before his attacker. Twin beams of green light exploded from his palms. The tentacle jerked away.

But Jackson had other problems. Two other tentacles had risen above the side of the boat.

"If you're going to do something, do it quickly!" Carl shouted at himself.

Carl screamed as two bolts of light shot from his palms to blast the nearest tentacle. The tentacle was blown from the ship, disintegrating as it flew away.

The other tentacles sank away, as if their owner thought better of this whole process.

Carl fell to his knees. He looked as though he couldn't catch his breath.

"Why?" he whispered.

Hyram thought about the nature of these things. The creature was quite definitely after Carl, or perhaps something that Carl possessed.

"Maybe your gems had done something to it," he suggested. "Those dragon's eyes in your palms do have quite a past."

Carl looked up at Hyram, then down at the stones in his hands. "That creature wanted me, because of Nunn? I have Leo stuck inside me because of Nunn! Can't I rid myself of Nunn?"

Hyram shrugged. "You get his dragon's eyes, I guess you get his baggage, too."

He knew, but didn't say aloud, that this all happened to Carl because he didn't take care of his lawn. As difficult and frightening as the experience had been, Hyram would miss being a part of Margaret. Her belief in Chestnut Circle was refreshing.

Jackson jumped to his feet. "I've had enough of you! Get the hell out of here!" He raised his hands, pointing both of his gems at the lawn god.

Hyram was surrounded by light.

Hyram saw the Circle clearly once again.

•   •   •

That annoying little piece of glowing green shit Hyram Sayre was gone. Carl hoped this time he had killed him. Around here, of course, you could never be sure.

He turned to the sailors.

"You!" he called.

"Yes sir!" The little man known as the Rat was the first to step forward.

Carl opened his gems on the Rat, both barrels, so fast the man didn't even have time to scream. The Rat was vaporized where he stood.

"There," Carl said, already calmer. "I just needed to know that I had really killed someone." He waved at Snake and Old Bill. "The two of you will just have to work a little harder."

Both the remaining sailors turned a most satisfying shade of pale. Old Bill raised one hand and pointed past Carl.

"Oh, I wouldn't get that upset. If I kill everybody, who would I get to do my work?"

"Behind you, sir."

What was it this time? Had the tentacles come back, or was it something worse? Jackson wheeled around to fight the new danger.

"I'm going to make sure you never kill again," one of the newcomers said. There were three of them in all.

But the one who had spoken was his good-for-nothing son.

O Twenty-eight

Snake couldn't believe it. The newcomers had actually brought him his daughter. He looked across the deck at Sala and smiled. She took a step behind that youngster she had run off with. It didn't matter. Snake and his daughter were meant to be together.

He had to think how he could use this to his advantage. The minute he got Sala alone, she'd do anything he wanted. But it was difficult to predict how this Carl fellow would react, except with anger. The new wizard seemed even more deranged than Nunn.

Not that Snake feared for his own life just yet. After all, Carl Jackson knew that Snake had connections. Snake could get him things, make his life as a wizard nothing but ease, set him up back in Snake's home port so Carl could be a king. Of course, they had to get out of the mess that was going on here first. This whole island and the waters that surrounded it were cursed with so many damned wizards and unnatural things it was impossible not to run into them.

Of course there was another battle going on a few feet away from him; that seemed to happen a lot around here, too. Carl started this one by shooting his blasts of fire out at all three of the interlopers, Sala included. It would be a shame to lose Sala. Snake had worked so hard to make her useful.

The two men—Todd, the upstart about Sala's age, and the other maybe as old as Carl—had dragon's eyes of their own, and returned the fire. There was a large explosion above the middle of the deck that seemed to burn nothing but air.

The battle was being waged in safely neutral territory for the moment, but he couldn't depend on it staying that way.

Snake had to figure out how to retrieve his property before
Sala got damaged. There was some market for girls missing
an arm or leg, but it was nowhere near the money he could
get for her whole.

He couldn't get any closer to the fighting without seriously
threatening his own health. But this ship held two ways be-
lowdeck, a set of stairs to the cabins and a ladder to the cargo
hold, with those two areas connected by a single padlocked
door. He could pass beneath the battle and, in a matter of
minutes, sneak up behind his daughter while the others were
fighting, spirit her away, and give her a little snuggle besides.
It was time for Sala to remember her place.

Snake took a cautious look around. Carl certainly wasn't
paying any attention to him. And Old Bill was cowering in a
corner behind a pile of rope, too concerned with his own ass
to worry about what Snake was doing.

There was nothing in his way. Snake walked away quietly,
heading for the ladder that led down to the cargo hold. It was
good to have a purpose again. If there had been no one about,
he might have started whistling.

Snake guessed there was nothing like family to cheer you
up.

"Stop here, my Oomgosh!" Raven called. The bird fluttered
down to land on Jason's shoulder as soon as he had stopped
running.

Jason couldn't see anything special in this place at all. It
was just another small clearing in the forest, not that different
from half a dozen others they had already passed through.

"This is the special place?" he asked.

Raven nodded sagely. "This is the center, around which
everything will happen."

"The dragon will come here?" Jason dug his toes into the
ground to talk with the roots that held the island together. You
are at the center, the roots told him, the island's heart.

"The dragon will be everywhere," Raven replied, "but it
will be here particularly."

Jason swore that half the time the bird talked in riddles. But
whenever he asked Raven to explain, the bird would say that
the Oomgosh already knew.

Sometimes Raven was right; sometimes Jason did know

things. They always came as a complete surprise, like the first time he realized he understood the insects that hid in the trees, insects that didn't talk so much in words as emotions, or how he was able to match his rhythms with those of the sap flowing through the trees so that he could hear their quiet music. As the Oomgosh, he might know everything, but as Jason, there was still so much that he didn't understand.

Raven raised his beak high in the air, as if trying to find a distant scent on the wind. "The dragon waits for blood!"

"Blood?" Jason frowned at that. "That's something I know nothing about."

Raven shook his beak. "It is not our place to kill. Blood is the business of others. But, when enough die, that is when the drama begins."

"Drama?" Jason asked.

"We get to see the dragon. Or at least as much as that fussy creature will show us. The dragon is nowhere near as direct as Raven."

Jason was still trying to understand. "And the dragon comes when there's enough blood?"

Raven paused for a moment before answering. "One in particular has to die."

"Which one?"

Raven cawed at that. "That would be telling, my Oomgosh. Besides, it is not always the same." The bird shook his head more slowly this time. "With the dragon, it is never the same."

Jason was beginning to understand something else. "You do not approve of the dragon."

"The dragon is melodramatic." He fluffed his wings dismissively. "Raven has seen it all before."

"There is one thing I've always wondered about, Raven," Jason said. "If you're the creator of all things, couldn't you just put a stop to all of this?"

"Stop it?" Raven squawked. "Where's the fun in that?"

Now Carl was good and mad.

First it was a couple of glowing green neighbors, then some other jerk inside his head, then some creature from the bottom of the sea, and now the do-gooder patrol shows up.

He tried to blast them right away, and found out both of

them had dragon's eyes of their own. What, were they giving these out to everybody?

It was still only a matter of time until Carl won. He had two of the eyes; he'd catch Todd or Mills off balance and *wham!* He'd deliver a double shot, laughing as the other guy died in agony. He'd let whoever was left plead for mercy before he killed him, too.

These eyes gave him the power he always needed, the power he deserved. He had every right to kill his son. He brought him into the world in the first place, after all.

Now, what right Mills had to be here was beyond Carl. Goddamned teachers tried to butt in every corner of your life. Tried to tell you whether or not you could even hit your kids! Well, he'd hit his kid now, and slap Mr. Mills besides.

He slammed bolt after bolt of energy at the newcomers, flashes of bright green that exploded blindingly in the night sky. He needed to keep them busy, keep them in the same place, so he could concentrate on both of them. If they split up, got on opposite ends of the deck or something, it might be trouble. Not that he couldn't handle it. He had two of these dragon's eyes, he could handle anything. But he didn't need something else to piss him off.

So he had come out with his fists swinging, sending one magical attack after another at his two foes. But so far they'd been able to match him blow for blow. He wished now he had paid more attention to Nunn, and how the wizard used his magic. Nunn was sneakier, more underhanded; that much Carl remembered. Well, he could be sneaky and underhanded, too. You just had to give him a chance.

A woman screamed.

Carl paused in his attack, startled. But the others had stopped as well. There, right behind the two with the eyes, was the sailor Snake. He had grabbed the girl around the waist with one hand while his other hand held a knife to her throat.

"Now me and my daughter are just going to walk away from here," Snake said. "Then you all can go on with your pretty battle."

The sailor had decided to do this on his own, without even asking Carl's permission. Carl would have to kill him for that, a little later. For now, this might be just the diversion Carl needed.

"No!" Todd shouted at the sailor. "No one is ever going to hurt Sala again!"

Carl shot a quick line of fire at Todd's back.

Mills countered with a blast of his own, deflecting Carl's magic harmlessly over the sea.

"Hurt her?" Snake cackled, waving the knife before Sala's throat. "Let me nick her a little to show you that I can."

But instead of moving closer to the girl's throat, the knife jerked away.

"What?" The sailor, caught off balance, stumbled back, losing his grip on his daughter.

"I gave the knife a purpose of its own," Todd called to Snake. "It's going to kill you."

Snake grabbed the knife with both hands as the blade turned around to point at his chest.

"We'll see about that!" Snake called as he dropped to his knees. He threw the knife down with both arms, driving the blade deep into the floorboards of the deck. "It can't hurt anybody now."

Snake's smile of triumph vanished as he looked down at the knife, jerking back and forth by itself, working its way free of the wood.

Even though Carl was going to kill Todd, he had to admire his son's moxie. Snake wouldn't just die, he would die frightened out of his mind. Carl would have to remember this sort of thing the next time he felt the need to casually murder.

What Carl was doing now wasn't murder. This was self-preservation.

Todd had glanced back at Carl, but then turned to the girl. The time was right to finish this.

"Todd! Look out!" Mills called as he intercepted one of two lines of energy erupting from Carl's palms. But Todd had barely half turned back to the battle, still raising his own gem with his hand, when he was hit by Carl's blow. Todd crashed to the deck like he'd been hit by a giant fist.

This time, Carl found the girl's scream much more satisfying.

◯ Twenty-nine

Bobby was horrified. What had happened to Charlie?

Obar had done something to the dog, and then the dog had turned on the wizard, tearing pieces out of the old man like some crazy beast.

Bobby felt like crying. With his mom and dad gone, the dog was all he had left. Now the dog had become a monster who could kill all of them.

"Stop!" Mrs. Smith commanded, and the huge thing that had once been Charlie froze. Not that it would do the wizard any good. It was hard to recognize that the pieces of bone and meat scattered around the clearing had once belonged to a human being.

Mrs. Smith frowned, and the huge beast lifted from the ground, surrounded by green light. "I think it may be best if we dispose of this."

No! Bobby wanted to run up to Mrs. Smith, to rip that glowing green piece of junk right out of her hands. This wasn't Charlie's fault!

"No," Mary Lou objected. "The spell is over. It died along with Obar. If you release the beast, Charlie will become a dog again."

"Killed by his own magic," Mr. Blake said. "There's a certain justice there."

"Does that mean our son will be freed from his sword as well?" Mrs. Blake asked.

"I don't know," Mary Lou admitted. "It's different. I believe that besides Obar's spell, the sword had magic of its own."

"Let us see if Mary Lou is correct." Mrs. Smith lowered

the frozen monster to the ground, the greenish halo disappearing. And, with the halo gone, Charlie shrank, becoming the oddly deformed dog he had been before.

"Apparently," Mrs. Smith remarked, "some of Obar's work was permanent."

Bobby frowned. What had they done to the dog? "He's lying awfully still. Is he all right?"

"He's sleeping now," Mary Lou replied. "He's been through an ordeal."

Bobby almost wanted to laugh at that.

Mrs. Dafoe shrieked. Bobby looked over at her and saw she was pointing to the spot where Obar had been torn apart. The remains of the wizard were now moving, shifting and bobbing around with a new purpose.

Was Obar coming back to life? The pieces of flesh and bone swirled around each other, pressing together with a series of odd, wet slapping sounds.

But the resulting jigsaw puzzle of flesh did not exactly look like Obar. It looked like a man, but he was far thinner, the remains of Obar's dirty robes somehow darker.

"Thoughtful of Obar to leave me a place to live, isn't it? Especially after I changed that last spell with his former dragon's eye."

It was Nunn.

But Bobby saw other movement closer to him. Charlie was up and walking toward him. Wizards could wait for a moment.

He squatted, his hands out toward the approaching dog. "Is it okay, boy? Are you all right? When I saw that thing—"

Not really me, the dog said in Bobby's head.

Charlie licked Bobby's hand, and for the moment everything was fine.

The wolves were barking. Even Nick had to admire the Captain's intricate code. Three barks meant all clear, a howl the enemy was approaching. One bark meant the enemy was approaching on the sentry's left, two on the sentry's right. With the ring of sentries the Captain had posted earlier, they could get a good idea of exactly where the enemy was and how fast they were moving.

"They're coming at us from—what?—four different directions," the Captain said with a grin. "They mean to surround us. A little bit more clever than the time before. A shame that this time we're ready for them." He let out three wolf howls of his own, quite good wolf howls, Nick thought. That signal meant that the surrounding groups of men and wolves should be ready to move.

"It's going to start at any minute," the Captain continued. "The best and worst of times, hey? It could be a glorious battle, or in a minute you could be dead." He laughed at the thought. "It's that sort of suspense that makes life worth living."

Another series of barks came from the surrounding woods. The Captain howled in response.

He glanced at Nick.

"Now," was all he said.

Carl had to laugh. Evan Mills, high-school-know-it-all-vice-principal, was staring at him openmouthed. Mills knew he was dead meat.

Something this good was worth rubbing in. "Why don't you beg for your life, Mills?"

Carl heard the clatter of feet running across the deck. Snake tried to rush past him in a panic.

"Not so fast," Carl said softly. "You could hurt somebody." Snake jerked to a halt, his hands reaching for his neck and the magic noose Carl had placed around his neck to keep him there.

Snake squirmed like his life depended on it.

"The knife, sir, the knife!" he gasped.

Carl shook his head. "It's going to get you sooner or later. Why not let it happen out in the open and let it be a show?"

Snake made strangling sounds as he tried to break loose from his bonds. Maybe he would die from lack of oxygen before the knife even got him. Carl was glad he could give the sailor another option.

But he was ignoring his business. "Now, where was I? Oh yes. I was going to kill Mr. Mills."

"Leo?" a woman's voice called behind him.

Her again? Carl thought. Why don't I just invite all the neighbors and have a party?

Margaret walked past Carl, stepping up to Snake. "I saw you rush past me down below. I wanted to thank you for waking me. I've got far too much to do to sleep the day away.''

Snake replied with some pathetic gurgling noises.

But the woman was standing between Carl and his enemies.

''Get out of the way!'' Carl shouted.

''Honestly. Some people can be so rude. But you're not Leo. I know I saw him around here somewhere.''

That was it. Carl didn't care if she was a crazy lady. From now on, if you didn't listen to Carl Jackson, you paid the price.

He sent a bright green fireball straight for her. Scratch one crazy lady. It should be quite spectacular in the dark.

''What?'' Margaret cried in outrage as the fireball bumped against her, pushing her back. The fireball didn't make her burn or explode or anything. Instead, it rushed on past her, lifting off into the darkness until it disappeared in the distance.

Carl couldn't believe this. It was as if she could resist the magic; by not believing in her surroundings, for her the magic wasn't there.

''I will not tolerate this!'' Carl shouted, but it wasn't his own voice talking. ''You will not attack my wife!''

''Leo. I've found you at last.'' Margaret took a step toward Carl and smiled. ''We always fought too much before. I didn't realize how much I missed you until you were gone.''

Carl could not stand this. What was happening to him? He raised his hands to give Margaret the full force of both gems. Even she wouldn't be able to withstand something like that.

He willed the gems to strike.

Nothing happened.

Margaret rushed into his open arms.

''Oh, Leo, I've missed you so!''

''And I've missed you, too, Margaret. I'm glad we can be together, if only for the moment.''

''Moment? What do you mean, Leo? Now that we've found each other, we can go home.'' She lifted her head and kissed his cheek.

Carl would not allow this for another second. He could do nothing with this cancer inside him. He had enemies everywhere! He would kill them all!

''Get away from me!'' He jerked his head back, pushing himself away from the woman's embrace.

Margaret looked hurt and confused. "Leo? What's happened to Leo?"

"I'm—" Leo began with Carl's voice.

"No, you're not!" Carl shouted to drown the other man out. If he was going to change things around here, he'd better start at home. "I'm going to burn you out of me!"

He turned the jewels toward his chest and told them to incinerate Leo.

He cried out as the eyes did their work, Leo's voice and Carl's both together. His whole body was encased in flame—green flame. Carl thought the jewels would protect him, but he had never known such agony.

"Stop!" he called to the gems.

The flame was gone, but his skin still burned. Carl tried to take a breath, but his lungs wouldn't cooperate. But he could still stand and think and see. And he still had the dragon's eyes.

"Leo?" he called out. "Leo?"

There was no answer. It was a painful solution, but it had worked. He was free at last, but he had no strength to stand. Carl laughed as he fell to the deck.

When Todd woke up, he had only one thought in his head. His father was going to kill him. His father had already tried.

Sala looked down at him. "Oh, Todd! I was so worried about you!"

Todd looked up at her beautiful face. He was glad she was safe. He got up to his feet slowly. He was sore, but otherwise all right. The dragon's eye must have protected him from the worst of his father's magic.

He turned to see his father screaming, wrapped in green fire. Margaret Furlong and Snake both stood nearby, both frozen by what they saw. What had happened when he was unconscious?

"He did that to himself," Mr. Mills said from where he stood nearby. "Carl's wizard form seems to contain Leo Furlong; some leftover gift from Nunn, I guess. Leo tried to assert himself with Margaret, and Carl wouldn't have it."

So he had set himself on fire? Todd's father was truly crazy. Todd realized he had been holding back in his fight with his father up to now. As much as he hated and feared the man, Carl Jackson was still Todd's father. How did you kill someone with whom you'd spent all your life?

Todd's father collapsed as the flames sputtered out. He mumbled something from where he lay on the deck, his voice slowly growing in strength.

"—eyes . . . pain . . . handle . . . pain . . . eyes can handle . . . pain . . . The eyes can handle the pain. The eyes *will* handle the pain."

He rose then, not through the use of his muscles, but by using his magic to rotate his whole body ninety degrees, so that the same straight, unmoving form that lay on the deck now stood in the exact same position.

"I am beyond the pain," the magician announced. He didn't look very much like Todd's father anymore. He hardly looked human, his flesh replaced by grey, flaking ash.

"I've gotten rid of Leo," the magician added. "Now I'll kill the rest of you."

Todd had often thought of his father as a monster. Now he looked like one.

"What say we consider that a challenge?" Mills asked.

But Todd wasn't about to let his father off that easily. "Sounds like raving to me. The raving of a pitiful old man who doesn't know what he's doing."

It had the desired effect. "You never had any respect. You never should have been born, and I'm going to make sure you don't stay here. I finally have a chance to put you where you belong."

Todd wasn't going to let his father's words hurt him anymore. "We both have that chance, Dad." What did you do to a crazy man if you wanted to win? Make him crazier still. "You're not even human anymore. You're falling apart."

Flakes of ash fell to the deck as Carl Jackson shook his fist at his son. "I've gone on to be better than human. Why do you need flesh and blood when you're a wizard?"

No, Todd thought, the only thing you needed as a wizard was a more clever plan than the other wizard. He couldn't burn something that was already ashes. Maybe he could create a great wind to blow his father away.

"What?" his father demanded. "What did you say?"

Todd didn't hear anybody say anything. But then he did,

though not in any normal way. He heard sounds like whispers that echoed through his head, a faint scratching inside of his skull.

"Look!" Mills called, pointing toward Todd's father. "In front of us!"

Shapes flowed across the deck, looking like shadows when there should be no shadows. Todd could hear their cries more clearly now although they made no real sound.

Nunn, the things called. *Nunn.*

"I am not Nunn!" Carl screamed back.

We have been waiting for you to fulfill your promise, the dark things said. *We want your power.*

The dark creatures swarmed across the deck toward the wizard. There seemed to be hundreds of them. Carl Jackson was no more. The ash creature could be anyone or anything. But the wizard possessed Nunn's jewels, the power these creatures had sought from whatever dark place they might have come.

"Keep away from me!" the ash wizard called. "I will kill you! I am nothing but power!"

The shapes swirled around Todd's father, coming ever closer. Carl Jackson sent out burst after burst of power, causing one or another of the shapes to move away. But the ash wizard waved his hands about him wildly. The few times the frantic shots hit one of the things, the shape would disintegrate. But the other creatures seemed not to notice. Their very numbers would overwhelm the wizard eventually, and the power would be theirs.

The whispers filled Todd's head as well. *Nunn. Power. Give. You owe us, Nunn. We will be strong. We will give you a sweet, cold death.* The voices threatened to freeze Todd from any action. He looked to Mr. Mills and saw that the vice-principal was covering his ears, as if that might keep the voices away. Sala stepped to Todd's side and took his arm. Her warmth seemed to make the voices a little more distant. Anything, he thought, to keep himself from going crazy, too.

Carl waved his arms about, looking frantically all around him for a clear space to escape. "You!" he called to the old sailor huddled out of harm's way. "Hiding over there! Come out here or I will fry you!"

The old sailor didn't move. It was plain even to him that

Todd's father was having too much trouble with the dark things to fry anybody.

"Won't anybody listen to me?" Carl looked to Snake, still struggling with his noose. "You! I'll give you your freedom!" The wizard waved one gem in Snake's direction, and the faint green noose evaporated. Snake stumbled forward, taking deep, rasping breaths, as if he still could not get enough air.

"Now!" Carl Jackson demanded. "Get these things away from me!"

"Lord, no." Snake looked behind him, to see the enchanted knife at last pull itself free of the wooden deck. "The knife!"

The weapon rose into the air and traveled about in a circle, as if even an enchanted knife had to get its bearings. The spinning stopped at last, the blade pointing once again toward Snake.

"I'll help you with the shapes," Snake called, "if you call off that damned knife!" He jumped behind the wizard made of ash as the knife rushed toward him. Carl glanced down in surprise as the speeding knife pushed through him, front to back, as if his ashen form held no substance at all.

Snake looked in horror at the knife protruding from his chest. He fell backward on the deck, very still.

"Dead," Mills said.

"He deserved it," Todd added.

Sala hugged Todd and began to cry.

Todd looked at the girl. He had thought she would be happy.

"I don't know why I'm crying," she answered before he could ask the question. "Maybe it's relief. Maybe I'm crying for the father I never had—the father I never can have."

Sort of like the way Todd felt about his father. Maybe that was one of the reasons he and Sala were together; they both understood those things.

Todd's father looked down at his chest. A hole had appeared where the knife had passed through, a hole that would have pierced the wizard's heart, had one remained. Ash swirled through the hole, drifted from the wizard's head and arms and chest, as if his whole form would slowly flake away.

He looked straight at Todd for the first time. "What have you done to your father?" he screamed.

The shapes spoke again.

Nunn. You are ready for us. You will die. Accept us at last. Give us your power.

"You're all coming for me," the wizard cried. "I don't care why, I don't care what I've done. I can kill everybody!"

Todd found his father's whining disgusting. "Can you, Dad? You've always been all talk. Can you do more than that?"

"I can do more than that! I can force you to help your father!" He reached out a hand toward Todd, the charred flesh flaking from his fingers with every move. The gem still glowed in his palm, though.

"What?" Sala called. "No!"

Todd looked to the girl at his side and saw that his father had surrounded Sala's waist with another tentacle of green, and was slowly drawing her across the deck toward him.

His father laughed as ash crumbled off his chin. "Now you'll do as I say, you ungrateful bastard, or I'll—"

"You'll do nothing!" Todd felt his whole form fill with rage. He would not let his father hurt another soul. He screamed as a great surge of power blasted forth from his dragon's eye.

His father shrieked in turn as he was hit by the power of Todd's blow.

"No!" he cried as the blast lifted him from the deck. "How dare you hit your father? I'll get you—"

Nunn. The shapes flew all around him now, seeking to cover him from head to toe. Great clouds of ash rose as they fluttered close to the wizard.

"No!" Carl screamed again. He propelled himself backward, over the ship's rail. Todd heard a splash.

Mills was first to the rail.

"Is he—" Todd asked as he stepped up behind the other man.

Mills called on his own gem to give off some light. "He's nowhere around. All I can see is a slight scum of ash on the water."

"And those shapes?" Sala asked.

"They seem to have gone with him," Mills answered.

"He's dead, then, just like my father. But what happened to the eyes?"

"Who really knows anything about the eyes?" Mills replied. "Perhaps the dragon will take them back when it arrives."

Todd didn't like this. He stepped up to the railing, but saw nothing but the dark water. He needed to see his father dead to know it was true.

Sala shivered at his side. "I want to get out of this place."

"You're all leaving?" the old sailor asked. Todd turned around to see the old man had stood and stepped out of his hiding place. "Shouldn't be surprised. It was always the way. Old Bill's always left to clean up the mess."

Margaret stepped up to the rail beside them and looked out to sea. She had seemed, in the recent battle, at least to regain some connection with reality. Todd wondered if she'd be able to keep it.

"Is Leo gone?" she asked.

Todd thought so, but before he could find a way to answer, Margaret pointed at something in the air beyond the ship.

"Look," she whispered. "How beautiful."

It was the owl, white wings spread, floating out over the ocean like some cross between a bird and the moon.

"You hardly ever see birds like that on the Circle," Margaret added.

For once, Todd had to agree.

Where was he?

The last thing Hyram Sayre remembered, he had been hit by a blast from Carl Jackson. There had been a moment of darkness. It had been very long since he had seen true darkness. When you were the lawn god, you didn't need to sleep.

When he opened his eyes again, it was all worth it. Everything around him was more so, brighter, faster, louder. He was traveling at unimaginable speeds, higher, ever higher, so fast that he thought he would never stop.

He knew instantly what was happening. Hyram was on his way to heaven. In the place where lawns were always green. At long last he would receive his just reward.

Hyram waved to a beautiful snowy owl as he went sailing past. Where he was bound there would be no more cares, an eternity of peace, a perfect world.

But first he would answer the doorbell.

○ Thirty

Nick saw the fire in the trees. Zachs was coming.

"We should be surrounded by now," the Captain said softly. "A pity the enemy doesn't realize they are surrounded as well."

The fire darted around the edge of the clearing, moving so quickly that most of the leaves it passed didn't even burn.

"Attack, my family!" The fire stopped and stood on its hind legs, its arms waving the troops to the clearing. "Attack for the glory of Zachs!"

The wolf at Nick's side growled softly as they heard a cry swell in the woods, as a score or more of the apes beat their chests and screamed. But the screams wavered and died, replaced by the cries of humans and wolves.

"No!" shouted the fire being in the trees. "Zachs will not allow this! No! No! No!" A great ball of fire appeared between Zachs's hands. He threw it into the forest below.

Some of the human and wolf sounds turned to cries of pain. Zachs could turn the tide of battle. He needed to be distracted.

"Zachs!" Nick called out. "Your real fight is with me."

The fire creature turned his head to look down at Nick. "The boy with the sword! He laughs at Zachs! No one laughs at Zachs and lives!" He shot another ball of fire at Nick. Nick raised his sword, which absorbed the fire easily.

"No!" Zachs screamed. "No! No one can do that to Zachs!"

Nick felt a wave of weakness overtake him. He staggered back and looked down at the ground, trying to regain his balance. For an instant he thought it had something to do with the fire, but it was different than that. It was a wave of change.

He felt, at that instant, that he could drop the sword and walk away from it forever. Except, of course, he would then be burned alive.

He wondered what had changed; if Obar had somehow changed the spell that governed Nick's life. Not that it mattered. It looked like he and his sword would be partners forever.

He looked up and saw that Zachs had flown down to stand before him.

Nick's blade shook in his hands, eager to attack. Would a fire being bleed? He might bake his sword and burn to cinders. Nick didn't care. He wanted this fight, to let out all the anger and grief and frustration he'd felt, not only with the sword and Obar's spell, but with his father and all the others who would act like his father, judging him, controlling him, Obar and the Captain included. At this instant his head seemed as clear as it had been at any time since he had come to this new place. He wanted to clean himself of all the anger and emotions, to burn it all away. How better than a trial by fire?

Nick stood up straight, his weapon before him. "You are no match for my sword, Zachs. And you're leading your family to their deaths."

The fire creature leaped from one foot to the other, as if he could not contain his anger. "Lies! All lies! Only Zachs knows the truth!"

Nick shook his head. "The only truth is in my sword."

"Fire is too merciful! Zachs will destroy you with his touch!"

The fire being leaped toward Nick with a shriek. Nick took a step away, almost overcome by the heat. But the sword kept his hands still, the point of the blade waiting for another offering.

He felt the blade penetrate the fire being as Zachs's burning hands encircled his throat.

Mary Lou knew that, sooner or later, her mother would get involved. As soon as there had been a pause in the battle between Nunn and the two women, Rose Dafoe had begun to shout.

"This is all too much. Mary Lou, I want you to stop this nonsense now."

Even Mary Lou's father, Harold, looked at his wife in disbelief. "Rose, what are you saying?"

Rose spun on her husband, happy, it seemed, to have someone closer be the focus of her anger. "Harold. Don't contradict me."

Harold raised his hands in self-defense. "But Mary Lou's been given a gift—something we can't understand."

Rose looked like she was about to cry. "I knew you would turn against me. You'll all turn against me."

"We'll all turn against each other," Nunn interrupted, "before the dragon is done with us. It would be easy for Mary Lou to give her gem to me."

That almost made Mary Lou laugh. Nunn wasn't about to change any more than Rose Dafoe.

"I'm sorry," Mary Lou added, "but I can't listen to my mother anymore." As if she ever should have in the first place.

Her mother started to cry for real. She shook off her father's attempts to comfort her. The world was coming to an end, but Rose wasn't getting her way. After all, her mother knew what was important.

Stanley stepped forward. "I think this would be a better place if we all turned against Nunn. You have two dragon's eyes to his one. Do we dare to kill him?"

Mary Lou shook her head. "How do we kill someone who isn't really alive? Besides, I know this is not the time to kill anyone."

"You know this, you know that!" Nunn demanded. "Who made you the one that knows everything?"

This was the one thing Mary Lou knew for sure. "The dragon."

That answer even stopped Nunn for the moment.

"When the dragon comes, I'm going to kill you all," Nunn said at last.

"If the dragon lets you." Mary Lou did not feel so sure of that. The dragon let her see how things should be for now. It gave her no glimpse of the future.

"Look!" Maggie called. "Up there in the sky!"

Mary Lou looked up. A huge white owl, wings spread wide, coasted across the night sky.

"Haven't seen one of those," Stanley murmured, "well, since we got to this place."

''This is something that happens only once,'' Mary Lou agreed.

All of them watched the owl fly silently overhead.

Mills had to leave the others from the ship; Todd, Sala, and Margaret. He promised he would meet them back at the clearing with the rest of the neighbors as soon as he had finished one last errand.

About time, another voice said within him.

You're back, Mills thought.

I never really left, Rox replied. *The battle had grown too intense. I just got a bit too caught up in settling old scores. I thought it best to retreat and think, perhaps gain some perspective.*

And have you? Mills asked.

How can you gain perspective when you have a dragon breathing down your back? Still, it was the dragon who separated us from Zachs. I think that reuniting the three of us has to be our first priority.

If we can coax him to join us.

We still have the stone. Zachs will have no choice.

Mills didn't know if he wanted an angry Zachs to coexist within him. Still, there seemed to be at least a little logic in this course of action; something you couldn't say about much else around here.

So we go after Zachs, Mills thought. The others had already left, leaving only the old sailor behind.

You're getting quite handy with that dragon's eye. That's another reason for me to vanish. You can't teach yourself anything if somebody else is always doing all the work.

Teaching the teacher, Mills thought. He hoped he'd learned his lesson well.

Now let us find Zachs. If I may use the eye, I know a few shortcuts.

Mills blinked, and they had gone from the deck of the ship to a clearing in the woods. Before them stood Nick and Zachs, unmoving, as if they formed a perfect circle of death.

Nick's blade had gone straight through Zachs's chest, while the fire creature's burning hands sizzled at the young man's throat.

It appears that the dragon has given us another obstacle.

"What should we do?" Mills asked aloud. "It looks like they were killing each other."

And were somehow stopped. Perhaps it wasn't time yet for either one of them to die.

"The dragon can do that?"

Who knows? Who else would do something like that? If we put Zachs inside us, we can probably repair the damage.

"But what will happen to Nick? I don't want to be responsible for his death."

He may already be dead.

"May?"

Nothing can ever be said with certainty about this place.

A low, mournful cry drifted to them from the edge of the clearing. Mills looked up and saw a great white owl nesting in a nearby tree.

The owl? We have to act now.

Mills looked down to see the jewel glowing in his hand.

No! he thought. He wasn't ready—

Nick and Zachs staggered together like they were a single being. Then both of them cried out in pain.

The Captain found himself with nothing to do. His troops had subdued the enemy in a matter of minutes, and Nick and his sword would handle Zachs. The Captain always found fire creatures a little out of his league, anyway. He had let the two combatants take over the clearing, and gone to check on his troops. There were hardly any casualties on his side. One man and one wolf had both been stabbed with poison sticks. A couple of the others had gotten bitten, but they would survive. Two of the apes had been captured, the rest were dead. All in all, it was a good night's work.

He could have gone back to check on Nick, to see if there was some way he could help the young man in his fight. But Nick and his sword could wreak havoc the Captain couldn't even dream about.

He felt that his best times were behind him; that the world was changing around him faster than he could keep up. He had helped to foil Nunn's army. There were no more challenges there. New wizards were taking over for the old, wizards with whom he had no connection. And everyone had done far too much living since he had left the Volunteers for him ever to rejoin them. Pator would chide him for having foolish thoughts, if Pator were still alive.

"Wherrre now?" asked the wolf with the broken fang.

"I don't know what to do with myself," the Captain admitted.

"Savorrrr the victorry," the old wolf suggested.

"Perhaps. I think I need a little quiet. A walk in the woods, perhaps."

"Prrotect yourrself," the old wolf cautioned. "Tonight is strrange."

"I've got my bow and my knife." The Captain touched the two weapons with his two hands. "That should be enough— I hope."

The old wolf nodded. "I returrn to camp." The animal turned and walked away from the Captain.

He found himself alone, on the edge of a new clearing. No, not exactly alone, for sitting on a tree branch on the clearing's far side was an owl, pure white in the starlight.

There was still a challenge or two left. The Captain had never killed an owl. He silently fit an arrow to his bow and aimed for the bird. The night was still, without the faintest breeze. The owl did not move, although its large dark eyes appeared to be looking directly back at the Captain.

One single note as the bow snapped taut, and the arrow was silently on its way. The owl still did not move, as if it were expecting this death right along, as if it were only waiting for the proper arrow.

The Captain took a step toward his prey as the arrow sank deep into the owl's chest. But the owl did not die.

Instead, the owl changed.

The spot where the arrow entered opened up, and it was filled with blinding light. And it continued to open, wider, and wider still, then impossibly wide, until it showed the first inklings of a creature on the other side, a creature so large that the great hole could only show its smallest portion.

The Captain had been waiting for this moment ever since he had come to this place. He had known this ever since the day he had fired the neighbors' gun, and had heard the dragon's distant answer. They were destined to meet, sooner or later. It was the last thing he was looking forward to. In killing the owl, the Captain would be the first to meet the dragon.

The Captain laughed and pulled the last weapon in his arsenal; his knife. Time for the final great adventure.

"Come on, you demon," the Captain shouted, waving his knife above his head, "I'll ride you to hell!"

The dragon obliged.

○ Thirty-one

The dragon was here.

Mrs. Smith saw it, a riot of color that filled the sky, shades of light beyond any she had ever seen. Was that its fire, or the sun reflected in a dragon's eye? If it was the last thing she was going to see, at least it was very beautiful.

The dragon was here.

Stanley and Maggie, the last of the Volunteers, held on to each other as the ground shook so violently they thought the whole world would shake apart. The sky had gone from darkest night to very bright. It was very different from the light of dawn.

The dragon was here.

Jason felt it in the dirt beneath his feet. The whole world was changing, coming alive in a way that would have been impossible before. Perhaps the world itself was the dragon, and they had spent all this time on the dragon's back. Or, more likely, the dragon had been somewhere else, and became the world when the proper moment came. If Jason, as the Oom-gosh, was a servant of the world, did he now become a servant of the dragon?

The dragon was here.

Rose Dafoe stopped crying. The air was so dry that tears were impossible. She wished she hadn't been so foolish, and could find the comfort of her husband's arms. Now she could see nothing but light, could hear nothing but a constant roar, could feel nothing but a certain dread that her life was over.

George Blake saw his son's imagination come to life, the impossible become reality, those things he had scoffed at become very serious indeed.

Nick saw a great yawning emptiness that stretched forever.
It wasn't death. Death was simpler. This was an emptiness that
threatened to stretch across eternity. Should he enter that place,
he would not only cease to exist, he never would have existed.

Todd felt a wave of emotion; happiness, grief, and anger,
especially anger, as if the dragon was made of all the feelings
in the world rather than scale and bone.

The dragon was here.

Mills and Rox and Zachs could feel the pain drop away and
the power grow.

Nunn could feel the heat within his newly constructed head;
a heat that spoke of fires beyond imagining.

For the first time Mary Lou could see the answer.

The dragon was here.

Joan Blake wanted to find her son. Rebecca Jackson just
wanted it to be over.

Margaret could see nothing but Chestnut Circle.

The dragon was here.

"Well?" Raven cawed to his old adversary. "You going to
do something, or just stand around and look pretty?"

O Around the Circle:
The Dragon's True Nature

The lore of the dragon has been handed down for year upon year, ever since that time, faintly remembered and barely spoken of, when there first were both a dragon and those who might speak about it. But the dragon came again and again, in times beyond counting. So it was that there happened in a certain time and a certain place to be a wise elder and a young student who wanted to examine all that had gone before. And the elder, to attempt to explain the nature of the dragon, decided to tell a tale.

This is how the elder began:

"The dragon has been described as many different things by many different people. Every time the dragon appears, there is another story that is handed down. And it is said that every time the dragon comes, it chooses a different path."

"Do you mean a different way to kill?" the student asked. For, to his understanding, the dragon always came to destroy the world.

"The dragon always brings change," the elder counseled. "Destruction is one of the dragon's tools. But there seem to be as many aspects of the dragon as there are visits the creature has made to this realm."

"I have heard that the dragon can make the world so hot that all that is living evaporates before it, leaving only shadows to mark their passing. And I have heard that the dragon's wings are so strong they can cause a wind far colder than the worst of winter, freezing people before they might take a breath. And I have heard that the dragon is so great that a single tear that falls from his eye can drown an entire city in an instant."

"All true," the elder acknowledged. "But let me tell you of a very different experience; the one time the dragon chose to come in peace; an ancient time when the dragon allowed itself to be in the presence of others.

"Even then, the dragon kept its secrets, for it waited until total darkness had fallen, for it did not wish its fearsome appearance to cause anyone to die prematurely.

"So it was that a man stumbled upon the dragon's tail, and upon close inspection, said that he had discovered a great worm, miles in length. But a woman in that distant spot where the dragon's head now lay felt the creature's mighty jaw, and declared that she had found some mighty wall that held back fire. Between the two, a small group found one of the great spikes that ridge the dragon's back, and declared it to be a shard of rare obsidian, a treasure as long as three men. And the woman moved away from the dragon, and found herself in the steam that came from its nostrils, and felt that she had stepped into the very cloud that brought the thunder.

"The people of that place had felt a worm and fire, obsidian and a cloud. And all of these impressions, in their way, were true. The dragon was all these things and a hundred more. Perhaps the dragon was a bit of everything."

The student nodded when his teacher was done. "I have heard a similar tale before, O wise one, but in the earlier version, it was about an elephant."

"Ah." At that the elder smiled a most enlightened smile. "My point exactly."

◯ Thirty-two

Mrs. Smith looked around. After a confusing jumble of images, sounds, and smells, an assault on all the senses, really, the neighbors were all here. But where was here?

They stood on a slightly uneven surface of neutral grey. So neutral was the color, in fact, that it was difficult for Mrs. Smith to tell where the floor ended and the sky—or perhaps a distant wall—began.

"This is still the same place where we stood before," Jason announced from the exact middle of their group. He had not even been with the rest of the neighbors a minute ago. Mrs. Smith had not noticed until now that Jason's skin had taken on a slight greenish cast.

"It is the world that has changed," Jason added.

Harold Dafoe stared at his son. "And what is that supposed to mean?"

"We're inside the dragon," Mary Lou announced in turn. "I think, at the moment, everything on this world is inside the dragon."

"If only we could protect our children from this," Rose Dafoe muttered.

Joan Blake peered up into the indefinite grey as if the answer might be just out of sight. "I don't understand. Has it eaten us?"

"It's playing with us before it destroys us," Rebecca Jackson suggested.

"No," Mary Lou replied firmly. "It will give us one chance before we die."

"Awfully nice of it," Evan Mills murmured, warily checking his immediate surroundings; more, it seemed to Constance, to guard against attack from human or wizard rather than some vague threat from the dragon.

"Before *some* of us die!" Nunn shouted from the edge of the gathering. "Those with enough power will survive!"

The bloodied flesh of Nunn's temporary form exploded into a thousand tiny motes of emerald light.

"This is the final battle," Nunn's voice called from somewhere within the sparkling mass.

Mills didn't know if this would work for a minute, let alone enough time to make a difference.

Let me out, Zachs screamed. The fire being was scrambling frantically around his prison within Evan Mills's physical form. It was enough to make Mills nauseous.

No, the wizard Rox chided. *This is where you belong. Together, we are strong.*

Nunn is getting away. Nunn hurt Zachs. Zachs has to kill Nunn.

All in good time. We all have reason to wish for Nunn's demise.

Rox's words actually seemed to quiet the fire being for an instant. For once, Mills thought, the three of them were in agreement.

Zachs had forgotten the feelings here. Zachs belongs?

It was the first time Mills had ever heard Zachs express doubt. Another good sign, Mills supposed. He still wondered how the three of them could effectively deal with some outside problem when they had so many problems just coexisting.

The three of us here together are greater than any one of us would be by themselves. That is what the dragon fears.

And that is what we have to use, Mills added.

Nunn is coming, Rox warned.

Nunn will die! Zachs shouted.

Mills just hoped the rest of them wouldn't die with him.

Nunn knew that time was at an end. He had to act now if he had any hope of winning.

Magic was mostly in the mind. So much of what he'd done before was illusion. Now, perhaps, he could use the dragon's tricks as well.

He would have to move quickly. His sorcerous allies of

years past were now his enemies, yearning for his power. The newcomers had power of their own, but they were naive in its use, and should be susceptible to surprise. He would have to depend upon his experience, and his treachery.

His own jewel would lead him to the others of its kind. His cleverness would capture them.

He had survived this once before. When the dragon was here, all things were possible.

Mrs. Smith was tired. The magic buoyed her, but she never seemed to have fully recovered from those assaults and accidents that had happened since she had been here. Her legs were still useless, and the shoulder that had been struck in battle felt like there was a wedge of ice in the bone. Maybe, if she were a better magician, she could become like Nunn, and be something no longer human, beyond the cares of the everyday. Maybe she was tired because she resisted the dragon's eye and would not surrender to its power. Obar and Nunn had both insisted the gem would take over her life. Their eyes had certainly taken over their destinies.

She looked back out into their nondescript surroundings. The grey, Mrs. Smith realized, was not so much floor or sky as a never-ending mist, a place where nothing looked quite real. She wondered if any of them—wizards, neighbors, dragon—were quite real anymore.

Other things were here as well. She could sense them with her eye, as if this grey plain might go on forever. There were thousands of things out there, millions perhaps; every creature from this world was somewhere inside the dragon.

She recognized some of them as her mind raced across that never-ending plain: those dark things that had fluttered about Nunn, and the thing that had come from beneath the sea, the Anno, the red-furred apes, all the people and things in that port town they had visited a couple of days before. First, the dragon had brought them all to this world. And now the dragon brought them here.

Mary Lou said that the dragon would give them a chance, whatever that meant. What was the dragon's purpose, after all? The stories about it could be interpreted in different ways. Did the dragon only destroy, or did it create the world anew?

There must be a secret to this mist; a secret to the dragon.

She would push her weaknesses behind and depend once more on magic, until the dragon took the magic away forever.

The voices wanted to pull Mary Lou away. Not the voices of the neighbors, or those others who seemed to stand just beyond their sight in the mist, but the voices of those no longer seen, the voices of the dead, the inner voices of the dragon.

"Mary Lou," the most familiar voice said.

"Garo," she replied, and a small part of her was still pleased to hear him.

"You're in my home now," his deep, reassuring voice continued. "Maybe we can be together at last."

Another voice spoke up. "Don't trust him for an instant."

Mary Lou knew that voice as well, a warmer voice than Garo's. "Wilbert?"

"At your service, volunteering in the afterlife." Wilbert laughed, and Mary Lou could picture his bearded, grinning face. "I live here now, too, if you can call this living. It's good to hear a voice I know."

"He doesn't know anything about this place," Garo said, sounding annoyed at the intrusion.

"I know enough to realize that you are working for the dragon," Wilbert replied.

Garo sighed, as if it was a great trial to make them understand. "We are *all* working for the dragon in this place. But there are many ways to do that."

"Garo?" Mary Lou asked. "Will you tell me the truth?"

"I've always had your best interests at heart," the gallant voice answered, "at least in those times that mattered." Garo hadn't changed. His pretty reply had avoided the question entirely.

"The dragon has rules," Wilbert insisted. "Even a newcomer knows that."

"We can *change* the rules," Garo insisted. "There are many ways here to shape reality."

Mary Lou never expected to be arguing with ghosts. But all her romantic notions were long gone. Garo couldn't be relied upon to tell her the truth. And Wilbert sounded like he hadn't been here long enough to learn his way around.

What did all of this really have to do with the dragon? Mary

Lou had work to do. Maybe Garo was merely meant to distract her until it was too late.

Nick's sword was confused, as though he and his weapon were swimming through a sea of blood. The blade spun wildly in his hands, jerking first left then right, as if it was right on top of a new victim and could not wait to plunge into his heart. Nick wondered what could cause this agitation. Perhaps the sword sensed a power greater than blood, a destination more attractive than the death of others.

They were lost, alone in the grey. Nick could hear voices somewhere in the distance, but could see no one in the fog. The flesh of his neck, which had sizzled and burned beneath Zachs's touch, flaked off if he touched the skin, but no longer seemed to hurt.

"Son?" a voice called out of the fog.

"Dad?" Nick turned around, looking for the source of the voice in the grey.

"I knew I could find you if I tried." Nick saw a vague shape now, approaching him through the grey. "That's the way things are supposed to work around here, isn't it?"

The mist swirled aside, and his father stood, perhaps a dozen feet away.

"Funny how I could do that." His father shook his head. "I've never felt like I fit in here for a minute."

His father tried to smile, but it wasn't in him.

"I've failed you many times before, and I'll probably fail you again. But it hurts me to see you in so much pain. I was hoping this time that I might do—something to help." He noticed how the blade in Nick's hands had turned to point toward him. "Maybe you could throw that sword to me. I wouldn't mind losing a little blood if it would set you free."

"You'd die, Dad." Nick shook his head. "And the sword is the only thing that gives me strength. I don't know if I can give that up."

That seemed to make his father sadder still. "If you don't, you know it will kill you."

Nick nodded his head. "Yeah. I know."

Dad walked forward and held out his hand. "Come on. Maybe this is something we can share with others. Maybe together someone can figure out a way."

Nick had never seen strength like this in his father before. Maybe he had strength in himself as well.

He pointed the sword away from both of them and took his father's hand.

Todd saw something moving toward him in the mist. Sala hugged him tight.

"Ah," the voice called out pleasantly. "There you are. I've been looking for you forever."

"I knew he wasn't dead," Todd said softly.

"Your father?" Sala asked, and her grip grew tighter still.

"It was all too easy," was Todd's reply. "With my father, nothing is ever easy."

Before Todd could even see him, he knew that his father had changed. The shadow emerging from the mist looked much thinner than before. He made a rattling noise as he walked.

"You didn't think you could leave me behind," his father called as he approached. "Not when you have to pay for all you've done wrong, Todd boy."

"Oh, God," Sala whispered.

The sorcerous flame that Carl Jackson had used to purge his body had worked all too well. He was nothing more than a skeleton, sporting a few bits of charred flesh and a dragon's eye protruding from each of his bony palms. But he was still Todd's father.

Carl Jackson laughed. "Something's missing."

Two dragon's eyes flashed amid the bones, and Todd's mother, Rebecca Jackson, was in his father's arms. She opened her mouth to scream, but nothing came out.

"A happy family, together at last." The grin on his skull seemed to get even wider. "Should I kill her first, Toddy, or would you like that honor?"

Mills stood in front of his classroom. He only had two students today. Their names were Rox and Zachs; an old man and a being made of fire.

Why were they here? He only knew that he had no time to spare. The lesson was very important. He turned to the blackboard.

TODAY'S LESSON was scrawled there in bold block letters. LEARNING ABOUT THE DRAGON.

Both his students held a shiny green stone. He looked down at his hand and saw that he did, too.

He remembered a little about this now. This was some sort of a scientific experiment. These green baubles might be pretty, but what good were stones anyway unless they could teach a lesson?

The classroom door opened, and a new student walked into the room, a tall pale fellow with a very happy face.

"Ah," he called. "Glad I'm not too late." He held up a shiny green stone of his own. "Three and one make—"

"Zachs knows!" the fire being shouted. The old man frowned, as if he was trying to remember something. He raised his hand. "I don't think I should be—" he began, but then stopped, and put his hand down again.

Mills had finally remembered the lesson. "The stones!" he announced. "We have to put them all together!"

"Exactly!" The new student grinned. "Then I'll show you a magic trick. They'll all disappear!"

Magic? Mills had problems with magic. Not scientific enough, for one thing. And, now that he thought of it, what was scientific about a dragon?

There was something about this that wasn't right. He hadn't been a classroom teacher for years. He'd been in another classroom, though, only a few days before. It had been an illusion, created by—

"Nunn," Mills said aloud.

The new student's smile wavered. "Yes, that's my name. Now give me those stones!"

The other students were on their feet.

"You can't trick us anymore, Nunn!" Rox called.

"Kill Nunn!" Zachs jumped up and down, his voice growing higher with every leap. "Kill him, kill him, kill him!"

"Don't let him escape!" Rox called. All three of them, Rox, Mills, and Zachs, rushed the wizard in their midst.

"This will not happen!" Nunn exclaimed, and for the first time Mills thought he heard fear in the wizard's voice. "This is an illusion of my construction! I am master here!"

"There is only one true master in this place," Rox replied calmly. "We are inside the dragon, and anything is possible."

"Let me out of here!" Nunn screamed as the others grabbed his clothes.

He vanished. Mills found himself holding a scuffed brown shoe.

"He can't get very far," Rox said. "Together, we can find him easily."

The classroom vanished.

Together, Mills thought, and two other voices said the word in his head.

"I've had just about enough of this, hey?" Stanley said to the neighbors around him.

Maggie looked at him skeptically. "And what are you going to do about it?"

"What I can, Maggie dear." Stanley shook his head. "Wizards and dragons, what a pain." He looked to Rose and Harold Dafoe, Joan Blake, Bobby Furlong, and even the dog Charlie. "What can we do when all this magic is flying around us? We can fight together, or we can die alone. We can die together, too, but at least that doesn't sound as lonely."

"I'm ready!" Maggie called. "Anybody know any stirring camp songs?"

"Are you looking for more volunteers?" George Blake and his son Nick strode out of the mist. "I'm getting pretty good at moving around in this stuff."

Joan Blake rushed to her husband and son. It was the first time Stanley had ever seen the woman cry.

"You want a song? How about 'A Hundred Bottles of Beer on the Wall'?" Bobby suggested.

Stanley nodded. "A fine old song, even where we come from. And sure to drive the dragon crazy, besides. What say we join hands and sing?"

Mary Lou said something aloud she had known silently for a long time.

"Garo? Are you the dragon?"

"I speak for the dragon. And for myself." Garo had the audacity to sound hurt. "You have to hurry, you know. Your moment will be over soon. The dragon is impatient to be done. It has already taken too long."

Too long? Mary Lou thought. How can an all-powerful be-ing be impatient?

But the dragon only seemed all-powerful. The creature had as many limits as the rest of them.

"The dragon can't do it, can he?" she said with a smile. "There's something in its way. We all have a moment more."

"The dragon will find a way," Garo replied self-importantly. "It enjoys a challenge. This current lot is one of the best."

"He's right there!" Wilbert added. "The dragon brought us all here for this moment, after all."

"Is the dragon talking through you, too?" Mary Lou asked.

"He tries, but old Wilbert's pretty good at bopping and weaving."

The mist swirled around them suddenly, as if it was being stirred by a great wind.

"What?" Garo cried in alarm.

It was Raven.

"Enough of this creature's inflated importance," the bird cawed at Mary Lou. "You are as great as the dragon. If it wasn't an even fight, the dragon never would have brought you here. This challenge is the reason for its existence."

Mary Lou had never been quite so happy to see the bird. "What do we do?"

The black bird fluffed his feathers for a moment before re-plying. "No; in this, Raven plays by the rules. You wouldn't want the dragon mad at Raven, would you?"

There was a new noise in the area, like three voices talking at once.

"Over here!" Raven called.

"Is Nunn here?" Evan Mills appeared abruptly at Mary Lou's side. But there seemed to be two others crowded with him. Rox and Zachs, Mary Lou realized.

"You've got them on the run!" Wilbert's gleeful voice called from very far away.

"Garo?" Mary Lou called. "Wilbert?" But all the dead voices were gone. "What was that?"

Mills and the two others shrugged as one. "Things happen when we're together."

Of course, Mary Lou thought. That was the answer. She had said it herself, when she had been speaking for the dragon.

They had to become the dragon. They had to use all seven eyes in unison. Only if they fought the dragon together would they have a chance to win.

"Always by the rules." The black bird cawed once more. "Except, of course, when Raven cheats."

"So where is Nunn?" Mills asked.

"I'll take you there," Raven replied. "It's the least I can do."

Raven flew off into the mist, with a levitating Mills in close pursuit. They could take care of themselves. Mary Lou had to do some traveling of her own.

Constance Smith had always thought that Margaret Furlong was a little different.

Margaret nodded pleasantly as she walked up to Mrs. Smith. "What is the matter with everyone? Oh, I see."

"Margaret," Constance replied noncommittally. No doubt Margaret did see in a different way.

"It's a lovely day on the Circle," Margaret added.

Constance nodded. No doubt it always was.

"Oh, well," Margaret chirped. "I have things that must be done." As she stepped away she rose as if climbing stairs. The mist seemed to buoy her up and carry her away.

Mrs. Smith wondered if she had just seen something profound.

With Margaret?

○ Around the Circle:
Margaret and the Dragon Take Tea

It was a beautiful day on Chestnut Circle. It was always beautiful now. There was never any reason to complain. And today was extra special, for Margaret had a visitor.

Still, there were always little problems, even in paradise, for otherwise even paradise would become too much the same and lose its charm.

She wondered, what exactly do you feed a dragon?

She peeked back into the living room, where she had sat the dragon after inviting it into her home. The creature was extremely polite, considering its reputation. And for someone who stretched on into infinity, it was surprising how the dragon just managed to squeeze into that overstuffed chair.

Great plumes of smoke would rise from its nostrils from time to time, great black soot to rival the factories downtown. But then the creature would conscientiously blow the smoke right out the window. She didn't care how terrifying it was, so long as it was polite.

The dragon turned and saw Margaret watching it. "You'll pardon me for mentioning this," it said with a soft rumble, "but I'm rather hungry. I only get to eat once a cycle, you know."

"Well, that will never do." Margaret fought a rising panic. She didn't wish to be incorrect.

"So long as I have your permission, let's take care of my little difficulty. . . ." The dragon opened its mouth.

Oh. The dragon had solved the problem for her. She stood quite still as the creature's great tongue lapped her up.

Fires danced all around her. She expected the flame to burn. Instead, she felt warm and safe and loved. She knew that Leo would be here somewhere.

Margaret could sleep at last.

○ Thirty-three

Todd had moved his father's hammer. There hadn't been any choice. The front step was broken. Someone could have gotten hurt if it wasn't repaired. And his father was too drunk to do much of anything besides hit his wife and son.

"Who moved my fucking hammer?"

Todd heard his father's heavy footsteps on the stairs that led to the basement. The hammer was on the kitchen table. How did it get there? Todd was sure he'd put it back where it belonged.

"I'm going to kill whoever did it!"

There was something wrong with the hammer. It seemed to have a human face.

Nunn, thought Todd.

His father appeared at the top of the stairs, but he was only a skeleton, and he held Todd's terrified mother in his arms.

The skeleton nodded at the table. "There it is! I'm going to take that hammer and open your fucking skull, you little bastard!"

This wasn't real. This was something plucked from Todd's memory, something that had happened long ago, being reenacted for Nunn's benefit.

"Dad!" Todd called as the thing that had once been his father reached for the hammer. "Don't!"

"Your whining won't save you now, Toddy—" His father grabbed the hammer. But the hammer didn't just sit in his hand. It twisted and jerked, causing his father to stop and stare.

Carl Jackson howled as the tool plucked the green stone out of his right hand.

"I've got it!" the hammer cried as it grew to the size of a

man; a wizard dressed in black who held dragon's eyes in either hand. The room from the house on Chestnut Circle faded away, replaced by swirling mist.

"Now give me the other one!" Nunn demanded. "They are mine, after all."

"Keep away from me!" The skeleton stumbled back. "One step closer, and I'll kill Rebecca!"

Nunn laughed. He didn't care about Rebecca. But Todd did. He felt the anger grow inside of him again.

"No!" Todd called. A wave of green light erupted from his gem.

His father stumbled backward from the force of the blow, his right arm limp at his side. Todd's mother pulled free and started to run.

"Rebecca!" Carl Jackson called as his wife disappeared in the fog. "You won't—you can't—"

But his wife was gone. Carl spun to stare at his son.

"I should have killed you first anyways."

The pale wizard was at his side. "Give me your last stone, and I'll be glad to kill him for you."

"No!" Todd had had enough of his father's hatred, enough of Nunn's lies. The mist was turned to a neon green as new power strobed from Todd's eye.

Nunn reeled back from the blow. "You can't do that to me. I've got two of these! I'm unstoppable!" He fell to his knees.

Todd's father still stood. He held his remaining gem high over his head, so that it bathed his whole skeletal form in green. "So your mother's gone. You're the one who really has to pay. I'll show you what happens to sons who jerk their fathers around."

Todd couldn't stand it anymore. Wouldn't his father ever leave him alone?

"No!" he screamed.

His father screamed, too, and collapsed into a pile of bones.

Nunn knelt to pick up the dragon's eye that was rolling away.

"No!" Todd shouted, but this time Nunn only smiled.

Jason heard them before he saw them.

"Ninety-eight bottles of beer on the wall, ninety-eight bottles of beer—"

He waved them to come over to the spot where he was rooted to the pulse of the world.

"Take one down and pass it around," they sang as they approached, "ninety-seven bottles of beer—"

The roots, the wind, the rivers, the birds all had songs of their own.

The neighbors came closer, singing on and on about bottled beer.

Now Jason wanted to sing, too.

Mary Lou had appeared before her so suddenly that Mrs. Smith took a step away.

"Together!" Mary Lou shouted. "That's how we defeat the dragon, by working together."

"You mean all seven dragon's eyes?" Mrs. Smith couldn't see how that would be possible.

"More than that." Mary Lou looked straight at her, and smiled. "I think all of us, everyone the dragon brought here, has to work together."

Constance frowned. This was all moving too fast for her. "Why? What will happen?"

"Something wonderful," was Mary Lou's reply.

Nunn could sense the faintest glimmer of life in Carl Jackson's bones. Jackson's dragon's eyes had kept him alive in extreme circumstances, and the one that remained could call him back again. Unless, of course, someone else took possession of that final eye.

Nunn's hand closed around the gem, and all signs of life faded from what was once Carl Jackson. A shame, really. In his ignorant, pigheaded, half-mad way, Jackson had done Nunn quite a service. It was through Jackson's efforts that Nunn held three dragon's eyes again, enough certainly to gain more of the precious stones, perhaps enough to defeat the dragon and rule the world.

He now held three dragon's eyes close to his flesh; his brother's flesh, really, which he had now reassembled twice. The power should be pouring into him. Instead, he had been staggered by an emotional attack from a teenage boy.

Something was wrong. The dragon was playing tricks again.

"Down here!" a voice called from somewhere overhead. It was that annoying bird, Raven.

The bird swooped down before him and landed on Todd's shoulder. "I've brought you a little help," the bird told the boy.

A man dropped from the sky a second later, or actually, three different men in one.

"We're getting pretty good at this," Evan Mills said with a grin.

"We simply had to wait for our time to come," Rox added serenely.

"Even Zachs is pleased!" enthused the fire creature. "Maybe soon I can introduce you to my family."

They were all against him, but what did Nunn have to fear? He had three dragon's eyes now, if he could only get them to work.

"Nunn," Evan Mills said. Or maybe it was all three of them together.

"As promised," the bird squawked. "Raven always keeps his word!"

"He took my father's dragon's eyes," Todd told the newcomers.

Maybe, Nunn thought, he could bluff his way out of here without having to use the gems at all. "I have three of them here!" He held up the three stones together, clenched in his right fist. "None of you will be able to stand against me!"

Evan Mills stared down at him. "You'll have to get off your knees if you're going to say that."

"He doesn't seem very powerful now," Todd added. "A single blast from my eye drove him down there."

Mills grinned at that. "Maybe the dragon is telling him his time is done."

"Zachs says kill him!"

"Rox agrees."

It couldn't end this way, with Nunn on his knees. He had to have some other trick, some way of breaking free until he could regain the use of his gems.

If only he could think of it.

Nick still held his sword.

"Ninety-two bottles of beer on the wall—"

The others had accepted his father and Nick as soon as they arrived, as if his sword meant nothing to them; all of them singing together, marching through the mist. Nick found it both totally silly and very cheering at the same time. His father would never have done something like this in the real world.

"Ninety-two bottles of beer. Take one down—"

But his sword was out and ready. He had drawn it to do battle with Zachs, and he had never had a chance to put it away. It refused to return to its scabbard. It was quiet for now, but soon it would need blood.

So the neighbors had traveled, most of them holding hands, until they had seen Jason, standing very straight and tall, his hands raised toward the sky. Nick could have sworn Jason had grown six inches since the last time he had seen him.

"Ninety-one bottles of beer on the wall, ninety-one bottles—"

Stanley had led them to gather around Jason, whose feet seemed to grow straight out of the ground. Together, they formed a ragged semicircle that marched around Jason now.

Together, they had strength.

"That's it exactly, strength." Nick looked up, and saw Mary Lou standing next to him. She smiled at him. "I may need your help." She turned and smiled at all the others. "I'll need all your help. I'll be back in a minute."

"Well, that was enigmatic," Maggie said.

"Wizards!" was Stanley's only reply.

Maggie turned to Nick, her smile even warmer than Mary Lou's. "It's good to see you again. I wish you could put down that sword so that you could really join the circle."

Nick wished that, too, more than anything.

Mrs. Smith was taken there before she could say a word.

"Here we are," Mary Lou announced. "Together."

"Together?" Mills frowned back at her. "We were about to take some of those eyes away from Nunn."

Mary Lou shook her head. "I don't think that's a good idea. The dragon gave us all these eyes for a reason." She looked at Nunn's raised fist, then turned to Todd. "He has three? What happened to your father?"

"There." Todd nodded at the pile of bones. "It was his own fault, really. He pushed the magic too far."

"He'll have some trouble joining us, then." She pointed at the pile. "Let's take one along, for luck."

Todd looked at her strangely, but didn't object when she removed a legbone from the pile.

"Here we are, together," Mary Lou continued. "All of us, working together. It's the only way we're going to meet the dragon."

"Together? I suppose it's worked for us," somebody in Mills's body murmured without much enthusiasm.

"I haven't agreed to a thing," Nunn objected.

Mary Lou shook her head. "You'll have to decide. The dragon is waiting."

The ground shook with a faint rumbling noise.

"We're going to see him very soon."

Rebecca Jackson smiled. Singing had never sounded so good to her in her life.

"—bottles of beer on the wall, eighty-eight—"

Her first thought after getting away from that thing that claimed to be her husband was to get out of the skeleton's reach. But as soon as she had gotten out of sight, she began to think about Todd. He seemed able to take care of himself, but he was still only a boy. Certainly, there was some way she could help. She tried to find her way back to the place she had just come from, and had gotten turned around completely.

The ground shook as she heard a distant rumble. She had panicked then, running blindly ahead through the nothingness for a minute, until she heard the voices. They had calmed her down immediately. Human voices, singing the sort of thing you'd hear at summer camp, something almost too normal in the middle of the totally strange.

She slowed down, took a deep breath, and began walking toward her goal.

"—wall, eighty-six bottles—"

She saw the first faint outlines of the group ahead. They saw her, too. Joan Blake waved her forward, singing all the time.

Maybe, Rebecca thought, she'd start singing, too. She certainly knew all the words.

Mary Lou looked at all those around her.

"It's now or never."

Nunn.

A dark shape fluttered past.

The wizard looked up. "I've stayed too long in one place."

"They're coming for you?" Evan Mills, or maybe it was the wizard Rox, said with great amusement.

Something that sparkled like morning sun on a lake flew overhead.

"Obar," a musical voice called.

"Whatever that is, it's a little late," Todd said.

"No," Mrs. Smith replied. "If I'm not mistaken, Nunn still carries some of Obar around with him. These creatures are awfully eager to see you—both of you."

"Nunn and Obar were always so good at making sorcerous bargains." This time Mary Lou was sure it was Rox who spoke. "Neither, however, was very good at paying when the bills came due."

"They seem awfully eager to collect," Todd said. "Maybe when the dragon shows up, all bets are off."

Nunn, the whispers called. *The time is now, Nunn. Surrender.*

"Obar," the music sang. "We only ask for some of your power. We have to survive, too."

"He combines two wizards, and two sets of debt." Mrs. Smith regarded the wizard as if he was some specimen in a jar. "I think that if he escapes from these, others will follow."

Nunn, on the other hand, looked quite beside himself. "They'll tear me apart!"

Mary Lou could think of no better time to remind them all of her plan. "Then I think we all should be going. Nunn, of course, can come if he wants."

A great roar shook the world.

"The dragon," Mills said, staring into the impenetrable mist, "right on cue."

"He's getting closer at last," Mrs. Smith added. "Whatever was in its way is gone."

"Zachs doesn't fear the dragon!"

"Zachs may have to learn a thing or two."

"It's time we were gone!" Mary Lou called. "Together! Now!"

Everyone, Nunn included, turned to look at Mary Lou. She looked down at her dragon's eye, and watched as it passed through her fingers and floated toward the others. From the cries of surprise, she supposed the other eyes were doing the same, finally beyond their human masters.

The gems rose together, and formed a circle of their own, spinning in the air.

"Is the dragon taking them away?" Todd asked.

"No," Mary Lou replied, relieved that the time had come at last. "They're simply leading the way. We're going with them."

And the world changed again.

O Around the Circle:
The Dragon's Dance

There is a dragon, the most fearsome of beasts, a creature who with a single breath can lay waste to the world. It has the neck of a serpent, which can twist about in such a way that there is no escaping its wrath, and two great, scaly wings that can travel in only a single moment the distance a man might walk in a lifetime. So great is its size that mortals can only glimpse it in parts, a claw here, a tail there, or a plume of fire come to destroy them. To see all of the dragon would surely drive them mad.

There is a dragon, and its fire cleans the world. So it comes, again and again, to destroy and create anew. But the dragon is not complete.

There is a dragon, and it is searching.

There came a time at last when the dragon saw something new; a time when mere mortals joined together to challenge its dragon might. If the great creature had possessed humor, it would have laughed at a confrontation from such tiny creatures as these.

But, in truth, their challenge was not without interest.

For one of these mortals was called Constance, and she held a dragon's wisdom. Another, Mary Lou, could see into the dragon's heart. The elder Nunn contained a dragon's cunning. There were three others who existed as one; three who would instinctively know the dragon's great secret, that it could be one thing or many things; an ancient legend, a distant bird, or the world beneath their feet. And the most necessary of all, the boy named Todd, whose anger was great enough to fuel a dragon's fire.

There were others, too. A boy named Nick, whose spirit spoke of courage and doom; another child, Jason, who was growing to great strength; and of course Raven, the dragon's emissary in the world, who held it all together. But there were more, many more, parents and children, humans and otherwise, all of whom showed great potential.

There is a dragon, and it has waited for one special moment for a thousand lifetimes. Could that moment be now?

Nick was not exactly sure what had happened, but he could guess. He had been standing with all of those who did not hold the eyes; the remaining neighbors, along with Stanley, Maggie and Sala. They had been singing about seventy-eight bottles of beer, and they could see the five who held the eyes disappear into a green glow. The glow spread out to include the singers, and time and space changed, but Stanley kept on singing.

Jason was their center, rooted to the soil, but the rest of them spun around him, still joined in song, a beacon that the fighters could hold onto. It seemed very important to be there now. Nick wished again he could drop the sword and join with neighbors to either side, making it a true circle. But other things drew his attention. He heard a great roaring, and saw flashes of those with the eyes.

"Stay together!" Mr. Mills called, and Nick got a glimpse of three men close together. "That's how we're going to beat this thing!"

"It's after me!" Nunn cried, and Nick saw a wizard in flight.

"Stay together!" Mrs. Smith echoed, and all Nick could see was her calming smile. "Our strength is in our numbers!"

Todd's angry face flashed before him. "I will kill the dragon!"

"Stay together," Mary Lou joined in, and her face seemed filled with light. "And stay calm. The dragon needs this battle. We will use its arrogance to defeat it."

The sixty-fifth bottle came down from the wall as Stanley continued to sing, as this strange new place grew stranger still.

*   *   *

The others changed, in a way the dragon had only imagined. They joined together and became one, their skin turned to scales, a lizard tongue darting from their great mouth. They beat great wings and cried out their birth to the cosmos.

A new dragon was born.

Where once there was one dragon, now there are two.

The dragon's imagination became reality, and the battle was joined.

The ancient dragon knew the best way to attack. It would separate the parts of its new rival, eliminating strength after strength, causing confusion and death.

Cunning could be dangerous. The ancient one attacked that first, but Cunning had disappeared, and the ancient one found itself raked by Anger's fire. Wisdom and Heart watched for now, planning strategies to come, while the Three were silent, keeping their secrets.

Cunning lashed out then, using Strength as a claw, and the dragon felt a wound open upon its belly. Not a great wound, little more than a scratch, but the first wound the dragon had ever known.

The ancient one backed away from attack. This was more than a simple battle. It was a true challenge.

The first dragon roared, a sound that in the past had caused great cities to crumble. "I am the ancient!" the roar cried. "I am all the power that ever was, or ever will be!"

"No," the new dragon cried with a voice every bit as great. "We are strong. We deserve this world as much as you."

But the ancient one could hear smaller voices still which spoke out within its new adversary.

"I want to understand you," said Heart.

"Why must you destroy?" asked Wisdom. "And why must I?"

"I will not let you hurt us again," Anger cried.

"Now that we have seen you," the Three said as one, "we will know you anywhere."

But the ancient one brushed past all these voices to find the one it truly sought.

"You will not have me," Cunning whispered. "I am nothing."

Anger lashed out at the ancient, but while the attack was full of passion, it lacked direction. The ancient dragon avoided it easily, and the onslaught was lost in the void.

"Attack the others!" Cunning screamed in panic as the ancient drew close. Cunning tried to mimic his fellows and hide among them, but his Heart was incomplete, his Wisdom twisted, his Anger bloated, and his secrets dark and deformed.

Nick realized that the dragon had singled out the wizard.

Nunn tried to hide among the neighbors. The wizard pushed Jason, and the young Oomgosh disappeared for an instant. They all heard a distant roar of pain.

Jason was back in their midst just as suddenly. "I must protect the world," he said.

"So you'll do nothing but defend this worthless place?" Nunn's voice was full of panic. And then the wizard, too, was gone.

Images jumbled together. Nunn tried to hide behind the images of others, but his magic failed him again and again. "Attack the others!" he screamed, but then he was lost in fire.

Nunn was gone. Nick could no longer detect his presence.

The ancient breathed a single breath, sending a lance of fire to cut Cunning from the rest. Cunning screamed in fright, and for an instant the ancient one could see the wizard Nunn, as he flailed about in his final moment, searching for a hiding place in the spaces between the stars.

There is a dragon, an ancient dragon, and it will triumph again.

"Together," Mills cautioned.

"I can't catch the dragon!" Todd's anger mixed with frustration.

"Work with the others," Mary Lou added. "Work with all of us."

"The dragon is coming back!" Mrs. Smith called. "Everyone! We must turn away!"

The song grew around them, then, helped perhaps by the remaining magicians, and it seemed to Nick that they were all wheeling about in space.

"Nick!" Todd called to him. "I need your help."

Nick looked before him at the blur that might have been Todd's face. "I'm glad you asked."

"I'm going to guide your sword," Todd told him, and Nick felt himself moving at tremendous speed, his sword crying out as it sliced through a mass of living tissue that seemed to go on forever. Blood poured forth, so much blood that the sword could take no more. The weapon bucked in Nick's hands, trying to escape the ocean of blood that overran it, but the blade still swept through flesh, cutting, cutting. The hilt grew so hot that Nick cried out in pain, his hands flying from his sword.

Mrs. Smith appeared before him for an instant.

"You'll need something to replace your sword," she said softly, and then her image was lost in the same fire that had claimed Nunn before.

Nick felt something small and hard drop into his palm as the images blurred and vanished, as the sound of the never-ending song once again grew louder in his ears.

Somewhere, Nick could hear Raven laughing.

The ancient one would finish this quickly, now. The time had come to aim for the new dragon's Heart.

But the new dragon twisted in an instant, as if Cunning still remained.

"Take me instead," called another, "because Wisdom can always be learned anew."

The ancient dragon, once committed, could not pull away. Wisdom it would be. He saw the human Constance for an instant, and she smiled the smile of the old and weary, but it was a smile of triumph nonetheless. Wisdom was consumed, and the ancient could see the smile no more.

Anger attacked again with Courage as its weapon, striking long and deep. The ancient reared back, full of pain and rage. Dragon's blood flared bright in the void. The newest cut would have been a mortal wound, had the dragon a mortal form.

Still, the ancient could fight no more. It had to retreat, to mend in those secret places where it hid to watch the world.

It turned for a final time to regard its adversary. The young dragon spread wide its great wings. Its scales showed bright in the starlight, containing every color that might exist.

The new dragon seemed to be singing, with a dozen or a

hundred or a thousand voices. For an instant, with wings spread wide to catch the subtle currents of the void, it looked like nothing so much as a butterfly the size of the world.

The ancient dragon is gone, defeated but not destroyed.
And the world is not changed.
But it is born anew.

⭕ Thirty-four

When Nick opened his eyes again, he was standing in the clearing in the woods. His sword was a lump of twisted metal at his feet. And in his hand he held a dragon's eye.

"Seven bottles of beer on the wall, seven—"

Stanley waved at the rest of the singers. "I think we can stop now."

"About time," Maggie agreed.

Nick's father looked up at the sky. "Is it all over?"

"Nick!" His mother ran over to him. "Are you all right?"

"He's probably a little tired," Todd said from where he'd appeared beside him. Nick wasn't sure if Todd had walked there or simply materialized. "He was the one who really drove off the dragon."

"No," Mr. Mills countered, and Nick was sure he hadn't been there a moment before. "We all did it together. All of us."

"Even the ones who are gone," Mary Lou added as she stepped out of nowhere, too. She looked at Nick. "Mrs. Smith gave you her dragon's eye, didn't she?"

Nick looked down at the stone in his hand. "Yes, I guess she did."

Mary Lou nodded. "So we still hold four of them. The other three are gone, back to the dragon."

"Is it really over?" Nick asked.

"For now," Mary Lou replied. "We've won this battle. The world is ours."

"Let me out!" Mills's appearance seemed to change, his face glowing a fiery red. "Zachs sees the one who hurt him with a sword! Zachs will kill him!"

"Zachs, no!" a deeper voice responded from inside Mills's chest. "You will stay calm. Rox commands it."

"Can't I get rid of you two?" Mills shouted. His arms and legs jerked as if he was a marionette with three sets of strings, dancing about for half a minute before he collapsed to the ground.

Sala was the closest to him. She knelt by his side. "He's still breathing. Just unconscious."

"Like all those people inside him got to be too much for him," George ventured.

Todd took Sala's hand and drew her close to him. "We'll find some way to help him." He sighed as if this was all still a bit too much for him. "I hope."

Rose Dafoe stepped forward. "Can any of us go home again?"

"I don't know, mom." Mary Lou smiled and shook her head. "Maybe. Once we learn more about these dragon's eyes, anything is possible."

"But what do we do now?" Nick's father asked.

"Well." Stanley stepped forward. "I could sure use some new Volunteers. The ranks have been depleted."

Nick's mom held out her hand, beckoning his father to join them. "Maybe we can get to know each other a little better."

"Maybe we could make a life here for ourselves for now," Mrs. Jackson added, looking skeptically out at the forest.

"Maybe we don't have a choice," Mr. Dafoe added. He cringed a little, laughing weakly, as his wife glared at him.

"I think it will get to be a little easier now," Mary Lou added. "That will help."

Bobby knelt down next to the dog. "I'm just glad Charlie is all right."

All Nick could do was stare at the dragon's eye, glowing softly in his hand. What a surprise to have this to replace his sword.

"Mrs. Smith is gone," he said to himself. "Nunn, too." He hoped that the four of them who now held the eyes, the new wizards, could work better together than Obar and Nunn. He remembered what Mary Lou had said a moment before. He looked up at the others and repeated it.

"Anything is possible."

The great black bird fluttered down to land on Jason's shoulder. "Of course all things are possible! Raven wouldn't have it any other way!"

Jason smiled at the bird. "So you were behind it all, my Raven?"

"Of course, my Oomgosh, for is not Raven the creator of all things?" The black bird flapped his wings impatiently. "But why are we standing here? There is a whole new world out there that Raven and the Oomgosh must explore."

"Lead on, my Oomgosh!" Jason called, and Raven flew into the air.

Jason turned to follow, pausing only to look back over his shoulder. "Any of you want to come along?"

A number of them thought that was a very good idea.

○ Epilogue

George Blake opened his eyes.

He was back in his bedroom, back in the real world, back on Chestnut Circle.

It was night, but he could see quite well in the moonlight. He was home, back from that other world he had never really believed in; that other world that at the time had seemed more real than this one.

He was lying lengthwise across the bed, as if he had simply fallen asleep atop the comforter. But he only had to look at himself to realize it was not a dream. His clothes were torn, his hands caked with dirt. They might have sent him home, but he would have to clean up himself.

"They?" he asked himself as soon as the thought entered his head. The dragon had sent him home. He had never wanted to be in that other place. It was only fair.

The house seemed so quiet after the chaos he had just survived.

"Nick?" he called. "Joan?"

There was no answer.

One of the dragons had sent him home. George wondered now which one. What would he do if he was the only one to come back, if none of the others had followed?

He stood from where he had been lying and walked to the window.

George Blake looked out at the dark, quiet houses that lined either side of Chestnut Circle. There was no way to tell, in the middle of the night, if there was a single soul in any of them. Somehow, though, George thought that all of them were empty, too. He was looking out at a neighborhood of ghosts.

He thought of his wife and son, and how he had almost gotten close to them. He had managed to help Nick at least, although he now felt the moment owed more to Nick's need to be rescued than to anything that had come from George.

A train moaned somewhere in the distance. Only when it was this quiet could you hear a train. George had no idea where the train tracks were hidden in this part of town. Somehow, the idea of a train in this part of town seemed even less believable than the idea of a dragon.

George Blake wished he held some fraction of his son's sense of wonder. He opened the window, hoping, he guessed, for some other sound to break the stillness.

The night was warm—it seemed to be summer—but there was a stiff breeze that rustled its way through the trees. George Blake felt a chill in the summer calm. The wind sounded very lonely this time of night.

He was back in the real world, the world he had wanted so much. He wondered now what he thought had been waiting for him here.

There is a pause in the battle. The battle is never over.

Deep within the world, the dragon has returned to its lair. It will sleep for an hour, a week, or a hundred years. Time is different for the dragon. When the time is right, its eyes will open, its wings will spread, its fire will burn all in its path.

Until then, it waits. The dragon does not think like others. Although its eyes are closed, it watches the world. The dragon does not see like others. The dragon knows of many worlds, and many times. Perhaps the dragon watches all the worlds at once.

The dragon has been turned away from its purpose, but it is not defeated. The dragon is never far away. The dragon will always return.

Parents will caution children, lovers will speak in whispers, the aged will feel it in their bones. All wait for the dragon. All know in their hearts that the wait will not be long.

The battle is never over. The battle begins again. The battle will not end until the day when the dragon destroys all.

Deep beneath the world, deep beneath every world, the dragon sleeps.

It will not sleep forever.

DANIEL HOOD

FANUILH 0-441-00055-X/$4.99

The wizard Tarquin valued the miniature dragon Fanuilh as his familiar—and the human Liam as his friend. And when Tarquin was murdered in bed one rainy night, both were left to grieve—and to seek justice.

WIZARD'S HEIR 0-441-00231-5/$4.99

Despite what people think, inheriting a wizard's familiar did not make Liam a wizard. But he is shaping up to be quite a detective. When his late friend Tarquin's magic artifacts are stolen, and then used to commit further crimes, Liam must solve a mystery that's already caused one death and threatens to start a holy war.

BEGGAR'S BANQUET 0-441-00434-2/$5.50

Liam agrees to help solve the theft of a priceless—and magical—family heirloom stolen from his business partner. And he recruits his dragon familiar, Fanuilh, to help. Because what's a little magic among friends?